"After years as a Christian bookseller, Kathy Herman knows both the necessity and the difficulty of weaving the gospel message into a story with clarity and relevance. She pulls it off with a natural sensitivity. The gospel unfolds as the plot expands in this mystery that won't let you go. I sat down with a cup of coffee to open this story. Two hours later, the coffee was cold and the cup untouched. I'm looking forward to introducing this new author and her first book to my customers."

STEVE ADAMS, PRESIDENT, EVANGEL CHRISTIAN STORES

"A very powerful book! Kathy Herman's descriptions are bold and clear, and her solid dialogue flows from one page to another as she swirls us up in a whirlwind of plot and adventure. *Tested by Fire* is a novel that's guaranteed to keep many a midnight light burning."

WAYNE HASTINGS, VICE PRESIDENT OF RETAIL DEVELOPMENT
THE PARABLE GROUP

"A suspenseful story of touching characters that is richly seasoned with God's love. Believer and nonbeliever will be moved by the depths of heaven's forgiveness and endless grace."

BILL MYERS, AUTHOR OF *ELI* AND THE FIRE OF HEAVEN TRILOGY

"As someone who loves the classics, I've wondered why there are so few great storytellers today. Seldom do I find a book that keeps me reading with such a sense of intrigue and mystery that I can't wait for the next turn in the story—or page of the book. *Tested by Fire*, Kathy Herman's new mystery, is masterfully told—making Kathy one of today's great storytellers!"

JIM REIMANN, WRITER AND EDITOR OF THE UPDATED EDITIONS OF
MY UTMOST FOR HIS HIGHEST AND *STREAMS IN THE DESERT* AND
PAST CHAIRMAN OF THE CHRISTIAN BOOKSELLERS ASSOCIATION

"Warning: *Tested by Fire* may be hazardous to your sleep! Kathy Herman has created a first-rate page-turner that kept me guessing and reading through the night."

CARON LOVELESS, SPEAKER AND AUTHOR OF
THE WORDS THAT INSPIRED THE DREAMS

TeStEd bY FiRe

THE BAXTER SERIES BOOK ONE

KATHY HERMAN

Multnomah®Publishers *Sisters, Oregon*

TESTED BY FIRE
published by Multnomah Publishers, Inc.
© 2001 by Kathy Herman

Cover image by Scott Goff/Index Stock Imagery
Cover design by Chris Gilbert/Uttley DouPonce DesignWorks

Multnomah is a trademark of Multnomah Publishers, Inc., and is registered in the U.S. Patent and Trademark Office.
The colophon is a trademark of Multnomah Publishers, Inc.

Printed in the United States of America

For information:
MULTNOMAH PUBLISHERS, INC.
POST OFFICE BOX 1720
SISTERS, OREGON 97759

ISBN 0-7394-2414-9

To Him who is both the Giver and the Gift.

ACKNOWLEDGMENTS

I owe a debt of gratitude to the late author, Bob Briner, who looked me in the eye back in 1994 and challenged me to use my talent to be a "roaring lamb" who makes it evident to the world around me where I stand in my faith. He changed my life.

A warm thank you to my editor, Rod Morris, and to my friend, Jimi Miller, each a gentle but inflexible taskmaster who played a significant role in nurturing me as a writer.

Special thanks to Matt Nash of the Tyler Fire Department, who helped me to create an explosion/fire scenario; to Lieutenant Lusk of the Smith County Sheriff's Office, who explained jurisdictional boundaries of law enforcement agencies, including the FBI and ATF; to Sans Hawkins, owner of Hawkins Electronics in Tyler, Texas, who schooled me on the sophistication of cell sites and tracing capabilities; and to Dr. Dick Hurst for his valuable input on medical issues.

To Bernie, Doris, Susan Kate, Missy, Susan, Suzanne, Ken, Belinda, and Carrie, the first to read the manuscript—thanks! I can never turn these pages without gratitude for your overwhelming show of enthusiasm.

To Rose, Sue, Remus, Jackie, and Erica, thanks for letting me brainstorm during our many hours of pool exercise. What a ball!

To Pastor Terry Cadwell, thanks for filling my cup and for your powerful prayer that helped me to breeze through a pivotal point in the book.

To my friends at LifeWay Christian Store in Tyler, Texas, and the ladies in my Bible study groups, thanks for your countless prayers.

To Deanna Tyler, my friend and prayer partner for life, thanks for your research and input on the history of the Irish McConnells.

To my friend Susan White, thanks for twenty-five years of cataloging my comments on three-by-five cards and insisting I had something to say. This one's for you.

To my sisters, Caroline Berry and Pat Phillips; my mother, Nora Phillips; and my aunt and uncle, Dorothy and Charles Allenbrand—thanks for your input, your constant encouragement, and for sharing my dream day by day. E-mail is a marvelous tool!

To our kids, Paula and Brad, Glenn and Kim, and Jody and Mark, thanks for getting excited along with me and for not complaining when I got lost in my writing.

To Glenn Herman, thanks for taking time to share important marketing insights with your dad and me. It changed the vision.

To Dave Lewis, thanks for good directions. We made it.

To Don Jacobson, Bill Jensen, and the entire team at Multnomah, thanks for your endless support and enthusiasm.

And to my husband Paul—the other half of my heart—you have a gift to identify and draw out potential. Had it not been for your encouragement, excitement, perception, and partnership, and your giving me boundless mental space, this book would never have been written. Thanks for your selfless hours of copying changes, struggling with unfamiliar software, printing and sorting and hole punching pages, and for patiently listening as I talked about the characters for hours, days, and weeks on end. We did this *together,* yet you allow me to shine. There's only One who loves you more than I.

And it's that One—the God and Father, the Lord Jesus Christ, and His Spirit, who indwells us—that I humbly thank for enabling me to contribute something to His people.

*For it is by grace you have been saved, through faith—and
this not from yourselves, it is the gift of God.*

EPHESIANS 2:8

PROLOGUE

Rhonda Wilson lay in bed, curled up with a pillow, resenting a huge golden moon that hung in the autumn sky outside her window as if to taunt her loneliness. It was eleven-thirty on Friday night, and she already knew this weekend would be a repeat of all the others.

Jed had come home shortly after nine, tipsy enough to be happy and just drunk enough to be anesthetized to her sharpened claws of silence. He had immediately retreated to the den. That's the way it was almost every night, and Rhonda was growing weary of this heavy burden of loneliness. Jed occupied his days with work and his evenings with his friend Mike McConnell and the good ol' boys down at O'Brian's bar.

The most maddening part of all was that Jed could stop drinking any time he wanted to. He imbibed just enough to deaden the pain of an old wound for which neither of them had a cure. Had Rhonda not understood, perhaps she could have despised him for having left her in the arms of indifference while he found solace in his precious pitchers of beer. Hating him would have been much easier than hanging on to the hope that someday he would love her again.

Upon hearing Jed's approaching footsteps, she wiped her tears with the corner of her pillowcase and pulled the covers up around her shoulders. The creaky bedroom door slowly opened and Jed's shadowy figure shuffled across the hardwood floor before finally flopping onto his side of the bed and turning his back to her.

The mantle clock struck eleven-forty-five, its chimes drowning out the sound of her sniffling. Rhonda held back the tears and exhaled slowly through her mouth. The last thing she wanted was his pity.

ONE

At 11:46, a brilliant flash ignited the midnight shroud, and a window-rattling explosion woke the sleeping town of Baxter with a jolt.

Rhonda and Jed Wilson sat straight up in bed.

"What in the world was *that?*" Rhonda threw the covers off and rushed to the window.

"It came from the direction of the lake," said Jed, sitting on the side of the bed, already pulling on his jeans. "I'll find out what it was. You stay here."

He ran down the porch steps and out to his red pickup, hopped in and backed down the long driveway. He sped off toward Heron Lake, leaving tire marks on the street in front of his house.

Within minutes he was driving along the eastern stretch of town only a stone's throw from the water's edge. He slowed when he saw people standing on the side of the road.

"Did you hear the explosion?" he asked.

"Yeah, look," said a teenager, pointing in the distance. "Must've happened on the lake."

Jed got out of his truck. Through a break in the trees, he spotted a number of fires burning on top of the water, none near the shoreline. He stood frozen, his eyes fixed on the location of the blazes.

"Sir, are you all right? Sir?"

He got back in his truck and pushed the accelerator to the floor.

At CR 157 he made a sharp right turn, his truck moving in a cloud of dust as he barreled down the gravel road that led to Mike McConnell's pier. He tasted smoke before he saw a conglomeration of vehicles and flashing lights.

When he spotted Mike's truck, Jed slammed on his brakes and jumped out, leaving the door to his pickup wide open.

"Let me through," he said, bulldozing through a wall of bodies. "I need to get through, let me through...."

He felt someone grab his arm. "Jed, wait!"

He broke free and fought his way until he was at the end of the pier looking toward the spot where Mike always anchored the houseboat. The explosion had spewed burning debris in all directions, giving the eerie illusion that Heron Lake was on fire. The largest fire appeared to have engulfed the entire hull.

Jed felt as if he were inside the head of someone else, watching the monstrous inferno, like some dragon from the deep, devour the McConnells' houseboat.

All he could do was stand there with friends, neighbors, and firefighters as the lake opened its mouth and swallowed everything that remained, pulling it down to the depths of an unholy grave.

Though the harvest moon shone bold and bright, midnight on Heron Lake never seemed darker.

As lights from emergency vehicles flashed all around him, John Washburn went through the motions of filling out preliminary paperwork.

As Norris County fire marshal, John had been exposed to many tragedies, but he couldn't remember a single time of standing there with all the water he could ever need, unable to do anything.

The moon shone like a searchlight on the water, and smoke hovered like the sinister fog of a horror movie. It seemed to him that even nature was determined to point out his failure.

"How could this happen?" mumbled a recognizable voice

nearby with barely enough energy to be audible.

John sighed. He didn't look up. "Don't know yet, Jed. There wasn't anyone else around. Nobody saw anything. We figure they were asleep inside the cabin when the thing blew. Let's hope they never knew what hit them."

"This isn't real," said Jed. "I was with Mike at O'Brian's just hours ago. We had a few beers and some laughs, unwinding like we always do. I can't believe…" His voice broke.

John forced himself to look up. "I'm sorry, Jed. There wasn't anything we could do."

"Twenty years, John. We put in twenty…."

"At the highway department. I know."

"Mike always said we've gone a few miles together…"

John sighed. He pulled the paperwork from his clipboard and put it over the visor. "Listen, I'm finished here. Let me take you home. We can come back for your truck tomorrow."

Jed looked at the ground, his thumbs hung on his jeans pockets, his feet rocking from heel to toe. "That's okay, you go on."

John reached out the window and gripped Jed's arm. He looked him straight in the eye. "Give it time, man. Trust me, you'll get through this."

John Washburn looked in the rearview mirror as he pulled away. He couldn't remember the last time he had seen Jed Wilson without Mike McConnell.

The breakfast rush at Monty's Diner was noticeably subdued, especially for a Saturday morning. Folks who didn't frequent the place wandered in to see what everyone else knew about the McConnell explosion. The *Baxter Daily News* arrived a little late, but after that, the conversation all but died. All eyes were on the headline story.

EXPLOSION RATTLES BAXTER
LOCAL FAMILY PERISHES IN FIERY INFERNO

Residents of Baxter were awakened at 11:46 on Friday night when an explosion on nearby Heron Lake blasted the sleepy silence with a powerful jolt. Michael S. McConnell (46), his wife Rose (45), and their three children—their daughter Erin (14) and twin boys Todd and Timothy (6)—are presumed to have perished in their flaming houseboat. Authorities believe the family's home was engulfed as a result of an explosion of undetermined origin. Officials in the sheriff's department and fire department have already formed a team of investigators to determine the cause of the explosion.

Heron Lake looked like a war zone when authorities and some Baxter residents arrived at the McConnell family's pier, less than a quarter mile northeast of town on CR 157. The houseboat had been anchored about one hundred yards from that pier, and flaming debris was scattered in a fifty-yard radius of the explosion. As far as could be determined, that was all that was left of the houseboat. Friends and neighbors watched in horror as the burning hull sank to the bottom of Heron Lake.

Divers will be working to recover everything they can find and to recover the bodies, but fire officials have cautioned that the intensity of the fire may make that effort extremely difficult or impossible. It is uncertain just how much was reduced to ashes. In addition, heavy rains are expected to drench Norris County over the weekend, making the search effort even more difficult.

Fire Marshal John Washburn said: "I have never felt this helpless in all my years of service. We weren't sure what blew, and by the time we realized where the fire was, we had no time to get a rescue team out on the water. It's ironic—all that water and we couldn't use a drop of it to save this family. It's going to take some time to get over this one."

Norris County Sheriff, Hal Barker, a long-time Baxter resident, said: "Every effort will be made to find out how this happened. Just give us a little breathing room to do our job. We've never had any real trouble on the lake before, and as far as I can tell, there's no reason to expect that this was anything other than an accident."

Another Baxter resident who stood by helplessly as this tragedy unfolded was Mayor Charlie Kirby. His comment to this reporter was: "We need to pull together as a community and comfort one another as we seek to find answers." Mayor Kirby asked that local residents cooperate with investigators by avoiding the area so that county officials needing to bring in equipment will have unobstructed access.

The investigation will be handled as a county matter since the explosion occurred outside the Baxter city limits, but the game warden and local police will be assisting the sheriff's department.

Though authorities could not say how long the investigation would take, the preliminary report could be filed as early as Tuesday.

Customers at Monty's Diner remained unusually subdued throughout the day. There were more questions than answers, certainly not the usual opinionated fare served up daily at this landmark gathering place on the town square. Hearts were heavy as friends and neighbors sought to make sense of this terrible tragedy.

Ellen Jones didn't like her job today. She sighed as she folded her personal hot-off-the-press copy of the *Baxter Daily News*. This much-better-than-average newspaper was a legacy passed down from the town's founder, Reginald T. Baxter, and had helped to foster the hometown spirit for a hundred years. For the last six of those years, she had been the editor and special feature writer, and her paper had met the challenges of reporting unpopular or upsetting news head-on. However, today's local headlines were the most tragic in her memory, and in such a close-knit community, no one was unaffected.

Ellen's phone rang. It was only 6:45 A.M., and she already guessed who it was.

"Good morning," she said.

"It's your husband, Guy Langford Jones. Remember me? Did you run away from home? Your side of the bed hasn't been slept in."

Ellen chuckled. "You don't have all the facts, counselor. I stayed here all night with the staff to get the McConnell story on the front page."

"Actually, I just read it. Good job."

"Good and bad, I guess. Good reporting. Bad news."

"Honey, you did what you had to do. Why do you sound disappointed?"

"Because this story really hurts, and reporting the straight scoop on tragedy is so…cold. It needs to be softened with a human interest slant."

"Well, that's where you shine, Ellen. You'll work out something. You always do. But it's not going to happen today, so…how about coming home? It's Saturday. I'm lonesome."

"Poor baby. Was it too hard to pour the cereal and milk by yourself? Or weren't you strong enough to push the 'on' button on the coffeemaker?" She giggled, glad for a temporary break in the gloom.

"None of the above, thank you very much. I'm quite the little homemaker when I need to be. Right now I'm looking at your empty chair on the other side of the kitchen table and happen to miss my wife. Now, having studied law, I know that's not a crime."

"No, the crime is my having gotten so bogged down over here that I've abandoned you on your favorite day off. Let me clear my desk and get out of here. I need twenty minutes."

"Ah, just enough time for me to brew a fresh pot of coffee and bake these cinnamon rolls," he said. "Tell me again how the oven works."

"Guy, don't touch anything. You'll burn the house down! Wait for me."

"Better hurry then.... I'm putting an apron on."

"An *apron?* You can't be serious." She laughed. "All right, all right, I'm hurrying."

Ellen was still smiling when she hung up the phone. The two of them knew when to rescue one another from obsessing over troublesome cases—hers in the newspaper, his in the courtroom.

Ellen quickly answered two e-mails and straightened the stacks on her desk. She yawned and rubbed her eyes, then leaned back in her chair and stretched. She looked up at the oil painting of Reginald T. Baxter, which had been passed down from editor to editor for more years than she had been alive. His eyes seemed to look into her heart as if he shared her shock over the McConnell tragedy.

Jed Wilson hadn't slept all night. He was holed up in the den, slouched in his easy chair. Rhonda picked up the morning paper and three more empty beer cans. It was only noon, but she had already counted eleven.

"Jed, you should try to get some rest."

"I don't want to rest."

"Well, at least let me fix you something to eat."

"I don't want to eat. Just leave me alone."

"I feel completely useless," she said.

"Duh. I wonder why."

"At least I care about how you feel." She positioned herself directly in front of Jed, trying to get him to look at her.

"You don't have a clue how I feel," he said.

"Maybe not, but I care."

"Yeah, well, I didn't ask you to care. What I asked you to do is leave me alone."

He got up from the chair. Rhonda went ahead of him and stood in the doorway.

"This isn't a good time for you to be by yourself," she said.

"I might as well get used to it."

"Jed, you don't have to go through this alone."

"That's right. I've got four six-packs to keep me company."

She glared at him. "This isn't the way to handle it!"

"Good grief, woman, will you back off?"

He pushed past her and staggered out to the kitchen.

"Jed, don't shut me out. You can't handle this by yourself—not this pain."

He turned around, his eyes unfocused and bloodshot. "Ever think maybe *you're* the pain?"

"I'm trying to help you. This is all so weird. There's no one to comfort, no one to make a casserole for, no place to send condolences—"

"So give it a rest!" He popped the top off another can of beer. "You're not needed."

Her green eyes brimmed with silent suffering.

"Don't start with the pitiful looks. And stop pushing. Just stay out of my way." Jed walked past her and stumbled toward the den.

Sheriff Hal Barker had been on the phone most of the day. Before he had one minute of quiet, the phone rang again.

"This is Hal."

"It's John Washburn. You sound hassled."

"Just tired. How's your part of the investigation going, John?"

"It's tedious, but the divers are pulling up all kinds of debris that should help us figure out what happened. How about you?"

"There's no indication of foul play," Hal said. "Just speculation that Mike's drinking may have been a factor. My deputies should wrap things up by Tuesday or Wednesday, especially with the police helping out."

"It'll probably take my team longer than that. Depends on what we fish out of the lake."

"What's morale like?"

"Everyone's bummed—it's a little close to home. But we're professionals. We'll get the job done."

"Okay, John, keep me updated."

"Yeah, I will. Get some rest."

Hal hung up and glanced over the top of his half glasses to a recent picture of his kids. He couldn't imagine losing Matt and Wendy, especially not in such a horrific tragedy.

His phone rang for the umpteenth time.

"This is Hal Barker," he said in a monotone.

"Hi, it's me. Do you realize what time it is?"

"Judging from the rumbling in my stomach, I'd say it's half past dinnertime," said Hal, suddenly realizing he was famished.

"I know what kind of a day you've had if you forgot to eat," Nancy Barker said. "We're having beef stew and cornbread. Dinner will keep until you're ready. Want me to feed the kids now so you and I can eat together later?"

Hal looked at his watch. It was twenty minutes until seven.

"No, I want to spend some time with Wendy and Matt before they go to bed. I'll be home in ten minutes."

"How are you doing?" she asked.

"I can't stop thinking about the McConnells, especially the kids. I keep seeing their faces."

"I know. We're all taking it hard. Wendy and Matt have been talking about it off and on all day. I suppose that's what everyone in town has been doing. Did you find out when the service is being held?"

"Two o'clock Thursday afternoon at Saint Anthony's. They want to wait until my investigation has been completed."

"By *they*, do you mean the relatives?"

"Actually, no relatives are coming. As far as anyone can tell, there are only two—Rose McConnell's sister in California, who just had surgery and will be in rehab for weeks, and Mike's father in Atlanta, who lives in a nursing home and can't travel."

"How sad," said Nancy. "Can you imagine losing your whole family and not being able to go to the funeral?"

"Well, everyone in town will probably show up. I have no idea where Father Donaghan plans to put all the people."

"Hal, come home. You sound tired. There's nothing more you can do tonight," she said gently.

"Okay, honey, pour the iced tea. I'll be home in a few minutes."

Sheriff Barker hung up the phone and fumbled with the piles of papers on his desk. When he was sure his emotions were safely locked up, he turned out the lights and headed home.

By late Tuesday afternoon the sheriff's deputies had interviewed scores of friends and neighbors, had checked out every aspect of the McConnells' lifestyle and routine, and had found no suspicious materials among the recovered debris. Now satisfied that there was no reason to suspect foul play, the sheriff's department was wrapping up its part of the investigation. Hal was just about to fill out his final report when the phone rang.

"Hal Barker."

"It's John Washburn. I need to come over there and show you something. It won't take long, but you need to see this."

"Sure, come on over."

Ten minutes later, John spread out several photographs on a big, round oak table in the sheriff's office.

"So what's this about?" Hal asked. "A snag in your investigation?"

John picked up one of the black-and-white Polaroids. "Here, take a look."

The sheriff looked through the glasses resting on his nose. "What is it?"

"Part of a jawbone—human remains."

Hal recoiled. "You mean, you actually found...?"

"Yeah, we did, and after those heavy rains over the weekend, we didn't expect to either. We just got lucky these were in the lake in spite of the undercurrent."

Hal stared at the photographs on the table. "John, maybe we should suggest the memorial Mass be postponed until we know more."

"I don't see why. We know the entire family was at home and had to have perished in the fire. Hal, you said yourself that no one suspects foul play. If we wait until we recover enough to identify all five of them, it could take too long for the memorial service to have any real closure for the community. I'd let it go forward as planned. But you'll need to authorize getting these remains over to Dr. Hicks for pathology to analyze them. Hopefully, there's something here that'll tell us who this is."

Hal sighed and leaned back in his chair. "John, I hate this! There's no dignity in the McConnells' being reduced to remains, scattered all over the place."

"Look, I'll keep the divers searching the lake, but we need to search downstream too. The longer the remains are out there, especially with the water still being warm, the less chance of identification and determining the cause of death. We don't have enough manpower to do this by ourselves."

"What about the ATF?" asked Hal. "Matt Nash offered his help if we need it."

"I think it's time to take him up on his offer."

"Okay, John. Get whoever and whatever you need to tackle this and keep me posted. Thanks for your effort. I know this isn't pleasant."

Two

When the bells chimed two o'clock on Thursday afternoon, Saint Anthony's Catholic Church was filled to
overflowing. Folding chairs were put in the aisle at
the end of every pew, and volunteers set three more rows of folding
chairs behind the back pews. When those seats were filled, mourn-
ers packed into the vestibule and the choir loft.

A large oil painting of the McConnell family was displayed on
an easel, set inside the center break in the communion rail. A talented parishioner had studied the family's photograph in the
church directory and then painted their portrait on canvas.

There was Mike McConnell—a rugged redhead with a spirited
disposition, hearty handshake, and contagious laugh. In Mike's
forty-six years, he had never known a stranger. A twenty-year vet-
eran of the state highway department, he rarely missed a day's
work, even when his morning-after head felt bigger than his ego. If
he could have earned a commission dollar for every mile of new
highway he helped to complete, Mike McConnell would probably
have given it away at O'Brian's by the round.

Mike enjoyed living on the lake and often bragged that his kids had
a free swimming pool and that his wife didn't have to nag him to mow
the lawn. But as curious as people were about his unusual lifestyle,
none of them had ever been invited to his home on the water. In spite
of Mike McConnell's outgoing nature, only Jed Wilson had been privy
to any part of his life beyond the smile and the handshake.

Nevertheless, many folks around Baxter had been recipients of Mike's spontaneity. He was known to show up unannounced to help with house painting, church cleanup, or town projects. If he saw someone struggling to carry groceries, straining to fix a flat tire, or having difficulty handling just about anything, he stopped to help. Mike even took flowers and chocolates to the ladies at Myerson Nursing Home last Valentine's Day and a huge puff of cotton candy to Sister Mary Frances when his sons' first-grade teacher sprained her ankle.

Rose McConnell was a quiet sort—friendly enough—but her deep blue eyes seemed distracted and gave the impression that she was mentally somewhere else. She kept to herself except for joining the ladies' altar guild at Saint Anthony's and regularly volunteering as a room mother at the grade school. Most of her time was spent with domestic duties and raising three kids.

Even at forty-five, Rose was a natural beauty. It was baffling to people why Mike seemed indifferent to Rose, since she turned the heads of other men in town. Perhaps not wanting to encourage any "lookers" was precisely the reason she kept to herself. About the only thing she hadn't kept to herself was her life's dream to some-day see New York City, though her travels in the past twenty years had scarcely taken her out of Norris County. Rose made the best of her isolation on the lake and grew close to her children and their friends.

Tim and Todd McConnell were six-year-old twin boys with copper hair, freckles dotting their Irish noses, and enough energy to drive Sister Mary Frances straight up the wall. Not that they were bad kids, but they were two times the mess, two times the noise, requiring double the effort. But now they seemed twice as charming, and Sister Mary Frances would miss their impish grins, endless energy, and creative antics.

Erin McConnell was a shy fourteen-year-old with deep blue pools for eyes and dark, shiny hair down to her shoulders. She had her mother's good looks, even at this awkward age of blossoming.

A simple girl, Erin had not taken on the faddish attire of adolescence or the weighty eye makeup that seems to define that right of passage. She was a ninth grader at Baxter High School and usually blended in to her environment without incident. She was not the scholastic sort, but she was a pleasant student who worked hard. Erin was never a problem to anyone, not even her peers. An intense people pleaser, she avoided the petty dialog that flows like poison from the lips of little women trying desperately to define their importance by drawing attention to those who are weaker. Her one close friend was Brenna Morgan, and without her, Erin was an island. The two girls spent many hours aboard the houseboat—giggling, dreaming, and finding themselves.

Many thoughts wandered through the minds of those gathered as they listened to Father Donaghan eulogize each member of the McConnell family. Many pairs of eyes gazed sadly upon the painting and the painstaking detail that had been put into it.

Father Donaghan managed to finish his eulogy, but not before he was overcome with emotion. He had no satisfying words to answer the question he saw mirrored in the faces of those who knew the McConnells, but he refused to hide behind stale platitudes. The inexplicable "why" of these deaths could be answered only by the God who saw fit to give life in the first place—but it was a question Father Donaghan would not negate.

Outside the gray stone walls of Saint Anthony's, one lone straggler lay hidden in the arms of a giant oak tree. The prayers of the memorial Mass escaped the open windows and could be heard above the rustling of October leaves. With the final, "Amen," the straggler climbed down from the tree and slipped away unnoticed.

THREE

Rhonda stood in the doorway to the den, holding a plastic trash bag.

"Jed, this place is a mess! All you do is go to work, come home, and drink yourself into a stupor."

"I'm not going to O'Brian's anymore, that should make you happy."

"You never drank this much before. You're destroying yourself."

"So what?"

"Wallowing in self-pity and living off beer and potato chips won't make the pain stop."

"So now you're a shrink?"

"You're completely closed off. I might as well live alone."

"Then why don't you?"

"Jed, I'm not the enemy. Please, just talk to me!"

He picked up the remote and began to channel surf.

She walked over and unplugged the TV. "I'm sick of talking to myself!"

"Okay, Rhonda, you want me to talk? Here's a bulletin—I hate my life! I hate coming home! There, does that make you feel better?"

She closed her eyes and took a deep breath. "I don't think either of us can trust how we feel at the moment. Losing Mike has been hard, but—"

"But what? I'll get over it? Is that what you think?"

Rhonda bit her lip.

"I saw him five days a week for twenty years. I'm not gonna just get over it. I can't remember a time when Mike wasn't there for me."

"We should all be so lucky," she said sarcastically.

Jed glared at her with red-rimmed eyes. "He also made me laugh, which is more than I can say for you!"

Rhonda pulled at the top of the trash bag and fought with it until it opened. She grabbed beer cans, potato chip bags, and newspapers and stuffed them in the trash bag. She tied the top, gave it an exaggerated yank, and dropped it in Jed's lap. She glared at him, but couldn't find words to express her fury.

"Hey, you wanted me to talk," he said.

"I need to get out of here. I'm going to Miller's Market."

"Good, get more chips. The big bags."

"Well, that'll sure fix everything."

"Spare me the sarcasm, Rhonda. Just get the chips."

"Fine," she said, turning on her heel.

He heard the front door slam. Jed could hardly believe he once loved her, and it was getting harder to remember how it felt. She no longer bore any resemblance to the cute little blonde he fell in love with so many years ago....

"I have a surprise for you. Close your eyes." Jed slipped his class ring off his finger, slid it onto a braided cord, and fastened it around Rhonda's neck. "Okay, open them."

"Jed!"

Her face told him what his heart wanted to hear, and before she said another word, his lips found hers.

"Excuse me, lovebirds, but I've got your order," said the carhop, putting the tray on the driver's side of Jed's faded red MG convertible.

"Jed just asked me to go steady," said Rhonda.

"Yeah? Congratulations."

"Thanks," they said in unison.

"Okay, looks like the usual—two cheeseburgers, two curly fries, and two cherry Cokes."

"That'll do it," said Jed, ready with the exact amount.

He held one cherry Coke and handed the other to Rhonda. "To us," he said, clinking the glasses together.

She giggled. "To us."

Their eyes smiled as they sipped from the straws.

"Jed, I have a surprise too—my dad's letting me stay out later on graduation night so we can go to the party!"

"Wow, that's great. But it's gonna go all night."

"I can stay until three. I'm so excited, I've already decided what I'm gonna wear. You remember that green mini dress.…"

He was distracted by what she was wearing now, her feminine curves outlined in a pink tank top tucked into a pair of white stretch jeans. He slid his arm around her. "You'll look great no matter what you wear. How come your dad decided to let you stay out late for the party?"

"He trusts me," she said.

"But not me?"

She giggled, her cheeks blushing with innocence. "My dad doesn't trust boys at all.… I'm debating on how I should wear my hair. Maybe I'll put Summer Blonde on it and leave it down. What do you think?"

"Yeah, leave it down. It's beautiful." He untied the ribbon that held her ponytail, letting the blond tresses fall past her shoulders down to the middle of her back.

"How come guys always like long hair?"

"I don't know, it feels soft," he said, stroking her hair with his fingers, studying her face.

"What?" she said.

"Nothing. I like the way you look, that's all."

"I'm too fat."

"No you're not. Why do girls beat up on themselves like that?"

She shrugged.

"How can you be so insecure when you're such a knockout? Come on," he said, starting the car, "this is a special occasion. It's time I showed you my favorite place."

"Where is it?"

"If I tell you, it won't be a surprise."

With the top down, he drove up the winding road to Cassie's Point, away from the city lights, until the night sky suddenly appeared as an infinite showcase of twinkling diamonds. He turned the car onto a gravel road and drove to a secluded clearing on a ridge overlooking the valley. He turned off the motor and put his arm around her. "What do you think?"

"I've never seen this many stars," she said. "It's awesome."

The scent of pine was pervasive; the only thing competing with it was the sweetness of Rhonda's perfume. Jed tenderly pulled her close, savoring the fragrance, enjoying the warmth of his lips melting into hers. Minutes passed and restraint gave in to eager, prolonged kisses. Soon his desire was at war with decency, the intensity of passion surpassed only by his father's voice resounding in his mind: "The right woman is a valuable gift, Jed. Don't treat her like a cheap commodity."

"I'm sorry," he said, suddenly letting go, his heart pounding. "That was stupid. It won't happen again."

"It'd ruin everything," she said, sounding out of breath. "We can't."

"I know...we won't, I promise...."

Jed popped open another beer and took a big swig, but what was in the can couldn't silence the truth. Long after tonight's hangover left him, the past would continue to point a finger just like it had for the past twenty-eight years....

"Here, Jed, have a beer," said a friend, tossing him a cold can from the ice tub.

Jed caught it with one hand. "Throw me one for Rhonda."

"Jed, I'm not eighteen. I told my dad—"

"Babe, it's graduation night."

Rhonda wrinkled her nose. "Maybe just one."

She took the dripping can and popped the top off a "cold one" for the first time. The sight of her tilting her head back and taking a gulp of beer was almost comical to Jed.

"You're a good sport," he said, squeezing her other hand. "Come on, let's see who's here."

A few beers later, they were having the time of their lives.

"Jed, do that John Lennon imitation again. Hey, guys, come here. You gotta see this."

Everyone gathered around. Jed borrowed a pair of round glasses and put on his best British accent, pretending to be John Lennon being interviewed by the queen. They loved it.

"What about Gomer Pyle, can you imitate him?" someone asked.

"Oh, he's easy."

Jed was laughing so hard it was difficult to focus. He turned an imaginary ball cap sideways and relaxed his face until he had the mouth just right. "Hey, Sergeant Carter, Gaaaw-ly." His audience was in stitches and begged for more. He kept on until, one by one, he did all the impressions he knew.

"That's it, that's all she wrote," he said, taking a bow.

"Somebody give that boy another beer, he's on a roll. Do Ringo again, it's hilarious."

"Ladies and gentlemen," said Rhonda, rising to her feet and taking his arm, "the talented Jed Wilson has saved the best for last. You're gonna love the finale."

She turned and whispered, "Do Principal Harris."

"Oh yeah, I forgot that one."

His imitation of the principal's well-known idiosyncrasies brought a round of laughter and applause.

Jed noticed that he wasn't the only one on center stage. Even the captain of the football team couldn't take his eyes off Rhonda. She was like a jewel in Jed's crown, and he felt like king of the hill.

"She's a real looker, Jed. So how come you got her?"

"The woman can't help herself. You can't resist me, right, Babe?"

Rhonda giggled and gave him an elbow in the ribs.

"When you get bored with Mr. Imitation here, just remember he's not the only game in town."

Jed put his lips to Rhonda's ear. "It's one-thirty. Let's go to Cassie's Point and finish celebrating—just the two of us."

"Leave the party?" she said.

"Yeah. I want you all to myself."

They staggered arm in arm, laughing all the way to Jed's convertible. They raced up the winding road to Cassie's Point, feeling the wind tugging playfully at their hair....

Jed wondered why he was thinking back on this. It always made him angry. One stupid mistake—and he'd spend the rest of his life paying for it. He kicked his shoes off the ottoman and popped open another beer. He didn't want to think about it anymore.

FOUR

al sat for a long time staring at the manila envelope in his hands. He pulled the papers out and scarcely began to skim the pages when the phone rang.

"This is Hal!"

"Man, do you sound edgy."

"Sorry, John. I've got the prelim from pathology."

"And?"

"I feel like I'm about to violate holy ground. Stay on the line; let's find out what it says."

Hal read through the report, mumbling to himself as he turned the pages.

"Come on, Hal, I'm chompin' at the bit over here."

"Just a minute. I'm getting to it.... Now *that's* a surprise."

"What?"

"Seems our Dr. Hicks found the remains of *two* individuals, but even with bone measurements and other testing methods, the preliminary report was inconclusive." Hal sighed. "They still don't know whose remains they are. Dental records will have to be obtained to establish identity. Just what I didn't want to hear."

"What a hassle," said John. "I was hoping we'd know something for sure; it's already been ten days since the explosion."

"I'll authorize further testing, but it'll be another week or so before we know. This waiting around stuff's getting old."

"No kidding. Let me know when you know."

"I will, John. By the way, why'd you call?"

"I don't remember, my mind's on overload. Whatever it was, it wasn't as important as this."

"Well, if you think of it, call me back. Give my regards to Mary Lou."

"Yeah. Same to Nancy."

After he hung up, Hal took off his glasses and rubbed his eyes. He sat quietly for a few moments out of reverence for the two unidentified McConnells and for the other three whose remains were still out there somewhere.

"Here's the final pathology report," the courier said. "Dr. Hicks said to call if you have questions. Says he's sorry it took a whole week to get this to you, but that he wanted to be absolutely sure."

"Yeah, thanks," Hal said.

He closed the door to his office and sat down at his desk. He opened the envelope and read the final analysis, line by line. He picked up the phone and hit the intercom.

"Gladys, I need you to call Mayor Kirby, Police Chief Henley, and Ellen Jones. See if they can meet in my office at eleven."

"Yes, sir."

Hal got up and looked out his office window from the second story of the county courthouse. He watched a UPS driver get in his truck and drive away. Today he would have gladly traded places with him.

He sat down at his desk and dialed John Washburn's cell phone.

"John? It's Hal. The final pathology report's in…."

Hal glanced up at the clock. It was ten-forty-five. He leaned back in his chair, his hands folded behind his head.

The view of autumn colors through the big arched windows

was distracting. He closed his eyes and tried to relax. The woody smell of oak paneling and hardwood floors took him back to the first time he walked into this office and sat down at this massive old desk. He was only thirty-three and never expected to win the race for Norris County Sheriff. He considered it a privilege to serve, and that hadn't changed with reelection. In the seven years he held the position, he never once took his title for granted or abused his power. He loved his job, but he was ready to get today's meeting behind him.

There was a knock at the door, and before Hal responded, John Washburn barreled through the door and across the creaky floor, the palm of his hand slamming into Hal's. "Hey, Sheriff. You look a little shopworn. You ready for this?"

"I don't know," Hal said. "How ready am I supposed to feel?"

"Are we the only ones who know about the IDs?"

"Yeah, John, I haven't told anyone else yet."

Police Chief Joe Henley shuffled through the door and flashed a big smile under a bushy white mustache. "Well, if it isn't the dynamic duo. I'm anxious to hear the results of your investigation. Quite an undertaking."

Hal shook Joe's hand, careful not to squeeze too hard on the chief's gnarled fingers. "Be glad this one's out of your jurisdiction. My guess is you're getting a lot more sleep."

"Looking forward to retirement, Joe?" John asked.

"Oh, mixed feelings. But with this arthritis, I won't mind taking it easy."

Hal noticed Mayor Kirby slip in the door and pour himself a cup of coffee. He stood by the window and seemed to be enjoying the view of City Park. As always, his fine hair was slicked down perfectly in place.

"Hey, Charlie," said Hal, extending his hand. "How's that pretty wife of yours doing with a new baby in the house?"

A proud grin spanned the mayor's face. "If Marlene hasn't figured out what to do by now, we're in real trouble."

John Washburn chuckled. "How many is that now, seven?"

Charlie nodded. "At last count. Getting harder to keep track unless I count heads. Speaking of counting heads...is everyone here?"

"They are now," Hal said as Ellen Jones walked in the door and paused to fluff her curls and straighten the jacket to her pantsuit. "Morning, Ellen. You're looking lovely, as usual."

"I hope I didn't hold up your meeting," she said.

"Not at all. The others just got here."

Her eyes surveyed the room. "Something's different...ah, you've added that wonderful plaid rug. Complements the wood nicely. I like it."

"Thanks. Nancy picked it out. Okay, are we ready to get started?"

The others nodded.

Hal seated them at a round oak table near the windows.

"You know the purpose for this meeting," he said. "So let me tell you straight out that my department's investigation didn't uncover anything that would lead us to believe this tragedy was anything other than an unfortunate accident.

"We interviewed eighty-three people who knew the McConnells, and not one could think of any person who would want to hurt them. Other than a few disgruntled wives annoyed that their husbands spent too much time at O'Brian's with Mike and Jed Wilson, no one had a bad word to say about anyone in the family.

"The events of that Friday night were in character for the McConnells. The houseboat was anchored out a hundred yards from their pier—usual for them on nice weekends clear into November. We know Mike had been at O'Brian's earlier in the evening with Jed. That, too, was usual. Jed said that Mike left for home around nine. Marvin Pearson saw Mike's truck pass his place about nine-fifteen. He remembers the time because there was a commercial on TV and he was headed for the bathroom. That would put Mike home about nine-twenty. We all heard the explosion around eleven-forty-five, and the rest, unfortunately, was witnessed live from the McConnells' pier.

"Our experts examined everything recovered by the divers." Hal took a deep breath. "Among the charred debris were severely burned human par—uh—remains, and after extensive testing, pathology was able to positively identify Rose and Tim McConnell from dental records." Hal's lip quivered and he forced the words out. "No remains of the other three McConnell family members have been found at this time. That's it, but I want John to fill you in on his investigation. John…"

"Thanks, Hal. My team did a thorough investigation. Let me tell you what we believe happened. The hull was found to be relatively intact, and the burn pattern on the back deck indicated that's where the fire started. Further lab testing revealed traces of gasoline.

"Judging from the condition of the debris and the degree of charring, we believe the fire happened first, then the explosion. Our conclusion is that a fire on the back deck of the houseboat produced heat capable of causing a propane tank leak. That's what caused the explosion.

"This is consistent with both the intensity of the blast and with the location and condition of the ruptured tank found in shallow water 275 yards down current from the site of the explosion.

"Since the fire occurred first, we believe the McConnells were probably overcome with smoke in their sleep and never knew what happened.

"By all indications, this appears to be an accident, though we can't be fully satisfied, knowing there may be additional remains that could tell us more. The undercurrent has probably carried any remains downriver. Since it's now been seventeen days since the explosion, we need to work methodically and quickly.

"We enlisted the help of Matt Nash at the Bureau of Alcohol, Tobacco, and Firearms, and he has sent an investigative team to help us search. Our only focus now is on recovering the remains of Mike, Todd, and Erin McConnell. That's the status. Sheriff…"

"Thanks for your hard work, John, and for a thorough analysis of the situation. Let me also say I've been in close communication with Rose McConnell's sister in California and Mike's father in Atlanta. They want us to continue our investigation until we have exhausted every effort to find the remains of the other family members. John will coordinate all efforts with Matt Nash and will keep me apprised of further developments. When that investigation has been completed, I will call us to meet again. Are there any questions?"

Chief Henley was quick to respond. "Do we know the cause of death on Rose and Tim?"

Hal shook his head. "The county coroner ruled the cause of death in both cases as 'undetermined.' Seems the remains were not intact enough to give us the whole story. Those dental records could tell us who they were, but not how they died."

Charlie leaned back in his chair. "Do you have reason to believe that Mike McConnell's drinking had anything to do with the accident? The rumor mill is working overtime."

Hal nodded at John to answer.

"Charlie, that's a question that'll probably haunt us. We know a fire started on the back deck and caused a propane tank to blow the place to kingdom come, but we can only speculate on how that came about."

Hal looked at his watch. "Any more questions?"

Ellen Jones studied her notes, twirling her pencil over and over like a baton. She finally looked up. "Hal, if my memory serves me correctly, your deputies found Mike's pickup at the pier."

"That's right. And Rose's VW bus too."

Ellen slowly leaned forward, resting on her arms. "Did you recover the McConnells' motorboat? You know, the one they used to ferry back and forth when they were anchored out on the lake?"

Hal looked quizzically at John who looked quizzically back.

"The divers made a report on everything they were able to identify," Hal said. "If you pose your question to them, I'm sure they can give you a definitive answer."

Ellen started to twirl her pencil again. "Hmm, I might do that, Hal...I just might do that."

Sheriff Barker shut the door to his squad car and looked at the stone house nestled in a stand of pine trees, a short distance back from the road. He started up the long sidewalk, and as he got closer to the house, he heard a TV blaring and saw lights on. He went up the front steps and rang the bell.

Seconds later the porch light came on. Rhonda Wilson opened the door, still drying her hands with a kitchen towel. "Oh...Hal. It's you."

"Excuse the intrusion, Rhonda, but is Jed home? I'd like to talk with him for a minute."

"He's home. That's about *all* I can say for him. Come in."

"Uh, thanks." Hal removed his Stetson and ducked slightly as he came in the front door.

Rhonda raised her voice above the blaring of the TV. "Jed, Sheriff Barker is here to see you! Jed? Jed! You hear me?"

Hal blushed. "Sorry. I picked a bad time to come by. I should've called first—"

"He wouldn't know the difference."

Jed stumbled out of the den smelling like a beer marinade.

"Hello there, Sheriff. What brings you out tonight?" He offered his hand to Hal, almost missing his aim.

Rhonda exhaled loud enough to make her point and then disappeared into the kitchen.

"Jed, can we talk?" Hal said.

"Sure, why not? Follow me." Jed bumped into the wall on the way into the den.

"Sit anywhere you like...just move something over."

Hal cleared the clutter from an overstuffed chair and sat down.

"I've got good news and bad news in the McConnell investigation. The good news is we feel sure there was no foul play in this case. A fire started on the back deck, spread to the cabin, and eventually caused a propane tank to explode. We think Mike and his family were asleep, probably overcome with smoke and didn't feel a thing."

Jed stared blankly. "If that's what you call good news, what's the bad?"

"Pathology has identified Rose and Tim McConnell from the remains recovered. But Mike, Todd, and Erin haven't been found. We've expanded the investigation to try to find their—uh—whatever we can that would enable us to make a positive ID. I know you were ready for closure on this, Jed. I'm sorry we're not there yet."

There was a long pause. Jed looked emotional.

"You really think they were asleep and didn't feel a thing?" Jed said. "Man, I have nightmares about that. I keep seeing Mike on fire, calling out for me, and I can't get to him. I see Mike's face and hear his voice and I do nothing. He's burning up before my eyes, and I just stand there like everyone else and watch. He dies and I watch. I just watch...."

"Listen, you're going to drive yourself crazy going over this again and again," Hal said. "Whatever happened out there, it's over."

Jed began to sob. Feeling awkward and inept, Hal got up and put a comforting arm around Jed and told him to let it all out. He was talking as much to himself as to Jed.

FIVE

Rhonda stomped across the bedroom and opened the bathroom door. She slammed the laundry basket down next to the hamper. How much more of this could she take?

After the sheriff left last night, she stayed in the bedroom and cried herself to sleep. She didn't know if she was more embarrassed for Jed or because of him. The way he acted, one would think his life was over because Mike McConnell died. It was as if she didn't exist.

Why did she think he would suddenly need her again? Jed's indifference began to divide them the minute they quit talking all those years ago....

Rhonda sat up. She worked to smooth the wrinkles on her green minidress. The giddiness had left her, and she felt nauseated. "Jed, please say something."

He gripped the steering wheel with both hands and stared at nothing.

"Are you mad at me?" she said, hot tears melting down her face. "You wanted to."

Jed didn't even look at her. He started the car and drove down the winding road from Cassie's Point.

That silent ride home was agony.

Jed said he didn't want to talk about it—ever. Anytime she brought it up, he shut her off. He acted like it had never happened.

သာ

Dr. Lucas called Rhonda into his office and closed the door. Her heart started to pound.

"Rhonda, I think you know what I'm about to say," Dr. Lucas said gently. "Your test was positive. You're eight weeks pregnant."

The lump in her throat gave way to sobs.

He put a Kleenex in her hand. "I know this isn't what you wanted to hear, but you have to face it. Does the father know?"

The father? The words sounded cheap. "My…uh…my fiancé will be okay with this. We'll get through it together." The lie scalded her cheeks.

She had no idea how Jed would take the news. More and more he found excuses not to see her. What if he left her? What if she were forced to face this alone? And—Oh, dear God—how would she tell her parents? When she left the doctor's office, she never felt more alone.…

Rhonda sighed. She grabbed the clothes from the hamper and stuffed them into the laundry basket. Little had changed in twenty-eight years.

Tuesday's warm spell drew Father Donaghan irresistibly to the outdoors. He parked his car along First Street and began a leisurely walk around the town square.

The towering oak trees looked ablaze in the midmorning sun, their flaming gold a stunning contrast to the reds and oranges of the competition. He marveled. Had there ever been a prettier fall? He couldn't remember when. Apparently, he wasn't the only one who thought so. Park benches around the square were filled with autumn's fan club, and numerous others were seated on the grass.

"Good morning, Mrs. O'Reilly," said Father Donaghan, tipping his hat.

The elderly woman smiled and methodically inched down the sidewalk with her walker.

He stopped to admire the county courthouse, which stood in the center of the town square, its reddish stone walls and white, rounded pillars echoing with Baxter's hundred-year history. The grounds of City Park surrounding it were *the* place for folks to gather, gossip, and lollygag. There was a crowd this morning and many faces he didn't recognize.

The lake brought scads of visitors to the area, and the town square lent itself perfectly to tourism. Quaint shops lined the brick streets and offered something for everyone, including an old-fashioned ice cream parlor, a specialty gift and toy shop, and a gallery displaying crafts and paintings of local artists.

As he reached the corner of First and Holmes, Father Donaghan saw Mark Steele standing in the doorway of Monty's Diner across the street.

He waved. "Hi, Mark. Beautiful day!"

"You can say that again!"

Monty's Diner had been there as long as Father Donaghan could remember. Famous for its authentic decor, home-cooked food, and home-simmered conversation, Monty's had loyal customers who were known to slide into a booth and stay for hours.

He turned right on Holmes and strolled along the back side of the courthouse. He tipped his hat to Mrs. Crenshaw and peeked in the baby buggy.

"How's little Cassie doing?" he asked.

"Oh, fine now. She's over her cold. The fresh air will do her good."

Father Donaghan made the turn and walked all the way down Second Street to the corner, where he spotted Ralph Miller setting up his hot dog stand—the same as for the last fifty years.

"Getting close to lunchtime, Ralph. Don't you love this weather?"

"It's good for business, I'll say that."

"Those dogs heated yet?"

"Ready when you are. Want your usual?"

Father Donaghan nodded and exchanged seventy-five cents for a hot dog smothered in pickle relish. He took a big bite.

"Ah. Ralph, some things never change."

"Yep, best six bits you'll spend today, Padre."

Father Donaghan turned and strolled along Baxter Avenue in front of the courthouse. Brandon Ensley whizzed by him on a pair of roller blades, followed by another youngster he didn't know.

"Why aren't you boys in school?" he hollered.

The only reply was the sound of giggling as the mischievous pair shot down the sidewalk at full speed.

Father Donaghan continued on to the corner, where the bronze statue of the town's founder, Reginald T. Baxter, stood. Golden leaves lay at his feet, dropped like thank-you notes from the giant oak trees in City Park. These beautiful grounds were just one of the founder's many gifts to the community.

Father Donaghan stood back and took in the whole setting. The town square was like an old friend. Even with the refurbishing of the courthouse, little had changed since he was a boy.

He was tempted to walk another lap, but he resisted. Good weather didn't cancel his responsibilities at the church. He popped the last bite of hot dog into his mouth and got in his car. He chuckled at Brandon Ensley and his friend. Sixty years ago, he might have played hooky too.

Father Donaghan walked in the side door of Saint Anthony's and was surprised to see a woman sitting in the front pew. He didn't recognize her as a parishioner. Not wanting to startle her, he gave a quiet cough. When she reacted to his presence, he proceeded toward her.

"I'm Father Donaghan. Is there something I can do for you?"

The woman seemed flustered. "Uh, I'm Mary, Mary Carter. I

don't go to your church, but I hope it's okay I'm here."

"Of course, Mary," he said, noting the initials RJW on her purse. "God's house is open to everyone."

She didn't look up. There was a long pause. "Listen, my real name is Rhonda Wilson. I was here for the memorial Mass for the McConnell family. Things in my life have been in turmoil since then—well, actually long before then—and I just wanted to find a quiet place to think. I thought maybe you wouldn't mind if I borrowed your church."

"Stay as long as you like," he said. "But it might help to talk about it."

Rhonda looked up into the face of the priest. "I want to pray but don't know how. Do you have a book of prayers or something to help me get started?"

He reached down to the book rack on the front of the pew, picked up a thin booklet and handed it to her. "There are prayers in this missal, but God already knows what you need to say, my dear. He knows what's in your heart. Perhaps it would be better if you just talk to Him in your own words."

"My own words?"

He nodded. "I'm going to work on my sermon for Sunday. My study is just through that side door and across the courtyard. I'll be there if you need me. Talk to God, Rhonda. He loves you and knows you better than anyone else ever could. Why, before you were born, He already had plans for you."

"Plans? *God* had plans for *me?*"

The priest smiled slightly, and so did his gentle brown eyes. "Of that I'm absolutely sure, but the details are between you and Him." He patted her shoulder and then left by the side door.

Rhonda studied the stained glass all around her but had no idea who most of these religious figures were. She did recognize a scene of the Last Supper. Once, when she was in grade school, a friend had invited her to Vacation Bible School. She was told about Jesus, the Last Supper, the Crucifixion, and the Resurrection. The teacher said that Jesus was God, but she had never thought much about it.

Rhonda thumbed through the missal, but nothing on the pages conveyed what was in her heart. Feeling awkward and incapable, she slid out of the pew and tiptoed toward the back of the church, hoping Father Donaghan couldn't see her. She pushed open the heavy wooden doors of Saint Anthony's and escaped into the waiting arms of an October breeze, relieved to leave conversation with God for another day.

Standing in the shadow of the ivy-clad bell tower, a young man in a plaid shirt and jeans watched Rhonda Wilson's every move. When she got into her white Ford Mustang, he was not far behind.

SIX

ary Beth Kennsington walked out of Cornerstone
Bible Church as the clock tower on the county courthouse struck twelve. She soaked in the sights and
sounds of City Park across the street and basked for a moment in
the noonday sun, letting its warmth melt into her face. What a glo-
rious morning it had been. The final preparations for Cornerstone's
annual carnival were completed. It was the one event Mary Beth
poured herself into because she had a heart for kids. The carnival
was open to the community and offered a comfortable setting for
building relationships with children whose parents didn't bring
them to church.

She got into her car and rolled down the windows. The mosaic
of color surrounding the courthouse was breathtaking. Mary Beth
drove her sporty blue Jeep Grand Cherokee to the parking lot exit
and turned left. She braked for a red light at the corner of First and
Baxter Avenue, and glanced in the rearview mirror just in time to
see a white Mustang before it plowed into the rear of her car. She
felt a powerful jolt.

Her hands shaking, Mary Beth unbuckled her seat belt and got
out of the Jeep. The front end of the car that hit hers was
scrunched beyond recognition. She walked over to the driver, who
was still inside—a woman who looked about her age.

"Are you okay?" asked Mary Beth.

The woman's eyes were red and puffy as though she'd been

crying. "I'm so sorry! I didn't see you until it was too late to stop!"

"Don't worry about that. Are you all right?"

"I think so. Good thing I had my seat belt on."

"What's your name?"

"Rhonda Wilson. I have insurance, it'll pay for the damage. I'm really sorr—"

"It's okay," said Mary Beth. "It appears that neither of us is hurt; that's the good news." She turned and looked at the broken glass on the brick street. "The bad news is your little Mustang didn't fare as well as my Jeep."

A young man in a plaid shirt and jeans was the first one on the scene.

Mary Beth noticed he instructed someone with a cell phone to call the police. She didn't see him after that, but several who witnessed the accident from City Park rushed over to offer assistance and to talk with police.

Forty minutes later the officer finished his report.

"Mrs. Kennsington, you're free to leave any time," he said. "I've got what I need from you. And Mrs. Wilson, your car's being towed to Jimmy's Garage. I'd be happy to drive you home."

"Thanks. I guess I need a ride," Rhonda said, her hands rubbing her neck.

"You sure you're not hurt?" he asked. "You really smacked into that Jeep."

"No, really, I'm okay. Just a slight headache."

Mary Beth extended her hand. "I'm so glad it wasn't a lot worse. I'm afraid I had you outsized by a ton. The Lord must really be watching out for you."

"Thanks for being so nice about it," Rhonda said.

"Come on, Mrs. Wilson," the officer said. "Let's get you home."

A young man in a plaid shirt and jeans watched as the officer's squad car pulled away from the curb. He had no intention of letting Rhonda Wilson out of his sight.

On Wednesday morning, Rhonda was working in the kitchen. The oven timer sounded just as the doorbell rang.

"Great. This day has barely started and already I hate it." After removing a square pan from the oven, she hurried to the front door.

"Hi, Rhonda. I hope you don't mind me stopping by like this," Mary Beth said. "I just wanted to make sure you were all right. Did your headache go away?"

"Uh, actually it did. I'm a little sore, that's all. Guess I was lucky. Would you like to come in?"

"I don't want to intrude. Just thought I'd check on you."

"No, it's okay. You're not intruding, really!"

Mary Beth laughed. "Climbing the walls, eh?"

"I'm not used to being without a car. Pleeeease come in."

Mary Beth stepped into the entry hall. "What a darling curio cabinet! Is it an antique?"

"Yes, it was my grandmother's. She gave it to me when we bought this house."

Mary Beth moved closer to the glass. Her eyes moved from figurine to figurine. "Which is your favorite?"

"The porcelain horse—there on the top shelf. I loved riding when I was a kid."

"Really? Me too. You've got a lot of cute things in there."

Rhonda led her from the entry hall into the living room where the morning sun squeezed through the lacy panels and spread across the creamy yellow walls like frosting on a cake. The delectable aroma of something freshly baked added to the imagery.

"I was about to have some coffee," Rhonda said. "Would you care to join me?"

"Sounds good." Mary Beth's eyes wandered around, taking in the character of the house.

Rhonda disappeared and reappeared with a serving tray. "I've got some brownies too, just out of the oven. Would you like one?"

"I smelled something yummy the minute I walked in. I've got to warn you, though. I'm a serious chocoholic. I'm not sure I can stop with just one." Mary Beth laughed.

"I can tell we're going to get along, Mary Beth. I can't stop with one either. You'll notice I brought a whole plateful."

Mary Beth took the first bite. "Mmm…a piece of heaven."

"They're my weakness. I can't sleep if I know they're in the house."

"Speaking of your house, I love all the homey touches. It's charming."

"Thanks. Jed and I bought this house when the kids were growing up. We've lived here for twenty years. A place grows on you after that much time."

"Tell me about your family," Mary Beth said.

"Well, Jed works for the state highway department. Actually, that's what brought us to Baxter in the first place. We've been married twenty-eight years and have two grown children, Jennifer and Mark. Both have moved away."

"Well, since you didn't mention grandkids, I'm sure you don't have any." They both laughed. "So where do your children live?"

"Jennifer's twenty-eight, single, living in Denver. She manages a natural foods store in a quaint section of the city. Mark's twenty-two, also single, and graduated from college last spring. He's our computer whiz. Got hired right out of school by a big company in Raleigh. Jed and I don't have close family other than our children. There's been a real void since they moved away."

"I can imagine," Mary Beth said. "We've got three—Erica's eighteen, Sherry's sixteen, and Jason's twelve. I'm having enough trouble just dealing with them growing up, much less moving away."

"Where do you live, Mary Beth?"

"Joe and I have an old, two-story brick house on Norris Street, near the high school. We've lived there for ten years. Joe's been principal of Baxter High School for the past two. Of course, our girls pretend he belongs to someone else. It can be awkward attending school where their dad's the principal, but they've learned to handle it pretty well."

"So that's where I know the name Kennsington from," Rhonda said. "It sounded familiar, but with my kids grown, I'm not in touch with what's happening in the schools anymore."

Mary Beth was enjoying her conversation with Rhonda and lost all track of time until she heard the mantle clock chiming.

"Oh my gosh, it's noon! I can't believe I stayed this long. You'll never invite me back." She giggled. "Actually, you didn't invite me—I showed up on your doorstep."

"I'm glad you did. And you don't have to leave. Let me fix us some lunch."

"I'm sorry, I can't. I have an appointment to get my hair cut at twelve-thirty. You know, Rhonda…our church is having a carnival this weekend where we reach out to kids in the community. We could use another hand if you want to satisfy that motherly instinct of yours. I need some help running booths and painting a few little faces. We have a wonderful time. I'm not sure who enjoys it most—us or the kids."

"It sounds like fun, and I'm not looking forward to being cooped up here all weekend. Could I hitch a ride?"

"Are you kidding? If that's all it would take to earn your help, lady, you're on."

SEVEN

"S on, your career as a petty thief is over—unless you want to end up behind bars." The phone rang. Hal gave the young-ster an I'm-not-finished-with-you-yet look.

"This is Sheriff Barker."

"Hal, it's John Washburn. Hope I'm not interrupting anything."

"Of course you are. But that's the good news. It's a normal Friday and there really is life beyond the McConnell case. What's up?"

"The ATF team found something. Can you spare a few minutes this afternoon, at say, two-thirty in your office?"

"Sure, John, I'll make time. How long?"

"Half an hour?"

"Done. See you then."

Hal hung up the phone. The young thief squirmed.

"I—I'm sorry, Sheriff," the boy said.

"Sorry isn't good enough. What about the fifty dollars in CDs you stole from Mr. Abernathy?"

The boy shrugged. "I don't have any money."

Hal got up and opened the door to his office and summoned in the boy's parents.

"All right, son. Here's what you're going to do. You'll come to the courthouse after school starting on Monday. You know where the janitorial office is. Be there. You're going to work harder for the next month than you ever have in your life—after school *and* on

Saturdays. At the end of one month, I'll pay you exactly fifty dollars. Then you're going to walk back in and pay Mr. Abernathy fifty dollars for the CDs you stole from him. Any questions?"

"No, sir."

"All right, then. Count your lucky stars that you aren't sitting in juvenile detention. You have a chance to turn this around. It's never too late to do what's right. I'd like you to sit in the waiting area while I speak with your parents."

The boy left the room. His parents looked scared.

"Listen, your son's basically a good kid. I took him on a carefully chosen tour of the county jail and had a heart-to-heart with him. He seems contrite enough, but I believe in applying my own version of 'community service' before this type of petty theft escalates into anything serious. For what it's worth, I rarely see repeat offenders once they've gone through this process. I appreciate your cooperation. Let's see if we can't get a good kid back on track."

After the parents left, Hal thought how rewarding it was to be sheriff in a community like this one, where people still had respect for the law, for each other, and for themselves.

At two-thirty, John Washburn arrived at Hal's office.

He pulled up a chair at the round oak table and took a stack of Polaroids out of an envelope and laid them out on the table.

"We won't know until pathology confirms it, but we may have found the remains of all the McConnells now," he said. "Look. These are more distinguishable—"

"John, these were people. Just give me the bottom line." Hal pushed himself up from the table and walked over to the window.

"Sorry. We think there's enough here to make positive IDs, but it'll take a few weeks to get the results back. Matt feels like we've gone over the area with a fine-tooth comb. His team was pretty fired up when they found this stuff. They were beginning to think it wasn't going to happen."

"Yeah, fired up. We can all get back to our lives now."

"I didn't mean to upset you. I thought you'd be glad we found these remains."

Hal turned around. "I am. I can't get past the mental images of the three kids. I'll get over it. You and Matt did a good job. Tell your guys how much I appreciate their hard work. I'll call Matt and thank him personally."

After John left, Hal leaned back in his chair and stared at the ceiling fan in his office. He was fortunate to make his home in Baxter. The brutal realities of his profession had taxed his reserve just a few times in the past seven years. Problems were more often break-ins, domestic squabbles, barroom brawls, or code violations. His greatest and most rewarding challenge was turning kids around, teaching them to be accountable.

Hal hated this case. Having the McConnells referred to and handled as remains hurt him somewhere deep inside. Knowing his former neighbors were being examined piece by piece, as if they were nothing more than charred wood from the houseboat, seemed criminal. Hal wondered how law enforcement officers in big cities could ever get used to seeing human beings reduced to nothing.

He wanted this case over with, but he also knew that the very thing he hated was the only way to end it. If they were ever to move past this case, identifying the victims was the closure they needed.

The sheriff sighed. For now the pathology waiting game would drag on.

EIGHT

Brenna Morgan took off her backpack and sat down on a log. She inhaled the damp smell of the forest floor. The sun filtered through the trees painting curious patterns of light on the fall foliage. She sat for a long time staring at the McConnells' pier and the water beyond. The place was deserted.

She picked up a bright red leaf and held it up to the light, twirling it by the stem. Red was Erin's favorite color. Tears stung her eyes. Brenna made a fist and crushed the leaf with all her might, letting what was left of it fall to the ground. She mashed it with her foot until it looked like ashes. After a minute, she found a stick and drew a cross in the dirt, slowly tracing it over and over again.

The sound of an idling motor caused her to look up at the pier. Her heart started to pound. Had he come back again? Brenna grabbed her backpack and started running. She wasn't waiting around to find out.

Donna Anderson was grading math papers on Friday afternoon when she became aware of someone standing in the doorway.

"Mrs. Anderson? Could I, like, talk to you for a minute?"

She looked up and smiled. "Why, Brenna, of course. Come in. Sit down." She pushed the stack of papers aside, offering her undivided attention. "What's on your mind?"

Her student stood there, trapped in a long pause.

"Brenna? What is it?"

"Uh…I saw something. Well, someone. I know I should tell, only I'm afraid."

Mrs. Anderson leaned forward. "Afraid?"

"Yes, ma'am. I should've said something when it happened, but I've been too scared to say anything. I can't prove it."

"But you're comfortable coming to me?" Mrs. Anderson asked.

"I have to tell somebody."

Donna saw the anguish in Brenna's watery brown eyes. "Start from the beginning. I promise I'll listen with an open mind."

"Thanks, Mrs. Anderson. It's been, like, really hard deciding what to do. I'm scared what this might mean."

Donna got up and sat at the desk next to Brenna and gently patted her hand. "You can trust me."

Brenna's voice was shaky. "It happened after Erin died. I couldn't sleep and I snuck out of my house real late one night and walked in the woods behind the McConnells' pier."

"Do you remember what night?"

"Yes, ma'am. It was the night before the memorial Mass. I just, like, needed to be there. Erin was my best friend and I was so sad…." said Brenna, choking back the emotion.

"I know, sweetie. Go on."

"I heard the sound of a motor. I could barely see a boat on the lake. It was dark, but the boat kept coming closer and closer and then stopped at the McConnells' pier."

"Where were you?"

"Hiding behind a tree. A man got out of the boat and tied it to the dock. And guess what?" Brenna lowered her voice to just above a whisper. "It was the McConnells' motorboat! I've been in that boat, and I know it was theirs because it had the number 08245McC on the side."

"How far were you from the water, Brenna?"

"I don't know, not very far. Like, maybe from here to the cafeteria. I could see, though."

"Did you get a look at who was in the boat?"

"Well, I think so—no, I'm sure I did. But what if people won't believe me? I might be in big trouble. I might even be in danger!"

Donna squeezed the girl's hand. "That's why you have to tell me. Who was it?"

"It was Mr. McConnell," she whispered.

"Are you absolutely sure? It was dark."

"Well, the moon was out, so it wasn't, like, totally dark."

"But did you see his face?"

"Yes, ma'am, kind of. But I just knew who it was by the way he did stuff."

"Like what? Can you be more specific?"

"Like, you know, how he walked and how he stood—and coughed. I recognized his cough. It was him."

"But did you actually recognize his face, Brenna?"

"Sort of. In the moonlight. But I know how he moves. I've seen him tons of times. I'm sure it was him."

Donna felt her heart racing. "Brenna, could you tell what he was doing?"

"Mostly he just, like, sat on the pier and stared. After a long time, he stood up and pulled at something on his left hand—maybe a ring—and threw it in the water in front of the pier. He kept blowing his nose like he had a cold or something. I didn't move."

"How long did you watch?"

"Until he got in the boat and left. Then I ran all the way home. Can't you see why I'm afraid to tell? If Mr. McConnell finds out I saw him, he might come after me.... Mrs. Anderson, he must've killed them."

Donna stood up and held out her arms. Brenna yielded herself like a rag doll and began to sob.

"Sweetie, we need to take this information to the sheriff. You know that."

A few minutes passed before the girl regained enough composure to say anything.

"Will you go with me, Mrs. Anderson?"

"Of course. Here, sit down for a minute and let's think." Donna walked to her desk and plucked several tissues from the box and put them in Brenna's hand. "We need to tell your parents first."

"But they don't even know I've been going there. They won't like it. They tell me I'm too morose, whatever that means. But they didn't know the McConnells. They didn't spend time with them. They don't have to feel this awful pain every day! Doesn't anyone care how sad I feel?"

Donna held Brenna's hand and let her cry. She felt the weight of grief—not just for Brenna, but also for Erin McConnell. What kind of situation were they dealing with here? She was almost afraid to find out.

Hal Barker slammed the door to his file cabinet. What was it about Friday? It seemed as if everyone in the county needed him for something. Mrs. Pickering was fed up with the Thompson boys teasing her prize bull. Mr. Norton reported a chicken thief out on CR 118. The Bullocks' dog thought the Nelsons' yard was a public toilet. After John Washburn's news this afternoon, these complaints seemed like nagging. He was ready for a quiet weekend.

The phone rang again.

"Hal Barker."

"Sheriff, this is Frank Morgan. You may remember my daughter Brenna was Erin McConnell's best friend. There's somethin' she needs to tell you. Could we come down there?"

Hal looked at his watch and rolled his eyes. It was already four-forty-five. "Mr. Morgan, can this wait until Monday?"

"Frankly, Sheriff, no. You need to know this right away."

"All right. How soon can you get here?"

"Ten minutes?"

"That'll be fine. I'll see you then."

∾o∾

Ten minutes later, Brenna Morgan, her parents, and Donna Anderson were seated around the oak table in the sheriff's office.

"All right. What is it you have on your mind, young lady?" Hal said.

Frank Morgan cleared his throat. "Sheriff, my girl's been sittin' on this 'cause she's scared. Keep in mind it took a lot of courage for her to come to you." He looked at Brenna. "Go on, darlin'. Tell him what you saw."

For the next twenty-five minutes, Hal listened intently to a frightened adolescent who knew far too much, yet far too little. The thought that Mike McConnell or any member of the family could still be alive was mind-boggling. He had been so certain after the investigation that foul play was not a factor—and now this. What else didn't he know? What other secret bullets were waiting to be fired?

By the time the Morgans and Donna Anderson left, Hal felt as if he were down for the count.

The sheriff sat alone with his eyes closed, enduring a splitting headache. Was Mike McConnell some kind of animal? Did he really kill his entire family?

Hal knew people here were unprepared for this turn of events. There hadn't been a murder in Baxter for a hundred years, and this case would break the heart of this community. He grieved over the death of innocence. He knew this family. He knew Mike McConnell. Why would he do such a thing?

In the solitude of his office, Hal put his head in his hands and wept.

NINE

On Saturday morning, Mary Beth pulled up in front of Rhonda's at exactly eight o'clock. She picked up the newspaper in the yard and skipped up the porch steps. Before she could ring the bell, the door swung open.

"Oops, sorry. You must be Jed. I'm Mary Beth Kennsington. Looking for this?" She handed him the newspaper.

"Yeah, thanks," he said. "Rhonda said you were picking her up for some church thing. How's your car?"

"It should be ready on Monday. I've got a loaner until then. I'm afraid Rhonda's little Mustang took the brunt of it."

"Sounds like it. Go on in. I think she's ready."

The second Mary Beth entered the house, Rhonda practically backed her out the door—right into Jed. Rhonda looked alarmed to see him standing there.

"So what's the big hurry?" he said. "She just got here."

Rhonda cheeks turned crimson. "Uh, I—"

"I'm afraid it's my fault," said Mary Beth, pretending not to notice his bloodshot eyes and disheveled appearance. "I've built up this carnival like it's the greatest show on earth. Hope you don't mind my stealing her for the day."

"Keep her as long as you want," Jed said. "*This* sinner is going to read the paper and do as little as possible."

Rhonda was silent, her jaw clenched.

"Hey," said Mary Beth, gently taking her arm, "have you been outside yet? The weather's perfect. We're going to have a great day."

Rhonda slung her sweater over her shoulder. "You're right. Let's go."

"Nice meeting you, Jed," said Mary Beth.

"Yeah. Bye, ladies."

Hal Barker nestled in his recliner—feet up, newspaper in front of him, and a fresh cup of coffee in his hand. Today he was husband, father, and Saturday-morning bum.

Ten-year-old Matthew darted by. "Evan and I are building a tree house. I'll be back for lunch."

Wendy, covered in a soccer uniform two sizes too big, stopped at Hal's chair. "Daddy, whaddaya think? Am I pretty?" She flashed him an irresistible smile with her front teeth missing.

"Princess, you're adorable." He brushed her blond pigtail aside so he could kiss her cheek.

Wendy crawled into Hal's lap and made herself right at home. She began chatting happily about a tea party at Holly's, and Claire getting a new bike, and Morgan's dolly getting a boo-boo—Hal loved these moments with his daughter. Her uninhibited chatter was music to his ears. Wendy's monologue ended abruptly.

"Daddy, you and Mommy are coming to my game. It's at three." She hugged him, crawled out of his lap, and bounced out the door.

Hal chuckled. There was still plenty of time to bask in the morning sun pouring in his window. Soon the peace he'd been hoping for settled over him, and he dozed off, a half-read newspaper covering his chest.

Ellen Jones sorted through her in box and made a few notations on Post-it notes. There was a message that Mitch Crawford, the head diver in the recovery effort, had returned her call. She dialed the number.

"This is Mitch."

"Mitch, this is Ellen Jones at the *Baxter Daily News*. I'm sorry I wasn't here when you returned my call. Do you have something for me?"

"Yes, ma'am, I do. I checked through the printouts of every itemized piece of evidence we recovered in the McConnell investigation. We found remnants of the houseboat and contents, but nothing that could be identified as part of a motorboat."

"Hmm…is the recovery effort officially closed, Mitch?"

"The recovery effort for debris is closed. I think the search for remains might still be active, but I'm not involved in that. You'd have to ask John Washburn."

"Is there anyone else I should check with regarding the motorboat?"

"No, ma'am. All the divers report to me. If I don't have it, it hasn't been recovered."

"Thanks, Mitch. I appreciate your willingness to check for me."

"You're welcome. Let me know if there's anything else you need."

Ellen hung up the phone and picked it up again. She wondered if Hal Barker knew about this.

The sheriff was snoozing when he was startled by the phone ringing.

"Hello," he said, trying to sound alert. He looked at his watch. It was twelve-thirty.

"Hal, this is Ellen. I'm sorry to bother you at home on a Saturday, but I followed up on something you said at our meeting. I'd be interested in your reaction."

"Refresh my memory, Ellen."

"I asked you about the McConnells' motorboat, and you told me to check with your investigators to see if it was found."

"And?"

"Not one piece of it has been recovered. Don't you find that interesting? If everyone in the family was on the houseboat when it exploded, the small boat had to have been out there. But if it wasn't there, then who took it? And why?"

Hal sat upright in the recliner. "Who'd you talk to?"

"Mitch Crawford. I just got off the phone with him."

"Ellen, don't get in a hurry to print this. It could be nothing."

"Or *something*. Hal, I'm not trying to interfere with your investigation, but this has bothered me from the beginning. This boat, or parts of it, should have been found, and there seems to be no trace. That should send up a red flag, shouldn't it?"

He lowered his voice. "Listen, Ellen, there's some stuff going on I'm not at liberty to discuss yet. Please trust me on this. I'll get back to you when it's appropriate. I've got a few irons of my own in the fire."

"Hal, this has to change the status of the investigation. How can you not suspect foul play?"

He sighed, switching the phone to his other ear. "Off the record?"

"All right."

"I don't know what to think right now. A lot has happened in the last twenty-four hours. I need to let the dust settle this weekend and go hard after it on Monday. I'm waiting on a few calls myself. I promise I won't leave you out of the loop, but I'm asking you, as a professional courtesy, not to say anything about this yet. When I have the facts, you'll get them."

"Fair enough. I'll stay out of your way."

"Thanks, Ellen. I need a little space."

"Rhonda, how do you like it so far?" said Mary Beth, her voice barely audible above the laughter. "I love the bunny face you painted on the little girl with the braids. Cute!"

"I'm having a ball. Doesn't take much to make them happy, does it?"

"Not really. I told you it was fun."

Rhonda nodded. "My kind of fun." She put the finishing touches on a ladybug. "How's that?"

The little girl looked at her face in the mirror and smiled. "Thank you."

"You're very welcome."

Mary Beth cupped her hands around her mouth. "Hey, Rembrandt! How about a kitty cat?" She sent a blond boy in Rhonda's direction.

"Sit right here, little man, and let me see what I can do. Hold really still for me. This might tickle."

The toddler sat like a statue as Rhonda turned him into a feline with a few strokes of stage makeup. She held up the mirror so he could see.

He squealed with delight. "I'm a kitty! I'm a kitty!"

The little boy threw his arms around Rhonda, who had forgotten how good it felt to be hugged.

A young man in a plaid shirt and jeans intently studied the crowd, aware of every move Rhonda made. He relaxed his watch. There was nothing here to worry about.

Hal gave his daughter a victory ride on his shoulders and put her down when they got to the front door. "There you go, champ."

Wendy looked up at him. Her giant blue eyes smiled even before her mouth did. "Daddy, whaddaya think? Am I pretty?"

"Princess, you're adorable," he said, looking beyond his daughter's chocolate mustache, tangled pigtails, and dirty soccer uniform.

The minute they walked in the door the phone rang. Nancy answered it and handed the phone to him. "Mitch Crawford."

Hal took the phone. "Any luck, Mitch?"

"Jackpot, Sheriff. We found a plain, gold wedding band in some underwater growth about sixty feet directly in front of the pier. What's this about anyway?"

"I'll tell you later," he said, lowering his voice and turning his head. "Were there initials engraved on it?"

"Let me get a magnifying glass. I'll be right back."

A minute later, Hal heard Mitch's voice again.

"Okay, let's see…there's more than initials. It's in script, kinda hard to make out…. It says…*Forever…without…*it looks like *thorns.* Does that mean anything to you—*Forever without thorns?*"

"Put it into evidence. And Mitch…don't mention this to anyone."

"Sure, Sheriff, whatever."

"I'll talk to you Monday. Thanks for the extra effort. I owe you one."

Hal hung up the phone and leaned his back against the wall. Mike McConnell was not going to get away with this on his watch—no way! How could anyone do something so unspeakable to his own kids?

One good ol' boy from O'Brian's bar just fell from grace.

Rhonda lowered herself into a folding chair. "Ooooooh."

Mary Beth laughed. "Well, tell me, O tired one, was it a success?"

"If the kids had half as much fun as we did, it was." Rhonda smiled at a handful of energetic children with wide brooms making a game of bulldozing paper cups across the parking lot.

"I know you're beat," said Mary Beth, "but I'm sure glad you came. Listen, I'm starved. Want to get a sandwich or something?"

Rhonda looked at her watch. "I can't believe it's already seven."

"Why don't we just walk over to Monty's. Unless you're too tired to walk across the square."

"Are you kidding? I've already got a second wind. Let's go."

Mary Beth closed her eyes, a smile spreading slowly across her face. "I'm craving something chocolaty...and gooey...and layered with calories."

Rhonda laughed. "*You* are the queen of chocolate. I believe I've lost the crown."

"You know they have mud pie parfait, don't you?"

Rhonda took Mary Beth's arm. "Come on. We'd better hurry before they run out!"

The sound of their schoolgirl laughter echoed in the chilly night. Watchful eyes followed the duo as they walked across the town square on the way to Monty's Diner. A young man in a plaid shirt and jeans never let Rhonda Wilson out of his sight.

TEN

I t's good to be home," Maxine Arthur said. "I can hardly wait to see how much the leaves have turned in three weeks. It'll be nice sleeping in our own bed. What's wrong, Hugh, won't the door open?"

"That's weird," he said. "I don't think it was locked, but I know I locked this thing before we left." He pushed it open slowly and flipped the light switch. "I'll get the luggage later. I'm dyin' of thirst."

He took Maxine's hand and they walked into the kitchen.

"I enjoyed seein' Europe," he said, "but there's no place like home."

"Hugh, I can't believe you left those out."

"What?"

"Those dish towels draped over the sink."

"Me? Why would I do that? You trained me better 'n a pet poodle to hang 'em on the rack."

She smiled. "I know. You must be slipping."

"Does that mean I don't get my water?"

Maxine opened the cupboard next to the sink. "Hugh! Where are my dishes?"

He saw the empty cupboard and opened the dishwasher. He pulled out the rack. "In here."

"But I put them away before we left."

"Aw, honey, it took a lot of plannin' to get ready for this trip.

Even a meticulous housekeeper like you can't remember every little thing."

"Hugh, I put them away; I'm positive. Just like you locked the front door and neither of us left out the towels. This is scaring me."

"All right," he said, "let's check out the rest of the house."

He walked ahead of her into the bathroom and immediately turned around, blocking the door. "Whoa, you're not gonna like this."

Maxine pushed past him. "Who's been in here? Just look at that messy soap in my marble dish! And dirty towels piled in the corner!" She stomped over to the bathtub and ran her finger across a dark ring of soap scum. "This is filthy! And look here—there's dried toothpaste in the sink and water spots on the mirror. This makes me so angry!"

"I wonder if anything's missing." Hugh took her hand and they walked across the hall to the master bedroom.

Maxine gasped. "Of all the nerve! Look at my pretty comforter, just wadded up on the floor." She started to cry. "Who would do this? They've probably been all through our things."

Hugh put his arm around her. "Somebody or bodies made themselves right at home while we were gone, and if I knew who it was, they'd be walkin' around with buckshot in their backsides."

"Hugh, I won't be able to sleep here tonight."

"Don't worry, I'm callin' the lake patrol. There's no excuse for this nonsense."

"What's taking him so long?" asked Maxine. She pulled an afghan around her shoulders as they sat together on the porch swing.

"Honey, it's only been twenty minutes since I called him. There, I see headlights. I'll bet that's him now."

A vehicle pulled into the driveway and a car door slammed. Paul Martin hurried toward them. "What in tarnation is this about a break in?"

"Come see for yourself. We've done more lookin' since I called you," Hugh said.

The couple led him into the kitchen and opened the pantry.

"Cleaned us out." Hugh motioned toward the trash container, which was overflowing with empty cans and wrappers. "Wiped out the freezer too—ground beef, bacon, frozen dinners, waffles. Drank all the beer in the house. Probably a bunch of kids up to who knows what." He pulled his wife close. "For cryin' out loud, they were in our bed."

Paul scratched his head. "Any sign of forced entry?"

"Follow me." Hugh led Paul out to the sunporch. "I found this broken windowpane; that's how our freeloaders got in. Wasn't hard to reach in and unlock the window. Of course, after that they just waltzed in and out the front door. It wasn't locked when we got home."

Paul wrote something on his report. "Hugh, what makes you believe there was more than one intruder?"

"I don't know. Just assumed it was kids. Can't imagine why any-one would hang out here alone. What's the point?"

"Who knew you were in Europe?" Paul asked.

"Everyone who knows us. We saw no reason to hide it. Never thought about somethin' like this happenin'."

"Your place is secluded up here in the trees. I doubt if anyone can tell when the lights are on."

"Only from the back."

"What about valuables? Anything missing?"

Maxine walked in the room. "I've got expensive diamonds in my jewelry box, but it doesn't look like it was even tampered with."

"Do you folks keep money anywhere?"

Hugh nodded. "I have a thousand dollars stashed in a cigar box in the closet. It's still there. Can you believe that?"

Paul Martin sat down at the kitchen table and finished filling out the paperwork. "Anyone looking for valuables would have torn this place up. Whoever was here ran the dishwasher and put the dirty linens in piles—my kids won't even do that! I'll file a report with Sheriff Barker tomorrow. Maybe he's run across something like this before, but it's the darnedest thing I've ever seen."

When Paul got up to leave, it was after 1:00 A.M. "I don't think you should stay here tonight. It may not be safe. Plus, I need to dust your place for fingerprints, and it's best if you don't go around touching everything."

"Hold on," Hugh said. "I'm not lettin' some no-good trespassers run me outta my own home. I'm stayin'. I'll just load my huntin' rifle—"

"Well, dear, you'll be here all by yourself because I'm driving to Ellison to find a safe place to sleep." Maxine walked over to the luggage and picked up her overnight bag and her purse. "Hugh Arthur, don't be an old fool. Let's get out of here until we get the locks changed."

"She's right," Paul said. "Whoever was in here could come back. Find a motel. Give me a call in the middle of the morning. I'll have an update for you by then. Try not to worry; we'll get to the bottom of this."

The grandfather clock in the hallway struck 2:00 A.M. Hal Barker sat in his recliner and doodled on a legal-size pad.

He believed Brenna Morgan's story, especially after Mitch confirmed that the McConnells' small boat had never been recovered. But could she be mistaken about the identity of the man she saw? Could it have been someone else? If it *was* Mike McConnell, he must have killed his wife and kids—why else would he run? Yet it didn't fit what Hal knew of the guy, and there didn't seem to be a motive.

Whoever threw the ring from the pier wanted it to be recovered so authorities would conclude that Mike McConnell had died in the fire. But why not drop it in the water at the scene? Why sneak back in the middle of an investigation and risk being caught?

Plus, Hal had no proof the wedding ring was Mike's. It wasn't much of a stretch that a wedding ring sentiment from a bride named Rose could read *Forever without thorns*. But without someone to confirm it, it wasn't solid evidence.

A great deal was riding on whether they were able to positively identify Mike McConnell from the remains. Anyone could have planted the ring—except a dead man.

ELEVEN

Rhonda sat in the fourth row at Cornerstone Bible Church with Mary Beth, Joe, and their three kids. She felt out of place.

Last night at Monty's, she had accepted Mary Beth's invitation to attend Sunday church with her family and then work the carnival the rest of the day. What started out as a quick dinner outing resulted in a marathon discussion and Rhonda's telling Mary Beth far more than she was comfortable with....

"Jed didn't used to drink this much, Mary Beth. It's gotten worse since Mike died. I'm embarrassed you saw him looking like he does."

"Don't be."

"But Jed's actually a handsome man—at least, he was."

"Does he talk about Mike?"

"Hardly a word. But then, he doesn't say much to me about anything. It's like his whole world blew up with the houseboat. He treats me like I'm not there."

"That must be hard."

"I can't believe I'm telling you all this, but I've put up with his indifference for twenty-eight years. To be treated like I don't exist is demeaning. It hurts...."

"I'm sorry," said Mary Beth, touching her hand. "I didn't mean to upset you."

"You didn't. It feels good to say it out loud. I'm so lonely. The saddest part of all is I've never stopped loving him. Pathetic, huh?"

"I don't think so. Doesn't it keep hope alive?"

"I don't know. I feel torn between hope and despair. Sometimes I think I hate him—but I don't." Rhonda sighed. "I'm tired of feeling like I live in a cemetery with all my dreams dead and buried. There's hardly any life in our marriage. I'm scared that one day we'll just decide to pull the plug...."

The organ began to play. Rhonda rose with the congregation and wondered if she had said too much last night. At least she hadn't told Mary Beth about getting pregnant with Jennifer.

Seeing Mary Beth with Joe made the canyon between her and Jed seem even wider. She lost herself in studying them. The couple's demeanor was open and receptive. Joe held the songbook with one hand, and slipped his other arm around Mary Beth's waist. They smiled at each other. The Kennsingtons shared what Rhonda longed for.

The congregation sat down and Pastor Thomas began his sermon.

"My message this morning is from Jeremiah 29:11. 'For I know the plans I have for you,' declares the LORD, 'plans to prosper you and not to harm you, plans to give you hope and a future.'"

That's all the sermon Rhonda heard. It seemed as if God Himself was speaking directly to her. Heat flooded her face and her heart began to pound. She remembered what Father Donaghan had said, but this time, she was so deeply stirred she couldn't move. The words were warm and comforting. The deep canyon in her heart stopped aching. It seemed as though God was sitting right next to her, telling her something, though it was no clearer to her now than when she fled Saint Anthony's. A welcome peace wrapped its arms around her, and she became lost in an intensely private moment.

A young man in a plaid shirt and jeans listened with interest to the words of the sermon and momentarily let down his guard. But Rhonda Wilson was never out of his sight.

Paul Martin's cell phone rang. "Lake patrol."

"Paul, it's Hugh. You finished at the house? Maxine and I would like to come back, try to make some sense of all this."

"If you figure it out, you can tell me. Guess I'll have to apologize to Maxine for taking some things from the house. I got more fingerprints and DNA evidence than Carter has pills. Shoot, I never got to do anything like this before."

"Don't sound so happy about it," Hugh said.

"I didn't mean it that way. It's an interesting case is all."

"Paul, as soon as you give us the green light, Lou Abernathy is gonna put new locks on the doors."

"You can go on back. I'm finished out there. I'm gonna check in with Sheriff Barker soon as he gets back from church. This is too weird to sit on."

"Okay, Paul, thanks. Keep us posted on what you find out."

"We'll keep an eye on the house, so don't worry. Tell Maxine everything's gonna be fine. Whoever was in there got the last free ride."

"Hal, why don't you lie down and take a nap," Nancy said. "You could hardly keep your eyes open in church this morning."

"I hoped no one noticed. I didn't sleep much last night."

"It was nearly dawn when you came to bed. Is anything wrong? I've never seen you this consumed with a case."

Hal looked into her understanding eyes. "There's a lot to tell you, but I need time to put it together. I promise I'll sit down with you after the kids go to bed."

"I knew something was up. But when you didn't tell me anything, I started to worry."

"I know, honey," he said, taking her hand. "I haven't said anything to anyone yet. Been trying to sort it out." He kissed her. "I love you. Let's talk later."

"Okay. I'll keep the kids quiet so you can rest."

Hal heard a gentle knock on the door. "The phone's for you," Nancy said. "Lake patrol. Do you want to take it?"

"Uh...yeah...sure." He put the receiver to his ear. "This is Hal."

"It's Paul Martin. Something strange happened up here on the northwest part of the lake, Sheriff. I wouldn't bother you on a Sunday, but I want to make sure I've done everything I need to. Never had one like this."

Hal listened patiently as Paul relayed the details about the break-in at the Arthurs'.

"Hmm...that is strange. I assume you dusted for prints and bagged all the evidence?"

"Yep. Didn't seem like the intruders were trying to hide anything. Hugh Arthur thinks it was a buncha kids."

"Okay, I'll meet you over there in the morning at seven-thirty, and we'll try to piece this together. You said the Arthurs are back in—with new locks, I hope?"

"Yeah. Good ol' Lou Abernathy insists on doing it himself even though the hardware store isn't open on Sunday. He'll have them fixed up yet today."

"Okay, Paul. I'll meet you out there in the morning."

"Maxine, I've finished unpackin' my stuff. There's a lot of dirty laundry here."

"That's okay, I'm glad to have something to do," she said. "I'm washing some of the older linens to put back on the bed. Paul took the things that were on the floor. I wouldn't have used them again anyway. Gives me the willies."

"Lou Abernathy just left," Hugh said. "The windowpane is fixed and the locks are changed. We're back in business."

"I wouldn't go that far. It's going to be a long time before I feel safe again."

"While you're doin' the wash, I think I'll go rake leaves. I need to burn off some nervous energy." He kissed his wife's cheek. "Honey, things are gonna be fine now. If it makes ya feel better, lock the door behind me. I've got a key."

Hugh went out the back door and grabbed the rake off the porch. He knew October wasn't finished covering his lot with a crunchy carpet of red, gold, and orange, but it felt good to be outside. He raked for a couple of hours and worked up a good sweat.

He stood and admired the view around Heron Lake. As far as the eye could see, the woods were covered in a patchwork of rich autumn colors spread between shimmering silver water and blue sky dotted with cloud puffs. Lake homes climbed the hillside and nestled among the trees.

The squabbling of a Great Blue Heron was an amusing contrast to the sound of children laughing, and the silence of trolling motors a welcome relief from the noisy jet skis of summer. In the distance, the whistle of the four-thirty train from Parker announced it was right on schedule.

Hugh felt a gentle hand on his shoulder.

"It's beautiful, isn't it?" Maxine said.

"Yep. Can't imagine livin' anywhere else. Good to be home. The sun's gettin' low. Think I'll put the rake in the boathouse." He smiled. "Ever miss the old pontoon?"

"I do. But I'm just as glad we don't have to worry about maintaining it now that you're retired. You've got enough to take care of, Mr. Packrat." She poked him with her finger.

"Hey, ya never know when ya might need somethin'."

"Phooey, the only saving grace is that the door faces the water. Thank heavens we can pull it down and hide all your junk. You have no shame."

He chuckled. "The empty boat slip is just wasted space. I could nail some boards across the cutout and create a big storage plank."

"You want to see an old woman throw a conniption?"

He laughed.

"It's getting chilly," she said. "I'm going back to the house. Are you coming?"

"Soon as I put this rake away."

"What's the hurry? It's only been on the back porch since August."

He walked down the steep stone steps to the back door of the boathouse. When he pushed the rusty door open, his eyes were instantly drawn to something that didn't belong in there. He stood frozen in the doorway.

"What the...?"

Paul Martin was cruising the lake about sunset when his cell phone rang. "Lake patrol. This is Paul."

"Paul, it's Hugh Arthur. You have any idea why Mike McConnell's boat is in my boathouse?"

"What are you talking about?"

"I went down to the boathouse to put away a rake. His john-boat is hangin' in my boat slip! What's goin' on? I'm gettin' kinda tired of surprises."

"Hugh, I'm on the lake about two miles north of the bridge. I'll be there in ten minutes."

"Maybe I'll just call that McConnell fella and ask him myself."

"Uh—it won't do any good, Hugh. Look, it's kinda compli-cated. I'll explain when I get there."

"I wish somebody'd tell me what's goin' on. I'm not runnin' Grand Central Station! People are comin' and goin' like they own the place. Maybe I oughta start sellin' time-shares!"

"Hugh, I'm on my way. Sit tight."

The phone rang at the Barker house. "Hello, this is Hal."

"Sheriff, this is Paul Martin again."

"Yeah, Paul. What is it?"

"Hugh Arthur discovered something very interesting in his boathouse. You might want to get over here."

"Paul, get to the point. I don't have time for this."

"Why do you suppose Mike McConnell's boat would be hanging in Hugh Arthur's boat slip?"

Hal sat straight up in the recliner. "McConnell's boat? Are you sure, Paul?"

"Sheriff, I'm standing here looking at it. It's his, all right."

Hal's squad car sped toward Heron Lake. Fifteen minutes later he stood in the Arthurs' boathouse, looking at the registration number Brenna Morgan had recognized: 08245McC.

"Paul, you need to dust this for fingerprints and put any contents from the boat into evidence. Also gather DNA evidence. Do it before it's impounded. I don't want *any* mistakes; get it done right."

"Yes, sir." A big smile stretched across Paul's face. "I'm on it."

"Mr. Arthur," Hal said, "do you have any explanation for the boat being here?"

"Absolutely none, Sheriff. I know—uh, knew—Mike. He used to come by here in that little johnboat and we'd talk some. He and his family lived year-round in that neat ol' wood houseboat."

"When's the last time you spoke to him?"

"Hmm…let me think…. Oh, the weekend before we left on our trip. I was down at the dock and he was out in the boat by himself, just cruisin' the lake. He stopped to say hi and we talked for a while. Friendly guy."

"What did you talk about? Do you remember?"

"Well, sir, not specifically. Just neighborly talk. He never said much about himself but always seemed interested in hearin' about what I was up to."

"This is very important, Mr. Arthur," Hal said. "Did Mike know you were going to be gone the following week? Did you talk about your trip and the time frame when you'd be out of town?"

"Sheriff, I reckon I did. I can't remember, but I guess I naturally would have since Maxine and I were excited about it."

"Do you remember what his mood was like when you saw him? Did he mention any dissatisfaction with his life, his family, his job?"

"No, Sheriff. He was friendly, just like always. Do you have any idea why his boat is in here? Do you think whoever broke into my house had something to do with the McConnells' dyin'?"

"Hard to say, but this boat's been unaccounted for. We're looking into it. We'll get it out of your way just as soon as we take some pictures and Paul dusts for prints. Sorry you and your wife came home to such a mess."

Hal shook hands with the Arthurs and walked back to his squad car. It was time to go home and tell Nancy before he took his finger out of the dike. The cruel flood of reality about to sweep through Baxter would leave a permanent watermark. He just hoped he wasn't in over his head.

TWELVE

O n Monday morning, Hal Barker, John Washburn, Mayor Charlie Kirby, Chief Joe Henley, and Ellen Jones sat at the oak table in the sheriff's office.

"I've called this meeting," Hal said, "because new developments in the McConnell investigation have caused us to change our entire focus. Over the past four days, new evidence has raised serious doubts to our earlier conclusion that there was no foul play in this case."

Four pairs of eyes looked searchingly into Hal's.

"I'll present this as objectively and concisely as I can, then I'll take questions. I'm due to meet with FBI Special Agent Jordan Ellis at twelve-forty-five, so let me get started. I don't want there to be any doubt as to where this department stands."

Hal laid out the events that began at their last meeting, starting with Ellen's inquiry concerning the recovery of the McConnells' small boat. He gave them every detail.

"Let me conclude by saying that John's team, working with Matt Nash at the ATF, also recovered additional human remains, which have been given to pathology for testing. We hope to know within the next few weeks whether or not Mike McConnell's identity can be confirmed. That's a key factor. I want nothing more than to find out Mike isn't responsible for this. But my gut feeling is that his remains will never be found because he didn't die in the explosion.

"These overwhelming doubts compel us to move this investigation in a different direction. From this point on, this is a *murder* investigation."

Hal waited for a reaction. Mayor Kirby coughed, but no one moved.

"Okay, let me wrap up what we know and don't know:

"First of all, Brenna Morgan claims to have seen Mike McConnell, but we have no physical evidence. We have dusted for fingerprints and collected DNA evidence in the Arthurs' house, in the McConnells' boat, and in Mike's locker at the highway department. Also, as I mentioned, we're waiting for the pathology report on the most recent remains recovered.

"Second, Brenna claims the suspect threw what appeared to be a ring into the water off the pier. Mitch Crawford recovered a man's gold wedding band, wedged in some underwater growth, sixty feet in front of the McConnells' pier. We don't know for sure if this was Mike's wedding band, but Rose's sister may be able to confirm it.

"Third, we know the registration number Brenna gave us matches the one on the boat found in the Arthurs' boathouse. We have verified with Fish and Game that this is the registration number given to the McConnells' boat.

"Another thing we know is this boat shows no evidence of damage and could not have been at the site at the time of the explosion. However, there is a small amount of scorching on the rope used to tie it to the houseboat.

"Rose McConnell's sister, Lisa Sorensen, will be here on Wednesday. Though she's recovering from surgery, she obtained special permission from her doctor to travel. She's shocked by these developments, and I think she may be able to help us piece some of this together. She knows more about Mike than any of us.

"That's all I have to say." Hal looked at his watch. "It's twelve-fifteen. Are there any questions? I need to leave in fifteen minutes."

"Do you believe the suspect has left the area?" Chief Henley asked.

"If he's smart, he did. We haven't ruled anything out."

Ellen twirled her pencil. "If he was the intruder at the Arthurs' home, he probably left the area either on foot or in a stolen motor vehicle or boat. Has anyone checked that out?"

"I've got my department working on it. We have a printout of every stolen vehicle reported in Norris County since the explosion."

"He could easily have hitchhiked," John Washburn said. "It wouldn't be hard to disguise himself. Even if he only got to Parker, he could've hopped a freight and ended up anywhere from there to the end of the line."

Everyone nodded.

"How will the FBI be involved?" Charlie asked.

"I'm about to find out," Hal said. "I've never handled a murder investigation. I hope they'll help us sharpen our senses in following leads, picking up on clues and using common sense. If it was Mike McConnell who fled that scene, we need to figure out how to begin looking, and how to work with other law enforcement agencies around the country. We're not equipped to do this by ourselves."

"Hal, would you mind if I pray?" Charlie asked. "I realize this is highly irregular, but so are the circumstances. When this news gets out, there's going to be everything from disbelief to outrage. God help us—one of our own is officially a fugitive. Maybe a murderer. Hard to believe."

"Go ahead, Charlie. Certainly can't hurt to have God on our side. I think everyone here agrees with that."

The five bowed their heads.

"Heavenly Father," said Charlie. "We come before You inexperienced and uncertain—not knowing how this will affect each of us and our community. But we know nothing escapes Your vision. You know what happened, why You allowed it, and how You will use it.

"Please help Hal and all those who will be assisting him in finding the truth. We pray that whoever is responsible for the deaths of this family will be brought to justice.

"But, Lord, if it is Mike McConnell, please use this to bring him to his knees, for You are a God of forgiveness and grace. No sin is too big, no sinner too hopeless to be pardoned if he confesses his guilt and repents."

Charlie stopped and the others opened their eyes. But when he resumed his prayer, Hal looked at Joe, who looked at John, who looked at Ellen. They quickly bowed their heads again.

"So wherever he is, Lord," said Charlie, with the voice inflection of a preacher, "please be with him and cause his heart to feel true remorse. Though we hate what he's done, help us not to hate him. We have courts to hold him accountable. And there will be consequences for his actions.

"But You are Judge over a higher court. Under Your system, Jesus took our punishment and finished out our sentence, so that anyone who asks to be forgiven and truly repents will be pardoned.

"Lord, bring Mike McConnell to repentance, for it's only then that he'll understand the riches of Your grace. In the Name of Jesus Christ, Your Son, we pray. Amen."

Hal hadn't expected Charlie's lengthy prayer and wasn't sure what to say to break the uncomfortable silence that followed. Finally he lifted his head, glanced at his watch, and rolled his eyes. "For cryin' out loud, Charlie, I forgot you went to seminary!"

The others burst into laughter.

"I do get carried away," said Charlie with a good-natured smile. "My wife won't put the food on the table until I've said the blessing. Otherwise it gets cold."

Hal patted him on the back. "That's okay. God doesn't keep track of time. But unfortunately the FBI has a schedule, and I'm on it. I've got to run."

Hal stood on the McConnells' pier and waited for Jordan Ellis to arrive. The day seemed unreal. He never considered he would be heading up a murder investigation with the FBI.

He thought about Charlie's prayer. Hal knew he should hate what Mike did without actually hating him, but at the moment, all he felt was contempt. He didn't feel mercy for a guy who could do something like that to his own family.

Hal looked up when Special Agent Jordan Ellis pulled his car behind the pier. He walked toward the car, aware that his six-foot-four frame clad in sheriff's attire, traditional Stetson, and gun in holster, might look like a figure from the old West. He wondered if he fit Ellis's preconceived idea of a county sheriff.

Ellis got out of the car. Hal sized him up—guessed him to be five-foot-nine, medium build. He was dressed in a dark suit, white shirt, and striped tie. His blond hair was neatly combed, dark glasses on his face, a bit of arrogance in his step. He appeared to be around forty years old, the same as Hal.

When they stood face-to-face, each had a hand drawn and ready.

"Jordan? Hal Barker. Thanks for coming."

"Good to meet you, Sheriff. I've followed this case in the newspaper, but until you called, I never got the impression foul play was a factor."

"Like I told you on the phone, the new evidence is overwhelming. We have no choice but to treat it as a murder investigation. Since it's been a hundred years since we've had one of those around here, this is way out of our league. We need to tap into your thinking. Maybe get some direction. Find out what resources we can use."

"Let's stand on the dock and you can fill me in," Jordan said. "No need to waste the sunshine."

Shortly after two, Hal pulled up in front of the courthouse just as Paul Martin was going up the steps carrying a large, brown envelope. By the time Hal got out of his squad car, Paul was all over him.

"Sheriff, the prints in the house and boat match. They also

match the prints on personal items taken from McConnell's locker at work. It was him, all right. The thumbprints even match what's on his driver's license record."

"Any fingerprints on the boat throttle and steering wheel besides Mike's?" Hal asked.

"Nope. Well, just his wife's—matched them to her driver's license record and stuff in her VW bus. But since she died in the fire, I'd say we got us a murder investigation, Sheriff."

"Sure looks that way. Is the report in that envelope?"

"Yes, sir." He handed the envelope to Hal. "Is there anything else you want me to do?"

"Not right now, Paul. I just met with Special Agent Jordan Ellis from the FBI. He's going to help us with this. God knows, we need all the help we can get."

"FBI? Really? Hot dog! Who would've thought this case would take a turn like this?"

"Yeah, who would've thought… Listen, Paul, I need to get quiet for a while, sort some of this out. My head's pounding." Hal rubbed the back of his neck.

"Sure, Sheriff. I'm outta here. Let me know if I can help."

"Yeah, okay. I will."

"Hello," said Rhonda, switching the phone to her other ear. She set a sack of groceries on the counter.

"Rhonda, this is Hal Barker. I have something I need to talk to Jed about, but I'd like you to sit in on it too. Would it be all right if I come by on my way home? I don't want to foul up your dinner plans, but I'm on a real whirlwind right now, and it's the only time I've got. I could be there in fifteen minutes. It won't take long."

"All right, Hal. Jed just got home."

"Rhonda…he may need a little moral support after we talk tonight. Are you planning to be home?"

"I'll be here. Hal, is something wrong?"

"I'd rather tell you when I get there. See you in a few minutes."

Hal removed his Stetson and rang the doorbell. He shifted from one foot to the other for what seemed an eternity. The porch light came on and Jed opened the door.

"Hey, Sheriff," he said. "Come on in."

Hal was surprised to see Jed looking sober. He followed him into the living room where Rhonda was waiting.

"Please, sit down," Rhonda said. "Would you like something to drink—coffee, Coke, water?"

"No, thanks. I'm fine."

"What was it you wanted to talk to us about?" Jed asked.

Hal had rehearsed what he would say, but decided instead to speak from his heart. He looked at Rhonda and then at Jed.

"Some new facts have surfaced in the McConnell case. I want to talk to both of you before the news hits tomorrow's headlines."

"What news?" Jed asked.

"Look, there's no easy way to say this—we don't believe Mike McConnell died in the explosion."

"What?"

"Hal, what are you saying?" Rhonda's eyes widened.

"Let me outline the new evidence that's surfaced since Friday." Hal told them everything that led to his meeting with Jordan Ellis.

"Are you sure those fingerprints are Mike's?" Jed asked. "There has to be some mistake. I know Mike better than anyone else. There's no way he murdered his family. No way. I don't buy it!"

"Then do you have another explanation for his disappearance? Or his entry into the Arthurs' house? Or Brenna Morgan's account of what she saw? Or the wedding band Mitch recovered? Or Mike's boat hanging in the Arthurs' boat slip? Jed, face it. His fingerprints were all over the place. The DNA evidence is just going to verify what we already know—Mike McConnell is alive. And he seems to be the *only* McConnell that is."

Jed heaved a sigh and leaned his head against the back of the couch. He closed his eyes and shook his head from side to side.

"I'm sorry, Jed," Hal said. "There's really nothing else I can say. If you think of anything—I mean *anything*—that would help us figure this out, I want to know about it, you hear me? Nobody wants to be wrong more than I do."

Hal got up. Jed and Rhonda accompanied him to the door, but nothing more was said. He put his Stetson on and left.

Jed stood there after the front door closed. Hal's news hung in the air like the feeling after a horrible nightmare. His heart was racing. He wanted to run.

For the first time in a long while, he looked into Rhonda's eyes and saw his own emptiness. Her eyes filled with tears at the same time as his, and after that, he couldn't see anything. He felt Rhonda's arms around him and he didn't push her away. Unable to hold back the flood of stored-up pain, he broke. Both of them were sobbing. Much more spilled over the dam than just sorrow over tonight's news. Jed knew it. He just didn't know what to do about it.

THIRTEEN

At Monty's Diner the morning sun shone through the east wall of windows and melted like warm butter across the blue-and-white checkered floor.

Rosie Harris picked up a freshly brewed pot of coffee and stuck two more breakfast orders on the clip. "Order!"

Leo turned around and slid two plates in front of her. "Order up."

Assistant Manager Mark Steele chuckled. The race was on. But he was momentarily engrossed in the reaction of the early crowd to Tuesday's headlines in the *Baxter Daily News,* which not only raised Mike McConnell from the dead, but also put him at the top of the prime suspect list.

"When did this thing change?" Reggie Mason asked. "We went through the memorial service and the whole nine yards. Now they're saying Mike McConnell's not only alive, but maybe murdered his entire family? If he did it, he deserves the death penalty."

Rosie poured Reggie a refill. "When they catch him, a jury'll decide that. Mike doesn't strike me as a cold-blooded killer. There must be extenuating circumstances."

"Yeah, like he's a no-good drunk," Dan Lockhart said.

"And likes playin' with matches," Mort Clary added.

Reggie raised an eyebrow. "Rosie, whaddaya mean he doesn't strike you as a killer? Since when do killers wear name tags?"

"Does anyone here know what happened?" Liv Spooner

whirled herself around on the stool. "Were any of you there? All I know is Mike McConnell stopped and helped me more than once when not one of you would lift a finger."

Mort grinned. "Liv, it don't take no rocket scientist t' figure this out. McConnell's guilty as sin. He did it, all right. He mighta got away with it, too, if it wasn't fer that Morgan girl. What I wanna know is—did he kill 'em first or just burn 'em all alive?"

"Stop rabble-rousing, Mort," hollered a voice from the back of the diner. "You're sick, man."

"He's just being realistic," Reggie said. "Maybe Mike set the fire so the houseboat would explode and cover up the real crime. I watch TV. I know what goes on out there."

"Oh, really?" Mark Steele folded his arms. "And what would that be, Reg? You know something the rest of us don't? Nobody knows what happened—get the facts before you go shootin' off your mouth."

Hattie Gentry gave a sigh. "We're heartbroken to think we might've witnessed a murder. George and I were standing right there when the houseboat was burning. It was hard enough realizing the family was inside. But now knowing that Mike McConnell is probably responsible? I can hardly stand to think about it! Where was he while his wife and children were burning? Watching? Laughing at the rest of us? This is awful. I don't see how you can joke about it."

Her husband George nodded and took her hand. "She's right."

Jim Hawkins stood up. "Hattie is right. This isn't TV or the movies—it's real. We knew these folks. This is the worst thing that's ever happened here. And there's nothing we can do to erase it. It's part of our history now. It's part of us. Maybe that doesn't affect you like it does me, but I always thought Baxter was a cut above everywhere else. This hurts all of us."

Things were starting to heat up when the door to the diner opened and let the morning light rush in. Heads turned to see who it was. All of a sudden things got quiet—dead quiet.

"I'm sure some of you are ready to lynch Mike McConnell after reading the morning headlines," Jed Wilson said. "But I'm here to tell you there's no way Mike did this. I've known him better than any of you for twenty years. He isn't capable of murder."

Mort snickered. "Jed, ol' buddy, you best wake up and smell the coffee, boy. McConnell's prints was all over the place. He broke in that lake house. The Morgan girl saw 'im. And them divers found a weddin' ring right where she said he throwed it. If he didn't do nothin', why's he runnin'?"

"You don't know that he's running. You don't know anything!"

"Jed, it's not looking good," Dan said. "You might want to read the morning paper again—if you're not too hung over, that is."

Reggie held up the newspaper. "The facts are here. Add 'em up."

"Yep," Mort said. "Too bad your buddy's a murderer. Charbroiled his wife and kids, then took off hidin' like some lily-livered snake. They'll find him, Jed, sure as heck. And when they do, he's gonna git the death pen'lty."

Mark took a mint from his pocket and threw it at Mort. "How about cutting Jed a little slack?"

"I don't need slack," Jed said. "I need answers."

Mort slowly leaned forward. "Whatcha gonna do if ya find out he did it, Jed? That'll really burn ya up, won't it?"

Mark grabbed Jed's arm. "Take it easy. Mort's a big mouth. Nobody takes him seriously."

"Yeah, like you're not taking me seriously?" Jed yanked his arm free. "I swear to you—I'll prove Mike didn't do this. Go ahead and laugh. But I'm right."

Jed spun around and left Monty's Diner. He didn't bother to close the door.

FOURTEEN

At noon on Wednesday, Hal Barker stood in the baggage claim area of James F. Ellison Airport and noticed an attractive lady in her forties moving toward him, using a cane. The woman bore a striking resemblance to Rose McConnell. Their eyes met with a question mark.

"Lisa?"

"Yes. You must be Hal."

"That's me." He tipped his hat. "I suppose the Stetson was a dead giveaway."

"It *was* a distinguishing feature. Probably the highest point in the crowd. Hard to miss." She smiled.

"Being tall has its advantages."

Hal sized up the woman he hoped would help in the investigation. Lisa Sorensen had shiny, dark hair like Rose, streaked with a little more white. She had the same striking blue eyes, was about the same size. Her smile was identical.

They engaged in polite chatter while waiting for her luggage to come around, and after only a few minutes, she pointed out which two pieces were hers. Hal grabbed the large suitcases, one in each hand, then walked slowly toward the exit door, careful not to move faster than Lisa, who struggled with the cane. His squad car was parked just outside the door, and after he got her situated comfortably in the front seat, he loaded the luggage.

He had spoken with her on the phone about the latest details of the case, but with an hour's drive ahead of them, he hoped to find out what she knew about Mike McConnell.

"Rose was the sweetest thing. I can't imagine why Mike would want to hurt her or the kids. It's still such a shock."

"Did they seem to get along?" he asked.

"In their own way, I suppose. Their marriage wasn't like mine. Rose and Mike lived in separate worlds. He certainly wasn't attentive to her, but I never got the impression he was abusive. She complained about her never getting to travel—that Mike didn't care about it. I know his drinking bugged her, too, but she seemed pretty positive when we talked."

"How often did you talk to Rose?"

"Oh…we talked three or four times a month—sometimes more. Rose and I were very close. She was my only sister—actually my only sibling. We were two years apart in age. I'm the oldest, in case you're wondering."

Hal smiled and let that one go by.

"Girls can get really close in a family, Sheriff. I made a trip to Baxter every other year, but Rose never visited me in California. Mike wasn't interested in going anywhere and never seemed willing to part with the money so she and the kids could make the trip either. But with long-distance rates so affordable, we could talk for an hour or two on Sundays, so that's what we did."

"Lisa, did you notice anything different about her the last few times you talked?"

"No. Nothing."

"What did you two talk about? I don't mean specifically, but generally."

"The kids, mostly. Some girl talk—recipes, new clothes, bargains. Rose was a terrific shopper. She saved that man a lot of money. Mike would ask her, 'How much did it cost this time for you to save me money?'"

"Are you saying they fought over the way she spent money?"

"No, Rose got a kick out of pinching pennies, and Mike kidded with her about it. That's all."

"Could there have been another woman?"

"I can't imagine. Except for working and hanging out with his buddies at that bar, Mike was usually on the houseboat, or at least on the lake, fishing or cruising around. Rose never seemed suspicious of an affair. She wouldn't have put up with it for a minute."

"You sound pretty sure about that."

"I am."

"How serious of a drinking problem do you think Mike had?"

"Serious enough to cause resentment, for sure. He wasn't mean or anything—at least I never got that impression. It seemed to me like he fell into a bad habit of drinking with the guys after work. He quit paying much attention to Rose a long time ago. She found other ways to fill her time."

"Like what?"

"Like she really loved those kids and stayed involved with them. Mike never did. He always paid the most attention to himself."

They rounded the top of the last hill and began their descent into Baxter. "There's the courthouse," Hal said.

"It's breathtaking! Like you see in travel magazines," Lisa said. "I've never been here in the fall."

In the distance, the gold cross atop a white-steepled church looked ablaze in the afternoon sun; and beyond, Heron Lake dazzled like a treasure chest of diamonds and precious stones, reflecting the resplendent color of surrounding trees.

"Lisa, there's something else I need to ask you. This is important. Do you remember if there was anything engraved on Mike's wedding ring?"

"Actually, there was. I don't remember the exact words, but I remember Rose was excited at the time because she thought it was clever—you know, like a play on words—something to do with thorns—about her being a rose but not having thorns. That was a long time ago, Hal. I really haven't thought of it since they got married. Why?"

"How about if I show you this afternoon? Right now I'd like to get you settled in at Morganstern's before we do another thing. I don't want you getting too tired."

"Morganstern's? Is that a hotel?"

Hal chuckled. "There are no hotels in Baxter. Morganstern's is a bed and breakfast." Hal slowed the squad car and pulled next to the curb. "There it is—that's Morganstern's."

The three-story Victorian house was painted gray with burgundy trim. The grounds were framed neatly with a black, wrought-iron fence, and carpeted with colored leaves from a variety of gigantic hardwoods. Even the high, angled roof had been buried in autumn's confetti.

"Oh my!" Lisa exclaimed, turning toward Hal. "I certainly didn't expect *this*."

The sheriff smiled. "We arranged for you to have the rooms out back—used to be the servant's quarters years ago. That way you won't have to climb steps. I know coming here was pushing it this soon after surgery."

"How thoughtful," she said, turning again to admire the beautiful old house. "Sounds like you thought of everything. My doctor wasn't too keen on my making this trip. Neither was my husband. He wanted to come with me, but he used up the last of his vacation time the two weeks after my surgery."

"Well, I promised your husband we wouldn't let you get too tired, and we'd provide time and space for you to continue your exercises. I think Morganstern's will work out."

"I should say so."

"Okay, let's get you moved in. Take as much time as you need to rest. When you're ready, I'll come get you and take you to my office."

FIFTEEN

After the *Baxter Daily News* ran the story that Mike McConnell was thought not only to be alive, but also to be the prime suspect in his family's probable murder, every significant media source in the state picked it up.

For those in Baxter, a probable murder was literally the news of the century. Ellen Jones expected newshounds to follow the scent. But she was determined to stay ahead of the pack.

As sorry as she was about the recent turn of events, Ellen found it stimulating to be sitting on top of a *real* news story—one with twists and turns and an uncertain outcome. She would make sure her newspaper was not only on top of it, but also behind the scenes looking for a human-interest slant. If people were drawn to this tragedy and couldn't seem to hear enough about it, then Ellen was determined to give them more of what they wanted. But she wanted it to be genuine, not media hype. This was their story, and who could report it better than someone who was intimately acquainted with Baxter and had emotional ties to the folks who lived here?

The first thing she did was set up an interview with Lisa Sorensen. Though Ellen spent most of her time in the role of editor, she was also the newspaper's feature writer. She loved opportunities to get back on the front lines. Ellen planned to get to Lisa before the electronic media even knew she had arrived in Baxter, and while she was still willing to talk.

The interview was set for two o'clock Friday afternoon at Morganstern's. There was a small parlor in the servant's quarters, a perfect place for Lisa to stay relaxed and off her feet. With only one crack at this, Ellen needed to win Lisa's confidence.

Just before two, Ellen pulled up in her white Buick Riviera and parked along the street. Lisa waved from the door of the old servant's quarters.

After they introduced themselves, she followed Lisa into the parlor, the scent of potpourri reminding Ellen of something she couldn't quite place.

An anniversary clock struck two just as they sat down facing each other on matching couches. Between them, atop a mahogany table, a silver tea service was arranged on a round platter.

"Would you like a cup of tea, Ellen?"

"Thanks, I'd love one."

"Did you notice the fireplace?" Lisa asked.

"The minute I walked in."

Built into the outside wall of the parlor was a small cherry fireplace with blue-and-white antique plates displayed on the mantle. Above it, painted in oils and elegantly matted and framed, was a striking picture of the town square.

"I love the ambiance," said Ellen, her eyes dancing all over the room. "It's cozy but elegant. Are you as taken with it as I am?"

Lisa handed Ellen a cup of tea. "Absolutely. I could hardly wait to get back here. This place is lovely. When I agreed to come, I wasn't expecting my accommodations to be so ideal."

"Have you been to Baxter before?" Ellen asked.

"A number of times, but never in the fall. It's gorgeous."

"Fall is my favorite season, but I think the color this year is as pretty as I've seen it. I'm distracted just driving down the street."

"I know what you mean. The trees look like they've been painted all those wonderful colors. Where I live in California, we don't have fall foliage, so this is an unexpected pleasure."

"Well, after what you've been through, you deserve a little pleasure. This has to have been a terrible time for you."

Lisa's face turned somber. "It has. There's no way to explain the grief. I'm trying to put up a good front, but sometimes I feel like I could cry and never run out of tears. It's the most profound sadness I've ever felt."

"I'm sorry, Lisa. I know how deeply this tragedy has affected the community. I can only imagine what you must be feeling."

"I just hope it goes away someday. The thought of feeling this bad for very long is overwhelming. I can't stop thinking about Rose and the kids."

"Lisa, you've already started to answer some of my questions. Do you mind if we begin the interview? I want to keep it as relaxed and natural as possible. I want us to talk just like we've been doing, so don't get intimidated by the recorder. It helps me keep my facts straight."

The anniversary clock in the parlor at Morganstern's chimed four times.

Ellen sighed and turned off the recorder. "Lisa, you've been so gracious about this. I promise to write a feature story that will make you proud."

"It actually felt good talking about it. I want to remember the happy things. I can still hear the kids' voices. My biggest fear is that I'll forget what they sound like...." Lisa dabbed her eyes.

"I'm so glad you packed these pictures of Rose and Mike and the kids before you left California." Ellen sifted through the photos. "I can use these with the feature story. Some of them are quite unusual."

"Those are all my favorites. They're all I've got left of them...."

Ellen was putting her recorder in her brief case when the phone rang.

"Oh, that scared me!" Lisa said. "Excuse me while I take this call.

"Hello.... Yes, it is.... Yes, I inquired yesterday.... Were you able to get that account credited so I can close it out? Why not...? When...?"

Ellen tried hard not to eavesdrop—but not too hard.

"That's impossible," Lisa said. "Of course, I reviewed it. They're unauthorized charges. Can you trace th... Oh, you have...? Yes, I've got a pencil. Repeat the number, please... 1-800... Uh-huh... Uh-huh... Okay, I've got it. Could you fax me something to that effect?" Lisa sounded annoyed. "Yes, that's the correct number.... I'm anxious to get this straightened out as soon as possible. Good-bye, Mr. Hawkins."

Lisa's mouth formed a straight line of disgust. "Wouldn't you know it; somebody stole Mike and Rose's credit card and made cash withdrawals in Atlanta, Nashville, and Kansas City in the last three weeks—to the tune of thirty-five hundred dollars. Maxed it out. One more hassle I don't need right now."

Ellen's eyes were wide, her thoughts racing. "Lisa...think!"

"What?"

"What if the card wasn't stolen? What if Mike's been using it? It makes perfect sense. He didn't waste any time maxing it out, but I'll bet he's a long way from any paper trail. My guess is he isn't anywhere near Atlanta, Nashville, or Kansas City."

Lisa sat there for a few moments, her hands tapping the table. "How could I be so naive? Deep down I didn't want to believe Mike did this—or that he's alive. But you're right! What other explanation could there be? If Mike died in the fire, his card would have melted. Mr. Hawkins said the card had been used. These were not telephone transactions. What kind of monster is he, anyway? Does he really think he can burn my sister and her kids like trash and then walk away like it never happened? Well, I won't let him get away with it! He deserves the death penalty for this!"

"Lisa..." Ellen said, gently touching her shoulder. "We need to call Sheriff Barker. He needs to be made aware of this right away. This is big! Now we know where Mike's been. Someone's bound to remember seeing him. I'd like to run this story and a special feature on you in tomorrow's *Daily News*. When the media jumps on this, Mike McConnell won't be able to show his face in public. He'll have to watch his back at every turn. Don't worry, Lisa, he's not going to get away with this. We'll get him. We'll definitely get him."

Ellen sat at her computer late Friday afternoon working feverishly to complete tomorrow's feature story. She, Ellen Madison Jones, got the first interview with a relative in the McConnell murder investigation! She knew her readers would eat it up. She also knew the networks would want a piece of the pie, especially after the breaking news she got during the interview.

From her window, Ellen spotted a media van moving down Baxter Avenue. *KJNX! Well, hello. What took you so long?* Ellen had no respect for the Myerson TV station that served Baxter from its ivory tower seventy-five miles away. She nicknamed it K-JINX because of the extreme measures they used to get a story. Once the network was positioned, it wasn't moving without a fight."

Ellen felt a little smug. No way would KJNX get anything special for the morning broadcast. They didn't have a clue about Lisa Sorensen or this afternoon's credit card development. Interviewing locals and creating some sound bites for the camera would not upstage the breaking news story or her special feature.

Ellen loved the print media. Racing to get the news out before the networks was a game of cat and mouse she enjoyed. She disdained the insensitivity and expediency of the electronic media and still held the old-fashioned notion that people's feelings deserved to be considered.

Tomorrow's handling of Lisa Sorensen's story would be truthful, would tug at heartstrings, and would evoke strong opinion. But Ellen would have done it fairly—by drawing Lisa out, not by chasing

Lisa down and shoving a mike into her face. Ellen smiled with satisfaction. She was way ahead of the game.

Late Friday night, Sean McConnell sat in his wheelchair in the residents' lounge of Southeast Colonial Manor. Most of the others had retired for the night, but he opted to wait until after the news.

He didn't mind being the last one down for the night. Just closing his eyes didn't make the loneliness go away, and falling asleep was an exercise that took time. Being eighty-three didn't change the fact that he was a night owl, and he had learned the hard way that fighting his nature usually resulted in his getting no sleep.

The old man reached in his pocket and pulled out a snapshot taken three years ago. How well he remembered his eightieth birthday. With this brood gathered around him, he was as proud as any man could be. Erin was barely eleven then. She was a pretty one—just like her mother and full of the blarney. Tim and Todd were three years old, the spitting image of Michael. Rose had dressed them like little gentlemen but could hardly hold them still long enough for their picture to be taken. He replayed the wonderful sensation of those last warm hugs, their soft skin next to his wrinkled cheeks.

His feeble eyes focused on Rose. She still looked like an angel to him. He had loved his daughter-in-law. This beautiful woman swept Michael right off his happy-go-lucky Irish feet. Sean couldn't have been more pleased with his son's choice. Even now, as he studied Michael's face next to hers, he felt that the love of this woman should have made his son's life rich and rewarding. What had gone wrong?

The old man's eyes brimmed with tears. He touched each of the faces with his finger. Grandfathers aren't supposed to outlive their grandchildren. They were going to come see him before Christmas. He told everyone at the nursing home.

Grief lay on his chest like a heavy weight. He didn't need a doctor to tell him his heart was failing.

Sixteen

On Saturday morning, Monty's Diner was bustling with activity.

"Order up!" Leo shouted.

Rosie Harris snatched up three plates and slid them in front of customers in booth four. "Here you go—two Monty's breakfast specials and an eggs benedict. Coffee refills coming right up."

Mark Steele caught Rosie's arm as she breezed by on her way to the coffeepot. "Hey, girl, slow down. You've got a lot of morning left."

She grinned and put her hand to her ear. "Listen...is Mort's breakfast order up next? Let me feed it to him! Maybe he can't talk with his mouth stuffed full."

Mark laughed. "Rosie, do I detect sarcasm? Surely you're not implying Mort's conversation this morning leaves a lot to be desired?"

"Nothing a good case of lockjaw wouldn't cure."

"Don't I wish," said Mark, turning his eyes on his least-favorite customer. "He's been on a toot since he read this morning's headlines."

"Didn't I tell ya from the beginnin' McConnell did it?" Mort said. "Woulda saved a lot o' fussin' if ya woulda just listened."

"Who wants to listen to you?" George Gentry rolled his eyes. "You're always so negative."

"Ya want positive, do ya? How's this—I'm positive Mike McConnell done it. He's a regular serial killer."

"As opposed to what—an irregular serial killer?" said Mark, unable to suppress his laughter.

"I call 'em like I see 'em."

Hattie Gentry sighed. "I wish we'd all agree on one thing. Rose and those poor children didn't deserve this. Ellen's story on Rose's sister is enough to break my heart. Just think about her loss—what all she's going through."

"Shoot, I didn't even know Rose had a sister," Hank Tolbert said. "Sounds like them two women was real close. Close to them kids too."

"Oh, the pictures of the kids about did me in." Rosie turned around to pour Hank a refill. "I used to sit by them in church, you know."

"Kinda hard to realize they were murdered," said Reggie, sounding uncharacteristically subdued. He seemed glued to the pictures in the newspaper.

"Know what surprised me?" Mark leaned against the counter with his arms folded. "How happy Rose's sister says Mike and Rose were when they were young. They never struck me as happy."

"Things change," Liv Spooner said.

Jim Hawkins folded his newspaper. "You know, I wouldn't be surprised if this story drew national attention. Of course, when KJNX does the story, they'll massacre it. They could learn a thing or two from how the *Baxter Daily News* is handling this."

"Well, one thing's for sure," George said. "They got the goods on Mike McConnell. That boy's in hot water."

"Gonna get a lot hotter. McConnell's gonna fry."

"Mort, they don't fry people anymore," said Mark.

"That so? Well the Almighty's got a place that jus' might do the trick!" Mort laughed his obnoxious wheezy laugh. "Them TV people, now they know howda tell a story. They don't go pussyfootin' 'round about what happened neither—"

"Then let *them* tell it," George said. "We've heard about enough out of you."

Mark Steele smirked. *Way to go, George!*

"It happened so fast," said Rhonda, her eyes staring at the skid marks on the pavement in front of Miller's Market. "It's all a blur."

"Sorry, lady. My foot musta pushed on the gas pedal instead o' the brakes. All o' the sudden, I was goin' faster than a chicken thief runnin' from a hound dog. Yer not hurt, are ya?" the man asked.

Rhonda thought he looked as old as the statue of Reginald T. Baxter. "I think I'm fine. I never saw your truck. I'm not even sure what happened."

"Name's Clarence Horton. I'm mighty glad yer okay."

"Ma'am, are you all right?" shouted a woman who raced across the parking lot toward her. "Do you want me to call an ambulance?"

"No, I'm all right," Rhonda said.

"Are you sure?"

"Hey, old timer," said a man with a cart, "maybe it's time to hang up the keys. You could've killed this lady."

"I wasn't hurt," Rhonda said.

"But it looked lik—"

"She wasn't hit." A young man in a plaid shirt and jeans stepped forward. "I saw the whole thing. It was a close call. No harm done."

"Well, then, I'll just be movin' on," said Clarence Horton, sounding sheepish. "Lady, I'm sorry fer almost hittin' ya. Glad yer not hurt."

"Me too," said Rhonda. She shook his dry, wrinkled hand. Clarence Horton was trembling.

The young man in a plaid shirt and jeans started to walk away—and then turned around. He gazed at Rhonda, his eyes penetrating. "Seems God has a plan for your life."

Rhonda heard Mary Beth's voice and saw her pushing her way through the onlookers. "Excuse me. Excuse me, please. May I get through? Pardon me, that's my friend…Rhonda! What happened? Someone said you got hit by a pickup!"

Rhonda shook her head. "It's all a blur. This young man saw everything. Ask him."

"Who?"

Rhonda looked all around her. He wasn't there.

Hal sat in the quiet of his office. He grimaced when the phone rang. "Not today. It's Saturday. I'm not answering it. I don't care who it is!"

…*Please leave a message at the sound of the beep.…* "Sheriff, this is Wilbur Manning. I got somethin' I need to tell you about that McConnell fella, but I guess I'll call you at hom—"

"Wilbur—wait! This is Sheriff Barker. What's this about?"

"Well, sir, I didn't say nothin' till now because I thought it was just my mind playin' tricks on me. I was home the day of the memorial Mass for the McConnells. I was down in the back—you know how I git."

"Yes, Wilbur, I know how you get. What do you mean your mind was playing tricks on you?"

"I was just gittin' to that.… Where was I? Oh yeah, I was sittin' in my rocker feelin' bad because I knew ever'body would be at the church. That's when I seen him—a guy who looked a lot like Mike McConnell snoopin' over on the church grounds. Now I figured I was imaginin' things. He was dead, right? So, this look-alike wanders kinda sneakylike around the side of the church. Pretty soon, he climbs up in a tree and just stays there fer the longest time. After maybe forty-five minutes or so, he comes down outta that big oak and scoots on down the hill outta sight. I didn't think much about it at the time. Like I said, I figured I was imaginin' it because Mike McConnell was on my mind. Well, sir, after this mornin's newspaper said they're sure he's alive, I knew I best tell you about this today."

"Did Hilda see him too?" Hal asked.

"Nah, she was in the church with most of the neighbors."

"Wilbur, would you sign a statement to this effect?"

"Yes, sir. I'd be right glad to do it. Sheriff, why do you think Mike McConnell would take a chance like that? I mean, if he was on the run for murderin' his family, why did he take a chance of gittin' caught? Don't seem smart in my book."

"I know, Wilbur. Nothing about this case is easy to figure."

"Kinda makes ya sad, don't it, Sheriff, to think that Baxter's gittin' more like them big cities? Who woulda thought we'd have us a murder?"

"Look at it this way, Wilbur. Even if Mike McConnell did this, it's the only murder in a hundred years. I'll still take Baxter any day."

"That's fer sure. Well, sir, when do you want me to sign my statement?"

"If you're going to be home, why don't I swing by in an hour?"

"That'll work. I'll just be here rockin'."

Jed sat at the kitchen table. He heard the front door open. He slid his notes under the newspaper and pretended to be reading.

"It's me," said Rhonda, her arms loaded down with groceries. "Could I get some help with these?"

"Now? I'm in the middle of something."

"Sorry to bother you, but I've got your truck full of perishables. This is double-coupon day."

Jed sighed. He threw the pen down on the table and got up. After making several trips back and forth from the truck, he realized Rhonda was in a good mood. He sat down at the kitchen table while she arranged things in the refrigerator.

"What do you think about the idea of my going to find Mike? I have three weeks' vacation, and right now I'm no good to anyone. Until this thing is settled, I feel like my whole life is on hold."

Rhonda looked over at Jed and suddenly realized he was sober. "Where would you go? How would you even know where to begin?"

"I don't know. Maybe I'll start at those banks where he used his credit card. I'm not sure yet, but I've got to do something. The rest of you think I'm the dumb one, but I know him. He didn't kill Rose and the kids...." Jed choked on the words.

"I don't think you're dumb," Rhonda said softly. "I don't know whether Mike did this or not, but I know it's hurting you, and it's a stumbling block in your life right now. If you really think you need to do this, Jed, go. See what you can find out."

"I thought you'd neg the whole idea."

"But if—and I'm just saying if—Mike is guilty, do you think he would hurt you if you found him?"

"No way, Rhonda. Mike's like a brother."

She studied his face. It was the first time she'd seen him sober on a Saturday since the explosion.

"Well...if you promise to be careful, maybe it's a good idea. I think. Well, I hope. I want you to be right about Mike—I really do."

Jed pulled her close and put his arms around her. She didn't budge...nor did she breathe. All she heard was the pounding of her heart. When he finally let go, an awkward silence stood between them. Rhonda felt the heat color her face.

"When are you leaving?" she asked, her cool hands pressed to her cheeks.

"In the morning."

"That soon? Jed, what am I going to do about a car?"

"I called Jimmy's Garage. They're still waiting on parts. Your Mustang won't be ready for another week, so our insurance agent arranged for a rental car. We can pick it up this afternoon, and you can keep it until the car's fixed."

"What about your job? You can't just up and leave without telling your supervisor."

"I already called Al. He said it was okay for me to take the time off. He said I could take all three weeks at once, so that's what I'm doing."

Her eyes met his. "You need to do this, Jed. You need to resolve it in your own mind." She didn't tell him what she really thought—that their marriage didn't stand a chance if Jed couldn't get past this.

"Okay then. I'll get my black bag and start throwing some things together."

"Take care of him, God," Rhonda whispered. "Help him to find the truth."

The young man in a plaid shirt and jeans sensed that Rhonda prayed. He served the One who would answer. And though the details were not disclosed, the mission had been made clear.

SEVENTEEN

"Uh, I guess I'm leaving now," said Jed. "Everything's in the pickup."

"Don't forget to call."

"I won't."

"Have you got your cell phone?"

"Yeah, it's right here."

"Did you get the snack I put in for lat—"

"Rhonda, I've got it. I'm not forgetting anything." He got in the pickup and rolled down the window. His sad eyes had a faraway look. "I'll call you, huh?"

"Jed..."

"Yeah?"

"Uh...nothing. Be careful."

"I will."

Rhonda went back inside and sat at the kitchen table. She skimmed the Sunday paper but couldn't concentrate. Why was she already missing Jed when he made her so miserable?

The entire week she had been watching him waste away with grief and self-pity, while she secretly relished her church experience from last Sunday. She almost felt guilty about feeling good. Then there was the strange comment from the young man at Miller's Market yesterday. Maybe God did have a plan for her life.

Rhonda was to meet the Kennsingtons at church at ten o'clock and then go to lunch at Monty's with Mary Beth and Joe. She had questions and hoped they had answers.

"It keeps coming up," Rhonda said. "Three times in less than two weeks I've been told God has plans for me, but I don't have a clue what it means. What do you think?"

Mary Beth wiped her mouth with a napkin. "I think it's exciting—Father Donaghan, Pastor Thomas, and that young man all touching on the same theme. That's the way the Lord works."

"But why would God have plans for *me?*"

"Are you kidding?" Joe said. "Before the world began God had plans for you and for every person who would ever be born."

Rhonda raised an eyebrow. "That seems a bit far-fetched. Not even every pregnancy is planned. There are accidents."

"Maybe to us, but not to God. He knew about each one and was ready with a plan. I find that incredible because no child can be a mistake, no matter how he got here. If people mess up, it doesn't mess God up."

"You're saying that in God's eyes, every child is planned? Come on," Rhonda said.

Mary Beth looked at Joe. He gave a slight nod and covered her hand with his.

"Listen, Rhonda," said Mary Beth. "I'm going to step out on a limb and share something extremely personal because it illustrates Joe's point better than anything I can think of. I didn't understand it myself until this past year, and I haven't told anyone except him and the girls.

"When I was seventeen, I was in a relationship that got way too serious…and I got pregnant. It felt like the end of the world. The father went off to college and left me to deal with the fear and embarrassment—and a hard choice. When I signed the adoption papers and the nurse took that baby boy from my arms, my heart broke. I didn't find all the pieces until years later. In fact, when Joe and I got married, I hadn't really dealt with my feelings. Guilt put a wedge between us, and I kept shutting him out."

"Obviously things got better," Rhonda said.

"Not for a long time. Not until after we got into reading the Bible and some similarities between spiritual adoption and physical adoption sort of jumped out at me."

"Like what?"

"Well, like from the moment we're born, all of us are stuck with the stigma of Adam and Eve's sin, even though it wasn't our fault. We inherited the sin and shame, and it's a part of who we are. It's only when we let God adopt us into His family that we get a new beginning, a whole new life, and a new name."

"I'm not following you," said Rhonda.

"Well, it's not much of a stretch to apply the same principle to my son's situation—once he was adopted, he no longer carried the shame of illegitimacy he inherited from his birth parents. Adoption gave him a new name, a proud identity, and a bright future. His new life had far more quality than the one I decided was never meant to be. After that, I let go of the guilt."

"Must've been such a relief."

"It was. But what blows my mind is that none of the pain was wasted. What I thought was an unfortunate mistake, the Lord used for something amazing."

"What do you mean?"

Suddenly, Mary Beth's chin quivered. She fought back the tears. "I—I met my son last year. Aaron is twenty-eight. He told me he was raised in a wonderful Christian home and that, growing up, he prayed I would come to know God's saving grace. Rhonda, that little boy prayed his birth mother right into the forgiving arms of God—and that was no accident either."

Mary Beth laughed and cried at the same time. "Sorry, it's just so awesome. The Lord knew what was going to happen, and He was waiting—not only to forgive my mistake but also to use it to create a wonderful human being who would impact my eternal life." She took a Kleenex from her purse and wiped her eyes. "God loves us so much that He has a plan even for our mistakes—that's grace."

Rhonda blinked the tears from her eyes. Whatever God was trying to tell her, she wanted to hear, but there was so much she didn't understand.

"What else can I get for you?" the waitress asked.

"Rosie, I've enjoyed a delicious lunch and the company of these two lovely ladies. I feel well-rounded." Joe playfully patted his stomach. "But you've got to help me out here before they muscle me into some gooey dessert or something." He lowered his voice. "We're talking a couple of chocoholics. This could get serious."

Mary Beth giggled. "Joe Kennsington, you party pooper. I want dessert—the chocolatyer, the better."

"*Chocolatyer?* Hmm…I'll have my students look it up in the dictionary."

"Oh, Joe, you are such an amateur," Rhonda said. "Monty's desserts are out of this world. There are no adjectives to adequately describe them."

"Here it comes, Rosie." He winked.

"I'll have a mud pie parfait with *double* chocolate," said Mary Beth, her defiant grin aimed at Joe.

"Same here!" Rhonda said.

He chuckled. "I see you've done this before. All right, it seems 'chocolatyer' is the name of the game. Let's go for it. Make it three."

Ellen put her car on cruise control and dialed her cell phone.

"Hello."

"Hi, Guy, it's me. I'm on the interstate, probably another hour out. I should be there around one."

"I hate your traveling alone," he said. "Don't get careless or too trusting. Nosing around Atlanta is a far sight different from Baxter."

"Have you forgotten you're married to a fair-minded, nicer-than-the-networks, but don't-let-go-until-it's-over pit bull? I have to keep going. My readers are eating it up. Timing is everything."

"Go heavy on the pit bull, all right? Atlanta's a tough town."

"I'll be fine. I just want to get this story before someone else does, especially KJNX. Those electronic gods from Myerson would love nothing more than to horn in and put their own spin on it. This is Baxter's story."

"Very well, then, Ellen Madison Jones, carry on. Just remember who loves you."

"I love you too," she said. "I'll call you before I leave Atlanta."

Sean McConnell lay in bed with his eyes closed. He hated visiting hours, especially on Sunday. Everyone he loved was dead now—except Michael. His heart ached thinking about it. He just wanted the day over with.

"Mr. McConnell, you really should get outside and enjoy the beautiful weather. We're not going to get much more of this."

He opened his eyes. The nurse was smiling at him.

"You can't fool me. Here, let me help you into the wheelchair. The fresh air will do you good."

"Think so, do ya?"

"There you go. Easy does it," said the nurse. "Now get outside in the sunshine. It'll feel good."

She patted his arm and left the room.

He sat, trying to muster enough desire to start moving. The phone rang.

"Hello, this is Sean McConnell.... Hello...? Hello...?" He sensed someone on the line. "Who's there?"

"It's me, Pop."

"Michael!" he whispered.

"Did you get my note?"

"Sure I did. I've got it hidden."

"No, you have to get rid of it. Flush it. I just wanted you to know I'm all right…. I'm sorry about Rose and the kids. I never meant to hurt you."

"The FBI was here yesterday. Son, tell me what happened."

"It's better if you don't know; then you can honestly say you don't. They'll try to get you to talk. I don't want you involved in this."

"But—"

"Listen, Pop, I've got to go. I can't chance them tracing this call. I'm in so much trouble."

"But, Mich—"

"I'm sorry. I've got to go." *Click.*

Sean McConnell's cold, feeble hands shook so badly that it was all he could do to wheel himself in a straight line down the hallway. His eyes stung with tears. He could barely see where he was going, but his pride pushed the wheels of the chair across the residents' lounge to the door that led outside. He felt a bump when the wheelchair crossed the threshold. He rolled across the courtyard and stopped under the familiar arms of a giant magnolia tree. There, the old man finally let go and wept.

Lord, forgive him. And forgive me. I don't know where I went wrong, but that boy needs Ya. Please keep him from being destroyed by this evil he's done.

Shortly after noon, Jed pulled his red Chevy Silverado into a service station on the outskirts of Atlanta. He had been so focused on Mike's situation that he missed a key turnoff. It cost him two hours, but what difference did it make? It was stupid to come on a Sunday when the banks were closed. At the moment he would have traded his pickup for a six-pack.

Jed filled his truck, paid for the gas, and then pulled over. He leaned his head back and closed his eyes. What made him think he could do this?

Whatcha gonna do if ya find out he did it, Jed? That'll really burn ya up….

Jed's eyes flew open. "He didn't do it, Mort. How about if I clear Mike's name, then take the proof and shove it down your throat? You and all the other know-it-alls."

He reached over the visor, grabbed the map of Atlanta, and put on his reading glasses.

A curious old man in a red cap and baseball jacket approached his truck. Jed rolled down the window.

"You look lost," the man said. "Can I help you find something?"

"Can you tell from this map where I am?"

"I'll bet I can." He poked his head in the window. "Let me see… Yep, you're right here." He pointed to the location on the map. "I suppose you're wantin' directions for the truck and auto extravaganza. Been people comin' and goin' all weekend."

"Uh…how'd you guess?"

"Get back on the interstate. Turn at the second exit, go to the stop sign and turn right. Keep goin' six blocks and you'll see the auditorium there on the left. Can't miss it."

"Sounds easy enough."

"The Magnolia Inn is down three more blocks. Reasonable rates. Real nice place. Won't find a nicer motel for your money."

"You're reading my mind. Thanks for steering me in the right direction."

The old man tipped his red cap. "That's what I do best. Glad to help."

Jed followed the directions without a hitch. Soon he was wandering down aisle after aisle of custom cars and trucks, enjoying the diversion. Tomorrow he'd have a plan. Right now, he was grateful not to feel lost.

Father Donaghan nestled in his favorite overstuffed chair, waiting for the kickoff to Sunday's game. He had just taken his finger off the mute button when the phone rang.

"Hello, this is Father Donaghan."

"Father, this is...uh...this is Mike—Mike McConnell. Could we talk?"

The parish priest dropped his potato chips and knocked over a Coke can. He turned the can upright, grabbed a napkin, and wiped the brown bubbles from his pants. His heart raced faster than the Atlanta Falcons now running down the field after the kickoff.

"Mike, where are you?"

"You know I can't tell you that."

"I was shocked when I heard you were alive."

"Yeah, I guess it's all over the news."

"So why not turn yourself in, Mike? Things can only get worse if you don't."

"I suspect they will.... Father, I called because I need to make my confession. You're the only priest I know to turn to. Whatever I tell you is protected, right? I mean, this is private between me and my confessor, no matter what I tell you?"

"Well, yes, of course, Mike. That doesn't change because of your...uh...circumstances."

"Then just because I do this over the phone doesn't mean it isn't valid?"

"Of course not. If you confess your sins to me, I am bound by confidentiality, but, Mike, God will expect you to do your penance, and I'm not sure you—"

"Then I need to do this now, Father. I need absolution. I may never get another chance. Frankly, I'm not sure God will forgive me for this."

Ellen pulled into Southeast Colonial Manor and was pleased when she didn't see a media presence. She parked the car and walked through the wooden doors to the information desk. After she learned Sean McConnell's room number, she walked down the long corridor to Room 301A. The door was open, but the room was empty. She walked back toward the desk.

As Ellen passed by the big picture window in the residents' lounge, she spotted an old man in a wheelchair, sitting outside under a magnolia tree. She was struck by how broken he looked. The prodding in her heart wouldn't let her pass him by.

She opened the door and walked across a small courtyard.

"Hello," she said.

He looked up from his wheelchair, his eyes red and puffy. He didn't say anything.

Ellen squatted down to eye level. "I'm Ellen. You look like someone I'd enjoy saying hello to."

There was a long pause. She noticed his eyes looked cloudy, almost as if he couldn't see. She was surprised when he spoke.

"Well, aren't you the sweet one. Rose was like that. She was always doin' for me and thinkin' about me. You remind me of her some."

"Was Rose your wife?"

"No."

Ellen imagined the clanking sound as the door to his heart slammed shut. "What's your name?" she asked.

"Huh? Uh…McConnell. Sean McConnell."

"Mr. McConnell, I have some time on my hands and could use someone to talk to."

"Why's that?"

"Well, I'm here on business. I don't know anyone in Atlanta, and it's too gorgeous of a day to spend just on myself. May I share it with you?"

"Grab one of those foldin' chairs over there and sit down beside me, why don't ya?"

Before fifteen minutes had passed, Ellen found herself chattering like they were old friends. Mr. McConnell listened with his heart, and she wanted him to talk to her the same way.

"Were you ever married?" she asked.

"Sure was. Fifty-one years. My sweet Margaret passed on nearly seven years ago. A gentle woman, she was. We came from Ireland when we were first married—immigrated to New York City. We were a little overwhelmed. I was an honest worker, but it was hard in those days workin' for anyone who wasn't Irish."

"How'd you make a living?"

"I learned cabinetry. I could do some pretty things with wood, Ellen. I love the stuff. Anyway, it was a good livin'. I could never complain. I always had more work than I needed. I once made a cedar chest for Franklin D. Roosevelt. Can you believe that?"

"Really? How did that come about?"

"Somehow he saw some of my work and had someone from the White House commission me to handcraft one special for him. Never got to actually meet him, of course. But I was one proud young man. Here I was—just an Irish immigrant—and the President of the United States was admirin' my work. Had to pinch myself to believe it."

"I can only imagine. What an honor!"

"Of course, that's the kind of thing a guy doesn't say much about. Now Margaret—she had to go tell everybody. I was content just knowin'."

Ellen lost all track of time as Sean McConnell poured out the memories of his life. His blue eyes were animated and his cheeks looked rosy as the afternoon's conversation drifted to happier thoughts. She decided he must have been a handsome man in his day. He had a full head of white hair that curled just a little at the ears. It was difficult to tell with him sitting in a wheelchair, but he looked to be tall and relatively trim. With a little sprucing up, he could still turn a few heads. Ellen couldn't get over how his eyes sparkled when he laughed.

This was better than an interview. It was an inner view of this proud old man, who, for one special November afternoon, remembered more about who he'd been than how sad he'd become.

"Did you and Margaret eventually have children?" Ellen was tempted to reach in her satchel and turn on her recorder, but she wouldn't violate her code of ethics.

"After many prayers to the good Lord, we finally had a son, Michael Sean McConnell. A fine boy, he was—red hair and a face like one of those porcelain figurines. Margaret used to say he was so beautiful that his features looked painted on. He was a special answer to prayer for us. It was fifteen years before the good Lord saw fit to give him to us—then I suppose we doted too much on the boy. Ellen, watchin' that child grow up was the joy of my life."

Ellen blinked several times to clear the moisture from her eyes.

"My only regret is we never took him to Ireland. I wanted Michael to feel his roots and meet some of his people. Of course, that woulda meant my havin' to deal with becomin' Catholic. Lovin' Margaret meant more to me than whether I was Protestant or Catholic. She was the religious one back then, so when I married her, I converted. Caused quite a ruckus with the McConnell clan, don't ya know? Woulda been risky for us to stay there.

"I always said we couldn't afford to go back, but truth is, somethin' in me always resisted ever leavin'. I kept on makin' excuses. The first time I saw the Statue of Liberty glowin' in the mornin' sun like a guardian angel, I vowed I was gonna live and die an American and never have to defend my religion. I guess I really didn't care to leave these shores 'cause even with all the talk, we never did get back to Ireland."

Ellen glanced at her watch. It was getting late.

"Ellen, ya mentioned bein' here on business, but ya never said what ya do."

"No, I didn't. I'm in the newspaper business."

"Ya don't say! And what's the nature of your business in Atlanta?"

"I came to meet a man and get a story," she said.

"How'd it work out?"

"A strange thing happened. I began to care less about the story and more about the man."

"I see. And what will ya do, seein' as how ya care about him?"

She saw the corners of his mouth turn up.

"Well now, that depends on how willing he is to trust me."

"Hello, Sheriff Barker."

"Hal, it's Jordan Ellis. Hope you don't mind a Sunday night call, but I thought you'd like an update. A couple of our agents paid Mike McConnell's father a visit at the Southeast Colonial Manor yesterday. The old guy played dumb. Had nothing to say. Hadn't seen or heard from his son—blah, blah, blah. You know the drill. My guys think he's holding something back. Do you want us to stay on him?"

"Jordan, how old is this guy?"

"I don't know—old. He's in a wheelchair and has a heart condition, but that doesn't mean he's deaf and dumb. He knows something."

"He's been a victim five times over," Hal said. "I don't want him put through any more. Let's wait and see if he gets visitors or phone calls. You've got authorization for a wiretap, right?"

"Yeah. It's a go."

"Then we can get what we need without leaning on the guy. He doesn't need to know we're there. Don't bother him anymore."

"I think that's a mistake, but it's your call, Sheriff. I'll tell my agents to back off. If McConnell's dad hears from anyone significant, I'll let you know. Also, I've got agents following the paper trail, but it's cold. Doesn't look like it's going anywhere."

"Okay, Jordan, thanks. Oh, wait—I forgot to tell you that I had an interesting call from a local resident yesterday. Seems Wilbur Manning may have seen Mike McConnell nosing around the churchyard during the memorial Mass. He blew it off at the time—thought Mike was dead and his mind was playing tricks on him. Now he seems sure. He sounds legit. I got his statement."

"Funny how things will surface in a case like this. People seem to crawl out of the woodwork when a case finally splits wide open."

"I guess so," Hal said. "I'm amazed at the evidence that's coming into play in a case we thought was cut-and-dried."

"Sheriff, for what it's worth, in a case like this there are two things you should always keep on—your thinking cap and plenty of coffee."

"Yeah, thanks, Jordan. I'll remember that."

"Hello."

"Guy, it's me. I'm leaving Atlanta."

"So how'd it go? Did you find him?"

"I'll say. What an afternoon! I went looking for an interview with Mike McConnell's father and ended up so intrigued with the man that I almost forgot about the case altogether."

"Really?"

"I can't explain it, but I was so into listening that I didn't even record it."

"No kidding?" Guy said. "So you didn't learn that much about Mike?"

"Yes and no. His roots were strong and deep—at least from his father's point of view. Makes me wonder why he turned out to be a killer."

"Come on, Ellen, don't you think Sean McConnell told you exactly what he wanted you to hear?"

"No. He didn't even know who I was until half the afternoon was gone. It's a little complicated. I'll tell you all about it when I get home. This is going to make a great story. Margie's saving space in tomorrow's edition. You'd have liked him, Guy. He's the sweetest old man I've ever met."

"Listen to you!" He chuckled. "I can't wait to hear all about him."

"Well, you know I can't talk on the phone and drive. Let me get both hands on the wheel and pull my thoughts together. I'll see you in about three hours. I love you."

∽◦∽

Father Donaghan sat in the dark. He didn't know who won the football game. He couldn't shake this afternoon's phone call. It was the first time he ever heard a confession over the phone. And the first time he was told something that could impact a murder investigation.

But he knew the commitment. He couldn't say anything. As far as anyone else knew, he never heard from Mike McConnell.

Father Donaghan could clearly picture all five members of the family seated in the second row of Saint Anthony's on Sunday mornings. He sighed. How did it come to this?

EIGHTEEN

On Monday morning, Jed awoke early and almost forgot where he was. Dawn peeked in through a crack in the heavy, lined drapes. Other than that, the room was pitch black.

He lay there a while longer and mentally mapped out his day. He would go to the Atlanta locations where Mike was known to have used his credit card. From there, he really didn't know—perhaps Nashville and Kansas City.

When he finally threw the covers off, he shivered. The room felt cold, a reminder that November had arrived. He wasted no time turning on the shower. Jed flipped on the coffeemaker and then stepped into the steamy tub and pulled the curtain.

When he got out of the shower, the coffee was ready. He enjoyed his first cup while he shaved, then picked up his cell phone to call Rhonda.

"Hello."

"It's me," Jed said.

"Where are you?"

"Some Atlanta suburb. Don't ask me which one; they all run together. Some friendly old guy suggested a nice motel called the Magnolia Inn. That's where I am."

"When did you get there?"

"A lot earlier than I needed to. Couldn't check out the banks until today. At least I got a good night's sleep."

"Jed, I'm really glad you called. Did you know that Mike's father is in a nursing home in Atlanta?"

"I guess I did. Never gave it much thought. Why?"

"Ellen Jones was down there yesterday. She interviewed him and wrote a very interesting story. He sounds like a dear old man who's just devastated by this whole nightmare. I'll save it for you."

"Yeah, okay, thanks."

"Jed, I was thinking... Do you suppose he knows something he might not tell the police or the FBI or a newspaperwoman, but might tell his son's best friend?"

"I don't know. Maybe. Did she say where this place is?"

"Just a minute. Let me get the paper.... He's at Southeast Colonial Manor in an Atlanta suburb. That's all she said, but how many can there be? It wouldn't be that hard to find him."

"Did she give his first name? I'm not sure Mike ever mentioned his father's name."

"Sean. His name is Sean McConnell. Maybe he knows something that'll help you."

"At least it's a starting place."

"So, what's your plan? Have you thought any more about it?"

"I'll try the banks to see if anyone remembers anything. But first I think I'll look up Sean McConnell and see if that leads anywhere. It might be nice talking to someone who still cares about Mike. Aren't many of us left."

"Will you let me know what you find out? Don't laugh, but I'm praying for you."

"Yeah? Well, good. Hope it works. Guess I'll go see what I can find out. I'll call you when I know something."

There was a long pause.

"Jed, you don't have to wait until you know something. I wouldn't mind if you called just so I won't worry."

"All right, sure. Talk to you later then, huh?"

"Okay. Good-bye," she said.

When he hung up the phone, Jed was struck by how little he had to say to her.

‍∾o∾

Hal Barker was having a cup of coffee and reviewing some files when the first call of the day came through.

"This is Hal Barker."

"Sheriff, it's Dr. Hicks. I've got the pathology report you've been waiting for. I decided to call you before I send the courier with the paperwork."

"Okay, Dr. Hicks, let's have it."

"We identified the remains of two more McConnells."

"And?"

"Before I say more, please understand there's no doubt. Our findings are conclusive."

"And what are your findings?"

"The remains are those of Erin McConnell and the other twin boy, Todd." Dr. Hicks sighed. "I guess that tells you what you need to know."

"Were you able to determine the cause of death?"

"Sheriff, the coroner will have to call it, but, unofficially, we just didn't have enough to tell. Same as last time—we know *who* but not *how*. Sorry. I know that would help your investigation immensely, but we don't know how they died. Only the killer knows if they were murdered first, and the fire and explosion were used just to cover it up."

"Yeah, and he's not telling. Well, thanks again, Doctor. I do appreciate the extra time and effort you put in on this. I'm much obliged."

"Sheriff...I'd like to say something off the record. After a month of this, I need to vent. I can only guess how hard this is for you since you knew these folks. I just want to say that after what I've seen here in the lab, I hope you get your man. Nobody should go to their grave in the condition these poor souls did.

"Sheriff, I rarely get emotional, but trying to piece these kids together...well, it hurt. I'd like to grab Mike McConnell by the collar and make him look at what's left of his family. Then I'd like to throw him to the piranhas, you know?"

"Yeah, I can relate," Hal said. "But on the record, I appreciate the professional job you did on this case. Thanks again."

Hal hung up the phone and picked it up again. He dialed John Washburn.

"Washburn here."

"John, it's Hal."

"Hey, what's up?"

"Dr. Hicks just called. The pathology report's in. The results were conclusive. Positive IDs on Erin and Todd."

"Well, isn't that what we expected? You sound surprised."

There was a long pause.

"John, are you absolutely sure that the ATF and your team have combed the area downstream as thoroughly as possible?"

"Don't go there. McConnell's alive. Get over it."

Hal sighed. "It's tough to accept. There's no motive. Nothing about his past and nothing anyone has said makes him seem capable of this. I kept hoping it was set up to look like Mike did it. I actually hoped he was dead. Is that desperate or what?"

"I realize this case is tough. So shuffle your cards. Cut the deck. Maybe a motive will come into play. How hard have you looked to find one?"

"Ad nauseam, John. Ad nauseam."

Jed took a huge phone book out of a drawer in the nightstand and put on his reading glasses. He scanned quickly down several pages—Southeast Car Care...Southeast Chimney Cleaning... Southeast Chiropractic...Southeast Colonial Manor. There was only one. The address was listed as Magdalene at Southeast Crossing. Something about that name sounded familiar. He must have passed it yesterday. He'd find it.

Jed left his room and stopped in the motel lobby for a complimentary breakfast. He picked up two bagels, cream cheese, a banana, and a glass of orange juice and sat down. He took the city map out of his pocket and marked the street locations of the downtown banks listed in Ellen's article. He also looked for Magdalene but didn't see it.

He finished eating quickly and walked to the front desk.

"I'm ready to check out. Jed Wilson, room 218."

"Sir, did you enjoy your stay? Was everything to your satisfaction?"

"Yeah, thanks. It was great. Say, I'm trying to find a place called Southeast Colonial Manor at—uh—let me see here…" Jed looked at his note. "Magdalene at Southeast Crossing. Any idea where that is?"

The clerk didn't look up. He politely cleared his throat. "Sir, turn around."

"Excuse me?"

"Turn around and look out the window."

Jed turned around. Directly across the street was Southeast Colonial Manor. He flashed the clerk a big grin. "Guess this is my lucky day. What are the odds?"

The clerk smiled and handed Jed his receipt. "Have a nice day, sir. Hope you'll stay with us again."

Jed left the building and walked over to his truck. He looked across the street and smiled. Things were starting to click.

When Jed pulled across Magdalene into Southeast Colonial Manor, an old man in a red cap and baseball jacket was not far behind.

Hal pulled up in front of Morganstern's and parked in the space designated for the handicapped. Media vans lined the street. Hal ignored the questions of journalists and turned away from anyone with a camera or a mike. He walked up to the servant's quarters and knocked.

He waited, knowing it would take Lisa a couple of minutes to make her way to the door. She greeted him with a big smile.

"Good morning, Sheriff," she said, a touch of sunshine in her voice.

"Uh—good morning. May I come in?"

She opened the door. "What's this about?"

They walked into the parlor and sat facing each other.

"Dr. Hicks called with the pathology report this morning. They've identified Erin and Todd. It's conclusive." He took a slow, deep breath and waited for the news to sink in.

Lisa gave him a questioning look.

Hal shook his head. "No ID on Mike. Sorry."

She bit her lower lip. "Well, now we're sure. This is hardly a surprise."

"You okay?"

"I will be. What now, Sheriff?"

"Well, first of all, I'm concerned about you and what you'd like to do to bury the remains and find some closure."

"It breaks my heart to think about it," she said. "I've arranged for something very simple for the family—four white crosses, one larger than the other three. No matter what's left of my sister's family, I want them buried togeth…" Lisa stopped midsentence.

"It's okay, take your time."

She wiped her eyes. "Patrick Dugan at Norris County Monument Company is making the marble crosses and they'll be ready any day…. Hal, I've decided to conduct my own private burial. Do you think people will understand? I don't want to offend anyone, but I've lost every member of my sister's family, and I don't think I can bear to share that final good-bye with anyone else…." she said, her voice cracking.

"Lisa, you just say the word. I'll make sure no one comes within a mile of that cemetery until you come out. When do you think you'll be prepared to do this?"

"Now that they're all accounted for, I think by Thursday or Friday."

"Is there anything I can do to help you with this?"

"You're sweet. You've been a good friend. But I don't think anyone can help with this part of it. I plan to keep it simple, but I'd like to do it privately."

"Whatever you want. Would you like to come back to the courthouse with me, or would you like a little time by yourself?"

"I don't want to be by myself right now. Please take me to the office with you. I'm ready to do anything I can to see Mike McConnell pay for this."

Hal looked outside. "Can you handle the cameras and the questions this morning? The wolves are ready to pounce."

"So what else is new? I'm not talking—it's the only control I have over any of this. They can ask all they want."

Hal offered Lisa his arm. "Okay then, let's get back to work."

NINETEEN

Mike McConnell heard the wind howl and felt a cold draft seeping through the wall. He pulled back the curtain and looked outside. Freezing rain was blowing in off the Pacific. Gray clouds covered the Washington sky like a plastic tarp thrown over patio furniture.

His confession to Father Donaghan yesterday had not cleared his conscience, even though he admitted everything and tried to believe God would forgive him. Who was he kidding? He couldn't even forgive himself. He knew hell awaited him at the end of the line. He wasn't in a big hurry to get there.

Mike closed the curtain and flopped on the bed. For the time being, he would hole up here at Evergreen Cottages. Three hundred dollars for the month—in advance. It was hard to beat ten bucks a day.

The oversized room had everything he needed—kitchenette, bathroom, bed, and dresser on one side of the room, living area on the other. A cushy plaid couch and chair gave it a homey feel. The brown carpet was outdated and worn but it felt better under his feet than an ice-cold floor.

This motel-turned-apartment wasn't a bad deal. The heat worked. Utilities were included. The TV had cable. It wasn't the Ritz, but it wasn't a dump either. Best of all, it was off the beaten path, hidden in the trees outside some dinky town called Harper's Grove. No one would ever find him here.

All Mike wanted was to stay hidden and to stay alive, safe from the punishment that awaited him if he got caught—and a worse one that awaited him if he died.

TWENTY

J ed noticed a small crowd gathered on the lawn of Southeast Colonial Manor. He parked his pickup and walked toward the entrance.

There was some commotion out front, and he spotted two TV network vans and camera crews filming the outside of the building. He noticed a policeman posted at the front door and several other officers milling around the premises. Jed wondered if this was going to be the beginning and the end of his lead.

An officer standing at the door saw him coming. "Excuse me, sir, what is the nature of your business here?"

"Uh—I'm here to visit the father of a good friend of mine."

"His name wouldn't just happen to be Sean McConnell, would it?"

"Actually, yes, but I'm not with them. I'm a friend of his."

"Yeah, right. We're not letting the media in here, so if you're trying to lie your way in, forget it."

"Look, my name is Jed Wilson. I'm a friend of the family's, and I'm here to see Mr. McConnell. I'm not with the media. I drove a long way to see him."

The officer's eyebrow went up. "Uh-huh. So tell me, why did you just happen to visit Sean McConnell today? I'm sure you don't know a thing about that small town newspaper story that started this circus."

"Of course I know about it. The reason I came is because I figured Mr. McConnell could use a kind word. Things are going to get tense for him now that his son is a fugitive." Jed took a step forward.

"Not so fast," said the officer, blocking the door. "Let's just see if Mr. McConnell knows you. Give me a photo ID."

He handed his driver's license to the officer, who handed it to another man. After something was said between the two, the man went inside. Jed put his hands in his jacket pockets. Had Mike ever mentioned his name to his father? He was about to find out. He liked a good challenge and decided he would push as hard as he could to get in. He looked around. The media presence was growing.

"Okay, you can go in." The officer gave the driver's license back to Jed. "But if you've misrepresented yourself, buddy, we'll haul you in."

"Haul me in for what?"

"Oh, we'll think of something. Go on," said the officer, nodding toward the door.

Jed entered the big wooden doors and was met by a nurse. "Mr. Wilson, follow me. We've relocated Mr. McConnell for security reasons. Seems everyone and his uncle wants to see him after that feature story. We can't be too careful. He's fragile enough without all this." She led the way down a long hallway and then stopped. "He's in there. Go ahead. He's expecting you." The nurse smiled and left.

Jed's palms were sweaty. Taking a deep breath, he knocked and then opened the door slowly and looked inside.

"Mr. McConnell? It's Jed Wilson. I don't know if Mike ever mentioned me, but we worked together at the highway department for twenty years. We were good friends, sir—very good friends. May I come in?"

The white-haired man seemed to be sizing him up. "Yes, of course...Jed. Michael talked about ya sometimes. He liked ya. Come on in. Have a seat."

Jed shook hands with Mike's father. He couldn't help but notice the resemblance. A sense of déjà vu caught him by surprise and put him at ease.

"What brings ya here, Jed? Hope you're not part of that mess outside."

Jed shook his head. "No, sir. I want to find Mike, but not for the reasons everyone else does. You see, I don't believe he killed his family."

The old man grimaced. "Ya don't, eh? And why's that? All the evidence points to guilty, don't ya know?"

"Maybe. Maybe not. There's a lot we don't know yet. The Mike McConnell I know isn't capable of this. He's just not. I came here hoping you could give me a clue where I might start looking for him. I've taken three weeks' vacation, and I'm determined to find him."

"What do ya hope to gain if ya do find him? He'll have to stand trial for murder. Ya gonna stick by him then?"

The emotion was caught in Jed's throat. "Sir, I'm not sure you understand. Mike was like the brother I never had. Something inside us just clicked. I would stand with him to his grave."

The old man's expression softened. "Michael did talk about ya quite a bit as I recall. Seemed real fond of ya. Said the two of ya laughed all the time and workin' with ya made the days go by real quick."

"We did bounce well off each other. Mike was the kind of friend I could count on. Sir, I've got to find him. I know he didn't do this."

Mr. McConnell seemed to drift off for a minute before his blue eyes held Jed in their gaze.

"Jed, how many media folks are outside, would ya guess?"

"I don't know, sir—eight or ten, maybe a dozen. Why?"

"And how many police officers and security guards?"

"Maybe a half dozen."

"Suppose ya were to walk out of here with the only clue to

Michael's whereabouts. Would I have your word that you'd never tell a soul? If you'll give me your solemn word, Jed, I'll tell ya what I know. Maybe we can find my son, but we need each other."

Ellen read Monday's feature story a third time. Reader reaction was already coming in, and she knew she had hit a grand slam. What surprised her was she was more satisfied with Sean McConnell's telling his story than her getting credit for writing it.

"Ellen, line three," said the voice on the intercom.

"Thanks, Margie.... Hello."

"Ellen? This is Lisa."

"Lisa! I'm glad you called. Things are moving fast since our breaking news and feature story on Saturday. How are you handling it?"

"Oh, I could do without the cameras, especially KJNX following me everywhere. But I'll eventually use them to my advantage. I called to tell you I enjoyed your feature story this morning."

"Thanks. I wasn't sure how you'd feel about it."

"I haven't seen Sean since Rose's wedding," Lisa said, "but he was a sweet man back then. Sounds like he hasn't changed much. Rose adored him, I know that."

"Well, believe me, the feeling was mutual. He was quite taken with Rose. I got the impression he loved her like a daughter. She seemed more attuned to the Irish heritage than Mike ever did. I think that touched Sean because he felt bad he never took Mike back to Ireland, to his roots. Rose was determined her kids would learn to appreciate them."

"Well, the article was wonderful, Ellen, it really was. But just because Mike had a nice father doesn't mean he didn't kill them. I want him to pay! Can you understand that?"

"Of course I can. I happen to agree with you. But Sean McConnell had a story to tell, and I thought it was worth running—just like the story on you. I hope you understand."

"I do. Listen, Ellen…the main reason I'm calling is I wanted to be the one to tell you the latest pathology report. It came back this morning."

"Lisa, you don't hav—"

"Yes, I do. I need to stay outraged until my scumbag brother-in-law gets the death penalty for this. The pathology report identified the remains as those of Erin and Todd—of course, you-know-who's weren't there. No big surprise to anyone," said Lisa, her voice shaking.

"I'm so sorry. I guess knowing for sure is better than wondering. What will you do now?"

"Well, that's the other reason I called. I've been thinking about this since I got here last week. I'd like to bury my sister and her kids in private. Ellen, I don't think I can bear to share them with the whole world. I just want to say good-bye without a crowd. Do you think the community would be offended? I mean, the way I feel right now, I don't even want Father Donaghan there. The memorial Mass has been said. I just want them all to myself. Am I being unreasonable?"

"I don't think so. You're the one having to bear most of the pain. You should do it your way. But I wouldn't tell anyone about it, if I were you. Pulling it off won't be easy with the media, especially KJNX. They've got you hemmed in."

"I know. Hal said if I told him when and where, he'd make sure no one came within a mile of the place until I came out."

"That's our sheriff. He means it too." Ellen paused to consider something. "Lisa, I have what may seem like a strange request, but I think it could work to your advantage."

"What's that?"

"You know I wouldn't violate your privacy for anything. So please hear me out before you answer. When you're ready to conduct the private burial, would you consider letting me take a telephoto shot of you at the grave site? I would be a long way off. You wouldn't know I'm there. Here's my thinking: I could use the picture by itself as a powerful good-bye the entire community could relate to. But more importantly, it would incite the public to demand justice in this case and keep authorities under pressure to find Mike. I could create a shot that would capture it better than words ever could. Will you trust me? I won't do it unless you say it's all right."

Lisa was quiet for a moment.

"Just you—no one else? And you would be too far away for me to notice?"

"That's the deal. You won't know I'm there. What do you think?"

"Just promise me you'll make it so powerful that people will…" Lisa's voice cracked. "Just make it powerful."

"I will, Lisa. I promise."

"Jed, I need arms and legs to find my son—and you need a clue. We're gonna have to work together. Ya seem to be the only one who thinks he's innocent."

"Don't you think he's innocent?"

Sean McConnell hesitated. "I honestly don't know. Either way, Michael and I have lost about everything. I'll never stop lovin' him, don't ya know? But I can't figure why he's runnin' if he didn't do it. Why doesn't he just turn himself in and let the authorities get at the truth? This isn't gettin' him anything but heartache. He's liable to get himself kill—" Mike's dad couldn't finish.

"But do you really believe he's capable of this?" Jed asked.

"Well, I never woulda thought so, but why wouldn't he face me? He just left me a note."

"A note!" Jed lowered his voice. "You have a note?"

"Well, of course I do. That's what I wanna show ya. Would ya mind checkin' the hall to be sure nobody's out there. This makes me a bit nervous. Don't know why, though, because no one else could figure out the note, and I can always say I don't understand it. The boy was nervous when he called, told me to get rid of it."

"Called?" said Jed in a loud whisper. "He called too?"

"Yesterday, just before that editor, Ellen Jones, was here. Real nice lady. Anyway, Michael caught me by surprise and didn't let me get a word in. Said he left the note because he didn't want me worryin' about him. Asked me to get rid of it, though."

Jed was beside himself. "Where is this note?"

The old man chuckled. "It's right here in my pocket. I was afraid someone might search my room while they relocated me. The way I figure it, they wouldn't think I'd be stupid enough to do what I am stupid enough to do—keep evidence on my personal body. Pretty clever, huh?"

"You really have the note here, in your pocket?"

"You wanna see it, Jed?" he asked, a twinkle in his eye.

"Sure I do."

"Jed, look at me, son. This might be considered withholdin' evidence, don't ya know? I suspect we could both be in some real hot water if the FBI found out. Are ya sure ya wanna get involved? Can I trust ya with it?"

Jed got a firm grip on Mr. McConnell's arm. "When it comes to Mike, you can trust me with your life."

Rhonda sat quietly with her legs draped over the overstuffed chair in her living room. The day crawled by since her conversation with Jed earlier. In her own awkward way, she was praying for him. She thought about her failing marriage, the feelings she had repressed for years, and about her conversation with the Kennsingtons after church yesterday.

Mary Beth and Joe had faced their problems, and they seemed so together now—so in love. Their type of relationship was what Rhonda wanted. Her heart ached at the realization of what she never had. Rhonda wondered if she and Jed could ever change the way things had been all of their married life. What would it take to turn things around? The phone rang and startled her.

"Hello," said Rhonda, her heart pounding.

"Mom? It's me, Jennifer."

"You sound funny. What's the matter?"

"Uh...I..."

"Honey, tell me what's wrong."

Rhonda heard sniffling on the other end of the line. The silence seemed endless.

"Jen, talk to me. Whatever it is, it can't be that bad."

"Mom, don't say that. Please don't hate me," she said. "I've...I've really messed up...bad. I don't know what to do...."

"Jen, I could never hate you for anything, but you've got to tell me what's wrong."

"Mom..." Jennifer's voice cracked. "I can't say it. It's too awful."

"Jennifer, you're worrying me. Honey, what is it? What's wrong? There's nothing you can tell me that would make me stop—"

"I'm pregnant. I'm so scared, Mom. What am I going to do?"

Rhonda was aware of Jennifer's sobbing, but her heart felt just like it had twenty-eight years ago in Dr. Lucas's office.

TWENTY-ONE

J ed, do ya see anyone?" Sean McConnell whispered.

Jed poked his head into the hallway and looked one way and then the other. He pulled the door shut. "There's no one out there. It's now or never."

The old man reached into his pocket and took out a folded, yellow square of paper. He sat quietly, holding it with both hands.

"Once ya know what this says, Jed, there's no turnin' back. I wouldn't do anything to get ya in trouble."

"I'm not looking for trouble, Mr. McConnell. I just want to find Mike so he can tell me what happened."

"Are ya ready then?"

Jed nodded, and the old man began to open the note, his feeble hands shaking as he unveiled each fold. Jed could hear his own heartbeat in spite of Sean McConnell's raspy breathing.

Come on, Mr. McConnell, get on with it.

There was a loud knock on the door. The old man jumped and dropped the note. Jed scooped it up and stuffed it into the pocket of his jacket just as a nurse opened the door.

The two men smiled angelically.

"Oh, *there* you are, Mr. McConnell. It's time to take your medication."

Jed was thinking if bladder control were an issue, both men would be emptying their shoes.

❧

Rhonda sat for hours, immobilized, distressed to consider what her daughter might be facing. She also felt the pain of her own past return with a vengeance....

"Oh, Rhonnie, you're a beautiful bride. You look like an angel," said Grandma, her hands holding a strand of pearls. "I wore these when I married your grandfather and fastened them around your mother's neck the day she married your father. Now it's your turn."

Rhonda glanced over at her mother, who struggled not to cry. She knew her emotion was from disappointment, not joy.

"I'll never forget the first time I held you in my arms," said Grandpa, taking her hands in his. "You were my sweet baby doll, still are. I always hoped I'd live to see this day. You look just like your mother did in that dress."

How she hated the deception! Only her parents and Jed's parents knew she was pregnant. She didn't deserve to wear white and certainly not the same dress her mother wore. The compliments and attention added to her guilt.

"Are you ready, honey? The music's started," Dad said.

Through her veil, Rhonda saw his eyes fill with tears. She knew it wasn't just because his little girl was getting married.

Six months later her life changed again. Rhonda never forgot the moment Jed laid eyes on Jennifer for the first time. He stood at the foot of the bed, looking cold and detached, almost angry.

"Don't you want a closer look?" Rhonda asked.

"I can see."

"Isn't she beautiful? Look at all this blond fuzz. Here, you hold her."

"No—uh, not right now. I need to call your parents."

"You waited this long. You can call them in a few minutes. Don't you want to hold her first?"

"They'll be plenty of time for that," he said.

But he never made time for Jennifer. Rhonda thought that would change with time.

"Jed, would you rock Jen for a while? She's teething, and if I put her down, she'll fuss.... Jed, did you hear me?"

"I heard you."

"I need to fold diapers. We're out."

"So I'll fold diapers. You rock the baby."

Rhonda bit her lip. "Jed, the baby's name is Jennifer."

"I know what her name is. I'd rather fold diapers, all right?"

"She's almost a year old, Jed—your own flesh and blood. How can you keep pushing her away?"

"I'm not pushing her away."

"Yes, you are! You treat her like she's not there. You can hardly say her name. She's your daughter! Someday she's going to wonder why you don't love her. What are you going to tell her?"

"I don't know what I'm going to tell her!" he snapped. "I've got a long time to think about it, don't I?"

Rhonda started to cry. "You don't love either one of us, and you never will!"

He left the room without saying anything else.

Rhonda didn't bring it up again. She decided she would love Jennifer enough for both of them....

The doorbell rang. Rhonda got up to answer the door and wished whoever was selling something would go away.

"Mary Beth! It's you."

"What's wrong? You've been crying."

"I'm not thinking too clearly right now," Rhonda said. "Come in."

"You really look shaken."

"If I ever needed to know God's plan for my life, it's now. I feel like I've just gone back twenty-eight years and history is repeating itself."

"What do you mean? What happened?"

"I got the worst news this morning, and instead of being able to step in and help, I'm acting like I'm worse off than the person who needs me."

"Rhonda, start at the beginning," Mary Beth said. "Tell me everything."

"All right, but I hope you can handle a little déjà vu."

"All right, Mr. McConnell, here you go." The nurse put his medication in a paper pill cup and handed it to him with a glass of water.

"Typical woman. Always fussin' over us menfolk, keepin' us in tow."

"Oh, stop your protesting," the nurse said. "You love being looked after."

He winked at Jed. The nurse waited until he took the medication and then left the room. The two men stared at each other and burst into a fit of laughter.

"Shoot fire, Jed, I thought we were discovered, don't ya know?"

"Man, that was close, Mr. McConnell. Let's get on with this. I don't think I can take much more!"

The laughter quieted down. Jed took the note out of his jacket and looked at Mike's father with a questioning look. "May I?" he asked.

"Sure. It's all yours now anyway, son."

Jed unfolded the yellow paper and instantly recognized Mike's handwriting. He carefully read each word and then read it again. "I don't get it, Mr. McConnell. What does it mean?"

"Read it to me, Jed."

Jed slowly read the note aloud.

"'When I was growing up, we walked together. You made me something to lean on when I got tired and wanted to give up. Well, Pop, I'm tired. I have no crutch, and I'm not sure I can stand alone. I think I'll go back to those roots. I'm in a great depression and I need a new deal. Everything you ever crafted was perfect, except me. I'm sorry.'

"Well, sir, this is clear as mud to me. Obviously it means something to you or you wouldn't have brought it up."

Sean nodded. "Yep—FDR."

"Excuse me?"

"FDR. That's what he's sayin'. Makes perfect sense to me, but then he knew it would too."

"FDR?" Jed repeated.

"Let me explain, son. I expect Michael must've talked some about my love for wood. My profession was cabinetry. I think Michael loved it too, even though he didn't inherit the talent. He loved that wood houseboat. Coulda had a newer boat made of synthetics, but I think wood was in his blood. Now, Jed, you probably don't know this, but once when I was a young man, I was commissioned to make a cedar chest for Franklin D. Roosevelt, and—"

"Oh, *that* FDR!"

"Right. Making that chest was the most excitin' thing I ever did. I called all over the state of New York tryin' to find the perfect cedar to do the job. I finally located what I wanted—an unusually high grade of western red cedar. Came all the way from Washington state, from Cedar Falls Mill near Olympic National Park. Jed, I worked on that chest until it was absolutely the finest work I ever did. I was right proud. Never got to meet President Roosevelt, but I still have his letter of thanks tucked away. Professionally, I never had a prouder moment, don't ya know?"

"Mr. McConnell, how does this relate to Mike and the note?"

"Now I'm gettin' to that.... Years later, when Michael was about eight years old, we got itchy to take a vacation, so we left New York City and took a long car trip. Went all the way to Washington state. In those days that was the other side of the world. Well, Jed, all those forests set my heart to rememberin' with pride all that went into makin' that cedar chest for FDR. My prize cedar was grown right there in one of those forests near Olympic National Park, and Cedar Falls Mill is where it was made into lumber. So I took Michael there. Let him see the whole amazin' process. Told him my story about FDR's cedar chest and how special this red cedar was."

Jed scratched his head and wondered if Sean McConnell was a doughnut short of a full dozen.

Mr. McConnell rambled on. "Near the mill, and not far from our campsite, were some hikin' trails. Little ol' Michael, he found him a huge red cedar branch and drug it all the way back to our tent. He wanted me to make somethin' special for him."

"Just like you did for the president." Jed shook his head and broke into a broad grin. "I should've known…Mike was born competitive."

"That he was. I worked a long time on that branch and made it into a fine walkin' stick. That little boy and that tall walkin' stick were inseparable from then on. Why, he even called it his FDR. He'd march all over the place sayin' as long as he had his FDR to help pull him along, he could go anywhere." The old man chuckled. "I got a big kick out of watchin' him with it, Jed. He was real proud that I made something for him out of the same wood I used for a president.

"But ya know the biggest difference between the cedar chest and the walkin' stick? I sold the cedar chest to the president of the United States, but ya couldn't've offered me enough money for that walkin' stick. When I fashioned it for Michael I was tryin' to say he was more important to me than anything—that he was the most special gift God ever made for his mama and me. Jed, that walkin' stick was a symbol between me and my boy. Do ya see where I'm going with this?"

Jed shook his head.

"Come here, Jed. Look at this with me." Sean held the note, and ran his finger under the text. Says here, 'When I was growing up, we walked together. You made me something to lean on for when I got tired and wanted to give up.' He's talkin' about that walkin' stick, Jed. Now when he says, 'I think I'll go back to those roots,' he's tellin' me he's goin' back to that forest. And when he writes, 'I'm in a great depression and I need a new deal', he's usin' words I think of with Franklin D. Roosevelt—FDR. What else could he be referrin' to except that walkin' stick?"

"Mr. McConnell, maybe I'm dense, but I still don't get it."

"Jed, it means he's in Washington state—close to Olympic National Park. My bet is he's not far from Cedar Falls Mill."

"How sure are you about this? I mean, 50 percent sure? 75? Washington state's a long way from here. It would take a big chunk of my three weeks just to drive up there and back."

"Jed, my guess is more like 98 percent sure. I know my boy. He wrote this note to tell me where he was goin'. He can't face me, but he doesn't want me to write him off either. And did you read this...?" The old man's voice cracked. He pointed to the words.

Jed read the last line. "'Everything you ever crafted was perfect, except me. I'm sorry.'" There was a long pause. "Man, he's really down."

"I don't know what the future holds for Michael or for us, but if ya would be my legs and feet, please go find my boy. Tell him that I still—no, that I'll *always* love him. Will ya do that, Jed?"

"Yes, sir, if he's where you think he is, I'll find him and I'll tell him."

Jed felt an awkward silence. His eyes burned with tears and when he looked up, Mike's fragile father was about to break.

"Jed, would ya mind much if I held on to ya for a minute? I really miss my son...."

"I can't believe I just told you the story of my life," Rhonda said. "I've never told anyone before. My getting pregnant with Jennifer completely changed my relationship with Jed. We had some years that were better than others, especially after Mark came along, but our marriage has never been happy."

"What about Jed and Jennifer?"

"Oh, Jed eventually got over the awkwardness and was civil to her, but he never completely accepted Jennifer. It still hurts me to see how superficial they are with each other."

"Have you and Jed ever dealt with what happened?"

Rhonda shook her head. "I'm ashamed to tell you, but no. He won't. Any time I've ever tried to broach the subject, he shuts me off. He's a master at shutting out anything he doesn't want to hear. That's why he drinks."

"Rhonda...what did you tell Jennifer this morning?"

"I'm not even sure I remember. I told her I wanted her to come home, that we needed to talk about this and decide what to do."

"Does Jennifer have any idea what she wants to do?"

"I think she's so stunned at this point she hasn't thought that far ahead. She seems scared and desperate. I know exactly how she feels."

There was a long hesitation.

"Rhonda, do you think she would ever consider an abortion?"

"I don't know. Politically, I think Jennifer's pro-choice, but I don't know if she would go through with anything like that herself."

"Well, where are you? I mean, would you support her if she had an abortion?"

"Absolutely not. But she's twenty-eight years old, Mary Beth. There's only so much I can do. I want to give her good advice. Right now my emotions are so tied up with hers, I'm not sure when I'm responding to her and when I'm responding to my old feelings. I really need to get this sorted out—and get *me* out of the way."

"When are you going to tell Jed?"

"Oh, I don't know. He's got so much on his mind in this search to find Mike. What good can it do for him to know while he's on the road? It'll just add more weight to his burden."

"When's Jennifer coming home?"

"She's trying to work out some vacation time. She'll let me know."

"Is the baby's father someone she's in love with?" Mary Beth asked.

"I didn't get that impression. Of course, she doesn't tell me all about her personal life either, but I never heard her mention anyone special."

"I can see why you're shaken up, Rhonda. Both of us know how it feels to be in her shoes. Would you mind if I prayed before I leave? I'd feel a whole lot better if we put this situation in God's hands."

"Oh, thank you, Mary Beth. I really wanted you to, but I was embarrassed to ask."

"Let's just sit here quietly for a moment…," Mary Beth said. "Father, Rhonda and I come before You with no pretense. We're both sinners. We've made mistakes. Lord, You know that. You knew it even before You died to release us from the pain of it. We ask You right now to enter into this situation and to take control.

"Lord, we ask your protection for Jennifer and her unborn child. We pray that You would give her wisdom and courage to make a decision that's pleasing in Your sight.

"Father, we also pray for Rhonda. Use these circumstances to heal her of the past and to create a strong relationship not only with Jennifer, but also with Jed.

"Lord, we lift Jed up to You. Wherever he is at this moment, we pray You would send angels to watch over him and keep him from harm.

"Most of all, Father, I pray this family will come to know You in a personal way and will be transformed as a result. I ask these things in the name of your Son, and our Savior, Jesus Christ. Amen."

The young man in plaid shirt and jeans was invisibly present when the fragrance of Mary Beth's prayer went heavenward. He never lost sight of Rhonda or of his mission.

TWENTY-TWO

Well, I trust you had a nice visit," the officer said.

"Yeah, I did." Jed glanced up and saw the crowd had grown.

"Well, I'm glad," a reporter said, "because you're the only one who got in there. You stayed a long time. Did you say you were a friend of the family?"

"That's what I said."

"So we're not going to find out tomorrow that you're some small-town reporter who lucked his way into another breaking story?" someone else asked.

"Look, I'm just a friend of the family who came to visit Mr. McConnell during a tough time. You people can make news out of that if you want to. I've got better things to do. Excuse me."

Jed couldn't get out of there fast enough. He was relieved when no one followed him.

As he opened the door to his truck, he looked up one last time and saw Sean McConnell watching him from the window. Jed maintained eye contact for a few seconds. Then after a nod of acknowledgement, he got in his truck and set out to find Mike.

When Jed pulled out onto Magdalene, the old man in a red cap and baseball jacket wasn't far behind.

◡◦◡

Special Agent Jordan Ellis was filling out a report when his phone rang.

"This is Jordan."

"Jordan, Nick Butler in Atlanta. I've got a tail on that Wilson guy from Baxter. He left Sean McConnell about one. Was in there for over four hours. Can't imagine what they talked about all that time. Anyway, I put our agents on him. Last I heard, he was headed north out of Atlanta. I guess his next stop'll be Nashville—pretty predictable. Poor sucker is wasting his time, though. We already checked out Nashville and Kansas City. Other than a couple of positive IDs on camera, dead ends—both of them. I'll keep you posted, but I think this is going to be a big yawn."

"Maybe. Don't get too laid back," Jordan said. "Did anybody else come to see the old guy?"

"No, police security was tight."

"Okay, Nick, keep an eye on Sean McConnell and let me know if anyone else comes calling. Did you take care of the phone?"

"Yeah, wiretap's in place. Anybody calls him, we'll know about it."

"Okay, then. Keep me updated. I want to know the minute he gets a call from Mike McConnell, whether he talks long enough to trace it or not. Got that?"

"You'll be the first to know."

Special Agent Butler tackled a mound of paperwork, which, unless he hit it hard and fast, threatened to preempt his viewing of Monday Night Football. The phone rang.

"Yeah."

"Sir, we're still tailing Wilson, but he's not going to Nashville."

"Sure he is. He's following the paper trail on the credit card statement."

"Well, then he's a moron because he's headed to Memphis."

"Memphis! Are you sure?"

"That may not be his destination, but that's sure the direction he's going. You can forget Nashville."

"Where is he now?"

"I-40 headed west, about twenty miles outside Nashville. Unless he's planning a detour, the next big stop is Memphis."

Butler sighed. "Not tonight, the Falcons are playing...."

"Sir?"

"Nothing. Don't let him see you. I'll get someone else to pick up the tail and tell you where to make the switch."

"It'll be interesting to see what this clown finally does. Maybe he's lost. Probably doesn't get out of Baxter very much."

"Don't underestimate him," Butler said. "This Jed Wilson knows exactly what he's doing. The key is don't let him spot you, and he just might drive us right to Mike McConnell's front door."

"Not to worry. We're as inconspicuous as a tick on a jackrabbit. He'll never know we're on him."

Sheriff Barker was at his desk when the phone rang.

"This is Hal Barker."

"Sheriff, it's Jordan Ellis."

Hal laughed. "Why is it when I hear your voice I get nervous like a kid in the principal's office? What's up?"

"Nothing—or maybe something. Special Agent Butler called. One of your local citizens paid Sean McConnell a visit this morning and stayed for over four hours. Then he headed north out of Atlanta. We assumed he was headed for Nashville and then Kansas City to check out the banks where our fugitive is known to have used his credit card. The boy isn't going to Nashville. He kept right on going and is headed for Memphis at the moment. You know this guy, Jed Wilson?"

"Jed? Sure, everyone knows Jed. He was Mike McConnell's best friend. They both worked at the highway department and hung out at O'Brian's together."

"Well, that makes it even more interesting. I've got a tail on him to see what he's up to. Thought you'd want to know."

"Okay, thanks. Let me know what happens."

Hal hung up the phone. He picked it up again and dialed.

"Hello."

"Rhonda, it's Hal Barker. Would you mind if I stopped by there for a minute on my way home? There's something I'd like to ask you."

Hal pulled up in front of the Wilsons' house. Rhonda met him at the door, looking worried. "Hal, what is it? Is something wrong? Nothing's happened to Jed, has it?"

"Now why would you ask me that? Isn't Jed home for dinner yet?"

Rhonda looked sheepish. "Well, uh—no, actually not."

"I wouldn't hold dinner if I were you. I got a call from Jordan Ellis with the FBI. After spending four hours with Mike's father, Jed seems to be tooling down the interstate headed toward Memphis. Wouldn't happen to know anything about that, would you? Rhonda, you want to tell me what's going on? I don't like surprises, and I was caught completely off guard when I got that call. There's a murder investigation going on. What in blazes is Jed doing in Tennessee?"

"Well…you see…Jed had some vacation time and he wanted to sort things out. He's really struggling with the idea that Mike is suspected of murder. He doesn't believe he did it."

"So what's he doing in Tennessee?"

"I honestly don't know that he is in Tennessee. That's what you're saying."

"Rhonda, don't mess with me. This could be serious. If he's trying to get in the way of this investigation, he could be in deep trouble. We're not playing cops and robbers."

"Jed isn't trying to interfere with anything. He's not breaking the law."

"Rhonda, look at me. I need a straight answer," said Hal, glaring at her from the other side of the screen door. "Is Jed trying to find Mike on his own? He doesn't know what he's doing. He could get hurt."

"Hurt? All he's trying to do is find Mi—"

"I knew it!"

"He just wants to ask him straight out if he did it. He's not going to believe it unless Mike tells him to his face. You know that!"

"Rhonda, you've got to talk some sense into Jed. Tell him to think about coming back here and calling off this crusade. If Mike McConnell is innocent, let him come out in the open and talk to us. There's a reason he isn't doing that—like maybe he's guilty. Did you ever think of that? So what if Jed finds him? Mike's a fugitive, a desperate man. He may not respond to Jed like a rational person. Frankly I'm concerned for Jed's safety."

"Hal, you're scaring me."

"Maybe you need a little scaring! And another thing: If Mike tells him he's guilty, do you think Jed's going to testify against his best friend? So then what? Does Jed lie about what he knows? Anyway you cut it, Jed's setting himself up to get in way too deep. Talk some sense into him. He needs to let the FBI do the looking. Rhonda, get him to come home. We've had enough tragedies around here. I don't want another one."

"I'll do what I can, but I promise you, he's not out to interfere with the investigation. He's tired of speculation. He wants it first-hand. Jed doesn't think Mike is capable of this and won't believe it until Mike tells him. Can you honestly blame him for that?"

"Just tell Jed to get himself back here and out of the line of fire."

"I'll relay the message, Hal, but I don't think it'll do any good."

Mike McConnell shut the door behind him at Evergreen Cottages and set a wet plastic bag on the counter. He put a six-pack in the refrigerator and slid out of his stiff jacket. The frigid wind had cut right through him and he was still shivering. He hated this weather.

After flipping on the TV, he turned the oven dial to preheat and reached in the freezer and pulled out a TV dinner. He opened the refrigerator, thinking a beer sounded good, but he put it back. It was too cold. Instead, he reached for the teapot and filled it with hot water. Something on TV caught his attention.

"…And so for now, authorities aren't saying where the clues are taking them in the McConnell case, but this sleepy town of Baxter has had a rude awakening to the violence that has knocked on the door of nearly every community in America. Mike McConnell remains a fugitive, while his friends and neighbors prepare to say a final good-bye to his victims. Marlene Roberts is standing by live in Baxter. Marlene…"

"I'm here in the community of Baxter where Rose McConnell's only living relative is preparing a private burial service for her sister, niece, and nephews. Reportedly devastated by the fire and explosion that killed her sister's family, Lisa Sorensen has asked the community to respect her privacy as she plans a private farewell in the cemetery overlooking this usually peaceful town. Patrick Dugan, owner of the Norris County Monument Company, told sources that Mrs. Sorensen is already making plans at this time. This follows a report earlier today that human remains, found in the Murdock River several miles downstream from Heron Lake, have now been identified as those of fourteen-year-old Erin McConnell, and six-year-old Todd McConnell. All four family members have now been identified. The county coroner said that, due to the condition of the remains, the cause of death was inconclusive. It is impossible to tell if the victims were murdered before the fire and explosion or if they were left to die as a result of it. Kent, back to you...."

"Authorities have released this picture of the suspect, Mike McConnell, and urge anyone who might have information as to his whereabouts to call the number at the bottom of your screen...."

The finality hit him. They'd all been found. Confirmed dead. And it was his fault. Mike McConnell—monster, murderer, miserable excuse for a man. Nothing could erase what he'd done. No one could forgive his offense.

He turned off the TV and paced back and forth, unable to escape the words still echoing in his mind: *It is impossible to tell if the victims were murdered before the fire and explosion or if they were left to die as a result of it.*

Mike leaned with his hands flat against the wall, hung his head, and wept.

Present, but unseen, a rugged man in hiking boots and a down jacket stood watch, ready to act should the forces of darkness make a move. His orders were clear—the only demons Mike McConnell was to encounter were his own.

TWENTY-THREE

J ed's red Silverado rolled out of Memphis and crossed over the
Mississippi River into Arkansas. From the bridge he could see
lights reflected in the winding waterway. He picked up the cell
phone and dialed.

"Hello."

"Hi."

"Jed, is that you?"

"Yeah, it's me. Why do you sound so anxious? What's wrong?"

"I've been worried."

"Why? I just talked to you this morning. I found Sean
McConnell. He gave me a clue I'm following up on."

"Where are you?"

"You're better off not knowing. It'd be awkward if anyone asks."

"Well, it's too late for that. Hal was here earlier. They know
you're in Tennessee."

"Who's they?"

"The FBI, I think. Someone called Hal and said they knew you
had been with Sean McConnell. Apparently they're watching you.
Jed, you aren't doing anything illegal, are you?"

"Of course not, Rhonda! Get a grip. I'm taking a message from a
sweet old man to his son, that's all. I think I know where Mike is.
I'm glad you suggested I talk to his dad."

"Jed, I'm scared. Hal seemed upset. He said to tell you to call off
this crusade and come back home. Let the FBI do the looking."

"No way, Rhonda. I need to find Mike and hear what he has to say. I'm not stopping until I do. I didn't come this far to give up."

"Well, where are you now?"

"In my pickup, calling you from my cell phone, but I'm not in Tennessee." The city lights of Memphis were barely visible in his rearview mirror. "So what's going on there—anything?"

There was silence on the other end.

"Rhonda, you still there?"

"Yes, I'm here."

"Why are you so quiet? Something going on?"

"I'm worried, that's all."

"Well, stop worrying. I'm fine. But it wouldn't hurt my feelings if you and Mary Beth said a few prayers if you want. Can't hurt to have God on my side. He may be the only one."

"Not the only one, Jed. I want you back safely."

"Yeah? I'll see what I can do. By the way, I haven't had a beer since I left Baxter."

"Really? Jed, I—"

"Go ahead and say it. You're glad I'm off the sauce. So now that you know I'm behaving, stop worrying."

"I'll try. It's really strange not having you here. Be careful."

"Yeah, I will. I'll call you tomorrow."

Agent Nick Butler was relaxing in front of the television, watching Monday Night Football. It was the end of the third quarter and the network had just switched to a commercial when his cell phone rang. He smiled.

"Hello, Jordan," he said.

"How'd you know it was me?"

Nick laughed. "I know you. You're looking for an update before the fourth quarter starts."

"Scary, isn't it—being so predictable? So, go ahead, tell me the latest on Wilson."

"I've had a string of agents tailing him from Atlanta," Nick said. "He beat it out of Memphis and crossed over the Arkansas line about thirty minutes ago. There are two Arkansas agents on him at the moment and others ready for the pass off. He's not going to get away from us."

"Good. Jed Wilson may be the only hot trail to Mike McConnell. If we lose him, we start from scratch."

"I realize that, Jordan. I've already put out the word. Hey, the game's coming back on. Anything else?"

"Yeah, did I mention your team's down by fourteen?"

"It ain't over till it's over. There's another quarter left."

"Well, Nick, let's hope your team out on I-40 is on top of their game."

Jordan hung up the phone and dialed.

"Hello, this is Hal."

"You're up late."

"It's football night. What's the latest on Jed?"

"He's in Arkansas."

"Already? Any idea where he's going?"

"None at the moment, but we're right on top of him. Wherever he goes, we go."

"Jordan, I talked to his wife earlier. She says he isn't breaking any laws, just wants to find Mike and hear from him what happened. I told her to get him to back off. Don't think it'll do any good."

"Well, Hal, McConnell's the guy I'm after. I don't particularly want Wilson to back off. He's our only lead at the moment."

"I know, Jordan. But I know him. You don't. I wouldn't want to see him get sucked into this thing and end up in trouble."

"His choice, Sheriff. All I care about is getting McConnell."

Jed had been wired all day, but somewhere between Memphis and Little Rock, fatigue finally set in. He pulled into a motor inn and noticed a white car exiting the off ramp not far behind him. He remembered seeing that same car when he stopped a few miles back for coffee, and he wondered if he should take the idea of the FBI's tailing him more seriously. He decided to get back on the interstate and see if the car would follow.

Jed drove back onto I-40, proceeded for two miles and exited at the next off ramp. He pulled into a motel parking lot and pretended to be reading a map, his head down but his eyes looking up. The white car pulled in slowly and stopped at the other end of the parking lot.

Jed was too exhausted to deal with it. He walked into the motel office and came out two minutes later with the key to a room on the ground floor. He threw his bag on the chair, slipped out of his jeans, and was asleep in a matter of seconds.

TWENTY-FOUR

The minute Jed woke up, his mind started to process the situation. Should he try to lose whoever was following him? Was it the FBI? Or was it someone who didn't want him to find Mike—or maybe someone else who did?

He stuck his head through a crack in the drapes and looked to see if the white car was still there. It wasn't. He squinted at the digital clock. It was 5:45 A.M. He showered and shaved, then headed over to the motel office.

Jed checked out, got in his truck, and pulled out of the motel parking lot. He saw nothing suspicious. Maybe he'd overreacted to what Rhonda told him. It'd been a long time since he was that tired.

Jed got back on the interstate and proceeded west until he saw a billboard advertising a fast-food place up ahead. When he pulled off, two cars exited behind him—one red, the other blue.

He placed his order for coffee and a sausage biscuit and pulled around to pay for it, then moved his truck to a parking space so he could look at the map. He noticed the red car was parked down the row. The driver was either reading a newspaper or hiding behind it. The passenger seemed to be asleep. Jed decided to leave and see if they would follow. In his rearview mirror, he spotted the red car pulling out just as he pulled onto the interstate.

He pulled off at the next exit and into a service station to top off the tank. While he still had the nozzle in his hand, the red car pulled into the station and stopped at the far pump. Jed walked toward the driver. He noted the man was dressed in slacks and a sport coat and looked rather sharp for six-thirty in the morning—except for a five o'clock shadow. The passenger had gone inside.

"Say, you wouldn't happen to know how much farther it is to Memphis, would you?" Jed looked the man right in the eyes, fishing for a reaction.

"I really couldn't tell you. I've never been there myself. Maybe you could get a map inside."

"Yeah, okay. Thanks."

Jed went inside to pay for the gas. He also picked up a map and unfolded it, keeping an eye on the red car. He had planned to angle up to Missouri. Maybe he should turn around and go back toward Memphis and really mess with their minds. He'd run them in circles all day if he had to. Jed got in his truck and turned onto I-40 east toward Memphis. He watched in his rearview mirror, expecting the red car to follow.

"Hello, this is Nick Butler."

"Sir, it's me. Listen, we're going a little nuts out here. Wilson must have made us."

"What? I told you not to blow your cover! What happened?"

"Hey, he prances up to the car asking for directions to Memphis—you know, playing the part of the lost traveler? I play dumb, tell him to get a map."

"So what's your problem?"

"I can't find my keys anywhere. The bum must have picked my pocket."

"What did you do, dance with him?"

"I can't figure it out. But the keys are definitely gone, and that's the only explanation I have. I put them in my jacket before I paid for the gas. I'm positive. I never leave them in the car."

"What about your partner, did he see anything?"

"No, nothing."

"Let me get this straight. You're the professional. He's the lost traveler. He's off to heaven-knows-where without a professional tailing him—and now you're the lost traveler? This is going to be a rotten day!"

While the FBI agents sent for a locksmith, the curious old man in a red cap and baseball jacket had long resumed his watch somewhere outside of Jed Wilson's vision.

Ellen Jones's phone had not stopped ringing, and she couldn't go anywhere without being pursued by the media.

Margie peeked her head in the door. "Ellen, line two is for you. It's Sean McConnell."

Ellen smiled and picked up the receiver. "Hello, Mr. McConnell."

"Well, hello there, young lady. Ya really are an editor, I see."

"I told you I was. And I've been shooting straight so far."

"Yes, ya have. That's why I called ya. This mornin' I got my copy of the story about me that ya wrote up for yesterday's paper."

"Oh, it came?"

"I've got it right here. Ellen, it's good. It—well—it touched me. You made me sound like some kinda special person. I don't see myself that way, but what ya had to say was right nice. I really appreciate the plug about the cedar chest. I'm kinda proud of that, but hardly anybody knows about it. Well, I guess they do now."

Ellen could almost see the twinkle in the old man's eyes. "Mr. McConnell, I believe this is what they call your 'fifteen minutes of fame.' Your story is warm and interesting, and it's all true. It's all right to take a bow and enjoy it while it lasts."

"Aw, I don't know about that, but I sure do appreciate all the nice things ya said, Ellen. I knew I liked ya even before ya did this. You have heart. One other thing: I'm grateful for ya not bein' negative about Michael. I still love that boy like life itself, and no matter how this thing turns out, he's still my son. Thanks for not makin' him out to be a demon or somethin'. He's still a par— Sorry, I get a little emotional. I was tryin' to say, he's still a part of me."

"Then I know there's good inside him, Mr. McConnell."

"Well, I just wanted to say thank ya for writin' somethin' that helped me to remember what things were like. I've had a good life, Ellen. I really have. I hope we get to see each other again sometime. I'd really like that."

"Because I remind you of Rose?"

"No, because I like ya."

"Well, you're my favorite celebrity. I'll make it a point to see you again."

"See that ya do, young lady. Bye now."

"Good-bye, Mr. McConnell."

Ellen hung up the phone. Her eyes unexpectedly brimmed with tears. *I've had a good life, Ellen. I really have.* Nothing he could have said would have meant more. Her story had given him back his dignity. Ellen looked up at the oil painting of Reginald T. Baxter.

"Well, boss, how am I doing?"

Hal Barker parked his squad car in the handicap place in front of Morganstern's. "Let's take a minute before we tackle this, Lisa."

"Good grief," she said. "There must be a hundred reporters and cameramen out there. They're like a pack of wolves."

"You've got that right. They can't get to Sean McConnell, so they're going to pace on your doorstep. Yesterday's pathology report sent them into a frenzy to get Mike McConnell. That's one positive thing that's come out of it."

"I can't believe Patrick Dugan told reporters I was going to conduct a private ceremony," Lisa said. "Might as well have sent them a written invitation. I feel betrayed. I asked him not to say anything."

"Some reporter probably preyed on him and caught him off guard. People here aren't used to this. All right, you ready to be escorted to the door?"

"I guess. But I'm not saying a word."

"That's fine. I'll hold onto your arm like always. It may feel a little claustrophobic with reporters closing in, but we'll just keep moving, okay?"

"I sure wish I wasn't stuck with this cane. It's not like I can outrun them."

"I know, and they're counting on that."

Brenna Morgan walked out the side entrance of Baxter High School on Tuesday afternoon and was besieged by reporters.

"Miss Morgan, is it true you saw Mike McConnell before anyone else?"

"Is it true you broke the story?"

"Brenna, weren't you Erin McConnell's best friend?"

"Could you comment on whether or not you think Mike McConnell is guilty?"

"How do you feel about the possibility that he killed your friend?"

"Do you hate Mike McConnell? Do you think he should get the death penalty?"

"Does it make you mad to think that your friend is now being talked about as remains?"

"Brenna, can you tell us how you feel?"

Hearing the commotion, Principal Joe Kennsington looked outside and saw Brenna begin to cry. He rushed from his office and pushed open the side door to the school. He elbowed his way through the chaos and put himself between Brenna and the cameras, sheltering her with his arms as he walked her back inside the building.

When she was safe, he turned and gave the reporters a look that told them they had come as far as they dared. No one challenged his authority.

Then he led Brenna into his office. "It's okay now, Brenna. They won't come inside the building."

"Mr. Kennsington, I'm not talking to any of them about Erin!" she said. "I'm so sad they found her remains. I know she's dead, but sometimes I pretend she's not."

He touched her shoulder and could feel her trembling. "I know." He looked out his window and then turned around. "A lot has changed since you first gave your statement, Brenna. This has turned into a murder investigation, and the media's all over it. They're looking for stories, and you're bound to be on their list. Sit here for a minute. I'm going to call the sheriff."

The principal looked through his Rolodex and dialed the number.

"Hal Barker."

"Sheriff, it's Joe Kennsington. I've got a big mess here at the high school with the media. They had Brenna Morgan surrounded the minute she left the building, and I literally had to go out and rescue her. I don't know what can be done, but I thought you ought to know."

"Yeah, I just left Lisa Sorenson at Morganstern's—almost couldn't clear a path through the media. Her place was covered up. Same down at the newspaper."

"I'm concerned about Brenna," Joe said. "This is probably not going to stop any time soon."

Hal sighed. "I think it's time for Chief Henley to get involved."

"Do you think we have enough police officers?"

"Probably not, but Chief Henley'll need to make that call. I've got deputies that can help out now that the FBI has taken on the bulk of the investigation, but everything inside the city limits is Joe Henley's jurisdiction. I'll give him a call. Is there anything else I should know before I do?"

"Just that I've got one scared young lady sitting in my office. I'm not sure how to get her out of here without her having to go through it all over again."

"I'll call the chief right now. If he doesn't have an officer to escort her home, I'll send one of my deputies. Somebody will be there shortly. Tell Brenna not to worry."

TWENTY-FIVE

Jennifer Wilson sat with her elbows on the kitchen table, her chin resting on her hands. A half-eaten plate of fruit was pushed aside, and Tuesday's edition of the *Denver Post* still rolled up with a rubber band. A calico cat jumped on the table and sniffed the plate.

"You won't like that," she said. "Come here."

The cat rubbed against her arm, leaving a trail of fur on the sleeve of her navy bathrobe. Jennifer laid her head on the cat's back, her golden brown curls draped over its side. She listened to the peaceful sound of its purring. The phone rang, and she instantly grabbed it.

"Hello, Mark?"

"Yeah, sorry it's so late. The big shots were in from Charlotte and I got tied up in meetings. I just got your message. Sounds serious. What's up?"

"Uh, a new development."

"Whaddaya mean?"

"Brace yourself.... I'm pregnant."

"Whoa! Have you told Mom and Dad?"

"I called Mom yesterday when I stayed home from work. She wasn't mad, but she didn't handle it well either. I knew she wouldn't."

"What was your first clue? Mom and Dad have never dealt with having to get married. They act like we're too dumb to do the math. It's weird, but they never talk about it at all—like if they don't talk about it, it didn't happen."

Jennifer sighed. "I know."

"I hope you're not gonna let this wreck your life like they did."

"Is that what you think Mom's getting pregnant with me did—wreck their lives? Thanks a lot, Mark. That adds meaning to my existence."

"Don't get all huffy. I didn't mean it that way."

"Besides, a child can't single-handedly wreck someone's life. They must've had other problems we don't know about."

"Come on, why do you think they've been so uptight all these years? They had to get married, and they never got over it. It's obvious. I mean, they never talk about their wedding even though they have pictures. They got married and you were born six months later.... Hello?"

"I think we shouldn't be so quick to judge, little brother. Like, we have no idea what really happened back then."

"Duh. That's my point, Jen—we have no idea. Why? What's the big deal? It's like this big secret that's always in the way. No one talks about it. Everyone pretends it's not there. Kinda sick, if you ask me."

"Well, for your information, I don't plan to let this ruin my life."

"So you're getting an abortion?"

"I didn't say that. I haven't decided what I'm going to do."

"Does Dennis know? Or does the creep even care?"

"Look, Mark, I know you can't stand him, but you don't know him. You've never even met him."

"Why would I want to?"

Jennifer sighed. "No reason, I guess, other than your sister is, like, carrying his child. What a time to find out I'm pregnant. I broke up with him a couple of weeks ago. Dennis certainly isn't the fatherly type. He's too full of himself. I'm not sure I'm going to tell him. I already know what his reaction will be, so why bother?"

"Jen, you never answered me about Dad's reaction. What did he say?"

"Oh, he doesn't know yet. He's out of town."

"Out of town? *Our* dad? Doing what—moonshining?" Mark laughed.

"He's trying to sort out his feelings since the McConnell case turned into a murder investigation. You know how close he and Mr. McConnell were. Mom says he's depressed. Dad doesn't believe he did it."

"I wonder if Dad's just plain dense. Mike McConnell's pond scum. How much evidence does Dad need? The rest of the world's already figured out he nuked his family. Why's he hanging on to this guy's innocence?"

"Mark, sometimes when you care about someone, you want to believe the best. I don't think that makes Dad dense. You should show a little respect."

"Yeah, well, that's about all I've got—a little respect. So, what are you gonna do about the kid?"

"Mark, I've got to go."

"Hey, I didn't mean to upset you."

"Don't worry about it. I'm, like, overly sensitive. I'm not handling things very well. I'll talk to you soon, okay?"

"Jen, don't cry. I hate it when you cry. I'll call you later, okay?"

"All right...."

Jennifer hung up the phone. The calico cat was back on the table, rubbing against her. She put her arms around it. "It's all right, Spicy."

Would her parents' lives have been happier had she never been born? Was it her fault they were so unhappy? She was afraid to ask them, but the answer might make all the difference in the choice she had to make.

Mary Beth hung up the phone and pulled her legs up on the couch in Rhonda's living room.

"Are you sure Joe isn't mad?" Rhonda asked. "It's nine. You've been here almost all day."

"No, not at all. He took the kids to Monty's for dinner. They had a ball. He's pretty good about understanding when I need to spend time with someone. Where were we?"

"You were saying that God sent Jesus to die for our sins. I don't get it. Couldn't He just forgive us? Why did He have to die?"

"Good question. Romans 6:23 says, 'The wages of sin is death.' Since we're all sinners, we're all under the same sentence. Only someone without sin could die in our place and remove it."

"So He was born to die?"

"Yes. But don't forget He rose from the dead. God had a plan for His Son's life too. John 3:16 tells us God loved us so much that He sent His only begotten Son, so everyone who believes in Him will not perish, but have everlasting life. It's amazing how far He was willing to go to not lose any of us."

"Because He knew us before we were born and already had a plan?"

"Uh-huh," Mary Beth said.

"And it's a free gift? I don't have to do anything?"

"What you have to do is realize the significance of what He did, believe and accept it, and repent of your sins. That means confessing to Him the things you know are wrong. It also means acknowledging that you need a Savior—that you can't remove the penalty. It's His gift to you."

"But what if I sin after I'm a Christian? What if I make mistakes?"

"Then you'll be like the rest of us. Jesus gave us the power to overcome sin, but it's a process of turning our lives over to Him and letting Him change us day by day. Since He already paid the price on Calvary, we don't have to worry about the areas of our lives that aren't perfect. When we become Christians, He adopts us as His children and removes the shame, remember?"

Rhonda nodded.

"Our part isn't to get hung up that we're not perfect, but to allow Him to help us become more like Him. We can't do this in our own strength anyway. When we fail, we ask His forgiveness and begin again. It's a process."

"So if we mess up, we don't lose it?"

"When you adopt a child, Rhonda, you don't unadopt him because he isn't perfect. You might discipline him, even apply some tough love to allow him to learn things the hard way, but he's yours forever. That's the beauty of God's grace. Once we belong to Him, we're His forever."

"So do you think this is the plan God has been trying to tell me He has for my life?"

"Well, I think it's the beginning and the end of the plan, but He also has something unique for you in between. You weren't an accident any more than Jennifer or my son Aaron was. He has a plan for all of us. When we walk with Him day by day, we begin to see how He's using us."

"How do you think God's using you?" Rhonda asked.

"Well, right now He's using me to help you. What are the odds that our paths would cross when they did, after we've both suffered the same pain in our past? Since I've been through it already, maybe something I've learned can help you. One thing I know for sure: God is offering you His gift of grace. He wants you to be adopted into His family and receive everything that inheritance offers. But you have to choose. It's a choice."

"Do you really think He wants someone like me? I'm a mess. My whole life is a mess!"

Mary Beth smiled "Oh, yes. I'm sure He wants someone like you. He's been tapping on your door for a long time, Rhonda. All you have to do is invite Him in."

"Well then, I'm ready to do that. I believe in Him, Mary Beth. I want Him to change me and make my life worth something."

"You'll never be sorry. This is going to be the greatest adventure you could ever imagine. I feel so privileged to be a part of it. Are you ready?"

"More than ready, Mary Beth. I think probably long overdue."

Jed was driving north on a two-lane highway in southern Missouri, headlights coming at him and only darkness behind him. After his early-morning showdown with the driver of the red car, he exited the interstate several times on his phony trek back to Memphis, but never saw the same car behind him twice. He played the game for a while and then decided to start up the secondary highways through northern Arkansas. He kept a careful eye in his rearview mirror, but never saw any sign that he was being followed. If he was, these guys were good.

Another radio station faded out. He fooled with the dial until he heard something distinguishable and decided a gospel station was better than nothing.

"Tonight's reading is from Psalms 9, verses 9 and 10. 'The LORD is a refuge for the oppressed, a stronghold in times of trouble. Those who know your name will trust in you, for you, LORD, have never forsaken those who seek you….'"

Jed wondered what it would be like to trust Him. Then again, what would be the point? *It's not like God cares what happens down here. Look at the pain and the injustice in the world. Where is He in all that?*

The Missouri sky was laid out like a billion diamonds on black velvet. For a moment, God seemed almost real. Cassie's Point was the only place he'd ever seen the stars look this amazing. He thought back to his getting Rhonda pregnant and the mess he'd made of his life. He was flooded with guilt and shame and anger. He didn't need this! He fumbled with the knob, but all he got was static. He shut it off. It occurred to Jed that he handled Rhonda the same way.

Without the radio to keep him awake, he'd never make it all the way to Kansas City. Up ahead he saw lights flashing at the EZ Rest Motel. He pulled in and paid just nineteen dollars for a room. It was nothing to write home about, but it was clean. Jed set the alarm and was in bed and half asleep before he had time to think about tomorrow.

As he drifted off, no one next to him in the bed, he felt a twinge of loneliness.

"Rhonda, after tonight you'll never have to wonder if God has plans for you or where you'll spend eternity." Mary Beth took her hand. "I'll say the prayer and you repeat after me.

"Jesus, I acknowledge I'm a sinner. I need Your forgiveness and grace, and there's nothing I could ever do to earn it. It's a free gift only You can give. I believe You died for my sins and that You're the only One worthy to pardon them. Please forgive me, release me from guilt, and adopt me into Your family. That kind of love is more than I deserve or can even understand.

"I ask You to come into my heart and change me and make everything new. Thank You for what You've already done and for what You will do. In Your holy name, I pray. Amen."

There was a long moment of silence. Rhonda looked up and noticed tears streaming down Mary Beth's face.

"What's wrong?"

"Nothing. Everything's right. Do you realize that in heaven right now, the angels are rejoicing because you repented and accepted God's saving grace?"

"Really? The angels rejoice?"

Mary Beth smiled. "Every time."

Hal heard a car pull up. He opened the door just as Joe Henley started to knock.

"Got your nose pressed against the window, Sheriff?"

Hal chuckled. "Not really, Chief. I heard you pull up. Come in."

Hal led the police chief into his study.

"What was it you wanted to run by me?" Hal asked.

"I spent the evening putting together a special team for media management. Got a few things nailed down. But we both know I don't have enough officers to handle this."

"Yeah, I figured. How about my deputies sharing the load? The FBI has taken over the bulk of the investigation."

"Thanks, Hal. I guess that's what I was hoping to hear. With the story drawing state and national attention, the situation's not likely to let up."

"What are you doing about Brenna?"

"I've assigned one of my officers to escort her to school and back. I think it's going to require having someone with her all the time, though. The media's camped outside her house now."

"Sorry, Chief. For a guy who didn't think this case would involve him, looks like you're in deep. You can count on my support. I'll give you everything I've got."

"Thanks, Hal. I thought you would. Well, let me get out of your hair." He stood up and stifled a yawn. "I've got an early meeting and need to get some sleep."

"If you figure out how, will you please let me in on it?"

"I think it's called age." The chief laughed.

Hal walked him to the front door and shook his hand.

"Talk to you in the morning, Chief. We'll pound out the details." Hal patted him on the shoulder. "Get some rest."

After the chief left, Hal went back in his study, sat down in his recliner, and replayed the entire day and all its implications. Media madness—just what he needed.

He also wrestled with lingering doubts. Sometimes he felt it was impossible for Mike to be a murderer. Other times, especially when he thought about the victims, he was ready to be the first one in line with a noose. But he was looking for a motive, and he kept drawing a blank.

A soft knock broke his concentration.

"I heard voices," Nancy said.

"Sorry if we woke you, honey. Chief Henley stopped by for a

minute. We're trying to get this media situation under control."

She slipped behind his chair and began to gently rub his neck and shoulders.

"Ohhhh, does that feel great," he said.

"You've wrestled with this enough today. Why don't you come to bed?"

Hal pulled her around to the front of his chair and held her hands in his. "I'll be up later. I need some time to think."

She brushed the hair out of his face and kissed his forehead. "See you in the morning, Sheriff. I suspect you'll be asleep in your chair when the sun comes up."

TWENTY-SIX

At Monty's diner, Mark Steele was going over his Wednesday morning checklist when he accidentally dropped a dozen eggs on the storeroom floor.

"Wayne!" he called. "Before you dump the water, would you be sure to mop up this mess? I'm a real klutz. Sorry."

"Hey, no problem, Mark. I prefer scrambled eggs." He grinned. "But actually, it's the smell of coffee brewing and bacon frying that lures me down here. I love working the early shift."

Rosie laughed. "You'll get over it!"

"Don't listen to her," Mark said. "She's getting old and cynical."

Rosie poked Mark in the ribs. "Hey, I don't mind being called cynical, but take it easy on the old part."

"So, Wayne, you like the early shift?" Mark asked.

"Yeah, after two months, these customers kinda grow on you. But Mort Clary sure keeps things stirred up. Is he a cup and saucer short of a full place setting?"

Mark slapped Wayne on the back. "Very perceptive, Mr. Purdy."

"Ol' Mort's a fixture," Rosie said. "He's been having breakfast at Monty's for as long as I can remember. Must not be the only one who thrives on the rabble-rousing. The others keep coming back." She looked at her watch. "Gentlemen, it's about that time."

Mark looked over at the cook behind the counter. "Leo, you ready?"

"Bring 'em on," he said. "Say, did you guys notice all the media around town?"

Wayne nodded. "Weird, isn't it?"

"I heard Brenna Morgan tangled with a bunch of reporters," Rosie said. "Yesterday afternoon at the high school."

"Oh, and I almost forgot to tell you," said Mark, "the big boss called me at home last night. KJNX did some sort of live interview with customers down here last night. Wanted their reaction to the influx of media in our fair community. They wanted to come back this morning, but I discouraged it. I didn't think the world was ready for a live interview with Mort. He'd have people believing the media was part of an alien invasion."

Rosie chuckled. She put on her name tag and looked at her watch. "Ten, nine, eight, seven, six, five, four, three, two…"

The front door to the diner opened. "Mornin' all." Mort hung his hat on the hook. "Did ya hear about them media people hasslin' that Morgan girl?"

"Yeah, Mort. We heard," Mark said.

"Makes ya wonder what all that girl knows she ain't tellin'."

"And why would she hold out on what she knows? She's the one who came forward and told the sheriff she saw Mike McConnell down at the pier, remember?"

"How much ya wanna bet she saw Jed Wilson too?"

"What?" Rosie said. "Where do you come up with this stuff?"

"Ain't ya heard? Jed's left town. Rumor has it he ain't comin' back neither. And just where do ya suppose he's off to?"

Mark looked at Rosie. "Did you know about this?"

She shook her head.

The door to the diner opened again. Reggie Mason hung his sweater on the hook. "Hey, did you hear Jed Wilson's missin'?"

"Oh, he ain't missin', Reg. He knows exactly where he is." Mort laughed his wheezy laugh.

The door swung open another time, and Hattie and George Gentry walked in, Liv Spooner on their heels.

George heard Mort laughing. "What's he wound up about? Sun isn't even up."

"Oh, now he's got some fool notion that Jed Wilson and Mike McConnell were in this thing together," Mark said. "His imagination's working overtime—like his mouth."

Rosie looked at Liv. "You live next door to the Wilsons. It's just a rumor, right?"

Liv looked blank. "Well, I haven't really talked to them for a while. But now that you mention it, Jed's truck hasn't been there for a few days. But this is nonsense. I'm sure there's some other—"

"Well, there ya go," Mort said. "Seein' as how Jed's flown the coop, I rest my case."

"Now if you'll rest your mouth," George said. "I might actually enjoy my breakfast."

Jed squinted until he could make out the numbers on the clock. It was almost nine! *How did that happen?* He was sure he set the alarm for 6:00 A.M. *I should be on the turnpike half way to Topeka by now!* He jumped out of bed, showered, shaved, and was out the door in fifteen minutes.

He threw his bag on the front seat of the pickup and walked over to the motel office to check out. A teenage boy was sitting on a bench just outside the office door.

"Good morning, mister," said the boy, his mouth forming the words slowly and deliberately.

"Hi, how are you?" said Jed, not expecting a reply.

"My dad was going to take me to school. But his doctor said no, and I hafta stay home."

"That's too bad. Hope everything works out for you."

"Me too, mister."

Jed opened the door and went inside, and while he was checking out, he noticed a gray-haired guy in greasy overalls limping across the parking lot from an ancient-looking gas station next door. The man made his way over to the bench, sat down, and started talking to the boy.

When Jed went outside, the gray-haired guy looked up and smiled. "Good mornin'."

"Good morning. Beautiful day, huh?" Jed said. "You guys have a good one."

Jed hurried over to his pickup and hopped in, anxious to get on the road. He put the key in the ignition and turned it. *Click.* He turned it again. *Click.* And again. *Click. Click. Click.* With a sense of dread, he got out and looked under the hood.

The gray-haired guy came over. "What seems to be the trouble?"

"I have no idea," Jed said. "It was working fine last night. It's only a year old and has never given me any trouble."

"Would ya mind if I take a look at it? I know how to fix just about anything. The name's Jessie Lasiter."

"I'm Jed Wilson. And I can use all the help I can get," he said, extending his hand.

Jesse shook his hand and then tinkered under the hood for about five minutes, whistling some indistinguishable tune over and over. Then he asked Jed to start it. When he turned the key, all they heard was the same troublesome clicking sound.

"Well, I know what the problem is, but I hope yer not in a big hurry."

Jed winced. "What's wrong with it?"

Mr. Lasiter leaned over the motor. "Well, ya see this little gizmo here and this little doomajiggey? These here parts ain't communicatin'."

"Can you tell me what I need to fix it?"

"Uh-huh. An alternator."

"An alternator?" Jed could see dollar signs and delays.

"Of course, you could have it tested at one of them places that does nothin' but work on cars, but there ain't none of them 'round here. I've been doin' this long enough to know. I'd stake my life on it. Now, I could fix this for ya. Thing is, I suspect it's still under warranty. No point in payin' for what's covered."

"Where's the nearest dealership?"

"That'd be Kansas City. You can git anythin' ya need up there. Probably could arrange to have yer truck towed to a Chevy dealer and git 'em to look at it. I suspect they'd git to it sometime tomorrow. You could git back on the road by tomorrow night or Friday mornin'."

"No, I've gotta get this fixed as soon as possible. Would you do it?"

"Sure I would, but I'd still have to order what ya need. I could do it 'bout as fast as them guys in Kansas City. But it'd take me till tomorrow to git the parts by FedEx. Either way, it wouldn't be done till late in the day tomorrow."

Jed tapped his fingers on the hood. "So my choice is either sit here and do absolutely nothing until the parts arrive tomorrow, which means I lose two days' driving—or get my truck towed clear the heck up to Kansas City, where it's probably covered under warranty, and then sit up there and lose two days' driving?"

"Sounds just awful when ya say it like that, but that's 'bout it."

"Can you call Kansas City and find out when the parts would be here? I think I'd just as soon have you fix it. Sir, I'm desperate. I...uh...I'm supposed to be in...Seattle...for a wedding...on Saturday night. I'm already pushing it."

Mr. Lasiter's eyebrows went up. "Seattle, eh? Let me go make that call. I'll be back in a couple of minutes. Stay right here."

About twenty minutes later he returned. "I got good news, and I got bad news. Which do ya want first?"

"The bad news, I guess," Jed said.

"Seems the highway between here and Kansas City is bein' rerouted. There was some kind of hazardous spill they're tryin' to git cleaned up. Authorities are sayin' the highway won't open up straightaway for at least twenty-four hours. That means a lot of hassle for FedEx, and they can't guarantee the parts will git here tomorrow. Of course, they might—just no guarantees."

"That's just great. So what's the good news? Probably won't make any difference after this dandy development."

Jesse Lasiter shot him a knowing look. "Well now, ya never know. It just might...."

On Wednesday morning, Rhonda sank into her overstuffed chair, feeling a joy she had never known. She basked in the morning sun, which flooded the living room the way grace flooded her soul. She felt completely together.

She thought this must be the peace that passes understanding. There was no other reason why she should feel this way. Her husband was off to who-knows-where with the FBI in pursuit. Her single daughter was pregnant. Her own life was a mess. Yet she was feeling happier than she'd ever felt.

Thank You, Lord, for caring about me. Whatever plans You have for me, I'm ready.

Rhonda's peace and calm was interrupted by the phone. She hoped it was Jed.

"Hello," she said.

"Rhonda, it's Mary Beth." There was a smile in her voice. "How are you this morning?"

"I'm wonderful! Why didn't you tell me it would feel this good?"

"You wouldn't have understood. There's absolutely no feeling that compares to being at peace with God. You have to experience it to know."

"And to think that all those years I thought Christians were phony baloney because they talked about this peace. Now I'm one of you, and I love the way I feel." Rhonda thought for a moment. "Mary Beth, do you think I should be baptized?"

"Yes. That's the symbolic part for what you did. We can talk to Pastor Thomas about it. You know, Rhonda, we should drive over to Cross Country Bookstore in Ellison and get you a Bible. I have a feeling that once you get into it, you won't be able to put it down."

"I'd love that. When?"

"We need to allow at least a half day. We can have lunch and really enjoy the time together. I'm as excited about this as you are!"

"I can be ready any time you're available," Rhonda said.

"Well, it's ten now. Do you want to do it today?"

"Really? That'd be wonderful. I feel so good today. Something's different. I can't explain it."

"You don't have to, Rhonda. I know the feeling."

"Mr. Lasiter, if there's good news, I'd like to hear it," Jed said. "I could use a little encouragement about now."

"Well ya see, I got a problem ya might be able to help me with. Casey here is supposed to be in school in Portland, Oregon, on Monday. I was goin' to drive him up there myself. It's a special school that helps young people like him learn to be self-sufficient. He's been beggin' me to git him enrolled, and he finally got accepted. Now my doctor tells me I can't take him. Says I'd be askin' fer it, drivin' with this bad leg. He says I'd be puttin' myself and my boy at risk. So here's the deal: What if I let ya borrow my Ford Explorer and you take Casey for me? He's got kinfolk up there who'll be lookin' after him. All I need ya to do is meet up with 'em. It's right on the way to Seattle—that is where you said yer goin', ain't it?"

Jed stood there flabbergasted.

"Now, if yer worried 'bout my car, don't be. It's only got thirty thousand miles on it—runs like a top. I keep it in perfect runnin' condition all the time. Ya shouldn't have a lick of trouble. Casey's a good boy and won't be no trouble neither. He don't need a whole lot of lookin' after, but he's got his heart set on gittin' up there. Whaddaya say?"

Jed put his hands in his pockets and glanced over at the boy. "I don't know...."

"Well, mister, it's up to you. I kinda hoped we could help each other out. I can fix yer truck either way. But I can't say fer sure if it'll be ready to roll before late Friday at the very earliest."

Jed sighed. "Well, Mr. Lasiter, I had planned to stay in Seattle for as long as two weeks. I don't know how you'd feel about your SUV being gone that long."

"Don't worry none 'bout the time, Jed. Just give me a rough idea when ya think you'll be comin' back through. I'll have yer pickup runnin' tip-top, and since I won't be needin' to drive, I'll just park it in my garage."

Jed's eyes moved from the Explorer to the boy to the old guy. "Mr. Lasiter, are you sure? I appreciate the offer and I'd take good care of your son and your car, but you hardly know me. Are you sure you want me to do this?"

Jesse Lasiter's faded blue eyes had a sparkle. "Well, Jed, I'm a believin' man. I prayed the Lord would help me find a way to git my boy up to Portland. What's the odds of a guy comin' along, just in the nick of time, that needs what I got—and I need what he's got? I think our paths was supposed to cross. I trust ya. Whaddaya think, Casey?"

The boy nodded. "Please, Mr. Jed, will you take me to school? Please?"

TWENTY-SEVEN

Mike McConnell took the last bite of a candy bar and threw the wrapper in the trash with the other one. He'd already read Wednesday's edition of USA Today and downed a pot of coffee. He was tired of playing solitaire.

He paced back and forth in the room. Outside, the sun was hiding and the chill was biting. He flipped on the TV and flopped on the couch. Same old, same old. He hated game shows and soap operas. He'd already listened to the news half a dozen times. He turned it off.

He paced some more. He was freezing! Nothing about Washington in November connected him to what he remembered as a boy. He felt isolated and lonely and knew if he were going to stay in Harper's Grove, he had to find something to do—some reason to make it through the day. He needed a contract labor job that paid cash at the end of a day. He knew those jobs were out there. He would nose around.

His red hair was longer now and dyed dark brown like his eyebrows and a newly grown mustache. And with all the junk food he put away, the roll around his middle hung over his belt. He laughed. How could anyone recognize him?

He walked into the kitchen and pulled out a clothing store coupon he'd found in his grocery bag. He folded the coupon and took three hundreds from his stash. He picked up his room key and put on his puny denim jacket. The outlet store was about a quarter of a mile from the main highway. He stepped outside and groaned.

"Go ahead and howl," he said to the biting wind as he started toward the highway. "But you've beat up on me for the last time."

Mike came out of the outlet store and stopped to put on a green Gore-Tex parka. He pulled a green stocking cap down over his ears and the hood of the parka up over it and tied the drawstring. He slipped on a pair of warm gloves. "Okay, put up your dukes, you big bully! I'm fighting back." He threw a couple of imaginary punches at the cold wind and laughed.

Mike trudged back to his log apartment carrying two large bags. The exercise felt good after being cooped up, and he felt almost toasty. The coupon got him an extra 20 percent off an already half-off sale, and he bought everything he needed.

When he walked in the door, he dumped the contents of the bags on the bed—jeans, flannel shirts, long johns, wool socks, underwear, boots. He sat down and put on a pair of wool socks and the hiking boots. He decided to nose around the small downtown area of Harper's Grove.

As he entered the city limits, he spotted a church steeple in the distance beyond some tall evergreen trees. He continued walking down a narrow street lined with huge old trees and quaint two-story houses until he stood facing the church. Calvary Community Church.

The structure was made from natural stone and topped with a tall steeple badly in need of stain. The same was true for the wood trim and the doors. *What a neat old place.* The tall windows along both sides of the church were made from squares of opaque colored glass, but the glass on either side of the entrance was clear.

Mike cupped his hands around his eyes and looked inside but didn't see anyone. He stepped back and noticed his reflection in the glass. The man staring back at him was a stranger. He was completely absorbed in the moment when someone tapped him on the shoulder, causing him to jump so hard that he nearly threw his back out.

"May I help you?"

Mike stood there, his heart pounding. "Buddy, you scared me to death. I didn't hear you coming. Just give me a second...."

"I'm so sorry. I didn't mean to sneak up on you. I'm Pastor Don Swisher. I saw you standing here and thought maybe you were looking for me. Is there something I can do for you? I don't think we've met, have we?"

"Uh, no—on both counts. I mean, no, we haven't met. And, no, I don't think there's anything you can do for me. I'm just killing some time, waiting to take on, uh...a new maintenance position in Doonesbury. I'm staying down at the Evergreen Cottages for a few weeks."

"I see. What's your name?"

"Mark McNeil," said Mike, offering a hearty handshake.

The pastor smiled. "Pleased to make your acquaintance."

"Thanks. Same here. It's nice to see a friendly face. I've been recently, uh...divorced and decided to come back to this part of the country. I have some happy memories of this area from when I was a kid. My folks brought me here one summer, all the way from New York City."

Pastor Swisher raised an eyebrow. "New York? You don't have the accent. I never would've guessed."

"Well, no. You see, we moved away from there when I was still a kid. I've lived all over the place, so I guess I sound kind of generic.... Pastor, what kind of a church is this? What denomination?"

"No denomination, just solid Christian. We're a bunch of good old Bible-believin' folks, that's all. Everyone's welcome. Maybe you'd like to visit sometime. People here are real friendly."

"Yeah. Sure."

"Have you seen the town yet?"

"Actually, I was just beginning to do that when you—"

"When I scared the liver out of you?" said Pastor Swisher.

Both men laughed and Mike was thinking how good it felt.

"Seriously, I was about to look around," Mike said. "I'm trying to find something to do with my time—you know, contract labor or something. I'm bored waiting on my maintenance position, and I'd really like to stay busy. Don't have time to apply and process paperwork and all that, but I'd sure like something to fill the time. The guy I'm replacing in Doonesbury isn't retiring until the end of the month."

"Did you say you were in maintenance? As in hammers and nails?"

"As in all sorts of things. I'm good with my hands."

"You know, Mark, this place needs some work. I'm sure you can see that. I keep putting it off, thinking I'll tend to it myself, but I never do. I get busy, and it doesn't get done. I could use a hand around here for a few weeks. I couldn't pay much, maybe $6.50 an hour, but—"

"Sounds great to me. When would you like me to start? Did I mention I'm very available, like bored out of my wits?" He laughed.

Mike's laughter was contagious and he could tell Pastor Swisher liked him.

"Why don't you come back at two. That'll give me time to make a list of things that need to be done. I can already think of a dozen things that need fixing. Do you scrape and paint and all that?"

"Absolutely."

Pastor Swisher looked toward the sky and raised his hands, a broad grin taking over his face. "Thank You, Lord! You really do know how useless I am with tools in my hand. Thank You for having mercy on the mechanically challenged! Hal-le-lu-jah!"

Mike couldn't tell which man laughed louder.

When Pastor Swisher hired Mark McNeil at the front door of Calvary Community Church, a rugged man in hiking boots and a down jacket was invisibly present. He was affected by neither the cold nor the lies and never let Mike McConnell out of his sight for a moment.

TWENTY-EIGHT

Special Agent Jordan Ellis paced the floor. Jed Wilson couldn't just drop off the planet! He picked up his cell phone and dialed.

"Nick Butler."

"Remember me—the guy who's running this show? On a good day, I've got a short fuse. So why am I wearing a hole in the carpet waiting on you to find Jed Wilson?"

"Jordan, you've got to give me more tim—"

"How much time do you need, Nick? It took your guys all of two minutes to lose him. You'd think that after two whole days, they could find him. How many FBI agents does it take to find one good ol' boy driving a red Chevy truck? If this is too hard for you, maybe we should call in the Girl Scouts!"

"Settle down, Jordan. Give your blood pressure a rest. I know there's no excuse for losing him, but no one has spotted him in nearly thirty-six hours, and it's not like we haven't been looking. Wilson must have crawled up some back-alley highway." Agent Butler sighed. "Realistically, he either found McConnell in Arkansas or beat the trap. This cat and mouse game is getting us nowhere."

"I don't want to hear that, Nick. He's our only lead. You lost him, you find him! I don't care how you do it—just do it!"

"Jordan, it's a lot of manpower just to find a guy who *might* know something about—"

"About what, Nick? About a guy who murdered all four members of his family? Gee, I wouldn't want the boys to strain themselves."

"It's like finding a needle in a haystack."

"Then get out the big magnets, Nick. We had Wilson. Get him back."

Mike opened the doors of Calvary Community Church at exactly two o'clock. Pastor Swisher stood in the hallway with another man.

"Well, here's our answer from heaven now," Pastor Swisher said. "Carlos, meet Mark McNeil."

"Hi, Mark. I'm Carlos Martinez. I'm responsible for cleaning the church."

"Nice to meet you," Mike said. "So, I'm an answer from heaven, eh?"

Carlos grinned. "Pastor Don says you know how to fix all sorts of things. Have we got some stuff for you to do!"

"I'm ready. Point the way. I've been sitting around just storing up all this energy. It's time to boogey." He slid his feet across the floor in a dance step that made all three of them laugh.

Pastor Don seemed pleased. "I'm going to leave the two of you to do your thing. Carlos, if you'd be kind enough to show Mark around and introduce him to...*the tools.*" As he playfully emphasized the word, his eyebrows raised. "I'm off to make my hospital rounds in Doonesbury. Gentlemen, carry on."

"Okay, tool man," Carlos said. "Let's see what we can find for you to do."

Carlos showed Mike around the church, and then took him into the basement to dig through the tool closet and workbench.

"Man, you've got every conceivable tool I'd ever need to repair or paint anything," Mike said. "Half this stuff's hardly been used."

"Well, like I told you, I clean the church on Wednesday and Friday afternoons. I'm not much of a handyman, and Pastor Don is downright dangerous with a hammer." Carlos laughed. "He says you're just passing through on your way to a good maintenance job in Doonesbury."

"That's right. Just passing through. What about you? Do you have a wife and family here in Harper's Grove?"

"Uh, not any more…my family was killed in a car accident last year." He turned his back to Mike and led the way up the stairs.

"Hey, man, I'm sorry. You must be having a hard time with the person who killed them."

Carlos stopped. He turned around and looked down at Mike. "Well, I'm still working on it. You see, the accident was my fault."

By Wednesday night, Jed was behind the wheel of Jesse Lasiter's Ford Explorer, rolling down I-70 toward Denver. Because of the hazardous spill, he lost time winding up secondary highways to the interstate. He reminded himself that he could be sitting in Missouri, waiting another two days for his truck to be fixed. At the moment, Casey was sleeping peacefully in the backseat.

He wondered what kind of faith made Jesse Lasiter naive enough to trust a stranger with his son's well-being. How could he know Jed was reliable? Yet the old guy seemed perfectly okay with the whole thing. Jed didn't understand the need for faith. Since God did whatever He wanted to do, faith was for the gullible.

With the cruise control set, the Explorer moved across western Kansas like it had a mind of its own. Jed picked up his cell phone and pushed the button to dial home.

"Hello."

"Rhonda, it's me."

"Jed! I've been so worried! Where are you?"

"You know I can't say. There's a pretty good chance the phone's tapped."

"Oh, come on, Jed. You've been watching too many movies."

"I don't think so. I can't say much, but everything's fine. I didn't want you to worry."

"Well, I have been." She sounded more tender than usual. "So, you can't tell me whether or not you're any closer to finding Mike?"

"Let's just say, I'm where I need to be. I don't think we should discuss this on the phone. Anything going on there?"

"You could say that."

"Rhonda, what's going on? Your voice sounds, well, happy."

"I am. I have so much to tell you, but I'll just have to wait until you're home. Something really neat's been happening with my faith."

"Hmm…seems to be a lot of that going around."

"What do you mean?"

"Oh, nothing. Listen, I need to go. I'm not sure how the FBI works. Maybe they tapped our phone, maybe they didn't. I can't take a chance. I can tell you this, I'm not breaking any laws, so don't worry about me. And, Rhonda…uh, it's all right with me if you pray some more. Can't hurt anything."

"Oh, I'm doing a lot of praying. Any idea when you'll get to wherever it is you're going?"

"Let me just say I'm not where I was, I'm right where I need to be, and for all anyone knows, I might already be where I was going."

There was a long pause. "Jed, do we have to play this game the whole time you're gone?"

"Yeah, I'm afraid so. I can't afford to take a chance. I mostly called so you wouldn't worry. I guess I'll go now. Uh, I'll be in touch when I can…. Okay, then, guess I'll talk to yo—"

"Jed, wait! Don't hang up! I…uh…"

"You what?"

"Well, I…"

"Rhonda, what?"

"I love you." *Click.*

Jed swallowed hard and blinked several times to clear his eyes. He stared at the interstate in front of him, trying to remember how long it had been since he'd heard those words. Lost in thought, he was only conscious of the rhythmic, almost hypnotic broken white lines moving under his high beams.

"Hey, Mister Jed, I gotta go to the bathroom!"

Jed let out a yelp he was sure they could hear back on the Kansas Turnpike. He felt his heart pounding over the thump, thump, thump of the highway noise. When finally he collected himself, his eyes met an innocent, smiling face in the rearview mirror.

"Casey," he said slowly, "don't ever surprise me like that again."

Rhonda was glad she finally said it. Until tonight, she couldn't remember the last time she told Jed she loved him. As she lay alone in their bed, she longed to be in Jed's arms—not out of a sense of entitlement as before, but with a renewed sense of commitment.

Rhonda turned on the lamp and got up. She walked over to the dresser and picked up the framed picture of Jed. She touched the glass with her finger and outlined his face. Her husband was still a handsome man, even though his thick, dark hair had nearly as much salt as pepper. She loved his irresistible, boyish grin, though she seldom saw him smile any more. Rhonda was drawn to his eyes—deep brown with long, thick lashes. She was helpless to find a remedy for the unhappiness she saw in them.

She put the picture down and walked over to the full-length mirror on the back of the bedroom door and took a long, hard look. Her blond hair was limp and faded. She carried fifteen pounds more than she needed. Her nightclothes, like everything else she wore, were nondescript and unflattering. If she didn't care about herself, how could she expect Jed to care?

But she also noticed the worry lines between her eyes seemed to have relaxed, and her countenance was more attractive. Instead of sullen and droopy, her mouth was turned slightly upward, more like a tentative smile. There was a sparkle in her eyes. Her grandfather used to say her eyes looked like polished jade, and tonight they really did. She was pleased to see the joy she felt reflected on the outside.

But what would Jed see when he looked at her? She should get her hair highlighted and shaped, cut down on the calories, and start jogging again. By the time he got home...well, maybe it was too much to hope that he would want her too. But regardless, she'd feel better about herself.

She knelt down beside her bed and prayed for Jed's safety. More than anything, she wanted him to come home so she could give him a part of her that had been missing all these years—self respect. By allowing God to love her, Rhonda was beginning to love herself. And as that happened, loving Jed again was not difficult.

Mike McConnell heated up a TV dinner and downed an ice-cold beer in celebration of his first day on the job. He dealt a game of solitaire and began to play out the hand. For the first time in four and a half weeks, he had enjoyed the day. Pastor Don was pleased that he replaced and painted the woodwork along the hallways and also the handrail along the basement stairs. The sight of all the progress had the pastor's wheels turning, and it didn't seem to Mike like there would be any shortage of work.

But even as he was thinking about the day's ray of hope, he felt the night's depression put its hands around his throat. He broke out in a cold sweat and felt like he couldn't breathe. It was about to start again. His mind would race out of control and drag him through a string of memories that served no purpose other than to point a finger....

"Mike, I'm over here!" Rose giggled as she took off running across the old Holman place.

"How'd you climb that fence?" he shouted.

"Bet I can get to the creek before you do."

Her shiny, dark hair bounced as she ran as fast as her bare feet could carry her. When he caught up with her, he took her in his arms and kissed her until she squealed.

"Be good," she said. She broke loose and jumped in the creek, up to her knees in the cool water.

"Let's go skinny dipping," he said.

Rose blushed. Her smile was coy. "You know I won't."

"Why not? Nobody out here but us."

"You're incorrigible!" She splashed water on him and laughed.

"Then marry me."

"What?"

"Let's get married."

She stared at him blankly. "You're serious!" She threw her arms around him.

"Is that a yes?"

"Yes!" she said. "Yes!"

The first time he woke up next to her, Rose looked like a fine doll with perfect features. When her eyes finally opened, they were as blue as sapphires against the white sheets.

"Good morning, Mrs. McConnell."

She smiled and nuzzled against him.

He felt the band of gold around his finger and smiled. He'd not been dreaming. Last night was real, and she was his forever....

"Oh, Mike, she's beautiful!" Rose said. "Look at all that dark hair. I'll be able to put a bow in it."

He carefully reached down and lifted his baby daughter into his arms. "What if I break her? She's so delicate."

"You're doing fine. Isn't she about the cutest baby in the world? The name Erin is perfect. It just fits her."

"Erin," he said. "She's a doll, all right. Looks like her mother." He handed the baby to Rose and then kissed them both. "We're going to be so happy...."

"What is it, Erin?" He put the remote on mute.

"I'm going to the freshman dance on Friday night. Could you, like, teach me how to slow dance? Mom said you were pretty good in your day."

He sighed. "Not now."

"But soon? Please, Dad? It's my first dance and I'm feeling, like, really clumsy."

"Yeah, sure, sometime soon." He hit the remote and turned the sound back on the TV. She was always interrupting him, just like her mother....

"Mike, would you help me give the twins their bath?" Rose said. "They're really wound up and I'm worn down. I've been chasing them all day."

"That's what mothers are supposed to do," he said. "I've worked all day too. The kids are your responsibility."

"When's the last time you chased a couple of toddlers for an entire day? My job doesn't stop at five, you know."

He turned up the TV and heard the bathroom door slam. That's right, Rose, lay another guilt trip. Like I don't have enough to worry about....

"Daddy, come play with us," shouted Todd, splashing lake water on the back deck.

"You promised," Tim said.

His twin sons looked like matching balls of copper wire hanging over an inner tube. The sound of their pleading was irritating.

"I'll play later." He popped open another beer and turned the page of his sports magazine....

Mike began to weep. Memories and regrets raced through his mind without permission. So many chances—and he blew it. After weeks of this nightly ritual, he knew how it would end. Nothing he did could stop what always came next.... He saw a flash of light at his back and heard the deafening sound of the explosion that ripped apart everything he ever loved....

The burden of guilt clawed at his heart. Being forced to relive it night after night, he wondered if he had already entered into hell.

"Mr. Jed, where are we now?"

"We're in Colorado, Casey. That's the state next to Kansas."

"It's far from my house," he said, matter-of-factly.

"Yes, but soon you'll be in your new home."

"In Port-land?"

"Uh-huh. That's in Oregon."

Though Casey Lasiter was seventeen, to Jed he seemed like an overgrown kid. He stood several inches shorter than Jed, but Casey was husky and probably outweighed him by forty pounds. The young man's hair was strawberry blond and straight as a pencil. His eyes were small and expressive. There was a band of freckles across his nose, which fit with his innocent demeanor. When he spoke, his mouth formed the words carefully and deliberately. Jed thought he was a sweet kid and enjoyable company.

"Mr. Jed, I miss my dad."

"I'm sure you do. But aren't you excited you get to go to school in Oregon?"

"Yes, and I'm going to haff my own desk, and I will get to ride the bus.... Mr. Jed, I'm sleepy. Could I get in the backseat?"

Jed spotted a billboard for a nice motor inn up ahead.

"If you can wait five more minutes, I'll take the next exit and get us a room. How's that sound?"

"I can wait, Mr. Jed," he said, stretching the words into a big yawn.

Jed exited as soon as he saw the turnoff. He pulled under the awning at the motel office, a little nervous about getting Casey settled for the night. He walked inside and stood where he could keep an eye on the car. He signed for a room with two double beds, got the key, and within five minutes they were both under the covers.

Jed yielded every tired muscle to the bed beneath him and began to drift off. He was somewhere between worlds when a voice invaded the quiet.

"Mr. Jed, I hafta say my prayers."

Jed's eyes opened. "Uh...go ahead, Casey. It's okay. Say them."

"No, my dad says 'em with me."

"Your dad isn't here, Casey. I'm sure he won't mind if you say them without him." Jed closed his eyes and drifted off again.

"But you're here, Mr. Jed. Would you say 'em with me?"

Jed closed his eyes tightly and hoped Casey would fall asleep.

"Mr. Jed?...Mr. Jed?...Mr. Jeeeeeed?"

Suddenly, a deep, childlike voice began singing "Jesus Loves Me."

Jed's eyes flew open. He was embarrassed, but by the time Casey started singing the second stanza, he just listened. There was something pure and uninhibited about this kid.

"Mr. Jed, did you hear me sing?"

"Yes, Casey, you sounded very nice."

"Did you know that, Mr. Jed?"

"Did I know what?"

"Jesus loves you?"

"Yes, Casey. I know Jesus loves me. Good night."

The room was quiet again.

"Then why won't ya talk to Him?"

"Because I'm asleep."

Casey giggled. "No, you're not."

"Yes, I am. My eyes are closed. That means I'm asleep."

"Well, if you die before you wake, did you pray the Lord your soul to take?"

Jed sighed. "I'll tell you what, Casey. How about if you ask Him for me tonight? Let's just get some sleep, all right?"

Casey drifted off to sleep in a matter of minutes. Jed lay there with the covers up to his chin, staring at the ceiling.

TWENTY-NINE

L isa, come in," said Father Donaghan, rising from the chair at his desk. "I thought we could meet here in my study. No one will bother us here on a Thursday morning. Please, have a seat.... Here, let me help you with that." He held her cane while she lowered herself into a chair and sat down facing his desk.

"Thank you," she said. "No matter how many times I do this, I'm not as coordinated as I'd like to be."

"Now, what was it you wanted to discuss with me?"

"Please hear me out before you comment. I want to break tradition, and I suspect there are some who'll think I'm wrong, maybe even you."

Father Donaghan lifted his eyebrows. "How's that, Lisa?"

"I've had four white marble crosses made to mark a family grave site for Rose and the kids. After thinking about the explosion and the miles between where the remains were found...well, I want the four of them togeth—" Lisa looked down, her lower lip quivering.

"Take your time, dear," Father Donaghan said.

"I want my sister and her kids together. The owner of Oak Hills was kind enough to donate the grave site. He said it was the least he could do for the family. There was enough insurance money on Rose to cover everything else."

"And so you want me to conduct the burial?"

"Actually, no. Let me explain. All the speculation about how

Rose and the kids might have died has become dinner-table conversation. People all over the country, people who never even knew them, are talking about it. It's been awful having their deaths exploited by the media. And the depressing ordeal of waiting for their remains to be…pieced together…well, it's caused the deepest sorrow I've ever—"

Father Donaghan handed her a Kleenex and patted her hand.

"Anyway," she said, "the memorial Mass was a public farewell that brought closure for this community. Can you understand that I don't want to share them anymore? I don't want to say good-bye with cameras flashing and people staring, and the media giving a blow-by-blow account of my grief. I want a private good-bye. Now, I'm not suggesting you don't say prayers at the grave site. I know Rose would like that. But I don't need to be there when you do. I know this may sound unreasonable, but I don't want to share one minute of this with anyone. Can you accept that?"

Father Donaghan rubbed his chin. "Certainly. But will this really be closure for you, Lisa? Can you let go of this by yourself? Wouldn't some spiritual support help to shoulder the burden?"

"With all due respect, Father, spiritual support has done nothing to ease the grief or the anger. I have to live with this the rest of my life. You or anyone else saying some hocus-pocus prayers over their remains isn't going to wipe away the pain like some religious magic wand."

"Ouch."

Her face turned red. "Oh, Father…that sounded just awful. I really didn't mean it the way—"

"Lisa, it's okay. You're still angry. It's going to take a while. I'd just like to be able to help you find closure."

"Well, answer me this: How do I find closure as long as the scumbag who murdered my sister and those beautiful kids is still free? Can you tell me that?"

"Lisa, hating Mike won't bring them back, but it will destroy you."

"Spare me, Father. I've heard all the clichés. No one else is walking in my shoes, and no one knows how I feel. If it takes the rest of my life, I'm going to see Mike McConnell pay for what he did!"

There was a lengthy pause.

"But, Lisa, rushing to judgment isn't justice."

"Oh, please! Don't talk to me about justice. One lousy life in exchange for four wonderful ones? Bad trade, don't you think? Even the death penalty is too good for that louse!"

Father Donaghan leaned forward, his hands folded on the desk. "My dear Lisa, if you don't let this go, I'm afraid you'll be the sixth victim."

"Sixth? You mean fifth."

He shook his head.

"You're insinuating Mike was a victim? I can't believe this!"

"Lisa, no one knows what happened. Until that comes out, everything else is speculation. I think I understand a little about how you must feel, but all this—"

"Stop, I can't listen anymore. First of all, you don't understand how I feel. I don't mean to be rude, but you honestly don't. And second, I don't have any mercy. If you want to feel merciful toward McConnell, that's up to you—just don't talk to me about it!"

Father Donaghan stood up. He walked around his desk and sat in the chair next to her. "Lisa, I apologize for upsetting you. I certainly didn't mean to. It's just that my perspective is different from yours."

"How can you possibly have a different perspective? Look at the facts! Mike killed all four of them, and I'm not going to rest until he pays for it."

"Lisa, most people never rest from hatred, even after someone pays for it. Seeing Mike pay for this won't change your heart."

Lisa hung her head in disgust. "Father, just let me get back to my original question, and then I've got to be going. Hal said he would come back for me in thirty minutes. What I want to know is—can you live with my saying a private good-bye without the religious ceremony? I don't object if you want to conduct a quiet Catholic burial service; I don't want to get into a major faux pas with the church. But I need to do my part privately. Can we agree on this?"

Father Donaghan looked at Lisa, but he saw Rose. His heart ached. "Yes, I can put together something simple that Rose would have liked. In a way, it'll help me say my own good-bye. The family grew up in this church, you know. I baptized Erin and the boys. When would you like me to do this?"

"I'd like to do mine sometime tomorrow. But if you don't mind, Father, maybe you could do something later today? I understand the site is ready. The people at Oak Hills can tell you how to find the grave site. I haven't seen it yet."

"Of course. I'll go by there this afternoon." He paused. "Lisa, I hope there're no hard feelings over our differing perspectives. One thing on which we agree is we both cared very much about Rose, Erin, Tim, and Todd."

Lisa's eyes filled with tears. "No hard feelings. I just need time. Thank you for your kindness."

Lisa Sorensen picked up her cane and struggled to her feet. Father Donaghan escorted her to the door just as Hal Barker was coming across the courtyard.

"Show me, Mr. Jed, show me," said Casey, holding up the map.

"We're on our way to Utah. That's the state right here next to Colorado." Jed pointed to the location on the map. "Now look straight ahead out the window. That's west. That's how we're going."

Casey put his finger on the map and moved it along the highway, pretending to be the car. "Mr. Jed, I miss my dad."

"Would you like to call him?"

"On the little phone?" Casey eyed Jed's cell phone.

"If you'll hand it to me, I'll show you how it works."

Casey handed the phone to Jed, his eyes alive with curiosity.

"Okay, let's see," said Jed. "You push this button to turn it on. I programmed the phone with your dad's number, so let's find that. Okay, just push this button, Casey, and wait for him to pick up. That's all there is to it."

Jed could tell Casey was having a difficult time pushing the tiny button with his big finger, but after a few tries, he giggled.

"It's ringing, Mr. Jed! It's ringing! Dad! Hi, Dad! Hi! I am Casey. Me and Mr. Jed are in, um…Mr. Jed, where did you say?" he whispered.

"Wy-o-ming."

"We are in Wy-o-ming. We're going west. I have my finger on the map 'cause Mr. Jed said I could."

"Well, Son, it's great to hear yer voice. I miss ya so much. Kinda quiet 'round here. I'm workin' on Jed's truck at the moment. Have ya been good? How're ya gittin' along with the driver?"

"Me and Mr. Jed slept in a big room and had pancakes. I saw a deer on the way to… Where did I see it?" he whispered to Jed.

"Den-ver."

"Den-ver. It had a white tail and ran real fast. I got Cracker Jacks 'cause I was being so good too. I like Mr. Jed."

Jesse Lasiter laughed. "That's just great. May I speak with him, Son?"

Casey handed the phone to Jed without comment.

"Hello? Jesse?"

"Well, hi there, Jed. Casey sounds mighty excited. I can always tell when that boy's enjoyin' himself. I assume he's tellin' me the whole story."

"Oh yeah. We're doing fine. Don't you worry. Casey's good company. I'm glad we decided to do this. It's working out great."

"FedEx got the parts to me in spite of the spill," Jesse said. "So I've 'bout got yer truck fixed. Ain't that a lick after all the worryin'? But just thinka how far you'd have to go if ya were still here." He chuckled. "See what a great head start ya got?"

"Truthfully, Jesse, I'm really glad we did it this way. Like I said, Casey's good company and I really do need to be in…uh…Seattle by Saturday night, you know."

"Well, ya got a long way to go, but I've been prayin', so I know yer in good hands."

Jed looked over at Casey who was itching to get back on the phone. "Uh—thanks. So far, so good. I think Casey would like to talk to you again."

Jesse laughed. "All right. I'll just say good-bye to him for a minute. Thanks fer the call, Jed. I really miss my boy. It's gonna be real hard havin' him on his own, but I know he needs to git independent. I'm not gittin' any younger, and he needs to learn… tak…care…himsel… Whoa, this here connection's cuttin' out. I'll just say good-bye to Casey. Thanks again for takin' care of my boy."

"You're welcome, Jesse. Thanks for letting me borrow your Explorer. We'll stay in touch. Okay, here's Casey."

Jed handed the phone back to Jesse's son and listened to the brief but loving exchange. He wondered what it would be like to be so trusting, without a care in the world.

Father Donaghan got out of his car. He put his hands on his lower back and stretched. From a high vantage point, he looked out across Oak Hills Cemetery. Nothing stirred except leaves being chased by the November wind. The priest had prayed over many grave sites during his thirty-eight years at Saint Anthony's, and little had changed except the size of the trees and the number of headstones.

The setting was picturesque and peaceful. Spread across twelve acres of rolling hills, the grounds were dotted with a blend of towering oak trees, hickories, gum trees, yellow poplars, and pines.

At the bottom of the hill he spotted the family burial place of Reginald T. Baxter, his wife Agnes Holmes Baxter, and several of their children and grandchildren. It was a well-known landmark, maintained by the proud people of Baxter.

Father Donaghan squinted. Through the trees he caught an occasional glimpse of Heron Lake, which shimmered below in defiance of the gray clouds. He began to walk. Lofty trees, now nearly bare, had laid down a crunchy carpet of color he trudged over on his way to the McConnell burial site. The whistling sound of wind in the pines and the inevitable scent that followed brought a reminder of the other times he had been here. He dreaded another good-bye.

As he approached the far side of the hill, he spotted the four white crosses just beyond a giant hickory tree. He walked over and stood silently for a long while, mourning the human defilement, which the fresh earth had mercifully hidden.

Father Donaghan remembered holding tiny Erin as Mike and Rose presented their firstborn for baptism. He recalled giving her First Communion. She had the face of an angel. He smiled as he thought about the two copper-topped imps who poured cherry Kool-Aid in the holy water font and then put turtles in the ladies' toilet before giggling their way right into his heart. How could it have come to this?

He wondered if there could ever be closure as long as the facts remained untold. His burden was great, knowing that he was perhaps the only person who could offer insight, yet he was bound by a vow of silence.

And so, as he grieved for the dead, Father Donaghan also grieved for two of the living, who seemed as good as dead. Though Mike McConnell's fate was in God's hands, Lisa Sorensen was determined to take it into hers. Meaningful life had now ceased for both.

On Thursday night, Jed and Casey sat in a family café, just off the interstate, a couple of hours from Ogden. Their heads were buried in the menu. "Casey, I'm going to have chicken-fried steak and mashed potatoes. How does that sound to you?"

"I like mashed po-ta-toes. I like drum...drumsticks."

"Then you want number three," said Jed, pointing to the menu. "I think we should have pie for dessert. We've both worked hard today. You did a great job helping me follow the map."

A big smile stretched across Casey's face. "I want ba-nan-a cream pie!"

"Then you shall have it, my man. Let's get dinner ordered, and when we're finished, we'll feast on dessert."

After Jed placed their order, Casey looked around the restaurant, taking everything in. Jed made some notations on the back of a napkin so he could keep track of expenses. Neither of them said anything for a few minutes.

All at once, Casey blurted out a question. "Mr. Jed, are you scared of Jesus?"

The people at the next table turned and stared.

Jed felt his face getting hot. He lowered his voice. "Casey, what kind of a question is that? Of course, I'm not afraid of Jesus. Why would I be?"

"Why won't ya talk to Him then?"

"Is that what this is about?" said Jed, slightly above a whisper. "Look, I just prefer to talk to Him my way, that's all."

Casey was distracted when the waitress brought their dinner. But as soon as he took the first bite of drumstick, he continued the conversation.

"My dad told me that people who won't talk to Jesus are hiding from Him. You don't hafta be afraid, Mr. Jed," he said, forgetting to chew with his mouth closed.

"Well, I'm not hiding from Him," he said.

"Then how come you pulled the covers up so He couldn't see you?" Casey's question drew a smirk from the couple at the next table, who were enjoying themselves at Jed's expense.

"Casey, look!" Jed pointed out the window. "See that big red rig? That's one of the new trucks. Wow! We need to check that out when we leave. Isn't that neat?"

"That's neat, Mr. Jed. Can I have my pie now?"

Jed called the waitress back and ordered dessert before they began to make a dent in what was already in front of them. She returned quickly with two generous pieces of homemade pie. Casey transitioned from mashed potatoes and drumsticks to banana cream pie without even looking up.

Jed poked at the meringue with his fork and avoided making eye contact with the couple at the next table. He was aware of Casey's jabbering all through dessert, but he wasn't listening.

After they left the restaurant, Jed drove northward in the dark toward Ogden. He thought about last night's conversation with Rhonda. He thought about Sean McConnell and about Mike. The closer he got to Washington, the more uncertain he was.

"Mr. Jed, are you hidin' from me?" Casey asked.

"What? What are you talking about now?"

"You won't talk to me like you won't talk to Jesus." Casey sounded as if his feelings were hurt.

Jed sighed. With Casey at the bat, there was no point in throwing him a curve. Even if he struck out, there was always another turn at the plate. "It's not that I won't talk to you, Casey. You just make my brain work too hard. I want to relax."

"Does your head hurt, Mr. Jed?"

"Sometimes. You see, Casey, I don't need to know God the way you do. I'm happy the way I am."

Casey looked alarmed. "But don't you care if you go to hell, Mr. Jed?"

"Now where did that come from? I never said I don't care if I go to hell. I just don't believe that a loving God sends people there." Jed thought he must have a screw loose to be involved in this conversation.

"My dad told me God does not send people to hell, everyone was going there anyway. God gave people the only way to stay out."

"Everyone was going there anyway? Why?"

"Because everyone does bad things and can't be good 'nough to live in heaven 'cause you haff to be holy if you want to live near God."

"Casey, no one can be holy. No one can live up to that."

"But, Mr. Jed, that's how come God gave us Jesus. He came and was like us, so we can be like Him. Get it? My dad says we got a good deal. I haff Jesus in my heart," he announced proudly.

"Oh? And how did Jesus get in there?"

Casey giggled. "Mr. Jed, you know."

"No, tell me."

"I just asked Him to come in!"

"Uh-huh, I see. And how do you know He's really in there, Casey?"

The boy's expression went blank, and then his eyes grew wide. "Bubbles! I feel Him like bubbles. He makes me happy. And I don't want to do bad things anymore. When I do, I get very sorry."

"Well, then I must have a little of God in me because suddenly I'm very sorry we're having this conversation!"

"No, you can't haff only a little of God, Mr. Jed! You're suppose ta trade!"

Jed sighed. "Trade what?"

Casey pointed to his heart. "You hafta give Him all of you, then He will give you all of Him. Get it? That's how the bubbles get in there."

"Casey, you're making my head hurt again! Let's just get to the next exit and find a place to sleep!"

Casey hummed to himself, counted on his fingers, and played with the edges of the map. Jed was grateful that he finally shut up.

After he cooled off, it was impossible for Jed to ignore the humor of his dilemma. He was trapped with a little wise-guy evangelist he couldn't shut off. The only way Jed knew to stop him was to resort to verbal cruelty. He wouldn't stoop that low. He liked

Casey and didn't want to hurt him.

Jed's head was spinning. It had been six days since he'd had a beer. He was beginning to remember why he drank.

THIRTY

O n Friday morning, Ellen Jones worked at her computer. She anticipated a call from Lisa Sorensen telling her what time to be at the cemetery. As far as Ellen knew, the media had not gotten wind of the details.

She heard the phone ring. A few seconds later she heard Margie's voice on the intercom.

"Ellen, line one is for you. It's Sean McConnell. I could barely hear his voice. I think the connection's bad."

"Okay, Margie. Thanks."

"Hello, Mr. McConnell. How are you?"

"Ellen…is that you?"

"Yes. I can't hear you very well, Mr. McConnell. May I call you back? I think the connection is poor."

"What's poor is my ol' body, not the connection."

"What's wrong?"

"Aw, it's my heart. The ol' ticker's givin' out. They've got me on some new pills, but I don't think it'll help much."

"Mr. McConnell, where are you? Are you still at the nursing home?"

"No. They brought me over to the Southeast Medical Center. I'm in a real hospital now. But, Ellen, if the ticker's gonna quit, my bein' here isn't gonna do squat. I'd rather be at the nursin' home. I've got friends there. I could do without all these medical people probin' and proddin' me all day, stickin' me with needles, don't ya know? I feel like a pincushion."

"Mr. McConnell, I'd like to come see you. Are you allowed to have visitors?"

"Well, sure I am, but there's no cause for ya to come all this way. I just didn't want ya to worry if ya tried callin' my room and they told ya where I was. I wanted to tell ya myself."

Ellen looked at her calendar. "I'd really like to come. Would you mind? I could drive to Atlanta tomorrow. Guy's working with clients, and I'm off most of the day and would enjoy the drive."

"Ellen, I didn't call to put ya through all this trouble, I—"

"Mr. McConnell, it's no trouble. You're my favorite celebrity, remember? Famous people are supposed to be surrounded by the press. I just happen to be friendly press." Ellen put a smile in her voice.

He chuckled. "That ya are, young lady. I sure would like to see ya if you're up to it. I'm not goin' anywhere. They won't even let me have my wheelchair right now—stole my wheels right out from under me. Plain stuck here in the bed, don't ya know?"

"Listen, I'll be there tomorrow, Mr. McConnell. I'm not sure what time, but as soon as I've finished my work here at the office, I'll head your way. You behave now, and don't give the medical staff such a hard time, you hear?"

"Aw, I don't have a lotta spunk right now. I'm lyin' around here doin' whatever they tell me to. Pincushions don't holler much."

"Well, I'll definitely be there tomorrow."

"Goodness, that'll sure give me somethin' to look forward to, Ellen. I'll see ya when ya get here. Bye now."

"Good-bye, Mr. McConnell."

Ellen hung up the phone and sat staring out at the crisp fall morning. Then she got on the intercom. "Margie, would you please find out the address for the Southeast Medical Center in Atlanta and then get directions for me?"

"Sure, Ellen. Is anything wrong with Mr. McConnell?"

"There's a problem with his heart. I'm not sure how serious it is, but I'm going to find out. See if you can get me there without my getting lost."

"No problem. I'll have your directions as fast as the computer spits them out."

Ellen turned her thoughts to the task at hand. She had an extraordinary photograph to take today, one she hoped would continue to fuel the search for Mike McConnell. She couldn't escape the irony of her working to ensure the son's capture while the father succeeded in capturing her heart.

Mike McConnell walked through the drizzle to Calvary Community Church. He was glad Carlos would be there this afternoon. Isolation was as much of a punishment as the nightly flashbacks he couldn't control.

Pastor Don was waiting for him. "Good morning, tool man." He laughed. "That is what Carlos calls you, isn't it?"

"That's me," Mike said. "So what's on the agenda for today?"

"Oh, this is so much fun. I get to choose, and *voilà*—the work gets done. How about a fresh coat of paint on all the classroom doors? There are gallons of paint just waiting for a home."

"I'm your man. Just point me to the paint."

Mike worked happily until one o'clock when his whistling was interrupted by the sound of footsteps. He turned around and saw Carlos approaching, a sack in each hand. Whatever was inside smelled so good that Mike's mouth began to water. He realized his stomach was growling.

"Hey, how's it going, Mark?" Carlos asked.

"It's going fine. What's in the sacks?"

A grin spread across his face. "Oh, just some…fresh…hot…delicious…authentic…Mexican food."

"Listen, bud, you could get rolled carrying stuff like that around. Ever think of hiring a bodyguard?"

Carlos laughed. "I don't need a bodyguard. I brought a second lunch to share with any would-be attacker. Interested?"

"You serious?"

"Sure. Made it myself. You like Mexican food?"

"You kiddin'? I love the stuff!"

"Well then, here you go." Carlos handed one of the sacks to Mike. "There are quesadillas, burritos, tamales, and chicken enchiladas. I even threw in a bottle of water, a fork, and plenty of napkins."

The two men sat down in the hallway and dug into the sacks.

"Did you really make this stuff, Carlos?" Mike surveyed the individual portions in sealed containers. He couldn't remember the last time he had eaten something homecooked.

"I made it up fresh this morning. No joke. Maria used to make everything. I watched and learned how. She was a great cook. I really miss her. She'd be proud of me for making my own. I admit it was hard at first, but I'm getting better at it."

The men sat with their backs against the wall, containers open, fingers and forks ready.

"You really miss her, don't you?" Mike said.

"I miss all of them. My three children too. Rosa was fourteen. Carmen was ten. And my son, Pablo, was just five. It's been eleven months, but it's still really hard."

Mike took his first bite. "Mmm…this is to die for, man! I can't believe you did this yourself. Ever thought about making this stuff for a living? You might be sitting on a gold mine, amigo."

"Never thought about it. Truthfully, this whole year has been so difficult that I'm just now coming out of it. Really some kind of nightmare."

"Well, if you don't mind talking about it, I don't mind listening."

Carlos hesitated. "It's depressing for other people."

"I'm just passing through, remember? Tell me what happened. It might help to talk."

"There's not a lot to tell. We were coming back from grocery shopping. It was raining and the highway was slick. It was kind of foggy too. I wasn't paying enough attention and didn't see a car stalled in the right lane. I swerved to avoid a collision and my car slid on the slick pavement. Maria...Maria was crushed...and killed instantly." Carlos struggled to say the words. "Rosa too. Carmen and Pablo were thrown from the car and sustained severe injuries. They were airlifted to Seattle...but, uh, Pablo died...before the helicopter landed. Carmen died two days later."

"Man, I'm sorry," Mike said.

"I was the only one wearing a seatbelt." He shook his head. "I should have made them! So I get the miracle, and my family dies. It should've been me, Mark. I'm the one who should've died. It was my fault. I should've seen that car. I don't know why I didn't. After that, my life had no meaning, and it was a struggle every day just to keep going. I even thought about suicide. But then I learned some things that helped me forgive myself. My entire perspective is different now."

"What turned you around?"

"Not what, *Who*. It was God."

"God? What did He do?"

Carlos looked at his watch. "Half your lunch break is gone. Are you sure you want to spend the other half listening to me?"

Mike nodded. He put the lids back on the empty containers and put them in the sack. He gave Carlos his undivided attention.

"Maria and the kids were attending church here. They were all Christians, but I didn't want any part of it. I didn't mind if they went to church, but I didn't want to. They kept trying to get me to go, and I kept making excuses. After this terrible thing happened, I started going mostly out of guilt, but it made me feel closer to them. I only wish I had gone with them when they were alive, you know?

"Anyway, Pastor Don's sermons really got to me. He talked about how God sent Jesus to pay the penalty for our sins—that nothing we do wrong is bigger than God's ability to erase the guilt.

We just have to confess it, ask for forgiveness, and let Him come into our life and make something out of it. Do you know what I mean?"

"I guess I don't."

"Pastor Don showed where the Bible says that if God is for us, nobody can be against us. I guess in my case, I was the one against myself. God has always been for me. He could forgive me. I couldn't forgive myself. Pastor Don said that my hanging on to guilt is like looking up at God's Son dying on the cross and telling Him that His death isn't good enough—that somehow my sin is bigger than God, and that even He can't help me. That got to me. But it was hard to believe that God's grace could reach into this black heart of mine and forgive me, you know?"

"Yeah, I think I do."

"I started talking with Pastor Don about my life and all this guilt. It took some time, but he got through to me because when I accepted Christ, I was finally able to let go of the guilt, and…"

"Hey, man, take it easy. You don't have to do this," Mike said.

"No, I want to say it. It was like I'd been set free. That horrible guilt was gone. The invisible brand I wore across my chest that said *murderer* was erased. I have to tell you, it was the most amazing thing I've ever experienced. I had a reason to live again."

When Carlos wiped the tears away, Mike struggled not to lose it.

"But, Carlos, you were never a murderer. It was an accident."

Carlos nodded, his eyes connecting with Mike's. "Maybe so…but my family is just as dead, aren't they?"

Jed glided down the Idaho interstate. Why was he missing Rhonda? A week ago he hardly had a word to say to her. What was different?

"Mr. Jed? Mr. Jed? Mr. Jeeeeed?"

"Huh? Oh, Casey." Jed reached for a sheet of paper over the visor. "Here's another game. I've made three columns. See the color at the top? One is for red, one for blue, and one for black."

"I see them, Mr. Jed."

"Okay, every time you see a car that's blue, make a mark in the blue column. When you see one that's red, put a mark in the red column. And when you see one that's black, put a mark in the black column. Do you understand?"

"Yes, and I can count to twenty."

"Go for it. Tell me as soon as you get twenty of the same color."

Jed's eyes were on the interstate, but his thoughts drifted....

He was holding Rhonda, dancing to the music of Kenny G. She was wearing that stunning green dress with the open back. With his arms around her, his hands caressed the soft warmth of her back as they danced, barely moving, relaxed in each other's arms. Her cheek nuzzled his; the smell of her perfume saturated his senses. His lips touched Rhonda's cheek and slowly inched their way down to her mouth....

"Mr. Jed, did you hear me? Mr. Jed?"

Jed snapped back to the present. "I'm listening."

"I counted twenty red ones, and...fourteen black ones, and um...nine blue ones!" He held up the columns so Jed could see.

"Way to go, Casey."

"I did good, didn't I, Mr. Jed?"

"You did real good. I'm impressed."

Casey yawned and laid his head on Jed's arm.

"Listen, sport, we have a long drive before dinner. Why don't you take a nap, and then we'll stop and get ice cream."

Casey nodded.

After Casey was asleep in the backseat, Jed resumed his daydreaming. He was surprised at the feelings he had for Rhonda. He looked at the cell phone on the seat, hesitated, then activated the phone, pulled up the address book, hit the button, and waited.

"Hello."

"Hi, it's me."

"Jed! Oh, I'm so glad to hear your voice. I miss you so much!"

"Uh…well…you know, I mis…uh, I just couldn't call, sorry." He could have kicked himself for not saying what was really on his mind.

"I suppose you can't say where you are," she said. "But are you where you want to be? Or are you still where you were?"

"I'm right where I need to be. I left where I was, but I can't say where that is, over the phone." Jed chuckled. "Sounds pretty crazy."

"Jed, I'm so ready for you to come home. There's so much to tell you. Things are going really well. I got my hair highlighted in golden sunlight and cut really cute. You're going to like it. I started up my membership again at the gym, and I've been down there using the equipment. I started jogging, and I started a diet. I've already lost two pounds and have only thirteen to go…. Jed? Are you there?"

For a moment, Jed thought he'd dialed the wrong number. "What else is going on?"

"Well, I've been reading my Bible, I can hardly put it down. I'm learning all sorts of things, and I feel happier than I have in ages, and I just can't wait to tell you about everything. Mary Beth invited me to her Bible study, and I started going last night, and I met some really nice ladies, and we went out for coffee and dessert— only I decided not to have dessert since I'm trying to get shaped up, but it was fun anyway. I seem to have so much energy now! Jed, I'm missing you so much. Do you miss me? Even a little?"

At that moment, Jed missed her a lot. She sounded like the girl he fell in love with. But for the life of him, he couldn't figure out how all this happened in just six days. He reasoned that if God could create the entire world in six days—information Casey volunteered in one of his theological ramblings—then He sure as heck could pull Rhonda back together.

"Yeah, Rhonda…I miss you." There. He said it.

"You do?" Her voice cracked with emotion.

"Yeah, I do."

The line seemed dead for a few moments.

"Jed, will you be home before the three weeks are over?"

"Probably not. I think I'm going to need all the time I planned on." Jed looked at the clock on the dashboard. "Listen, Rhonda, I need to get off. I don't want the FBI tracking me. But I...uh...want to respond to something you said last time."

"Last time?"

"Yeah, I..."

A few seconds of dead air seemed like minutes.

"I wanted to say, uh...I love you too." *Click.*

Jordan Ellis dialed his cell phone.

"Hello, Hal Barker!"

"Hey, take it easy, cowboy. Sounds like you need a vacation."

"Sorry, Jordan, hectic day. I'm about ready to pack it up. What's up? Did your agents find Jed?"

"Not yet. I don't know what's with this vanishing act, but I'm getting antsy. I know McConnell's dad told him something. I think we should lean on Sean McConnell and see where that goes."

"What are you going to do with an eighty-three-year-old man?" Hal said. "Torture it out of him? Threaten him with prison? Withhold his social security checks? FBI agents have already questioned him, and he obviously doesn't have anything he wants to say. Sean McConnell is not the criminal here. He's been through enough. Let him live in peace at the nursing home."

"He's not at the nursing home right now. They transferred him to a hospital. I hear he's not doing well. Sounds like his heart is going."

"Even more reason to leave the old guy alone."

"If Sean McConnell is really bad off, he might be willing to talk. He knows something, Hal. The guy's playing dumb."

"Let it go. Find Jed Wilson, and you'll find Mike McConnell."

"All right, Hal, it's your show, but I think you're too soft."

"Oh, I don't know, Jordan, call me an old softy, but there's something about us pushing an old man with a failing heart straight over the edge that seems to cross the line. There are already four McConnells dead. I'm not too anxious to make it five. If your agents hadn't lost track of Jed, we wouldn't even be having this conversation. I'm not going to victimize Sean McConnell because we can't get our act together."

"Okay, Okay, Sheriff. I hear you.... Listen, Jed Wilson's been calling his wife pretty regularly. In fact, he called her a little while ago, but we couldn't get a fix on him. He's onto us. He won't stay on the line and won't hint at his whereabouts—not even to her. We know he's using a cell phone, so we're getting ready to intercept his little game with bigger toys."

"Why am I sure you're smiling?" Hal said.

"And why not? With more electronic sophistication, we can correlate cell sites and pinpoint his location. Next time he activates his phone to call his old lady, we'll know where he is to within a ten-mile radius."

"Great, Jordan, that's more like it. Let me know when you find him. I trust we're in agreement about leaving Sean McConnell alone?"

"Hey, after what you said, I'm thinking maybe the bureau should send him candy and flowers and a personal note of apology."

The silence on the other end told him Hal was not amused.

"Okay. I do tend to be, let's say, overly zealous. Comes with years of dealing with creeps."

"Well, as long as we're overly zealous about finding Jed Wilson and remember who's a creep and who isn't, I think we'll get what we want."

❦

Late Friday afternoon, Lisa Sorensen walked away from the four crosses, tears streaming down her cheeks, the cold wind chilling her to the bone. It was a private good-bye, as she had hoped, but there was no closure. As she struggled down the hill with her cane, Hal ran up to her and put his jacket around her shoulders.

"Here, put your weight on me. Don't lose your footing," he said.

"I can't believe they're gone, Hal. I still can't accept it. I don't want to leave them out here. It's not fair."

"I know, Lisa. I'm sorry."

"I'll never see them again...."

Lisa fell into Hal's arms. As she sobbed, his arms sheltered her from the cold, but not from the pain. She left the cemetery as empty as she came.

Ellen blinked the tears away. She had shot one roll of thirty-six-exposure film, certain she got a photograph that would earn the top portion of tomorrow's front page.

She sat in her car and looked out across Oak Hills. There was a century of history represented there. Ellen knew the McConnell murder case would be a dark blotch that could never be erased. In years to come kids here would grow up and tell their children about it and would bring them to the McConnell grave site.

She wondered how Mike McConnell could ever live with himself. And as she thought about Lisa standing over the four white crosses, Ellen hoped he lived just long enough to regret it.

THIRTY-ONE

M ike lay across his bed, staring at water stains on the
ceiling. What a way to spend a Friday night. He
wished he were at O'Brian's with Jed. What was an
extrovert like him doing holed up in Harper's Grove? If the FBI
didn't do him in, the loneliness would.

The depression began to overtake him as his struggle to resist
failed, and his mind began its nightly race through its list of regrets.

He wondered what Pastor Don and Carlos Martinez would
think of him now, as he lay across his bed soaked in the sweat of
his guilt. Mark McNeil was the nice guy passing through; Mike
McConnell lived a lie.

How was Carlos able to trust God with his guilt? How did he
let go of the self-condemnation and let Jesus erase it forever? Mike
wanted to believe it was possible, but it made no sense. It was too
simple after what he had done.

No matter how hard he tried to put it out of his mind, that last
night on Heron Lake replayed itself over and over....

Mike parked his truck and walked to the pier. Rose had already
moved the houseboat and anchored it. What time was it anyway?
His eyes tried to focus on his watch. Oops! After nine. She was
ticked. He knew how to handle her. He loaded two cases of beer, a
bag of ice, and a fresh can of gasoline in the johnboat and started
the motor.

He felt really good. A huge golden moon sat just above the

horizon. The night air was unusually warm and damp. Autumn was hanging on to summer for all she was worth. It was going to be a great weekend.

Mike pulled up next to the houseboat and killed the motor. He tied the smaller boat to the larger. He climbed aboard in time to see Rose turn away and go inside the cabin. Oh boy, another weekend in paradise.

He knocked softly on the cabin door.

"Come on, Rose, let me in."

"Keep your voice down, Mike; you'll wake the kids."

"What's your problem?"

"You're my problem," she said, trying to shut the window, which was stuck halfway and wouldn't budge.

He laughed. She didn't.

"You're drunk. It's late. It's always late when you get home. The boys were hoping you'd take them out in the boat for a while. You said you would."

"I never said *when*—just that I would. Come on, Rose, give me a break."

"Always some feeble excuse. It's hard to have a serious conversation with you about anything."

"So lighten up," he said.

She unlocked the door and came outside.

"Let's not wake the kids up. They hear enough already. Mike, did you ever stop to think about the feelings of the other four members of this family? You go out and have your little party time with the good ol' boys—but what about *your* boys? And what about Erin? She sees you for minutes a week."

"Okay, Rose. What's this really about? You're always mad at me about this stuff. There's something else going on here."

She glared at him.

"Okay, have it your way." Mike walked over and picked up a can of beer. He popped the top, which he knew would make Rose even madder.

"What happened to the money I was saving for a trip to New York?" she said. "I had a thousand dollars in savings. It's gone. It took me two whole years to tuck that away. What gave you the right to take it without even telling me? You know what that trip means to me. Just because you couldn't care less doesn't give you the right to treat me and what I want like it's nothing. Where's the money?"

He downed the rest of the beer and popped open another one.

"Well, that's the answer to everything, isn't it?" Rose said. "Just pop open another beer and all is well. Taking that money is about the lowest thing you've ever done, and unless you have some explanation, you just nee—"

"I lost it, Rose…in a bet. I've been really ashamed. I wanted to double the money and get you to New York faster. But I lost it. What can I say? I messed up."

She started to cry. "You lost it? How could you? You know how badly I want to go to New York City! Sean talks about it with that sparkle in his eyes. He and Margaret built such happy memories there. It's where they had you, and where you went to school as a little boy."

"Yeah, Rose, I know that."

"Then why doesn't it mean anything to you? I want to see the old building where Sean made his prized cedar chest for FDR, and O'Bannion Park where Margaret used to take you to swing. I want to see their old neighborhood and try to picture O'Toole's grocery and Michael Leary's dairy. I want to see the apartment where you lived as a boy, and Saint Edward's grade school while it's still standing. I want our kids to see the life their grandparents made for themselves when they came over here from Ireland. Is that so much to ask? It's part of their heritage! It's part of you! It's what makes them McConnells!"

Mike leaned casually against the back rail.

"But you never care about anything that's important to us. Jed and the boys down at O'Brian's—that's where your heart is. What's happened to us, Mike? You used to love me. You used to care about me and the kids. Now all you care about is doing just enough to keep us off your back. But this? It took me two solid years of cutting the budget to put that much away! I'll never forgive you for this!"

He didn't say anything.

"Do you hear me?" She picked up a can of beer and threw it at him. It hit the side of the deck with a loud thud and rolled around until it rested against the wooden frame of a chaise lounge. Mike never flinched.

Rose turned on her heel and stormed back to the cabin. She locked the dead bolt. He popped open another beer....

Jed pulled out of the restaurant parking lot and drove back up on the interstate. He and Casey were nearly to Boise. He felt good inside, glad that he had told Rhonda how he was feeling. Before today he couldn't remember the last time he'd said the words *I love you* to anyone. He'd forgotten it felt as good saying the words as it did hearing them.

"Mr. Jed, I like I-da-ho potatoes."

"Me too, sport. They were good, weren't they? How do you suppose they got all curled up like that?"

Casey giggled and shrugged.

"Mr. Jed, tomorrow I will be at my aunt and uncle's house?"

"We should be there by dinnertime."

"And I will go to school."

"You will for sure. You're pretty fired up about that, aren't you?"

Casey sounded homesick. "I miss my dad."

"Well, how about if we call him again. Want to?"

"Yes!" Casey clapped his hands and reached for the phone.

"Hey, you know what? It's too dark to do this in the car," Jed said. "How about if we stop at the next exit? We can get a place to stay for the night, and we'll call your dad. Okay?"

"I will talk to my dad!"

Jed drove two miles to the next exit, which was on the outskirts of Boise. He spotted the Longview Motor Inn when he drove down the exit ramp. He turned right onto the main street and left into the motor inn. He parked the Explorer in the lot.

"Okay, Casey. This time you push the buttons. Let me show you which ones, and then you push. Here we go…"

Casey giggled the whole time and his eyes grew wide when he heard the phone ringing. Jed could tell when Jesse picked up the phone.

"Hi, Dad! Hi, Dad! I am Casey! I had Id-a-ho potatoes and they were curly, and Mr. Jed is lettin' me count red and black and blue cars and hold the map, and we had ice cream today and more Cracker Jacks 'cause I was good. I'm going to see my aunt and my uncle and go to school, and I'll get there tomorrow when it's dinner-time, and Mr. Jed is nice."

Jed envied the relationship between Casey and Jesse. He never had that level of intimacy with his kids. He would miss Casey after tomorrow night. Being in Casey's company had almost made him forget the pressure of finding Mike.

Jordan Ellis put the TV on mute to answer the phone.

"This is Jordan."

"Sir, this is Morris. Checkmate."

"You picked up Wilson's signal? Where?"

"I correlated the strong signal in cell 259 with the weaker signal coming from cell 260 and cell 258. He's stationary in the triangle."

"In English, Morris. Where is he?"

"Oh, sorry, in Idaho. Near Boise. The signal is strongest in the southern half of cell site 259, near the interstate."

"Okay, thanks, Morris. You know what to do. Get the resident agency in Boise on the phone. Our boys are back in the game."

Jordan hung up the phone and dialed.

"Hello, this is Hal."

"Sheriff, it's Jordan. Sorry to bother you at home."

"That's okay. What's up?"

"Wilson's in Idaho. Near Boise. We just picked up his cell signal, and our agents are practically there. The strongest signal was near the interstate. I'll let you know as soon as we have him spotted."

"Great, Jordan! That's the best news I've had all day. Idaho? That's a little out of the way. He's really truckin' along—obviously on a deliberate track to Mike McConnell."

"Well, hang on to your hat, Sheriff. We're about to find out."

Mike McConnell lay across the bed, the flashback still playing in his mind....

"Rose, wait a minute. Come back here."

He wasn't going after her. She had every right to be mad, but she'd sulk for a week. The woman never let go of anything. He felt guilty enough without her turning the knife. Mike leaned on the back railing, lit a cigarette and popped open another beer. Let her pout if she wanted. He was going to enjoy the last of this balmy weather.

He couldn't get over how huge and bright the moon was or how it was reflected on the rippled water. Good thing the weather was mild if he had to spend the night on the deck.

Mike lay down in a chaise lounge and covered up with a couple of the kids' beach towels. He lit another cigarette and lay there a while, looking at the moonlit sky. More and more, Rose was on his case about everything. He felt empty. He wanted another beer and remembered the bag of ice he brought home was still sitting out. Mike snuffed out the cigarette and flicked it into a trash container next to the window.

When he got up, he tripped over the can of beer Rose had thrown earlier. He stumbled into the side railing and knocked over the gas can, which sent the loose lid rolling into the darkness.

Gasoline poured all over the back deck. He tried to set the can upright but stumbled and knocked it over again.

He grabbed a beach towel, got down on all fours, and frantically tried to sop up the mess. Gasoline soaked his pants and continued to run under the chaise lounges and table, threatening to seep into the storage bin. He grabbed the other beach towel and continued to sop up the mess. When he got it all, he threw both towels in the trash container.

The gas can was nearly empty. He set it upright and groped around until he found the lid and screwed it back on. A whoosh caused him to spin around. The trash was burning out of control!

He scrambled to his feet. The fire had already ignited the curtains in the window closest to the trash container.

He pounded on the cabin door. "Rose! Open the door! Rose!"

Mike kicked the door twice and then shoved it with his shoulder, but it didn't open. He moved to the other window and tried to raise it up all the way. It still wouldn't budge.

"Rose, open the door! Fire!"

The fire was spreading rapidly. Mike grabbed a broom handle and broke the glass out of the window frame, but there wasn't enough room for him to crawl through. He stuck his head inside and shouted.

"Rose! Rose! Erin! Boys! Get out! Fire! Fire!"

Mike jumped back from the window when flames spread across the cabin door and ignited the curtains. His skin felt like it was melting. Perspiration dripped into his eyes. Smoke and fumes sent him into a coughing spasm. It took a minute to catch his breath. He felt woozy. The thick, black smoke made it impossible to see inside the cabin now.

"Rose!" he shouted.

He thought he heard her call out. His pulse raced.

"Rose? Can you hear me? Rose!"

Mike listened, but all he heard was the roar of the fire. Smoke burned his eyes. The heat was almost intolerable. The cabin was completely engulfed. Flames were shooting from the roof. Smoke and fumes poured inside.

Mike remembered the propane tanks.

"Rose, you've got to get out now!" he screamed. "Erin! Tim! Todd! Do you hear me? It's going to blow! Get out!" Mike shouted until he was hoarse.

He jumped into the johnboat, and his hands shook as he struggled to get the rope loose.

Mike started the motor and pushed the throttle as far as it would go. Terror seized him. He hunkered down and looked straight ahead. A bright flash preceded the deafening explosion. He covered his head with one arm and ducked, fearing for his life.

A few seconds later, hissing debris fell all around him. Mike dared to glance back. From under a thick blanket of smoke, he looked out in horror and disbelief. What was left of his home and his family was scattered across the lake as a hundred fires.

"It's all my fault!" he cried. "I killed them! *I* did it! *I* did it! *I* did it!"

Mike McConnell sat straight up in bed, soaked with sweat and trembling in terror.

His guilt was so deep, so black, and so ugly that it seemed to breathe. Every night he faced this demon, and every night it condemned him.

"Welcome to the southern half of cell site 259. I don't see any red Silverado," said the young FBI agent. "Why am I not surprised?"

"That signal was stationary for thirteen minutes before it cut out," said his partner. "Wilson had to be seen somewhere. Let's nose around. There's a truck stop up ahead. And the Longview Motor Inn. Also a pizza parlor, a MacDonald's, and a tavern. Maybe somebody remembers seeing him."

The FBI agents inquired at each place of business. No one remembered seeing Jed Wilson or his red Silverado. They got back in the car.

The young agent sighed with frustration. "His signal was picked up just fifteen minutes before we got here. We're right in the middle of the action and we get nothing. So how far could he have gone?"

"Doesn't matter. The interstate's covered from here to the other side of Boise. We'll find him. Just a matter of time. I have a feeling his luck just ran out."

THIRTY-TWO

At eight o'clock on Saturday morning, Ellen Jones sat at
her desk, ready to leave for Atlanta. She was waiting for
her copy of the morning paper, eager to see if the picture
of Lisa was as poignant as she envisioned.

A knock at the door was followed by the aroma of freshly
brewed coffee.

"Good morning, boss." Margie handed Ellen a copy of
Saturday's edition of the *Baxter Daily News*. "You're gonna love
this."

"Am I?"

"Ellen, what you do with words, you do equally well with a
camera. I don't know where it comes from. It's a gift."

"Thanks for the coffee, Margie." Ellen smiled and touched her
arm. "And the vote of confidence. Oh, and the map. I'm all set to
leave for Atlanta."

"You're welcome. Take a few minutes to enjoy your handiwork
before you leave. I think you'll be pleased."

Margie shut the door. Ellen sat back in her chair. She took a
deep breath and unfolded the paper. "Oh my," she whispered. "It's
perfect."

The top portion of Saturday's newspaper consisted of a close-up
shot of Lisa Sorenson standing on the hillside, looking down on
four white crosses, one larger than the other three. The bare trees

took on an almost human form, looking mournful in the misty gray autumn backdrop. The vacant look of devastation on Lisa's face needed no comment. The headline simply read, "Good-bye…"

Ellen blinked the tears away and sat quietly for a moment. Then she folded the paper on her desk and got up to leave.

"Okay, Lisa, let's see if this pushes a few buttons."

"Mr. Jed?…Mr. Jed?"

"What is it, Casey?"

"I'm not sleepy anymore."

Jed looked at the clock. It was already nine-thirty.

"Can't believe I slept so late. Hey, this is the big day, isn't it?"

"Yes, and I will see Uncle Ray, and I will see Aunt June! See, I put my clothes in here!"

Jed saw Casey's suitcase, stuffed full and zipped. "You all ready?"

"I go to Portland, Mr. Jed."

Jed laughed. "All right, Casey. Let me shower and shave and we'll get on the road. First stop, breakfast. Then on to Portland, my man."

After the call to Jesse last night, Casey was wound up, so Jed decided to drive into Boise and treat Casey to a piece of pie. They found a motel and watched a movie and didn't get to sleep until well after midnight. Jed was surprised Casey was up first.

"Mr. Jed?" Casey stood by the sink while Jed finished shaving.

"Just five more minutes, Casey."

"No. How much before I see Uncle Ray and I see Aunt June?"

"You'll be in Portland by dinnertime. I'm going to call them when we get closer, and they'll give us directions to their house. Have you been there before?"

"Oh yes. I haff been there. They haff a kitty named Pork. He's real big and fluffy. Uncle Ray says he eats too much."

"What else do you remember?"

"Mmm...Aunt June makes banana cream pie. I like banana cream pie, Mr. Jed."

Jed chuckled. "I know you do, Casey. What do you want for breakfast this morning?"

Jed could have said the answer right along with him. He just didn't know for sure which flavor.

"Pancakes! I want...strawberry!"

"Okay, strawberry it will be." Jed put the key in his pocket and picked up the bags. He handed the light one to Casey. "Let's hit the road."

"Portland! I go to Portland!"

At eleven, Ellen pulled into a parking space at Southeast Memorial Hospital and got out of her car. A crisp November wind sent a chill right through her, which prompted her to reach in back and get her all-weather coat. She didn't like hospitals much, but she liked Sean McConnell, and she was looking forward to spending the day with him.

After she got his room number at the patient information desk, she walked down two long corridors before arriving at Room 176. She knocked gently. "Mr. McConnell? It's me, Ellen. May I come in?"

"Why sure ya can, young lady. Come over here and let me look at ya. Goodness, you're lookin' mighty pretty. You're a welcome sight. I'm real glad ya came."

Ellen heard fear in the old man's voice. "Well, me too. I thought you could use a visitor, just to help break in the new room. Besides, somebody has got to make sure you're behaving."

"Don't feel like doin' much else. The ol' ticker's bad, don't ya know?"

"What does the doctor say, Mr. McConnell? When can you go back to the nursing home?"

"Oh, ya know how they are. They won't tell ya anything, but

I…well, I don't think I'll be goin' back, Ellen. I don't think I'm gonna get better. A body just knows when he's not doin' well."

Ellen noticed he looked gray and tired. "Are you sure you're not doing a little too much self-diagnosis?"

"Well, sure I am, but who knows what it feels like in this body except me? All those doctors—they have equipment to tell 'em how I'm supposed to be feelin', but I'm the only one who really knows. And I know it isn't good. I think I'm failin'…." The old man was emotional. "Now, Ellen, ya have to understand that I'm not feelin' sorry for myself. I just didn't want to die until I saw Michael and told him one more time…that I love him…and forgive him." His eyes welled with tears. "I don't think that's gonna happen now. Makes me kinda sad because the boy'll always wonder if…"

"It's all right, Mr. McConnell." Ellen held his hand and sat with him while the tears rolled down his cheeks and onto his hospital gown.

"You know, I'm sure Mike knows you love him. And because you do, he already knows you've forgiven him," she said.

"Maybe so, Ellen, but I really want to say it to him. I also want him to turn back to God. Sure, he needs to know I love and forgive him, but nothin' I say will set things straight with his Maker. I still don't know what happened or what my boy's actually done, but I do know that whatever it is, only God can make it right. Are ya a religious woman, Ellen?"

"Not in the traditional sense. I mean, I believe in God, but I don't dwell on it a whole lot. I've never been a churchgoer, if that's what you mean."

"Nah, I just mean are ya a prayin' woman?"

"No, I guess I'm not, Mr. McConnell. I probably should be, but I've never been around it much."

"Well, ya see, Michael has. His mama and I took that boy to church. We taught him right from wrong. He learned it at Saint Edward's too, when he was comin' up. He never fussed much about all the trainin' he got, but when he grew up, it was Rose who pulled him along. Michael has always known about God, but I'm not sure he's ever really answered the door, if ya get my drift. God has been knockin' on Michael's door for years, and I'm not sure that boy has answered Him. I worry about that. With Rose and me both gone...well, Ellen, the boy's gonna be completely on his own. He needs God."

"Mr. McConnell, God has been knocking on Mike's door all his life, right?"

"Yes, I believe He has."

"And Mike hasn't answered that knock?"

"No, I think not."

"Well, isn't it entirely possible that God will just knock louder, since Mike is in trouble? I'm assuming God can do anything."

The worry lines between Sean's brows began to relax, and a hint of a smile returned to the corners of his mouth.

"Young lady, ya just might have somethin' there."

After a few minutes, Ellen and Sean talked about all sorts of things. Ellen told him about Guy and their life together. She talked about Reginald T. Baxter's legacy that kept the daily paper going and how much fun she had in the role of editor. Sean told her more about his life with Margaret and about some special times he had spent with his grandchildren. Ellen thought his color looked peculiar. He seemed exhausted.

"Mr. McConnell, I think you should lie down now and get some rest."

"Aw, I'm fine. I'm enjoyin' our visit. I don't get to talk like this with anyone. You're real easy to be with, Ellen."

"Thank you. I feel the same about you. I just think you need your rest. How about taking a nap?"

"Ya really think I need to, do ya?"

"Just for a while, Mr. McConnell. I'll go to the gift shop and get a magazine and sit here and read. I'll be here when you wake up."

"Ellen, don't ya think it's time ya called me somethin' besides Mr. McConnell, seein' as how we're friends and all? How about just callin' me by my name. It's Sean, don't ya know?" His tired eyes were smiling.

"Well certainly. I'd like that very much, but it might take a little getting used to."

"Now I'll just settle down here for a spell. You'll be here when I wake up?"

"Glued to the chair like press to a celebrity."

They both chuckled. Ellen realized she felt more like his daughter than just a friend.

THIRTY-THREE

I t was another dreary Saturday. Mike McConnell was about to go stir-crazy at the thought of spending the entire day locked up at Evergreen Cottages. He decided to hitch a ride to Doonesbury. There was bound to be something going on over there.

Mike picked up his wallet and room key, put them in the zippered pocket of his new parka, and set out on foot toward the highway. When he had made the decision to return here, he knew it would be a good place to hide. But he also hoped the memories would comfort him. They didn't.

The forests that stood tall on either side of the road caused Mike to think about how much his father loved wood. The man could make something beautiful out of any piece of wood—raw or cut lumber. Mike could never do that. He was good with his hands, but not in the creative way his dad was. He admired it. He admired him.

FDR… He smiled and shook his head. As young as he was when his dad made him that walking stick, Mike understood its significance. Right now he missed his father with an aching that wouldn't quit.

Looking down the long, misty stretch of road in front of him, Mike felt like he was alone at the end of the earth. A part of him wished he could keep on walking right over the edge. A part of him was sure he already had.

When Sean McConnell woke up, Ellen was sitting in the chair beside his bed, absorbed in the magazine she bought in the gift shop.

He studied her for a few moments—the way the curls framed her face and the area around her eyes showed no lines. She seemed relaxed and at home dressed in khaki slacks and a dark green turtleneck. Sitting in the chair with her shoes off and her legs drawn up, she looked to him like a child lost in her favorite story-book.

He coughed politely so as not to startle her.

Ellen looked up and smiled. "Hi."

"You look mighty engrossed, young lady. I hope I haven't been sleepin' so long ya gave up on me."

"Not at all. I've been enjoying the quiet and reading my maga-zine. It's nearly four o'clock. You had a nice nap."

"Aw, I didn't want to sleep that long. I'm wastin' our visit. Ya came all this way to see me, and I'm not bein' neighborly."

"I'm not leaving yet, Sean. We can do a lot more visiting." Ellen bent down to slip on her loafers. "Your dinner should be here before too long. Are you getting hungry?"

"Not really. I almost forgot what that's like. I haven't had much appetite since all this mess with Michael happened. It was real hard thinkin' I lost my son and daughter-in-law and all my grandchil-dren in that horrible fire and explosion. But then havin' Michael turn up alive, just to be accused of bein' their murderer…hadn't gotten over feelin' one way before I had to start feelin' another. I don't think the rest of me's caught up yet, don't ya know?"

"Well, it's no wonder. Your emotions were dealing with his being dead before all this turned a new direction. You've been through a very traumatic loss. I think the nap did you some good."

The phone rang. Sean looked surprised.

"Ellen, would ya mind gettin' that? It's probably the wrong number."

Ellen walked over and picked up the phone. "Sean McConnell's room, this is Ellen Jones speaking.... Hello? Is anyone there? This is Sean Mc—"

"Yes, may I speak to him, please?"

"Certainly. May I tell him who's calling?"

"Uh...I'd really like to surprise him, if that's okay."

"Please hold on for just a moment." Ellen handed the receiver to the old man, shrugging her shoulders. "It's a surprise."

His white eyebrows lifted. "Hello, this is Sean McConnell.... Michael! Is it really you?"

Ellen's eyes widened and she motioned to Sean that she would wait outside. He nodded.

"It's really me, Pop. Listen, I can't talk long, but be careful what you say. I imagine your phone is being tapped. Was that Ellen Jones from Baxter who answered the phone?"

"Ellen's been real good to me. She's just visitin' me here at the hospital. She's left the room now, so we can talk. Son, I've been so worried about ya. Are ya all right?"

"How come they moved you to the hospital? I called the nursing home and they gave me this number. Are you okay?"

"Oh, ya know, the ol' ticker's growin' weak. I'm doin' what they tell me. Did ya make it to—Oh—I mean, what do you hear from FDR?"

"He's still around. Looks a lot different these days. Awfully cold and wet."

"Glad ya found him. Are ya doin' all right, Boy? Are ya makin' it?"

"Makin' it, Pop. Growing weary, but makin' it."

"Michael, there's some things I want to tell ya. I want ya to please listen and not hang up. I'll just say 'em outright, and then ya can say whatever's on your mind. Michael..." Sean started to cry. "I want ya to know there's nothin' ya could have done that would make me not love ya. You're a part of me. You were given to me by God, and I love ya, no matter what. The other thing that's been on my mind is that ya need to get right with God. Now, ya know I don't go preachin' at ya, but this is one time I'm gonna. Michael, the good Lord's been knockin' on your door since you were a boy. I think it's time ya let Him in. I may not always be around for ya, Son…but He will. Besides, ya better be decidin' where ya want to spend your time after ya die. It's a choice you've gotta make, Michael. No one else can do that for ya." Sean McConnell took a deep breath. "That's most of what's on my mind. I just miss ya so much…. Are ya there, Michael?"

"Yeah, Pop, I'm here. I heard what you said. I've been thinking a lot about stuff like that. Don't worry about me. I have a lot to work through. Uh, there're some things I want you to know. I…uh…I love you too. I know I'm the most importa—" Mike had to stop. "What I mean is, I know how much I mean to you, and I know I haven't done things right. What happened with Rose…" Mike stopped again to get his emotions in check. "What happened with Rose and the kids…was my fault, but I never meant to…it should never have happened. I'm so sorry. I think about them all the time. If I could just go back, I'd trade my life for theirs. I'd give anything to go back…." Mike began to sob. "I'm glad you don't hate me. I'm doing enough of that for both of us. Listen, Pop, I've really got to go. I'm afraid they'll trace this call."

"No, wait! Michael, tell me, did Jed ever make it? Did he find you?"

"Jed? I don't know what you mean, Pop, but I've really got to get off this line. We've been on too long. I'll talk to you." *Click.*

Special Agent Butler's cell phone rang.

"Hello, this is Butler."

"Sir, we got a fix on McConnell, and listen to this…."

Agent Butler listened to the taped conversation between Mike and his father. A smile took over his face.

"Great job! Call the resident agency closest to Doonesbury and have them pick up McConnell. I'll take it from here."

Special Agent Nick Butler hung up and dialed Jordan Ellis's cell phone.

"Hello, this is Jordan."

"Jordan, it's Nick. We nailed McConnell on a call to his dad. He got careless and talked too long—a real emotional conversation with his old man. Sounded like a confession, even got kind of religious. Anyway, while father and son got carried away, we got a fix on Mike McConnell. He was using a pay phone in some town called Doonesbury in Washington state. The RA will pick him up."

"How clever of you, Nick! You threw away Jed Wilson and went right for McConnell. I'm in awe."

"Just a little technique I was saving for a rainy day."

"Yeah, sure you were. Well, we don't have to wonder where Jed Wilson is headed now. Let me know when you have McConnell in custody."

Casey sang another round of "This Old Man," and Jed enjoyed the pure innocence of the moment. He wondered how much he missed by not being closer to his kids when they were growing up. In just four days he felt closer to Casey than he ever did to Jennifer and Mark.

Jed tapped Casey on the arm. "I need to call your Uncle Ray and Aunt June. We need to get directions to their house. I'm going to pull off so you can use the bathroom if you want."

He took the exit and pulled into a service station. Jed knew Casey wasn't about to leave while he made the call.

"Hello, Mr. Lasiter? This is Jed Wilson."

"Well, hello, Jed. Jesse's told us all about you. Where are you?"

"We're about three hours out, should be in around six."

"Please plan to stay for dinner. June's made her famous lasagna."

"Lasagna? Wild horses couldn't keep me away from lasagna."

Jed looked at Casey who was clapping his hands with excitement.

"Mr. Lasiter, you'd better give me directions fast. There's someone else who wants to talk to you." Jed wrote the directions down. "Sounds easy. I don't think I'll have any problem. Let me turn this call over to the star of the show. We'll see you around six."

Casey grabbed the phone. "Hi, Uncle Ray, I am Casey! Mr. Jed got me pie, and we saw a movie, and I counted cars and had Cracker Jacks...." Casey listened and smiled the whole time his Uncle Ray talked to him.

Jed filled the car and started to wash the windshield. When he looked down again, Casey was watching him. The boy knocked on the window and waved. Jed smiled, then reached in and shut the phone off.

"Did you have a nice visit with Uncle Ray?"

Casey nodded. "Mr. Jed, will you sing 'Knick Knack Patty Whack' with me?"

Jed had listened for the last fifty miles, and the words were forever-and-a-day ingrained in his memory. He smiled. "Hey, why not."

He put the credit card receipt in his pocket and got back in the car, feeling more like a kid than he had in years.

Just as Jordan Ellis reached for the phone to call Sheriff Barker, it rang again.

"Hello, this is Jordan."

"Sir, it's Agent Morris. We've got another signal on Wilson. Looks like he's on his way to Portland."

"Are you sure?"

"The strongest signal is between Boise and Portland. I'll let you know when we get something else, but ten to one, that's where he's headed."

"Thanks, Morris."

Jordan Ellis hung up and dialed Hal's number.

"This is Hal Barker."

"Hello, Sheriff. It's Jordan Ellis."

"What have you got?"

"Pay dirt! We have McConnell using a pay phone in Doonesbury, Washington. And we have Jed Wilson heading that way via Portland. Our guys are practically on top of McConnell. I'll let you know when we have him. Looks like we'll have a big surprise for Mr. Jed Wilson when he gets there. He's going to be ticked after traveling all that way, only to discover that we beat him at his own game."

"This is great news, Jordan. Thanks for all the effort. I'm anxious to get Mike extradited to Norris County. I have a string of questions I can't wait to ask him."

"Oh, Hal...I thought you might be interested to know that we got the fix on McConnell when he called his dad. Those two were definitely on the same page. I told you the old man knew something."

"And I told you that as long as we remembered who's a creep and who isn't that we'd get what we want. It's about dignity, Jordan. Don't you feel better that you got this without running over Mike McConnell's feeble father?"

There was a long pause.

"You're not going to let me gloat, are you?"

Hal chuckled. "Not on my turf."

THIRTY-FOUR

Mike McConnell sat on a curb in Doonesbury and tried to pull himself together. He hated the helplessness! He hated the uncertainty, the isolation, and the loneliness! And after the call to his dad, he hated the distance!

He couldn't take much more of this. The thin thread holding him together was breaking.

Suddenly aware that people were staring, he got up and started to wander around. When he crossed Knowles Boulevard, he noticed activity at Doonesbury Park and decided to go take a look.

A small crowd was gathered, and he heard music. As he entered the park, he saw some young people playing guitars. He maintained a comfortable distance and stood listening to what they were singing.

"Just as I am without one plea, but that Thy blood was shed for me, and that Thou bidst me come to Thee, O Lamb of God, I come...I come."

The song's gentle melody and the tender message of acceptance touched him. He stood and listened to the other verses, then walked to a park bench and sat by himself. He wished he understood more. This sounded like what Carlos talked about.

The crowd was growing around the young people, who began to sing something else. "Amazing grace, how sweet the sound, that saved a wretch like me. I once was lost but now am found, was blind but now I see."

This tune was familiar to Mike, though he had never really listened to the words until now. He felt lost, all right. What did it mean to be found?

Someone tapped him on the shoulder, and Mike felt a surge of adrenaline. He looked up and saw a rugged man in hiking boots and a down jacket. He was holding a piece of paper.

"I think this belongs to you," the man said.

"I don't think so. What is it?"

"Why don't you take a look and see if it's yours." The man's eyes were insistent.

Mike opened the paper. Written on it was Jed Wilson's name and cell phone number. It was Mike's handwriting, but where had it come from?

"Uh...thanks."

"You're welcome. Are you enjoying the singing?"

"Actually, I am. It's nice. Kind of relaxing."

"I know what you mean. Well, Mike, enjoy the music."

A second later, it hit him—*Mike?* He stood up and turned around to get a better look at the guy—but he was gone.

Ellen finished eating dinner in the hospital cafeteria and sat there dying of curiosity—if only the hospital had a cure for that! She guessed the conversation between Sean and Mike would be over by now, so she returned to room 176. She pressed her ear to the door and didn't hear anyone talking. She knocked softly.

"Come on in," Sean said.

Ellen cracked the door. "Finished with your phone call? I don't want to interrupt anything."

"You're not. It's been over for a while."

"Did the discussion go the way you hoped?"

"I said what I had to say. Michael tried to say what was on his mind, but the poor boy is pretty torn up. Sounds like he's been doin' some soul searchin', Ellen. I still don't know what happened. He never said. He said he was sorry and it shouldn't have happened, but thinkin' back now, he really never said…" The old man looked sad.

"Did he say where he is?"

"Not directly."

"What will you do now? Anything?"

"If ya mean talkin' to the authorities, what could I tell 'em? Deep inside, I think there's more to this than any of us knows. That boy was awful torn up. He didn't sound like a murderer to me. But then, I'm his father." Sean looked grieved. "Ellen, you'll forgive me if don't say anything else to ya about this. I don't want ya drug into the middle. The less ya know, the better."

"I saw the food cart in the hallway. Your dinner is coming. Try to eat something," she said, touching his hand. "Then maybe you can rest again. You look a little tired." She didn't say what she really thought—that his skin was an awful shade of gray and his eyes looked hollow.

"If ya don't mind, Ellen, I think I'll just lie here and sleep for a while."

Agents Rick Barnes and Don Ames pulled up in front of the public telephone booth on Piedmont Street, next to the Pizzeria.

"I don't expect McConnell to still be hanging around," Barnes said, "but he might be in the area. It's only been thirty minutes."

He parked the car, and the two of them began to walk the sidewalk, looking for any sign of the suspect. With all the coats, hats, and umbrellas, it was difficult to spot any distinguishing feature among the people they passed.

"We're wasting time," Ames said. "Let's cruise around."

They got back in the car and drove around.

"Hey, look over there. Something's going on at the park," Ames said. "Let's check it out."

Barnes made a U-turn on Knowles and headed back. He parked the car.

"Let's split up," Ames said. "Let's walk the perimeter of the park in opposite directions and meet back here."

Mike McConnell still sat alone on the park bench and surveyed his surroundings with a wary eye. How'd that guy know his name? But the sound of the guitars and the words to the songs again vied for his attention. He didn't understand why, but listening to the music gave him hope. He remembered what his father told him about answering God's knock on the door. Mike never felt comfortable getting too close to God. There were things he was ashamed of, especially how he messed things up with Rose....

Mike was in love with her. Their early years were happy. Eventually the distractions of raising kids reduced her passion to a flicker. Rose was no less beautiful, just less available. Mike felt justified when his Irish eyes went roving way over the line, and he had a fling with some gal named Nancy.

He couldn't even remember her last name. It didn't mean anything to him, but it meant everything to Rose. She said she forgave him, and that was it. They got on with their lives, hoping the pain would go away. What went away was their happiness. The anger and guilt never went away—and the passion never came back. Neither did the closeness. When Rose was in his arms, she may as well have been somewhere else. So Mike spent his evenings drinking at O'Brian's. He knew it hurt her, but he didn't care. She withheld herself from him. Two could play that game. It seemed so stupid now. He would have done anything to turn back the clock and make things right....

The music stopped, and when Mike looked up, he noticed the musicians mingling with the crowd. One of them worked his way toward Mike's side of the park, handing out some kind of leaflet. Mike decided to move on, but just as he stood up to leave, the young man hurried over to him.

"Hi. Glad you came by the park today. I hope you enjoyed what you heard."

"Uh, yeah. I did. I was just leaving, but thanks for the music. It was nice."

"I don't think I've seen you here before."

"Just passing through."

"Well, thanks for coming." The young man turned to go and then suddenly turned back around. "Uh, I feel like I'm supposed to give you this. Maybe it's something you need. Anyway, God bless you."

Mike took the leaflet and stood there until the young man was out of sight. He sat back down and looked at what was in his hand. There on the cover was the familiar picture of Jesus—like the one that hung in his parents' bedroom for as long as he could remember. Below it was the caption, "Behold, I stand at the door and knock." His hands began to shake.

Mike McConnell broke down and sobbed, unsure if it was because he was running from God or to Him.

Agents Barnes and Ames walked in opposite directions around the park without spotting any suspicious-looking person. They met back at their rendezvous point, just behind the third park bench on the Knowles Boulevard side. Barnes dialed a number from his cell phone.

"Hey, it's Barnes. We haven't spotted McConnell anywhere. We've checked out the park and two square blocks around ground zero. Nothing so far. We're going to move on. Check with you later."

After the two FBI agents got back in their car and drove off, Mike McConnell looked up from the park bench, where he sat frozen in fear and disbelief. He overheard every word and wondered if it was safe even to go back to Harper's Grove.

Mike knew he should have been more careful when he called

his dad. But he had no idea they could find him so quickly. He didn't know which way to turn. For the moment, he sat on a damp park bench in Doonesbury, Washington, afraid to do anything.

Jed and Casey pulled into the Lasiter's driveway at 6:05 P.M. Casey was out the door before Jed turned off the motor. He ran toward the front porch, where he was met by his Uncle Ray. Jed was struck by how much the man looked like Jesse.

"Howdy, pardner. How was the ride?" He put his arm around Casey and tickled him with the other hand.

"Me and Mr. Jed had fun. I counted cars and pointed to the map. We had pancakes and french fries."

Ray Lasiter looked up and walked toward Jed, his hand extended in greeting.

"Jed...Ray Lasiter. Welcome to Portland."

"Hello, Mr. Lasiter. I'm glad to meet you."

"Please, call me Ray. You already seem like family."

"Thanks. I sure have enjoyed Casey these last few days. He's good company."

Ray smiled. "That he is. We're sure glad you made it safely. We've been praying for angels to watch over you. Sounds like they have."

Jed looked up and saw a rotund woman come down the steps with her arms outstretched.

"Come here, Casey, and let Aunt June take a look at you." She hugged and kissed her nephew, who yielded completely and seemed to love every minute of it.

Then Casey looked past her and pointed. "Look, it's Pork! Come here, kitty."

Standing at the top of the stairs, looking self-assured and in control of the spotlight, was a giant gray-and-white cat. He meowed and walked side to side. Then he came down the stairs and rubbed against Casey's leg.

"Come on, Pork. Let's play." Casey looked at Aunt June. "Can I find his toys?"

"Sure you can. They're in the same place as last time."

Jed caught her eye. "Mrs. Lasiter, I'm Jed Wilson."

"Yes, Jed…so nice to make your acquaintance. You've been in our prayers since you left Missouri. I feel like I already know you."

"Seems I've been prayed for more than I realized. Casey did a little of that too."

"That youngin' has always been spiritually tuned in. He amazes me sometimes," she said. "Now, Jed, please call me June."

"Thank you, June. I was telling Ray how much I've enjoyed Casey's company."

She chuckled. "I'm sure you have. We're looking forward to spending some time with him before he goes off to school on Monday. You know, that's going to be a major step in his life. Jesse isn't getting any younger, and he wants to be sure Casey is as self-sufficient as he can be. The Brighton School is supposed to be the best. If it's possible to get that boy to where he's capable of being on his own, they can do it. Say, are you guys hungry? Dinner can be ready any time you are."

"I'm more than ready," said Jed. "I've been thinking about the taste of homemade lasagna ever since Ray told me on the phone that's what you were serving. It's one of my very favorites."

"Then you're in for a real treat," Ray said, "because June here makes the best."

"Well, come on, boys. I'll have it on the table in five minutes."

As they were walking into the house, June turned around. "Jed, I thought you had to be at a wedding in Seattle tonight. I do hope your plans aren't ruined."

"Uh, well, no. Actually, the wedding is tomorrow night. I missed the rehearsal dinner this evening, but I called and it's not a problem. I'll drive tonight until I get tired. I'll get in there tomorrow in plenty of time for them to fill me in on what I missed." He hoped he could keep his story straight. He hated lying to such nice people.

"Well, we better get you fed so you can do what you need to."

Jed grinned. "Thanks. Right now, that lasagna is about *the* most important thing in my life."

Ellen looked at her watch. It was 10:00 P.M., and Sean McConnell was still asleep.

"Sean?" Ellen said softly. She watched the slow rise and fall of his chest. She put her hand on his shoulder and gently massaged it. "Sean, I hate to disturb you, but I need to leave and want to say good-bye."

There was no response. She tried a third time to rouse him but was unsuccessful. Ellen summoned the head nurse. "I can't get him to respond. He seems to be breathing fine, but he's not reacting to voice or touch."

The nurse tried to rouse him, but her efforts failed. "Would you please step outside? I'd like to examine him."

Ellen left the room. She paced outside Sean's door for ten minutes before a doctor arrived and went inside, closing the door behind him.

A few minutes later, the door opened. "Hello, I'm Dr. Rosburg, Mr. McConnell's cardiologist. And you are…?"

"Ellen Jones. I'm a close friend of Sean's. He doesn't have family here. Is he going to be all right?"

"I really should be talking to a family member. I'm aware of the recent loss he's suffered, but isn't there someone in the family I can call?"

"No, I don't think so, Doctor. I'm all he's got at the moment. Is he going to be all right?"

"Mrs. Jones, your friend's heart is failing, and he's slipped into a mild coma."

"What are you telling me, Doctor? Is he going to wake up?"

"He might. Sometimes these things are temporary, but his condition is deteriorating. He's resting comfortably right now. It won't hurt if you'd like to stay with him. I'll check back later and see how he's doing. We'll just have to wait and hope for the best."

Jed couldn't remember when a meal ever tasted better or when he enjoyed such good company. It was eight-thirty. He needed to get on the road.

"June, I have to agree with Ray. That's about the best lasagna I've ever had in my life. If this were a county fair, you'd win the blue ribbon."

"You're sweet to say so, Jed. I do love making it. Seems most everybody likes it. Would you like another serving?"

"Sure I would. But any more and they'll be flagging me down at one of those trucker weigh stations. Isn't that right, Casey?"

Casey looked uneasy. "I don't want Mr. Jed to go."

"I know. But I need to get back on the road."

"Aunt June made ice cream pie, Mr. Jed. You can have some."

"I think I'm going to have to pass on that too. I don't know where I'd put it." Jed pushed himself back from the table and stood up.

"Let's see," Ray said. "We got all of Casey's things out of the car. Have you got directions to where you're going?"

"Yes. I sure do. Thank you both for your hospitality. It's been nice. And the lasagna—June, you outdid yourself." He patted his stomach with satisfaction.

"We're the ones who should be thanking you," Ray said. "We're so grateful you were willing to bring Casey here. Without your help, he'd be sitting back in Missouri, probably pouting with disappointment. I know Jesse would be."

"You know, it worked out great all the way around. Casey, my man, would you like to walk me out to the car so we can talk man-to-man before I leave?"

Casey grinned. "Yes! I will race you!"

Casey ran to the door. Jed shook hands with Ray and was surprised when June hugged him.

"Thanks again for everything," June said. "You're a good man, Jed Wilson."

"Jed," said Ray, extending his hand. "Take care now. If you get back this way, you're always welcome here."

"Thanks. I appreciate that." Jed turned to Casey. "All right, Casey. Ready, set...GO!"

Mike McConnell sat on the park bench for hours, afraid to move. He was the only one left in Doonesbury Park. For the first time since he became a fugitive, he felt the pressure of being cornered.

The wet wind made him shiver, and he put his cold hands in his pockets. He felt the note. He took it out and wondered again where this piece of paper came from.

He'd give just about anything to talk to his friend. If he called Jed's cell phone, would he get an answer? And if he did, would Jed even want to talk to him? More than anyone else, Jed had the right to feel betrayed.

As he sat there in the dark, it started to drizzle. Mike McConnell was running out of time and options.

"I beat you, Mr. Jed. I win! I win!"

"You did win, Casey," said Jed, huffing and puffing in jest. "This is hard on an old man."

Casey looked up. His face was somber. "Mr. Jed, you hafta go now? I want you to stay. I will miss you."

I'll miss you too, Casey. We've gone a few miles together." Jed winced when he said it.

"Will you come back, Mr. Jed?"

"I really can't say for sure, Casey. I hope I'll see you again, but I live far away from here."

Casey's face lit up. "But if you ask Jesus in your heart, we would be brothers. Then I would see you in heaven! How about you talk to Jesus? He cannot get in your heart if you won't talk to Him."

"You don't think so, huh?"

"Jesus will only come in if you ask Him, Mr. Jed."

"Casey, why do you think I need Jesus in my heart?"

"Because it's dark in there, and He can make the light go on."

"Well, tell me why I need the light on."

"Because when the light is on, the dark cannot stay. Then you can see, so you never hafta be afraid. Get it?"

"But what am I afraid of?"

"What is hiding in the dark, Mr. Jed. You know that."

Jed was quiet for a moment. He did know. "Casey, come here a minute."

Casey moved over and stood facing Jed. Jed put his arms around him and held him close. Casey was completely relaxed in Jed's arms, and they both felt warmed in the November chill.

Jed smiled. "Casey, I hope I'm as wise as you are when I grow up."

Ellen sat next to Sean McConnell, holding his hand. Though his breathing was regular and he seemed comfortable, his lack of presence was disheartening to her. Ellen walked out in the hallway and dialed her cell phone.

"Hello, Ellen?"

"Yes, it's me."

"Is everything all right?" Guy asked. "I just got home and was about to call you. I was surprised you weren't back yet. Where are you?"

"I'm still at the hospital with Sean McConnell."

"Ellen, it's almost midnight. I don't like you on the highway this late."

"I know. Something awful has happened. Sean has slipped into a mild coma. The doctor says his heart is failing. He might come out of it, and he might not."

"I'm so sorry. Are you going to spend the night at the hospital?"

"Yes. I can't leave him this way."

"Do what you need to. Are you all right by yourself? Do you want me to meet you there?"

"I'll be fine, Guy. It's Sean I'm worried about. He looks just awful."

Ellen started to cry.

"Honey, are you sure you're okay by yourself?"

She took a slow, deep breath. "Yes. There's nothing you can do, and there's no reason for you to drive here in the middle of the night. You've had a tiring day yourself. I'll be fine. Really."

"Call me as soon as you know something more. I don't care what time it is.... I love you."

"I love you too."

Ellen turned off the phone and went back in Sean's room. She looked down at this precious man. Tears clouded her vision. Just when she found him, he was slipping away.

Jed was on Interstate 5, traveling north out of Portland. He had to laugh that it took someone childlike to drive home the same spiritual truths he had rejected so often in the past. Jed knew he was avoiding God and was afraid of what was hidden in the darkness of his heart. But he didn't know what it meant to invite Jesus in. It was all religious lingo to him, but he thought Rhonda would know. After all, she had been talking to Mary Beth about this stuff, and she was sure changing for the better. Jed smiled. Bubbles. That's what Casey said it felt like—and happy. Jed could use a little happy. He realized he was grinning.

It was already nine Pacific time, which was midnight in Baxter, and Jed wondered if it was fair to call Rhonda so late. He hadn't checked in today and was missing her. He knew she'd forgive the intrusion. He activated his phone, pulled up the address book, and pushed the button.

"Hello?" mumbled her sleepy voice.

"Hi, Babe, it's me." *Babe?* He was surprised he said it. He hadn't called Rhonda that in years.

"Jed! I've been worried. How are you?"

"I'm sorry. I wasn't where I could call easily. I can't explain, but I'm fine. How are things there?"

"Uh, they're fine. Yes, it's him." She whispered, sounding like her head was turned.

"Rhonda, is someone else there?"

"Jennifer's here for the weekend."

"Really? Is everything all right?"

"She's okay, Jed. We'll talk about it when you get home. Can you tell me anything more, or are we going to talk in circles again?"

"Well, you know. Round and round and round he goes. Where he stops, only Jed knows."

Rhonda chuckled. "Cute, Jed. Real cute."

"I can't say anything else about the Mike situation. But I met this kid. He got me thinking about all sorts of things, kind of like the stuff you and Mary Beth talk about. Can't explain it over the phone. But I've got a lot to tell you too. I'll save it until I get back."

"Any idea when that will be?" she asked.

"None. Right now don't count on less time than what I originally planned on. Uh…Rhonda, I may not be calling you for a few days after this. I can't explain, but I may need to drop out completely for a while. I don't want you to get worried if I don't call. Maybe you and Mary Beth can keep praying for me. I wouldn't mind."

"We've prayed for your protection all along, even asked for angels to watch over you. Do you know God does that, Jed—sends angels?"

"Uh, that's what I've been hearing."

"What do you mean?"

"Oh, nothing. Well, I guess I'll be going then."

There was a long, awkward pause.

"I love you," said Jed at exactly the same time as Rhonda.

There was another long pause.

"Uh…good night, Babe. See you soon."

"I can hardly wait until you're back. Be really careful, Jed."

"Yeah, I will. You take care too."

THIRTY-FIVE

J ed traveled north on I-5 and decided to drive until he got sleepy. He was wound up after his good-bye with Casey and his close encounter with Rhonda. But it was time to shift gears.

He had a massive maze in front of him. With no more to go on than Sean McConnell's interpretation of the note, Jed's finding Mike would take time—if he could find him at all.

His plan was to drive to Olympic National Park and start making inquiries about the location of Cedar Falls Mill. He had no idea how vast an area that might encompass.

Jed was deep in thought when the ringing of his cell phone nearly sent him into a ditch. What if it was the FBI? But what if it was Rhonda? She was the only one who ever called him on the cell phone.

"Hello."

"Jed? Jed Wilson? The same Jed Wilson who once walked a mile in my shoes?"

"Mike! Is that really you? Tell me what kind of shoes they were."

"Those rattlesnake boots were a size eleven. How are you?"

Jed laughed. "It's great to hear your voice! I'm fine. The question is, how are you?"

"Lousy, Jed. Really lousy. Things are coming down around me, and I'm not sure what to do. I found a note with your cell phone

number on it and debated whether or not to call you. My dad said you were on your way up here."

"I've been on my way up there since Monday. I want to know what happened, but I want to hear it from you, Mike—nobody else. We can't talk specifics on this phone. The FBI tailed me out of Atlanta clear into Arkansas. I ditched them after that, but I'm pretty sure they can pick up this signal. We can't stay on long, but let me ask some questions. Don't get real specific. Let's figure out a code like you did on paper with you-know-who. Understand?"

"Loud and clear."

"Okay, did you find FDR?"

"Yep. Same old guy."

"Are you with him now?"

"No."

"Can you give me a hint where you are?"

"Jed, the FBI already knows where I am. I called Pop this afternoon from a pay phone in Doonesbury, Washington. His phone must've been tapped because right after that I overheard two guys in the park who I'm sure were FBI. I don't know what to do, but I can't stay on this phone. I don't know what their capabilities are, but if they're picking up your signal, maybe they can track me from that. For all I know, they might be watching me right now."

"Mike, we've got to talk. I need to see you. I'm not that far away. Tell me where. When. Think fast, man. There's got to be a way."

"How about in front of FDR's. I'll be *milling* around. What time can you get there, Jed?"

"Uh, how about tomorrow, at the same time we always split a Snickers?"

"Great, that'll work. If you get there first, Jed, wait for me. I'll have to hitch a ride or do some walking, so I can't control the time exactly. You won't be able to recognize me. How will I recognize you? Are you in your usual vehicle?"

Jed paused to think. "Mike, listen carefully. When Johnny

Holcomb traded his old Ford, do you remember what he got that he was so proud of?"

"Yeah, I do. Is that how I'll know you?"

"Uh-huh. Only it's a darker shade with out-of-state plates."

"All right, Jed. Be sure they're not tailing you. I'll see you out front at FDR's. The ol' boy might be open on Sunday, so be careful."

"Wait! Mike, don't hang up. I know what FDR is, but not exactly where it is. You-know-who didn't remember how to find it."

"All right, listen up. It's on the highway, eight miles west of…okay, remember the bartender who was at O'Brian's when we first started going there? He went by his last name. Six letters, Jed. Think…"

"Yeah, I remember!"

"Okay, I'll be out in front of FDR's, eight miles west on the highway that runs through the town with the bartender's name—at the time we used to split a Snickers. Are you following me, Jed?"

"I think so. Yeah, I got it, Mike. Now get out of there before they find you. Go!"

Jed turned off his cell phone. His heart was pounding. He watched every set of headlights in his rearview mirror. He probably shouldn't have called Rhonda. Since the FBI was monitoring Mike, it was reasonable to assume they were monitoring him too. They probably tracked his location every time his cell phone was activated, meaning they knew he was on Interstate 5 headed north. The only advantage he had was the FBI didn't know what vehicle he was driving. He hoped.

Jed decided to pull off the interstate, maybe find a motel somewhere off the beaten path, and give himself some time to think his plan through. He guessed the only heart pumping faster than his was Mike McConnell's.

After Mike hung up the phone, he slid open the door of the phone booth and looked up and down the sidewalk. He didn't see anyone.

It was almost nine-thirty, which gave him a little more than twelve hours before his rendezvous with Jed. He began walking nonchalantly away from the phone booth, trying not to draw attention to himself. He didn't know where to go. It was drizzly and cold.

After walking three blocks, Mike slipped into a small, dimly lit café and sat at a table next to the front windows. There was only a handful of customers, all sitting close to a wood-burning stove in the rear.

The waitress took his order for the corned beef and cabbage special and black coffee. Soon the warmth of the café offered a sense of safety, and Mike felt less tense. He was grateful for a place to get the chill off before he started his walk toward the main highway to hitch a ride back to Harper's Grove. He thought about Jed and how good it would be to see him tomorrow. But Mike still had to figure out where to sleep tonight. With the FBI this close, he'd have to be crazy to go back to Evergreen Cottages.

Thirty minutes later, he left the café. He surveyed his surroundings and didn't see anyone who looked suspicious or any parked vehicles that hinted of FBI surveillance. He proceeded on foot toward the highway, annoyed that the afternoon's stress had zapped his strength. This was not a time to give in to it. He kept pushing.

After walking several blocks, Mike had an eerie feeling he was not alone. But after he left the downtown area and moved out in the open near the railroad tracks, he felt as conspicuous as an FBI wanted poster and began to walk briskly toward the old section of town, which looked deserted. He had a strong sense he was being stalked, and he was too exhausted to run. Mike walked as fast as he could and turned down the first street, looking for a place to disappear. He ducked into a recessed doorway under an awning that hung over a strip of storefronts. For a moment, he didn't breathe. Then he peeked out. He saw nothing but heard footsteps on the sidewalk. He pulled his head back into the shadows and stood with his body flush against the inside wall, to the left of the door.

The footsteps moved slowly and methodically and then paused. Mike stood plastered against the wall, his heart banging so loudly he was afraid the sound might give him away.

Jordan Ellis was ready to call it a night when his cell phone rang.

"Yeah."

"Sir, it's Morris again."

"What is it?"

"McConnell and Wilson just had a conversation. Looks like our Baxter boys have planned a little rendezvous for tomorrow."

"All right!" Jordan said. "Speak to me."

"Wilson's cell signal indicated he was north of Portland on Interstate 5 and was talking to McConnell, who's still in Doonesbury. They made up some personal code so we can't figure out what Wilson's driving or where they're meeting. Our agents in Doonesbury haven't found McConnell yet, but he's still there because he talked to Wilson a little while ago."

"Morris, you said they devised some kind of personal code. Like what?"

"They kept talking about FDR and splitting a Snickers—really weird stuff that makes no sense."

"I'm not letting two guys from Podunk outsmart the FBI. When are they meeting?"

"Uh, at whatever time they used to split a Snickers. Catchy, huh?"

"Does Special Agent Snyder know about this?"

"Yes, sir. He's right here. Heard the whole conversation."

"Put him on."

"This is Special Agent Snyder."

"Crack the code, Snyder. Call their employer. Talk to coworkers. Do whatever you have to do, but figure it out."

"Uh…sir, it's well after midnight, and tomorrow's Sunday. Half of Baxter will be in church an—"

"I can tell time, Snyder! Just do it. I don't care if you have to get people out of bed. Crack the stupid code and let's get McConnell. So what if you have to inconvenience a few folks in his hometown? After that picture in the morning paper, they want the creep as bad as we do. We're too close to lose him now. Am I making myself clear?"

"Perfectly, sir."

"And, Snyder, I'm holding you personally responsible for this one. Get the job done. Don't disappoint me. I'm counting on you."

"Yes, sir. I'll get back to you when we have something."

Sean hadn't moved. Ellen was sleepy, but she was awake, sitting in the chair next to his bed. They had enjoyed such a nice visit before Mike called. Ellen wondered if Sean had been holding on just until he said whatever he planned to say to his son.

"You know, Sean, I've grown very fond of you in a short period of time." She leaned over and kissed his forehead. "I never got along with my father. He objected to my entering the field of journalism. He's of the opinion that a woman should stay home and have babies and take care of her man. I did raise two sons and I've been devoted to Guy for twenty-five years. But I've never been able to repress the passion for reporting the news. It's who I am. My father still disapproves of me. And it still hurts."

She took Sean's hand, and her eyes filled with tears. She wasn't ready to let him go.

Mike McConnell's heart pounded like the wild, rhythmic beat of a tribal drum. A shadowy figure paused in front of the doorway, then slowly moved forward until Mike could see the flash of a big silver blade and an arrogant, threatening smile.

"You wanna die? Jus' cross me, man."

"What do you want?"

The voice laughed. "Whaddaya think I want? I want whatever you got. Now turn around, nice and slow, and put your hands against the door. Don't do nothin' stupid. This knife's been used before."

Mike turned around and leaned with his hands up against the door.

"Gimme your wallet!"

Mike felt the knife tip pressed against his back. With one hand he reached in and unzipped the inside pocket of his parka and removed the wallet. It contained $250 minus what he spent on dinner and on the phone call to Jed. He reached behind his back and handed it to the thief.

"Oh, looky here! Payday! Looks like a lotta bills in here, rich boy. All right, let's see what else you got. Empty your pockets. Just drop it all on the ground."

Mike reached in his zippered pocket again and pulled out everything he had—his room key, the note with Jed's cell phone number, and the leaflet he got from the young man in the park. He dropped them on the ground, furious that this creep was about to leave with almost a month's rent, and there was nothing he could do to stop him.

"Keep your hands on the door, rich boy. Let's just see if you're holdin' out on me." He patted Mike down.

In the next instant the mugger kicked Mike's feet out from under him, causing him to drop to the pavement. His attacker laughed, delivered several hard kicks, then ran into the dark night, leaving Mike doubled up in pain.

There were no headlights behind Jed's car. He double-checked his cell phone for the third time to be sure it was off. He went ten miles down some back highway and entered a dumpy little town called Howling. He saw a run-down motel with a vacancy sign lit. There were no cars parked in front of the rooms. From what Jed could see, that was its only appealing feature—that it was virtually deserted.

He pulled in and parked the Explorer. There appeared to be ten empty rooms at The Backwoods Lodge, which was surrounded by trees on three sides. He walked into the motel office and found the elderly manager snoozing next to a pint of peach brandy. Jed had to wake the old guy in order to pay for the room and get a key. It cost him fifteen dollars. Jed cringed to think what fifteen dollars might look like when he opened the door to his room.

The crunching sound of gravel under his tires seemed exaggerated as he pulled the Explorer in front of the room on the far left.

He grabbed his bag and walked up to the door of room one. He turned the key and pushed extra hard to get the warped door to open. He was met with an unpleasant musty smell. The room had orange shag carpet and dingy beige walls. The bedspread was some faded red fuzzy material that reminded him of Rhonda's bathrobe. The drapes were a hideous shade of turquoise. The overhead light was dim. Just as well. He decided ignorance was bliss.

He threw his bag on the bed and sat in a chair in the corner. He unfolded a map of Washington. He put on his half glasses and took a pen and marked his location on the map. He searched for Harper. No Harper, but he found a Harper's Grove, which looked to be about thirty-five miles from Doonesbury. That must be what Mike was trying to tell him. Jed traced his route for tomorrow's drive. He'd get up and be out of there by five-thirty. That should give him extra time for breakfast, and more than enough time to find Harper's Grove and be in place for the rendezvous at Cedar Falls Mill.

Jed got up from the chair and turned out the light. He walked over to the window and peeked through a crack in the drapes. He saw no one. He felt certain he hadn't been followed. The old windup clock read 10:23. There was still plenty of time to get a good night's sleep and be alert for whatever tomorrow would bring.

Jed set the alarm, slipped out of his jeans, and crawled under the covers. He lay there a while thinking about the day. So much had happened. After the adrenaline rush of Mike's call, Rhonda and Casey seemed far away. He wondered what it would be like to see Mike again. Jed had been through the entire gamut of emotions concerning Mike McConnell, but all that was behind him. He was going to be with his friend tomorrow, and Mike would set the record straight. He was starting to doze off....

Bang! A shot shattered the stillness. Jed's eyes flew wide open.

Bang! Bang!

Jed heard footsteps walking down the sidewalk in front of his room. They stopped. They started up again.

Bang!

He jumped out of bed, leaned against the wall, and pulled on his jeans. He looked out of a slit in the drapes and saw a shadow sneaking across the parking lot. He didn't know who was out there, but he couldn't believe the FBI would shoot at him. He never felt so defenseless in his life.

Bang!

He heard a male voice mumbling something, so he hid behind the door and strained to hear. His knees got weaker as the voice got closer to his door. The footsteps stopped again. Then he heard gravel crunching under someone's feet and feet running toward the tree line to the right of his door.

Bang!

There was silence. Jed heard footsteps shuffling toward his door. He grabbed the base of the pole lamp, pulled the plug, and tore off the shade. He stood behind the door, ready to take on any intruder.

"Dang coyotes!" a male voice shouted.

Jed looked out of the peephole in time to see the old manager in his long johns staggering toward the motel office, his rifle in hand.

Jed collapsed on the bed, trying to regain his composure. It was open season in Harper's Grove—only the one being hunted was Mike McConnell.

Mike lay in the recessed doorway for a few minutes. Finally he pulled himself up. His ribs were throbbing, his right leg hurt, but there didn't seem to be anything broken.

He found a puddle and used the water to wash the mud off his parka and his face. The cold water caused him to shiver. So much for staying warm. Mike bent down slowly and picked up his room key and the note with Jed's cell phone number and zipped them in the pocket of his parka.

A biting wind kicked up, and Mike pulled the hood over his head and tied it. He put his hands in his pockets and started walking. He noticed a piece of paper in the middle of the street, one end being blown up by the wind, the other flat on the pavement, as if someone had a foot on it. *How weird.* He picked it up and held it up to the streetlight. *A twenty-dollar bill? That creep must've dropped it.*

Mike planted a kiss on the twenty and carefully tucked it in the zippered pocket.

Present but unseen, the rugged man in hiking boots and a down jacket remained at Mike McConnell's side as his charge trudged toward the main highway, hoping to thumb a ride back to Harper's Grove.

THIRTY-SIX

al...Hal," Nancy whispered.

"Huh? What's wrong?" he asked.

"There's a man on the phone who needs to talk with you. He says he's from the highway department and that something weird is going on."

"What time is it?"

"It's one-thirty."

Hal took the phone. He cleared the cobwebs from his head, and then cleared his throat. "Hello, this is Sheriff Barker."

"Sheriff, this is Al Cuppertine. I don't know if you remember me or not. I'm the supervisor at the highway department. Mike McConnell worked for me. You interviewed me as part of your investigation in the explosion."

"I remember. What's the problem, Mr. Cuppertine? It's late."

"Yeah, I'm sorry to bother you, but the FBI just left here. They came banging on my door at one-fifteen in the morning asking me what time Jed Wilson and Mike McConnell used to split a Snickers. Is that not weird? They were polite enough, but they were evasive. As far as I'm concerned, they were invasive too. What gives them the right to do that—get me and my wife out of bed in the middle of the night?"

"Did you know the answer to the question?" Hal asked.

"Sure. Ten in the morning. That's when the guys took a break."

"Then that's what gave them the right, Mr. Cuppertine. This is a murder investigation. We may be close to arresting Mike and getting him back here. The FBI has its reasons for inconveniencing you. I'm sorry it was so late, but for some reason, they needed to know the answer tonight. Did they say why?"

"Sheriff, these guys don't tell you anything. They politely walk in, ask the question, get the answer, and apologize for the inconvenience."

"Mr. Cuppertine, if I were you, I'd go back to bed now and not give it any more thought."

"That's it? Just forget it?"

"Unless you have a better idea, that seems like it'll get you the most sleep. You did your civic duty. If you told them the truth, I'd just go back to bed."

"Well, of course I told them the truth…. Okay, Sheriff. Sorry I woke you up. I don't have any experience with this kind of thing."

"No problem."

Hal hung up the phone. He rolled over next to Nancy.

"What was that all about?" she asked, sounding half asleep.

"I'm not sure, but sounds like Jordan is on a roll. We're getting really close to Mike. Go back to sleep, honey."

Hal went downstairs and sat in his recliner, amused that Mr. Cuppertine had apologized for waking him. It had become a routine part of Hal's weekend that his home had become like a second workplace.

At 2:05, the phone rang.

"Hello, Sheriff Barker."

"Sheriff, this is Cliff Hodges, the manager down at O'Brian's. I'm sorry if I woke you up."

"Actually, you didn't. What can I do for you?"

"Two guys from the FBI were just here, questioning my regulars and my bartender. Do you know what that's all about? I run a clean establishment. I've never been cited for anything. Why are the feds nosing around here?"

"What questions were they asking, Cliff?"

"A lot of questions about Jed Wilson and Mike McConnell, but mostly wanting to know the name of a bartender who worked here years ago and always went by his last name."

"Well, did they get their answer?"

"Sure. Just about everyone down here knew it was Harper. He always went by his last name."

"Then it seems the FBI got what they were looking for."

"Sheriff, what's going on? I don't like all this mystery. What's the big secret?"

"Cliff, the FBI has a whole bagful of secrets. They don't tell us because it doesn't concern us while they're trying to nail somebody. I suspect they're on to Mike McConnell and had a reason for asking the question. I'd close up and forget about it."

"All right, Sheriff. I just thought it was really odd. Nothing like that has happened down here before."

"Cliff, we've never had a murder in Baxter before."

At 2:31, the phone rang again.

"This is the sheriff."

"Sheriff, this is Margie Jorgensen down at the newspaper. I'm sorry to wake you, but we were working on tomorrow's edition when the FBI showed up here asking a bunch of questions. Ellen is in Atlanta for the weekend, and I wasn't sure what to do. They wanted to see every feature story written about anyone related to the McConnell investigation. I got out back issues of those papers and turned them over. I hope I did the right thing. I felt a little intimidated."

"They were polite, weren't they?"

"Very. Almost to a fault."

"Did they say what they were looking for?"

"Not really, but when they saw the feature on Sean McConnell, the two agents looked at each other and smiled. One of them said,

'Bingo.' I don't understand FBI lingo."

Hal smiled. "Margie, did the men show you their badges?"

"Oh yes. They were FBI. I'm convinced of that."

"Well then, you did everything right. Whatever they were look-ing for, they must've had a reason to go searching in the middle of the night for it. Maybe they're closing in on Mike McConnell and needed something in one of those features."

"Maybe so, but their showing up like that was unsettling—especially with Ellen gone. She leaves me in charge, you know."

"I'm sure they apologized?"

"Well, yes. They did."

"Margie, sounds like you handled it just fine."

"Thank you, Sheriff. I feel better about it now. I think I'll get back to work. Good night."

"Good night, Margie."

Jordan Ellis's cell phone rang.

"Yeah, it's Jordan."

"Sir, it's Snyder."

"Snyder, this better be good. It's three-thirty in the morning."

"The best, sir. We think we've cracked the code our Baxter boys devised."

"Let's hear it."

"The long version or the short version?"

"Give me something in between," said Jordan, still half asleep.

"Okay, we talked to their supervisor at the highway depart-ment. They split a Snickers at 10:00 A.M.—that's when the guys took a break. The bartender's name was Harper. There's no Harper, but there's a Harper's Grove, Washington, about thirty-five miles from Doonesbury. Now this is the really good one, sir. Are you ready?"

Jordan was wide awake now. "Go."

"We talked with some guys at O'Brian's, a local bar where

McConnell and Wilson hung out. Several people told us that FDR was mentioned in a feature story written by the editor of the local paper, some lady named Ellen Jones. So we went down to the newspaper building and talked to the woman in charge. We got copies of back issues with feature stories relating to the case, and there was one written last Monday on McConnell's old man. Seems he made a cedar chest for FDR. You know, President Roosevelt— back in the old days. We tried to make a connection between FDR, the cedar chest, and Harper's Grove. Get this: There's an old mill eight miles west of Harper's Grove called Cedar Falls Mill. The way we figure it, our boys are meeting at ten tomorrow morning at Cedar Falls Mill eight miles west of Harper's Grove. How's that for cracking the code?"

"Excellent! What about Wilson's car—what's he driving?"

"That's the only part of the code we haven't cracked yet. No one here has ever heard of a Johnny Holcomb. We'll stay on this, but at least we know exactly where and when. I thought you'd want to know."

"Good job, Snyder. Keep on it until you find out what Wilson's driving. Our agents will be waiting to ambush Wilson and McConnell. We'll beat them at their own game."

Jordan hung up and dialed Hal's number.

"Hello."

"Sorry to wake you, Sheriff, it's Jordan."

"You didn't wake me. I'm sitting here waiting for your call."

"Oh yeah?"

Hal chuckled. "Seems your boys caused quite a stir among the locals. I've had a few calls. What's the deal?"

"McConnell called Wilson."

"So that's what this is about?"

"Well, let me tell you how it's going down...."

THIRTY-SEVEN

M ike watched the truck's tail lights slowly disappear in the ground fog. It had taken him a long time to hitch a ride from Doonesbury, and this was as far as his ride could take him—where the main highway and the road to Harper's Grove intersect. He'd walk the rest of the way, though his ribs were throbbing and his back and leg were stiff and sore.

As Mike trudged through the misty fog, he was watchful of his surroundings. The woods were close to the road, and when he saw approaching headlights reflected in the fog, he hid behind a tree until the vehicle passed. When he entered Harper's Grove, he saw nothing out of the ordinary but decided to take the back way to Calvary Community Church, cutting through yards and avoiding streetlights.

Mike remembered seeing a rusty, worn-out lock on one of the basement windows at the church. He hoped he could work it loose and crawl down there for the night. If he got caught, he would just say he was employed there and had lost his room key, couldn't get in at Evergreen Cottages and didn't have anywhere else to go. At worst, he would suggest Pastor Don be called. The pastor liked Mark McNeil and would never press charges.

He moved stealthily in the darkness and continued to look around him in all directions until he arrived at the church. The sound of a dog barking alerted him that he needed to move quickly. Mike slipped around to the back of the old church and found the basement window he was looking for, pleased to find it hidden from view by a large evergreen tree. He slipped in behind the tree and squatted down. He jiggled the frame of the wood window then pounded it with his palms. After several good jabs, he felt the lock give way. The window was hinged at the top. Mike pushed it open from the bottom and slid down through the opening, letting go of the window as he dropped to the basement floor. He landed feetfirst, just as the window slammed against the casing. He paused for a moment to let every muscle in his forty-six-year-old just-mugged body groan.

The basement was cold and damp and black as coal, but it was the most welcomed place he could think of. No one would find him down there. Pastor Don never came down in the basement, and Carlos wouldn't be back until Wednesday afternoon.

Mike shuffled slowly across the pitch-black basement in the direction of the workbench. He bumped into a ladder and kicked an empty mop bucket. He continued on with his arms held out in front of him until he felt the familiar shelving. Then steadying himself against the sturdy structure, he let his hands be his eyes, moving them over to the first drawer, then down to the second, and down to the third. He slid that drawer open, put his hand around the flashlight and turned it on. Fortunately the basement windows had been painted. No one outside would see the flashlight beam moving in the dark.

The basement had a tiny bathroom with a crude toilet and sink. On a cart next to the workbench sat a coffeepot with everything he needed to make coffee once the breaker switches were turned back on. A fresh package of Fig Newtons was stashed next to the cups and might be all he had to eat tomorrow.

Mike shone the beam of light in the tool closet and grabbed some paint tarps and a stack of hand towels. He spread the tarps under the stairwell and crawled on top. He turned on his back, spread another tarp over him and pulled it up to his neck. He placed the hand towels under his head and turned off the flashlight.

Mike lay in the thick darkness, listening to the sounds of the ancient basement. He was spent. Every muscle in his body hurt. Worst of all, his soul hurt. How could his life have come to this?

THIRTY-EIGHT

A
t five-thirty on Sunday morning, Jed drove out of Howling. He winced when he passed the sign, suddenly realizing the implication of the town's name. The coyote incident had left him unable to drop off to sleep until after midnight.

Jed felt an urgency to call Sean McConnell and let him know what was going on. He spotted a pay phone next to a service station that was closed and decided not to risk using his cell phone. He pulled in and got out his phone card, then decided against using it. He reached into his mound of change and got out of the car to place the call.

"Hello, Sean McConnell's room. This is Ellen."

"Uh…Ellen who?"

"This is Ellen Jones. Who's speaking, please?"

"Oh…Ellen! I wasn't expecting you to answer. This is Jed Wilson. I'm trying to reach Mr. McConnell. I called the nursing home and they gave me this number. May I please speak to him?"

"Jed, there's something going on here I can't discuss, but Sean can't come to the phone."

"Listen, I only have about forty-five seconds. This is urgent. I really need to talk to him."

Ellen heard the tension in Jed's voice. "What's the urgency? Oh my…Jed, are you with Mike McConnell?"

"Ellen, I can't say. I need to talk to Mr. McConnell. Will you please put him on?"

"Sean's very ill. He's taken a turn for the worst. Jed, you need to get a message to Mike. I'm not sure he…I'm not sure he's going to make it. He's been in a mild coma since Mike talked to him yesterday afternoon. It doesn't look good. If Mike wants to see him, he's going to have to come back here."

"Ellen, that's impossible! The FBI is all over both of us!"

"The FBI?"

"Listen. I've got to hang up. Your phone is tapped and I don't want them knowing where I am. I'll call back in a few minutes." *Click.*

Ellen paced back and forth, waiting for Jed to call back. She could hardly believe she had been so oblivious. How and when had Sean talked to Jed? What was their plan? Where was Mike? Her being this close to a story and not knowing the facts was about as maddening as anything could be.

Ellen took Sean's hand and held it to her cheek. "I'm so sorry you had to bear this by yourself."

Sean didn't feel her warm teardrops against his skin. He was still trapped somewhere between worlds, and she couldn't reach him.

Mike McConnell turned on the flashlight and looked at his watch. 3:28? It felt like he'd been lying down much longer than three hours. He struggled to get up from the basement floor. He moaned. Everything hurt.

He walked to the tool closet and picked up the step stool, carried it to the window, and climbed up. He pushed the basement window open and saw daylight.

What time was it? He felt panicked. The evergreen tree blocked most of the light, and fog made it impossible to tell the position of the sun. He didn't hear voices or footsteps upstairs, which meant it wasn't eight-thirty yet.

And he hadn't missed his meeting with Jed.

Mike climbed back down and leaned against the wall. By the time of their meeting, the feds would have had twelve hours to work on cracking their code. Did he dare take a chance?

Mike felt compelled to change the plan. It didn't seem smart to meet at Cedar Falls Mill. He had no idea what time it was, but he had to get word to Jed.

Jordan Ellis had done little more than doze all night. Things were going down fast. He heard his phone ringing for the tenth time this morning.

"Yeah, this is Jordan."

"Jordan, it's Special Agent Harlan Smith, calling you from beautiful downtown Doonesbury."

"Harlan? You old goat! We haven't talked since the Remington case in Seattle. Please tell me you're working the McConnell case."

"Yep—head honcho of the Northwest. That's why I called. Listen, my agents have surveillance around Doonesbury, Harper's Grove, Cedar Falls Mill, and the main thoroughfares connecting in and out. We also have a roadblock set up on the main artery into Harper's Grove. Wilson and McConnell have to go that way to get to the old mill. Even if they spot the roadblock and opt out, we'll see them. They can't get away from us. One way or another, they're as good as got."

Jordan chuckled. "Same old spirit, I see."

"Hey, watch that *old* stuff. And when are you going to tell us what Wilson's driving? It might help to know what we're looking for." Harlan laughed.

Jordan didn't. "I've been asking myself that same question all night. My agents cracked the code—except for Wilson's vehicle. Right now, we still don't know. Burns me. Going in half right is still going in half wrong."

"Well, lighten up, Jordan. Either way, we're going in. But not to worry, I'm going to get the job done for you."

"Thanks, Harlan. I'm glad you're so optimistic because you owe me one, remember?"

"Like you'd let me forget. So, how do you want this *pomme de terre*—mashed or french fried?"

"Oh, let's not get too dramatic. How about you leave the peel on and just deliver it hot? I'll take it from there."

Mike McConnell poked his head out of the basement window and didn't see anyone. He pulled himself up and crawled out.

The pain was excruciating. He paused for a moment behind the evergreen tree and thought he was going to throw up. After taking a few deep breaths, Mike decided he didn't have time to give in to it and began walking defiantly up the gradual slope behind the church.

At the top was a narrow road that came to a dead end at the back of the churchyard. A half mile down the road was a log grocery store that Mike hoped was open this early on Sunday.

He remembered seeing a pay phone outside the grocery. All he had was a twenty-dollar bill, and a lot of good it would do him in a pay phone. Mike started walking down the road and soon realized he was favoring his right leg. He didn't need a watch to tell him the clock was ticking.

Jed was headed straight up Interstate 5. He had decided not to call Ellen back. Too risky. The closer he got to Harper's Grove, the more nervous he felt. He had one mission, and one mission only—to meet with Mike McConnell.

Jed reached to turn on the radio and was shocked—then horrified—by the ringing of his cell phone. Had he left the phone on by mistake?

"Uh—hello," he said.

"Jed, it's me, Mike. How close are you?"

"I'm not sure, maybe thirty minutes ahead of schedule."

"Okay, listen up. I'm going to talk fast. Abort the first plan. Got that? Forget what we agreed on. We're going to plan *B*."

"All right. What now?"

"Remember when Johnny Holcomb was after the men who stole his brother's motorcycle? Do you remember where he crashed when he was chasing them…? Hello, Jed, you still there?"

"Yeah. Sorry, Mike, I'm drawing a blank."

"It was an establishment, Jed. A very specific type."

"Oh yeah—initials MG, right?"

"Yes! Now, Mrs. Armister's dog…do you remember his name?"

"Yeah, Mike, that one I remember."

"All right. Do you remember what we used to say about Lester—that he was *blank?* You fill in the word. Fill in the blank."

"I remember!" Jed said.

"Okay, put it together. Here's where I'll meet you: one-half mile east of an establishment like the one where Johnny Holcomb wiped out, at a location having a name that's a combination of Mrs. Armister's dog and what we used to say about Lester. Go through it in your mind, Jed. Does it make sense? This is the only chance I've got to call you. Have you got it?"

"Got it, Mike. I'll be there by the time you split a Snickers."

"Wish I could say it outright, Jed, but I have a sense they're closing in. I really need to see you. Get here, man. Now get off the phone." *Click.*

Jed felt a flood of adrenaline. He turned off his cell phone then double-checked to make sure it was off this time.

Jed took the next exit, turned right at the stop sign, and pulled off onto the shoulder. He got out his map and looked for Dusty Hollow. It wasn't listed. He looked again. His heart was racing. No Dusty Hollow. Rats!

He made a U-turn and took the ramp back up to the interstate. There were no cars behind him. He looked again to be sure his cell phone was turned off. He shook his head. How could he have made such a careless mistake? Oh well, it worked out for the best this time.

The old man in a red cap and baseball jacket was present, but unseen, and was in no way hindered by the limitations of earthly technology. His instructions were clear: Remove all obstacles.

Mike devoured two sausage muffins and downed a large bottle of orange juice on the way back to the church. He had also bought a bottle of Advil and a Snickers. He was almost out of money.

When he reached the back of the churchyard, he stopped and looked down from the road. People were starting to arrive for the early service. He guessed it must be between eight and eight-thirty.

He hobbled down the slope and slipped behind the evergreen tree, opened the window and dropped down to the basement. He grimaced. Even though the Advil had kicked in, his injuries were going to play hardball.

When Mike looked up, he realized the basement was light. The breaker switches had been turned on. He went into the tiny bathroom and turned on the hot water, then took off his parka and peeled off the rest of the layers above his waist. He was surprised at the amount of bruising around his ribs and knew his leg probably looked the same. He'd like to take a swing at the creep!

Mike stood over the sink and cringed at the sorry reflection staring back at him in the mirror. The creature's hair was wild, and he needed a shave. The mirrored cabinet was slightly ajar. He opened it and was surprised to find a razor, shaving cream, after-shave, soap, deodorant, a bottle of mouthwash, and a hairbrush. This stuff wasn't in here yesterday! Carlos must have put it there.

He used the bar of soap to wash his hair and body. He dried off with the same towels that had been his pillow the night before. The hot water kept him from becoming chilled as he stood there shaving. When he finished, he dried his face and hands, then squatted in front of the space heater and combed his fingers through his hair until it was dry.

When he stood up, he looked and felt much better. Without his parka, he didn't even look that bad. At least his shirt and jeans looked clean.

Mike heard the sound of organ music upstairs, and something in him stirred. When the singing started, he crept up the stairs and tried the door. It was still locked. He went back downstairs and crawled out the window.

THIRTY-NINE

M ike McConnell walked through the main door of Calvary Community Church, donning a big smile and with a handshake ready and waiting.

"Good morning, and welcome to Calvary Community," said the greeter, offering his hand. "Glad to have you with us this morning. My name's Greg Loftin."

"Mark McNeil. Pleased to meet you, Greg."

Mike spotted an empty seat in the back pew and sat next to a young couple that returned his smile.

The organ began to play "Amazing Grace." Once again, Mike liked the way it made him feel. As the choir sang, he listened to the words, "Amazing grace, how sweet the sound that saved a wretch like me. I once was lost, but now am found, was blind, but now I see...."

When the singing stopped, his attention was directed to Pastor Don, who looked straight at him, then nodded and smiled.

"Good morning. I'm glad for each and every person gathered here this morning. It's no accident you're here. God drew you. No matter how you got here, God was behind it. He's sovereign. Nothing escapes His notice, amen? And no one, no matter how lost he thinks he is, is outside of His infinite plan. You see, God has a plan for your life. Now some of you are rolling your eyes. Some are chuckling. Some are just plain skeptical. Others of you are painfully quiet. You wonder how God could have a plan for your life. You've messed up. You've even done some things that are so horrendous, so despicable that they're outside of God's ability to forgive. You don't deserve to be forgiven.

"Well, let me agree with you right off the bat. You surely don't. None of us deserves to be forgiven. I want you to think right now about the most secret sin in your life. You know, the one you hide from everyone else. The one that makes your heart ache or makes you blush. The one that would break your heart if put on the front page of every newspaper in America. The one you have a horror of it ever getting out. Have you identified the one I'm talking about? You know what it is. So can we agree that none of us deserves forgiveness? Well now, that's the bad news.

"The good news is there's nothing we can do to earn it anyway. Grace is unmerited favor, and that's what Jesus Christ has offered all people. It's free. It's available. But it's a choice. It's the only thing you can take with you when you take your last breath, and it will determine where you spend all eternity.

"Sometimes I wonder when we'll get it through our thick heads that Jesus did it all. It's finished. He paid the price. He did the time. Our verdict is guilty, but our sentence has already been served. People, when we accept the completed work of God's Son on the cross, we get to go free! Can you say 'amen'?"

Mike had never heard this message put quite this way before. He felt as guilty of murder as anyone could. Because of his stupidity and mistakes, four people were dead. Was Pastor Don actually saying his eternal sentence could be removed? Forgiven? Mike McConnell expected to spend eternity in hell. He had it coming. That's why he was afraid to die.

"This morning I want to introduce a special guest. This man spent thirty years in prison for the stabbing death of a coworker. He's been to hell and back—not literally, though the flames of guilt and despair nearly consumed him. He tried twice to take his own life. He had a nervous breakdown. His wife divorced him. His parents disowned him. His friends deserted him. He was a man with no hope. His story is one of grace. It's about the unlovable being loved. It's about a tender God staying with him every day of his life until he could accept what had been his all along: forgiveness and grace. Unmerited favor. Being loved when you don't deserve it. That kind of grace melts people's hearts. That kind of love turns even murderers into willing vessels for God. God doesn't make junk, people—we do. But He can take whatever mess we've made of ourselves and fashion it into something that puts a smile on His face. That's what happened to our guest. His deep understanding of grace has blessed me. Listen carefully. You're in for a real treat. People, please welcome Donovan MacGruder."

Jordan Ellis was reading the Sunday paper, his cell phone not more than an arm's length away. With Harlan Smith handling things on the Washington end, he figured McConnell was as good as in the bag. His cell phone rang.

"It's Mark Snyder. We've got a problem." He sounded tired.

"What problem?" Jordan said.

"McConnell called Wilson. Our Baxter duo has pulled a switcheroo, and we're not sure where to go from here."

"Snyder, don't tell me that!"

"Sir, Agent Morris picked up Wilson's cell phone signal and placed his location at more than halfway to Harper's Grove. The problem is their rendezvous point has been changed and so has the code. They switched to plan *B* and we have no idea what the code means now."

"So get out there and figure it out, Snyder! You know how to do it."

"We've already been working on it, sir. The problem is, no one we've talked to in Baxter recognizes the references this time. I think the guys got wise and pulled a number on us. Truthfully, sir, we may not be able to crack it."

"Crack it. I don't care how you do it, just do it!"

"All right, sir. We're still on it. I understand Harlan Smith has surveillance on all the main arteries and a roadblock set up on the main highway into Harper's Grove. Maybe Wilson will walk right into it."

"No, we're right back to square one," Jordan said. "I'm going to tell Harlan to get rid of the roadblock. Wilson is our only ticket to McConnell, and we can't afford to scare him off. But I need to know what he's driving, got that? And, Snyder, I don't want to wait all day! Do you hear me?"

"Okay, sir. You got it."

"God had been knocking on my door for many years. I just never answered it."

Mike McConnell's eyes widened. Donovan MacGruder had his undivided attention.

"You see, God knew me before I was ever born. He knew exactly how many steps He had for me to take. None of them was wasted, not a one. He already knew the mistakes I'd make, the sins I'd commit—even the ones I called unforgivable. He knew I'd lose my temper and stab Stan Martin to death. He knew I'd try to kill myself. He knew that I'd never understand how much He loved me without His help. But He loved me anyway, whether I understood or not, whether I chose to accept Him or not. He knocked on my door for thirty-five years—whether I answered it or not.

"Then one night, when I was so consumed with guilt and despair that I felt like the flames of hell had already found me, I opened that door, and His love and forgiveness poured into my heart. Me, Donovan MacGruder, imprisoned for murder, deemed unfit to live in society, yet forgiven and accepted by God! Set free from eternal condemnation, not because I deserve it, but because Jesus ended it at the cross and said it is finished. That's grace!"

The speaker paused to regain his composure. "Friends, understand something. I was raised in a home where I was taken to church. I was taught right from wrong. I knew about Jesus. I just didn't really know Him. I never understood grace, that wonderful unmerited favor that it won't do you any good to work for because you'll never be good enough. Our goodness comes through Jesus taking our place. He died so we can live. He took our sin, so we could take His righteousness. Because of His sacrifice on the cross, our Father in heaven looks at us as if we had never sinned. You see, we can't do it. We can't be good enough. We can't give enough money or say enough prayers or go to enough church services.

"Many of us think that if we aren't all that bad, then we must be good enough. The Bible says we aren't. No one is good enough. It's Christ's sacrifice on the cross that bought us our worthiness. It was no different for Mother Teresa, Princess Diana, or Jeffrey Dahmer: There's only one way to forgiveness, to heaven and to God, and that's through His Son Jesus Christ. The Bible says there is only one name under heaven by which we must be saved, and that's Jesus Christ. Folks, if you want to get there, He's the only way.

"If there's anyone here today that hasn't answered that knock and made the choice to open his heart to the Son of God who purchased him with His own blood, don't leave here today without setting things right. God loves you. There's nothing you could have done that could make Him not love you. But you need to invite Him in. You need to turn from the sin in your life and let Him change you. I'll be up here to pray with you. It's a choice, and only you can make it."

Mike knew what it was to be loved by his dad, so understanding the love of his Heavenly Father wasn't that big a stretch. The thing he had to reconcile in his mind was Jesus. The One who took the punishment for his affair, for his years of neglecting Rose and the kids, for his foolish gambling that lost Rose's dream money, and for his irresponsible drinking that ultimately caused his family to die such a horrible death. That was an awful lot of black for a King to wear. Mike wondered if he could heap anything so ugly onto the Son of God. But something inside him was ready to trust Jesus with his life.

❦

Jed steered with one hand and held the map with the other. He was getting more nervous by the minute. It was nine o'clock, and he still had no idea where to find Dusty Hollow.

He noticed the car was steering funny, pulling hard to the right. He sighed with disgust and pulled off at the next exit, his eyes peeled for any sign of company. As far as he could tell, he wasn't being tailed.

He pulled into a service station and went inside.

"Could someone here check a tire for me real quick? I think I'm getting a flat. I'm supposed to meet a friend who's going to be stranded if I'm late."

The young mechanic looked at the Missouri plates and smiled.

"I'm sure I can fix you up. Pull it right in here."

Jed pulled the Explorer into the garage and stood nearby as the mechanic checked the tire for leaks.

"Mister, when's the last time you checked your air pressure?" he asked.

"I don't know. Seems like it's been fine."

"Well, the only thing wrong with this tire is that it needs some major air. Fill this puppy's lungs back up, and it'll be as good as new."

Jed couldn't imagine why that one tire was so low or why it came on suddenly.

"Nice SUV you got there. Guess you're taking it down to Dusty Hollow to hit the off-road trails?"

Jed perked up. "Actually I am looking for Dusty Hollow. Can you tell me how to find it?"

"Sure, look way over there." The young mechanic pointed off in the distance. "See the sign?"

Jed turned and squinted. "No. Where?"

"Right down there to the left of that billboard. That's Dusty Hollow Road."

"Oh yeah, I see it now."

"It goes up through the woods for miles. Not much on that road except Dusty Hollow and the forestland owned by private investors and realtors. The road dead-ends at some old church in a little town called Harper's Grove."

"Is there a log grocery on this road?"

"Uh-huh. On the other end."

"That's what I'm looking for." Jed's pulse was racing.

"The road got its name because it used to be gravel. But now that it's paved, the only dust flying is from the four-wheelers pounding those trails. Right now with all this rain, there's more mud than dust. But man, there's some great off-road action waiting for you."

"Looks like I stopped at the right place. How much do I owe you?"

"Not a thing. Have a blast out there."

"I sure didn't expect you to check the tire for free."

"Hey, welcome to Washington," said the grinning mechanic. "If you like rain, you came to the right place. Enjoy the mud."

"Thanks a lot. You made my day." Jed couldn't believe his luck. He thought maybe Rhonda was praying.

Invisibly present, the old man in a red cap and baseball jacket stood with Jed. He knew the Master, the mission, and the man. What he didn't know was the outcome.

Jed turned onto Dusty Hollow Road. It was already nine-fifteen. In his rearview mirror, he spotted a Jeep coming at a fast rate of speed. He accelerated and waited to see what would happen.

The Jeep came right up to his bumper. Jed saw two men. They had long hair and wore leather jackets. These guys were climbing his bumper, honking, flashing their lights, and waving their arms.

They acted like they were on something.

Jed hit the accelerator. The Explorer wasn't exactly a Corvette, but it was impressive enough at the moment.

The Jeep stayed right on his tail, driver and passenger yelling and waving their arms. Jed didn't know how much longer he could continue speeding around these curves on this unfamiliar road.

All at once the Jeep pulled up on his left. Jed assumed he was about to be shot or run off the road into a ravine. He looked straight ahead and avoided eye contact. *What are these guys on? They're nuts!*

He decided to take his foot off the gas and fall back. When he did, the Jeep went ahead of him and slowed. Anytime Jed tried to pass, the Jeep moved to the left and blocked his access. They were slowing to a stop. Jed's heart was in his throat as the men climbed out of the Jeep.

He sat there as the men knocked on the glass and waved something in front of the window. They motioned for him to roll it down. Jed shook his head. They knocked on the window again. Jed didn't see a gun, so he didn't budge.

Finally one of the men shrugged in frustration and pushed something against the windshield in front of Jed's face. "Mister, you dropped your wallet!"

Jed felt embarrassment color his face. He opened the window.

"You guys nearly gave me a heart attack!"

"Sorry. You dropped your wallet back at the station, and since you're from out of town, we figured you'd be really stranded without it. Didn't mean to scare you. Didn't you see us waving it in the air?"

"I had no idea what you were doing. My imagination was working overtime. I really would've been stranded without it, though. That's no joke."

"Yeah, we thought so," the driver said. "Have a nice day."

"Hey, thanks, guys. You went to an awful lot of trouble to get this back to me. Sorry for the chase."

The two men got back in the Jeep, made a U-turn, and left. Jed sat there for a moment, his heart still pounding. Okay, he'd try this again. Mike would be waiting.

Suddenly, he was amused at how ridiculous the last few minutes must have looked. He pulled back on Dusty Hollow Road, a broad grin claiming his face. "McConnell, you're going to get a kick out of this one."

Mike watched a half dozen people get up and go forward to make their profession of faith. He wanted to go. All of it made sense to him. He glanced back at the clock. It was already nine-forty-five!

Mike grabbed his parka and headed out the door. When he walked behind the church and started up the slope, Pastor Don's words about grace came rushing back to him. *It's the only thing you can take with you when you take your last breath, and it will determine where you spend all eternity.*

He looked down at his watch and realized for the hundredth time today it didn't work. Time stood still. Mike looked up at the road and back at the church. If he was willing to trust God with his life, surely he could trust Him to take care of Jed.

"Harlan, have you spotted Wilson yet?" Jordan Ellis asked.

"No. We're checking every out-of-state plate that comes up Highway 101 Alternate. Of course, it would help if we had a clue what vehicle we were looking for. Has Agent Snyder cracked any of the code? Do you have any idea at all where their rendezvous is taking place? Look at the time, Jordan. We're out of it!"

"Yeah, Harlan, believe me, I know! Unless they're getting divine intervention, there's no way they can get by your spotters. Keep your people in place. Wilson's got to go up 101 Alternate. He doesn't have a choice."

FORTY

J ed pulled up to the log grocery store, nervous that he was late. He turned the Explorer around and drove east.

When his odometer indicated he had gone almost a half mile, he slowed to a crawl and soon came to a deep clearing. A sign along the road confirmed his hope—Dusty Hollow. He pulled off the road and parked behind a stand of pine trees. It was 10:25. No sign of Mike.

He rolled down his window. A refreshing scent of pine lingered in the misty air. The woods around him were thick, and he felt a sense of security.

Jed heard a sudden rustling behind the car. A nervous doe went bounding past him. That was the third time in the past twelve hours he'd almost had a stroke. He sat there and let his heart quiet down.

Three cars went by, but none slowed. He looked at his watch— 10:32.

Down in the hollow, Jed spotted a small lake that disappeared in the mist and then reappeared. He counted six Canadian geese sitting atop the water before the mist hid them from sight. He knew the off-road trails were in the woods, but he hadn't seen any 4x4s. He no sooner had that thought when an SUV, oozing with mud, zoomed by on Dusty Hollow Road. Jed smiled. It would have been fun to kick up a little mud.

10:36. Jed tapped his fingers on the gearshift. What if he'd missed Mike? What if he'd already come and gone? He was afraid to activate his cell phone, but what if Mike needed to call and couldn't get through?

He heard twigs cracking and then the sound of feet swishing through fallen leaves. In his rearview mirror, he spotted a man about twenty yards behind the car, walking his direction. The man had dark hair and a dark mustache, a green parka and blue jeans. Jed didn't recognize him, but nothing about the guy's demeanor caused him alarm. Jed kept his eyes on the man and observed his every move. He had Mike's walk!

Jed got out of the car and faced the stranger.

The man kept coming. He flashed a broad smile. "Well, if it isn't the return of the Jedi!"

"Mike?" Jed laughed. "Is that you?"

"What? You don't like the mustache?"

"I would never have recognized you, man."

In the next instant they were wound up in a bear hug.

"Ouch." Mike groaned.

"What's wrong?"

"Nothing now, Jed. We're on the same page, buddy. You understood the code." Mike produced a Snickers and broke it in two.

Jed smiled and took his half. "Who would ever have thought we would need *Trail Blazers* to come up with a code to get us past the FBI?"

"Not me," Mike said, "but that's probably the only reason we're standing here right now.... Jed, it's so great to see you!"

Jed studied Mike for a moment, trying to acquaint himself with the new look. Mike looked like he'd really been through it, but he had a sparkle in his eyes that Jed was surprised to see there. "I can't believe it's really you."

Mike laughed. "What's the matter, Jed, having trouble recognizing this ol' Irishman without the red hair?"

"Nah, I'm just not used to seeing you without a cigarette." Jed smiled at the understatement.

"Well, those are history. I've got so much to tell you. Where can we go to talk? I don't know if the FBI knows where we are or not, but I don't want to lose this chance to tell you the whole story. I'm turning myself in." Mike winced, his arms holding his ribs.

"You all right? That's twice now."

"Just sore. I got rolled last night in Doonesbury right after we talked. Some creep stole almost $250 and then used me for a soccer ball. I'm okay. But man I'm sore! Just about everything hurts—big time."

"You look like you're miserable."

"So get my mind off it. We've got important things to talk about."

"You're really going to turn yourself in?"

"Yeah, but first we need to talk."

"Okay, McConnell, hop in. Let's take this mean machine on one of those off-road trails. I don't want the FBI showing up before I've had a chance to hear you out."

"Jed, where did you get these wheels?"

"Hey, I've got a few stories of my own to tell."

It was two o'clock. Ellen looked at her watch again, just as she had done every five minutes for nearly twenty-two hours. She sat beside Sean McConnell, who had shown no response since he closed his eyes late yesterday afternoon. She was beginning to lose hope that the sweet old man would ever come back.

Her cell phone rang.

"Hello."

"Hi, honey, it's me. How are you holding up?"

"So-so, Guy. I can't tell if Sean even knows I'm here."

"There's nothing you can do. Why don't you just come on home?"

"I can't leave him. Not like this."

"Ellen, how long can you just sit there and wait for something to change?"

She sighed. "I don't know. But this is where I need to be. Please say you understand."

"Honey, you know I do. I just don't want you to get too down."

"I'm all right, Guy. Don't worry."

"Are you going to stay another night?"

"I don't know. I keep hoping he'll come out of this."

"Say the word, Ellen, and I'll bring you some clean clothes."

"Let's wait and see what happens today. The nurses let me use the shower, but I don't think I want to wear these clothes a third day."

Ellen glanced at Sean. "Guy, hold on for just a moment." She got up and walked out of the room. "I want to tell you something—attorney-client privilege?"

He chuckled. "Ellen, you're my wife."

"Pretend I'm your client."

"Honey, what's going on?"

"Guy, Mike McConnell called here yesterday."

"What?"

"I don't know what he said. But it was after his call that Sean slipped into the coma. And there's more. Jed Wilson called this morning. I think he's with Mike! He said the FBI's all over both of them. He called to let Sean know he found Mike."

"Did you tell him what's going on with Mr. McConnell?"

"Yes. Jed sounded nervous. He said the FBI had tapped Sean's phone. He got off quickly and said he'd call back. But he never did. I've been pacing the floor all day, wishing he'd call."

"Why? What more could you tell him?"

"Nothing really, but my curiosity is on tilt. I can't believe I didn't see this coming. Sean and Jed had a meeting, and they've been in cahoots to find Mike. Sean never mentioned any of it. I was shocked to find out the FBI is following Jed and the phone here at the hospital is tapped."

"If the phone's tapped, the FBI already knows everything. You don't have to get involved. What could you tell them anyway? You don't know where Jed is."

"You're right. I've been worried about that. I just don't want to betray…"

"Ellen, are you all right?"

She swallowed the emotion. "I don't want to betray Sean. He's so fragile. He's tried to keep me out of it so I wouldn't know anything."

"Well, as your attorney, I'm advising you to stay out of it. If the FBI has the phone tapped, they already know everything you do. Let them handle it."

"So it was an accident!" Jed said. "You didn't murder them. I knew it! I always knew you couldn't do it."

"Not so fast, Jed. I did kill them. I didn't set out to hurt them, but hey, they're just as dead, aren't they? It was my irresponsible behavior, my drinking, that killed them. I guess that's why I ran. I felt as guilty as if I'd shot them all."

"Aren't you being a little hard on yourself?"

"I ran. I never confronted it. I was a coward. And I put a lot of people through the mill. Just look at what it did to you."

"What happened after the explosion?"

Mike sighed. "I panicked. Drove the boat out of the smoke and kept on going. I knew Hugh and Maxine Arthur were out of town. His boathouse wasn't locked, so I hid the boat in there and walked up to the house. I broke a window and let myself in. My hands were blistered. I was covered with black. I remember showering and digging through Hugh's closet for something clean to wear. It's kind of a blur."

"Mike, Wilbur Manning said he saw you outside the church during the memorial Mass. Were you there?"

"Yeah, I really needed to…to hear for myself what Father Donaghan had to say. I couldn't believe they were dead. I mean, I saw the houseboat engulfed, and I heard the place blow. But it was still hard to believe. I can't explain it."

"You don't have to. I felt the same way when I stood there and watched...." Jed paused to get his emotions in check. "I thought I was watching you burn up. It was a nightmare."

"Yeah, nightmare. That about describes it. I haven't touched a cigarette since." Mike's lower lip quivered. "My hand still shakes if I even think of lighting up."

Jed sat quietly for a minute. The honking of Canadian geese echoed in the distance.

"Some girl named Brenna Morgan says she saw you down at the pier in the middle of the night. Says you threw something in the water. Hal found a wedding ring."

Mike looked surprised. "Brenna saw me? I didn't know that. Yeah, I was there. The night before the memorial Mass, I was climbing the walls, so I went back to the pier. It was awful. I stood there and stared at nothing...." Mike's hands were clenched. "I told Rose I didn't mean to lose the money, that I was sorry for what I put her and the kids through—the way they died...." Mike was overcome with sorrow, his whole body shaking. "It was over. Everything was lost...."

"Hey, it's okay, man. You don't have to talk about this anymore."

"I want you to know, Jed...I threw my wedding ring in the water—right where it belonged! Rose was at the bottom of Heron Lake, and my kids were down there.... I never felt so lost. If a heart can break, mine did...." He put his head in his hands and sobbed.

"Mike, you don't have to do this—"

"Yes, I do.... I went back to the Arthurs'. I knew I had to get out of there. I decided I'd leave town after the memorial Mass. I walked out to the highway, disguised in one of Hugh's hats and a pair of his dark glasses. I hitched a ride to the interstate with some teenage boy, and kept on hitching all the way up here. Most of the time I rode with truckers. Caught a few winks between stops. Ate one big meal a day at a truck stop, and the rest of the time ate junk food."

"But you stopped in Atlanta, Nashville, and Kansas City, didn't you? Your credit card record showed you made cash withdrawals. It was all over the news."

"Yeah. I went to Atlanta to see Pop. But I couldn't face him. That's when I left the note you read. I've never had an ATM card, so I used the credit card several times to get cash there. Then I hitched a ride to Nashville and Kansas City. I made a bunch of cash withdrawals at banks there, but not in huge amounts. I was trying not to create suspicion. People in Baxter thought I was dead, but to people everywhere else, I was just the name on a credit card with a photo ID to prove it."

"Man, weren't you nervous showing your ID? What if someone heard about the explosion and recognized your name?"

"What choice did I have? I figured I had maybe two weeks to get my cash limit. It's surprising how bold you can be when you're desperate. Plus, I didn't want to leave a trail up to the Northwest."

"Sounds like you were thinking pretty clearly."

"Survival instinct, Jed. I knew the financial records were destroyed in the fire. So how would anyone know what credit card to close out until the statement came in the mail? I figured that 'anyone' would be Lisa. I'll bet she hates my guts. Probably thinks I deliberately killed them."

"You can't worry about what anyone else thinks. Think about yourself and how to get this mess resolved. You know what really happened. No one else does."

"That's the problem, Jed. No one else does. It isn't something I can prove. Sometimes it still doesn't seem like it really happened. It's like I'm trapped in some horrible dream."

Jordan Ellis tried to enjoy Sunday's football game with his family, but his incessant tapping finally drove them out of the house. He didn't like the feeling of being helpless. He picked up his cell phone and dialed.

"Harlan, it's Jordan. What's going on up there?"

"Same thing as the last four times you called—nothing. It's a morgue. We can't figure out where Wilson could've gone. Jordan, every highway into Doonesbury, Harper's Grove, or any surrounding community is covered. It's like these guys have vanished."

Jordan paced the floor. "It makes no sense, Harlan. Two amateurs completely evading us? What about Wilson's cell phone? Anything else?"

"Nothing. After McConnell called him on the way up here, his phone's been deader than a doornail. Wilson knows we can trace him. I don't think he's going to take any more chances."

"Sure he is, Harlan. They all do. Stay right where you are. Wait him out. I want to know if anything happens. I mean anything."

"Yeah. Sure, Jordan. I want him almost as bad as you do. I'll let you know when somethin's cookin'."

Jordan hung up the phone. He tapped his fingers on the table and watched the inexperienced quarterback overthrow the receiver by a country mile. The ball was intercepted. That's what he needed about now—a turnover. Who was he kidding? He hadn't found out yet where his game was being played.

"What a hoot!" said Mike, laughing and grimacing while he held his ribs. "That would be a good one for *America's Funniest Home Videos*. Wish I could've seen it.'"

"Hey, no joke. I really thought I was history." Jed stifled his laughter, trying to look serious.

"That's almost as good as the coyote story."

"I was thinking funeral arrangements, and they were returning my wallet! Talk about red in the face!"

"Oh, don't get me *howling* again," said Mike, doubled over with laughter. "Pleeeeeease, no more, Jed. It hurts."

The laughter slowly died down and things got quiet.

"Jed, there's something else I want to talk to you about. Something happened this morning that, well, kind of changed my life. I'd like to tell you about it before we run out of day."

"Sure, Mike, what is it?"

"Well, like Paul Harvey says, I'd like to tell the rest of the story."

∽◦∾

Rhonda marked the page in her Bible and closed it. Jennifer was on a plane to Denver. What was going on with Jed? She still couldn't believe he had called her Babe. Or told her he loved her—twice! He hadn't done that since before Jennifer was born. Something was happening inside him, but she didn't know what. She couldn't put her finger on it.

For the first time in ages, Rhonda could hardly wait to see him. Her heart was full of all she was learning, all she had received. Each day she discovered some new truth from the pages of the Bible. She could hardly put it down.

Lord, Jed needs You too. If he felt Your love like I do, maybe he'd be able to love Jennifer. Maybe we could be a real family. Watch over him, Father. Draw Him to You. Protect him from harm and bring him safely home.

Jed was used to Mike's exuberance, but not about serious things. He wondered if he was seeing the bubbles Casey talked about.

"Let me get this right," Jed said. "You asked Jesus Christ into your heart, told Him what you'd done wrong and asked Him to forgive you and change you? That's it?"

"Yeah. But don't forget, I also acknowledged that He's the only one who can forgive me. He loved me enough to tra—" Mike's voice cracked unexpectedly, "to trade places. Jed, he took my punishment. He paid for my mistakes. I'm the one who deserved to be on that cross, not Him. But He did it anyway. Blows my mind. What kind of love is that? I went to church all my life and never understood grace. Pastor Don says it's unmerited favor."

"Unmerited favor?"

"Means we don't deserve it, but He gives it to us anyway. This guy, Donovan MacGruder, said grace is God's giving us what we don't deserve, and mercy is God's not giving us what we do deserve. I never understood when all those fanatics talked about 'being saved,' but that's what we're talking about here, Jed. It's a free gift, but He won't push it on us. We have to ask for it. Is this making sense?"

"Yeah, sort of. Casey said I'm afraid of God and that's why I won't talk to Him. And if I won't talk to Him, He can't come into my heart—I have to ask Him in. Isn't that what you're saying?"

"Yeah, exactly."

"But get this: When I asked Casey why I needed Jesus in there, he said it was because it was dark and He could turn the light on so I wouldn't have to be afraid." Jed chuckled. "The little wise-guy evangelist also said that I can't have just a little of God, but I have to trade—give him all of me, and then He would give me all of Him. You two are on the same page. I can't believe it."

Mike laughed. "Sounds like God's ganging up on you, Jed."

"But who would've thought a mentally challenged kid could be so spiritually tuned in? The stuff he said really got to me. I've got so much baggage, I can't believe it. I've been running from God most of my life. A part of me knew it; I just kept stuffing it."

"Yeah, I suppose I did too," Mike said. "It's not like I never heard people talk about it. I was never interested until I realized I was a sinner." He sighed. "The joke is, I've always been a sinner. God knew it. I just hadn't figured it out. It took something this horrible to wake me up. I guess I'm a little slow."

"Well, that's two of us. You know, Mike, there's something going on with Rhonda too. She's into all this. You should hear her. She's different. I'm actually looking forward to going home. Can you believe that?"

Mike's eyes filled with tears. "Jed, that's great. I know you two have your problems, but at least you can go home and get it right. Make every day count because you never know what's around the next corner. Don't waste it, man. I did. All those years I spent being mad at Rose—I'd give anything to get it all back. I guess it's true what they say: You don't know what you've got till it's gone. And in my case it's even my fault it's gone...."

"Mike—"

"It's okay, Jed. I know God's forgiven me. I'm sure of that. But the consequences of what I've done won't go away down here. I'm about to find that out. But I can handle it better now."

It was a few minutes before Jed decided to tell Mike what he'd been holding back.

"Uh, Mike, I've got some serious news to tell you. I saved it until last because you can't do anything about it, but you need to know. I called Atlanta this morning. I don't know how else to tell you this. Your dad's condition is deteriorating. He's slipped into a coma. Ellen Jones was there with him. It doesn't sound good. I'm really sorry."

Mike grimaced.

"You okay?" Jed asked. "You've been doing that all day."

"I got rolled, remember? I suspect the soreness will get worse before it gets better. That goon really kicked me hard. I've got some Advil in my pocket. Have any water?"

Jed reached underneath the seat and pulled up a bottle. "Here you go."

Mike counted out four tablets and swallowed them with big gulps of water.

"I couldn't get details," Jed said. "I called from a pay phone and didn't stay on the line more than a minute because you said the FBI's tracing the calls. I feel really bad about this. I like your dad. The guy really loves you. Like I told you earlier, that's part of the reason I'm here. He wanted me to find you and tell you that. It's good you got to talk to him yesterday so he could tell you himself."

"I want to call him before I turn myself in. He may not be able to talk to me, but Ellen can put the phone to his ear. At least I can tell him what's on my mind. I know the FBI can trace the signal, but it won't matter now if they know where I am. I need to talk to him."

Jed activated the cell phone. "I programmed your dad's number into the phone after I called this morning." He hit the button and handed the phone to Mike.

"Yes!" Agent Morris picked up the phone to call Jordan Ellis.

"Yeah, it's Jordan."

"It's Morris. Wilson's cell phone's been activated. Hang on a second while I correlate cell sites.... Let's see, the signal is really strong in cell 986 and hardly detectable at all in 987...almost nothing in 985...these signals are overlapping. Hmm...the signal seems stationary."

"Morris, I don't need a blow-by-blow. Just tell me!"

"Hold on just a second, sir.... Okay, that's it—the extreme western third of cell site 986. That's where you'll find our man."

"Thanks, Morris. I'll tell Harlan to move in."

"Hello, Sean McConnell's room. This is Ellen Jones."

"Ellen, don't faint. It's Mike McConnell again."

"Mike? I wasn't sure you'd call at all. Jed called earlier and said he'd call back, but he never did."

"Yeah, I know about that. He was worried about the line being tapped."

"He found you then?"

"Uh—yeah, he did. We've been talking all afternoon. I'm going to turn myself in. How's my dad?"

"Not good. He hasn't responded at all since right after your phone call yesterday. He seemed totally wiped out and immediately fell into a deep sleep. He hasn't opened his eyes since."

"What does the doctor say?"

"That he's in a mild coma and that his heart is failing. The doctor says it's possible that he'll pull out of it, but not likely. I don't think..." Ellen choked back the tears. "I wouldn't count on him getting better, Mike. I don't think he's going to make it. I think he's dying. If you want to see him, you're going to have to get here quickly."

"Ellen, you probably have no use for me, and I don't blame you, but if you care about my dad, would you do something for him? Would you put the receiver to my dad's ear? There are some things I want to say to him. Please? It may be my only chance."

"Okay, Mike, hang on for a second.... All right, I'm holding the phone to his ear. Go ahead."

"Pop, it's Mike. I took your advice. I answered God's knock. I asked Jesus Christ into my heart this morning. I'm forgiven. You already forgave me; now He has. I know I'm right with God, and He's not holding this stuff against me anymore.

"What happened on the lake was an accident. But I was responsible. I was drunk and accidentally started a fire.

"I tried to save them, Pop, I reall—" Mike fought the emotion. "The fire was out of control. Rose locked the cabin door. I tried to get it open. I tried crawling through the window. I called out to each one of them by name, but they didn't answer. The propane tanks were about to be engulfed and the place was going to blow. I kept calling, but they didn't answer! I got scared and ran for my life. I'm sorry I kept running, Pop. That was the worst of it. I felt so guilty, I just kept running. I'm not going to run anymore. I would never have hurt them on purpose. Never. I'm so sorry...."

Ellen heard everything Mike said. When she wiped her eyes, she saw Sean McConnell's mouth forming words. His eyes were opened wide; his countenance was glowing.

"M-M-M-Michael?" he whispered.

"Mike, he's back! He's back! He's trying to say something to you. Listen..." Ellen put the receiver to Sean's lips.

Mike's father seemed to push the words out slowly and deliberately. "I'll...s-s-s-s-seee...you on...theeeeee...other...s-s-s-s-side."

The old man's twinkling blue eyes looked right at Ellen and smiled into her soul. He moved his hand to touch hers. "I l-l-l-love y-y-you, Ellen."

"Ellen! Ellen, what's happening? What's going on?" echoed the voice in the phone. "Ellen, are you there?"

She stared at Sean McConnell's face and took a shallow breath. "Mike, he's gone. Uh, your father has...died. He looks beautiful... so radiant...and peaceful. I think he was ready to die and was just waiting to hear from you.... All the color has come back to his face, and his eyes are smiling. I've never seen anything like it...." she said, fighting back the tears. "Mike?"

Mike didn't answer, but she could tell he was still on the line. She heard Jed comforting him.

"Ellen, this is Jed. Mike's in no shape to talk. I'm not sure what to tell you. He's obviously not going to be able to get back there to make the funeral arrangements. When I get back, I'll stop in Atlanta and—"

"I'll take care of it," Ellen said. "Sean had everything pre-arranged. I'll call the nursing home. They'll have it on file."

"That's an awful lot to ask. Are you sure?"

"Yes. Uh, tell Mike that I'll make sure it's done with dignity.... I—I loved Sean. It's the least I can do."

"I can't believe you'd do this," Jed said.

"Ellen? This is Mike...thanks...." Then all she heard was the sound of Mike McConnell's sobbing. The line went dead.

It was a few minutes before Mike could talk again.

"Jed, do you think I'll ever get anything right? I should be there to bury my father. It's not going to happen. As soon as I turn myself in, I'm going to be extradited to Norris County. I already know that. There won't be any family there for him, and it's my fault. He was a good man. He deserves better."

Jed sighed. "I don't have any frame of reference for this, Mike, but maybe there's some provision in the law for this type of thing. He's your father. Surely they have compassion for that."

Mike winced. He was holding his ribs.

"I wish I knew what to do for those injuries."

"This'll go away, Jed. I hurt a lot worse deep inside. I can't believe I'll never see Pop again...."

Agent Morris sat quietly, feeling like he had listened in on something sacred. He waited for a few minutes. Then he made the call.

"Hello, this is Jordan. Whoever's calling, this better be good news."

"Well, sir, that will depend entirely on your perspective. There's been an unexpected twist in the McConnell case. Uh...the father just passed away during a conversation with Mike. I've got it on tape. It's not what you're expecting to hear, and it doesn't sound like a setup either. This is pretty emotional stuff. I think you'll want to hear it, sir. McConnell says he's going to turn himself in."

"Okay, Morris. Let's hear the tape."

Ellen sat staring at an empty bed. She could hardly believe that Sean had looked so vibrant just when he was on the brink of death. She'd heard about things like that happening but hadn't witnessed it before today.

As she sat there, remembering Sean's last words, she was never more aware that she had longed for a father's acceptance most of her life. At the moment she felt a void, but in that void echoed the dear old man's last words, "I love you, Ellen." She felt privileged to have been loved by him. The joy she saw in his eyes touched something deep inside her, and she wondered if God was trying to tell her something.

FORTY-ONE

Where are those four-wheelers?" Harlan Smith shouted. "It's almost dark!"

Harlan's cell phone rang. He hoped it wasn't Jordan Ellis again.

"This is Harlan."

"It's Jordan. How close are you?"

Harlan sighed. "We're sitting on Dusty Hollow Road with no way to get on those off-road trails. The mud is atrocious. We've already had two cars stuck and we'll have to get something to pull them out. The four-wheelers are almost here, but it's getting dark. If only we'd had that signal earlier."

"Harlan, is everyone ready to roll when the 4x4s get there?"

"Are you kidding? They're chompin' at the bit. We know Wilson and McConnell can't get out without bumping into us. But if they aren't coming out, we're going in. Jordan, you seem subdued. How come? I don't hear the fire-breathing, just-get-it-done-now attitude I've grown to love." Harlan sensed his humor fell on deaf ears.

"Oh, just something we picked up on McConnell's phone call to his dad. I'll tell you about it later. Just get him in custody."

"Yeah, sure. I'll let you know when we have him."

"All right, I'm ready to turn myself in," Mike said. "It's kind of ironic: The FBI has probably listened in on every phone conversation we've had, but I don't know how to call them."

"I can get the number from information. Are you sure, Mike? Maybe you should take a little more time. Losing your dad is a big shock."

"I know. But there's no point in putting it off any longer."

Jed reached for the phone and activated it. He dialed information. "Yeah, Harper's Grove... I need the number for the FBI.... What about the FBI office closest to Harper's Grove?... Yeah, that'll work...."

When Mike saw Jed jot down the number, something tugged hard at his heart.

"Wait, Jed...before you make the call, there's something else I need to say."

Jed turned off the phone.

Mike winced, his hand rubbing the back of his leg.

"Is the pain getting worse?" Jed asked.

"I don't know, I guess. Every place I got kicked hurts, and the Advil isn't helping that much. But not to worry, the FBI'll take good care of me. After all, they want me in one piece so the prosecutors can dice me up." Mike smiled wryly.

"I'm glad *you* can joke about it. You said there was something else you needed to say?"

"I'm just going to ask it straight out: Are you going to answer God's knock on your door, Jed? You can't be sure you have even one more day, and like Casey said, you can't have just a little of God; you have to trade. Why not give Him what's in your heart and let Him fill you with what's in His? He can turn your life around and get your relationship with Rhonda back together. You need her. You've missed something special."

Jed listened.

"Plus, I suspect I'll be in prison on four counts of manslaughter or reckless endangerment or something. They're not going to let me off without time. We probably won't see much of each other. You're the best friend I've got, Jed. I'd like to know we get another crack at this when we get to heaven. We've gone a few miles together. Why not take it to the limit?"

Jed smiled. "The sky's the limit?"

"Well, heaven's forever, and the only way to get there is to confess our sins and accept Jesus' sacrifice on the cross. You have to decide if you're willing to do that. I'm not trying to push you. But if you're ready, Jed, please don't wait. No decision you'll ever make is more important. That's really all I had to say."

"To be honest with you, Mike, I believe it. I just don't know how to do it. I mean, what do I say? I thought maybe I'd ask Rhonda when I get home."

Mike felt a boldness he never felt before. "If you're saying you're ready, I'd be, well, honored to pray with you. Hey, it may be awkward since we're both new at this, but it's not like we can pull a preacher out of these woods to show us how it's done. The only experience I've had with it was this morning when Donovan MacGruder prayed with me. But you and I have tackled new jobs before. We learned as we went. We can wing this too."

Jed grinned. "You realize the guys at O'Brian's would never believe this. If you're willing to stumble through this with me, I'm ready to turn my life over to someone who can do a better job."

Mike felt the tears fill his eyes, and he blinked them away. "Okay, then, let's do it!"

Just barely able to see through the dusk, Mike and Jed got out of the car and walked a short distance. Mike was touched by the irony of their kneeling side by side on a soggy cushion of November leaves—two good ol' boys from O'Brian's bar about to improvise a sinner's prayer under a revival tent of Washington sky.

Mike said the words and Jed repeated. "Jesus, You know I've really messed up. Though I don't deserve it, You said if I believe in You and confess this stuff, that You'd erase it just like it never happened and let me start over. I believe what You did on the cross is the only reason that can happen. So I'm asking that You come into my heart and forgive my sins. That You take control of my life and make something better out of it. I don't know why You do, but thanks for caring so much about me. Amen."

Mike looked over at Jed and wiped away a couple of runaway tears. "Looks like we're in it for the long haul.... Can you believe this?"

Jed blinked the moisture away. "Absolutely."

Present but invisible, were a curious old man in a red cap and baseball jacket and a rugged man in hiking boots and a down jacket. Neither had lost sight of his charge for a single moment.

"You're leaving," said the first to the second.

"Yes, the Master calls."

Jed and Mike walked back to the Explorer in silence.

"Okay, I'm ready to make that call now. Would you do the honors?" Mike picked up the phone and handed it to Jed.

Jed dialed the number and then handed the phone back to Mike.

"Federal Bureau of Investigation. How may I direct your call?"

"This is Mike McConnell. I know you're looking for me. I want to turn myself in."

"Stay on the line for just a moment while I connect you with the special agent in charge of the case."

Mike looked at Jed and grinned. "Now I'm a desperado on hold." He winced. "Would you get me some water so I can take some more Advil?"

"Mike McConnell? This is Special Agent Harlan Smith of the FBI. I understand you want to turn yourself in."

"Yeah, that's right. I'm going to have my friend Jed Wilson drive me back to Dusty Hollow Road. We'll meet you one-half mile east of the old log grocery store, just outside Harper's Grove. We're unarmed. We're in a dark green Ford Explorer. We should be there in less than twenty minutes." *Click.*

Jed handed Mike the bottle of water. He started the motor and put the Explorer in reverse. As he turned to look behind him, he saw Mike wince and grab his chest.

Jed hit the brake.

"Mike, there's something else going on than just soreness because that goon kicked you."

"I think you're right. Ohhhh...my chest. The pain is really...bad...." Mike stopped talking for a moment, then pushed the words out. "I feel weird...Jed, I can't breathe."

"Mike, don't try to talk. You might be having a heart attack." Mike was doubled over, the color gone from his face.

When Jed reached for the cell phone, Mike latched on to his arm.

"They can't...find us...any quicker...than we can...drive back."

"Well, my guess is they know exactly where we are. I'm calling for an ambulance."

"Ohhhh..." Mike grabbed his chest and coughed up blood.

Jed flung the door open and ran around to the passenger side. He opened the door to the backseat, reached for his bag, and pulled out a T-shirt. He wiped the blood off Mike's face.

"Jed...I'm not...going...to make it."

"Yes you are! I'm calling for help!"

Mike clutched tightly to Jed's arm.

"Jed, I'm ready. I've made my peace with God." Mike labored, gasping for air.

"Don't die, Mike! Let me get help!"

Mike coughed again and nearly choked. Jed couldn't imagine where the blood was coming from.

"Jed...I...love ya, man.... Thanks for...finding...me...." He suddenly let go of Jed's arm and seemed to be losing consciousness.

Jed grabbed his cell phone, but before he could dial the number, he heard Mike's raspy voice struggling to say something else. He looked at his friend in time for their eyes to lock.

"Don't worry...Jed...I'll see...you...on the...other...side."

"I know you."

Mike McConnell recognized the face of the rugged man in hiking boots and a down jacket, who had spoken his name in Doonesbury Park and then disappeared. Transformed and radiant, he now stood as a towering giant in a flowing white robe, with massive wings and a fiery sword. His eyes were intense and penetrating. Power and strength emanated from him.

"We meet again, Mike. Come now, and you will see what lies beyond."

Someone was standing with the angel—someone Mike recognized, not as he did on earth, yet he knew him.

"Pop?"

His father's smile was unmistakable. The two men moved toward each other and embraced, shedding every pain and sorrow that had ever burdened their hearts. Then the three stepped into eternity.

Jed sat in disbelief, caught in an emotional replay of the night he thought Mike had died in the explosion. Now, just when he found his friend alive, he experienced Mike's death a second time. If the first left many questions, the second answered them.

For one sacred moment he realized that Mike McConnell was already in the very presence of God. The reality of it was overwhelming.

A sudden awareness of traffic on Dusty Hollow Road brought Jed back to raw reality. He took a deep breath and then dialed the FBI's number.

"Uh...this is Jed Wilson. We need—I mean, I have an emergency out here. Your suspect, Mike McConnell, needs an ambulance." *Click.*

With tears searing his eyes, Jed looked one last time at his best friend. A lifetime of memories tore at his heart. The peaceful look on Mike's face made Jed grateful that his friend didn't have to run anymore. He was home.

FORTY-TWO

Jed shifted his weight in the straight-backed wood chair. He looked at the clock on the white wall. It was 5:27 P.M. He'd lost track of what day it was.

"All right, Jed. You're free to go," Harlan Smith said. "We appreciate your full cooperation. I know the questioning seemed long and tedious, but it's standard procedure. We've got Mike's phone conversation with his dad on tape. That'll serve as his statement of what happened. You filled in all the blanks."

Jed sat with his hands folded, his eyes fixed on nothing. He heard the rumble of a jet taking off nearby. He was surprised to feel Special Agent Smith's hand on his shoulder.

Jed looked up. Harlan's eyes suddenly looked human.

"You were a good friend, Jed. Mike McConnell was lucky to have somebody like you. Are you heading out tonight?"

"Uh, yeah. I need to return the Explorer to Mr. Lasiter and then head home."

"You sure you're all right?"

"I'll be okay, thanks."

"Jed?"

"Yes, sir?"

"There was nothing you could do. If you want to blame someone, blame the mugger. But blood clots are unpredictable. You couldn't have saved him."

Jed nodded slightly. "Thanks. Can I go now?"

"Whenever you're ready."

When Jed left the FBI office in Seattle, he didn't even call home. All he wanted was solitude and looked forward to the long drive ahead.

Finally alone with the truth, Jed was spent. His eyes felt as heavy as his burden, and he made it only as far as Portland before stopping for the night. He checked in to the first decent motel and fell asleep as soon as his head hit the pillow.

When he woke up the next morning, Jed lay there a long time, thinking about the significance of what happened between Mike and him. After he showered and shaved, he decided there was one phone call he needed to make.

"Hello. I am Casey."

"Hi there, Casey. It's Mr. Jed."

"Mr. Jed! Hi, Mr. Jed! I'm going to school today!"

"I know you've started school. I'll bet you really like it."

"Yes, and my teacher is Mr. Hall. He went with us on the bus."

"That's great. Someday you'll be able to do that by yourself. Listen…I'm not going to be in town long enough to see you. I have to get back to Missouri and return the car to your dad. But there's something I want you to know, something I think you'll be happy about. I asked Jesus into my heart. I'm a new man."

"You talked to Jesus, Mr. Jed? You asked Him to come in?"

"I did. And I want to thank you. You showed me the way. If it hadn't been for you, I might never have let Him turn the light on."

"Now we are brothers, Mr. Jed, and we will be in heaven with Jesus!" Casey exclaimed, sounding satisfied.

Jed smiled. Mike McConnell would be there too. "Well, little brother, I have to get going. I have a long drive ahead of me. Maybe sometime you could come visit me in Baxter, where I live. I'll talk to your dad about it when I return the car. I don't want to lose track of you. Well, I guess this is good-bye for now."

Casey was quiet for a moment.

"Mr. Jed?"

"Hmm?"

"Do you have bubbles in your heart?"

"Yes, Casey," Jed said, a smile stretching across his face. "I really think I do."

During those many hours of solitude on his journey home, Jed Wilson cried. He laughed. He grieved. He prayed. He began trusting God to fill the void in his heart with something new.

Jed would never forget Mike McConnell. But even more importantly, somewhere on the other side of the country was a green-eyed blonde whose heart he had broken, and he wanted the chance to put the pieces back together.

By the time Jed left Missouri, the burden began to lift as his thoughts turned toward home. He picked up his cell phone, finally ready to talk to Rhonda, and wondered if he started talking, if he would ever stop....

Multnomah Publishers

The publisher and author would love to hear your comments about this book. *Please contact us at:*
www.multnomah.net/baxterseries

Dear Reader,

I think you'll agree that Rhonda and Jed Wilson and Mike McConnell are no different from many people we know or hear about every day—and, in some cases, from the people we once were. There are countless individuals struggling without forgiveness and hope because they don't realize that God intended grace to be the sole solution.

My hope after writing this book is that we be more attuned to those around us who haven't heard the message and more confident to convey the truth in a simple way.

Let me encourage you to share this book with someone. It might well open a door of discussion enabling you to share how God's saving grace has impacted your life. It won't matter whether your response is simple like Casey's, conversational like Mary Beth's, or poignant like Donovan MacGruder's. God can use any words except those that are never said.

I also invite you to come back to the Baxter series for book two, *Day of Reckoning*. You already know a number of the characters. What you don't know is how hard it will be to put it down!

I'd love to hear from you. You're the reason I do what I do. Feel free to e-mail me at: www.multnomah.net/baxterseries.